'I was caught up in the drama as questions unravel shocking truths . . . *Deception Creek* is another great read that combines suspense and romance in an authentic rural Australian setting.'

Book'd Out

'Cybercrime, financial fraud, murder and more—this page-turning book will keep readers enthralled. There's even a touch of romance!'

Blue Wolf Reviews

'One of the best of the Dave Burrows series . . . Fans of McDonald won't need a lot of prompting to pick this up, but new readers should also give it a try.'

Beauty and Lace

'I loved how [McDonald] uses her experiences and knowledge of working on the land to make the story both informative and sound authentic.'

Mrs G's Bookshelf

'*Deception Creek* is another outstanding, tense suspense novel which I absolutely loved . . . a phenomenal read which I highly recommend.'

Reading, Writing and Riesling

'I simply can't get enough of Detective Dave Burrows! Fleur McDonald knows how to add mystery into every element of the story, leaving her readers eagerly turning the pages.'

The Burgeoning Bookshelf

Fleur McDonald has lived and worked on farms for much of her life. After growing up in the small town of Orroroo in South Australia, she went jillarooing, eventually co-owning an 8000-acre property in regional Western Australia.

Fleur likes to write about strong women overcoming adversity, drawing inspiration from her own experiences in rural Australia. She has two children and an energetic kelpie.

Website: www.fleurmcdonald.com
Facebook: FleurMcDonaldAuthor
Instagram: fleurmcdonald

FLEUR McDONALD

Deception Creek

ALLEN&UNWIN
SYDNEY·MELBOURNE·AUCKLAND·LONDON

This edition published in 2022
First published in 2021

Allen & Unwin
83 Alexander Street
Crows Nest NSW 2065
Australia
Phone: (61 2) 8425 0100
Email: info@allenandunwin.com
Web: www.allenandunwin.com

A catalogue record for this book is available from the National Library of Australia

ISBN 978 1 76106 817 1

Set in Sabon LT Pro by Bookhouse, Sydney
Printed in Australia by McPherson's Printing Group

10 9 8 7 6 5 4 3 2 1

What was, still is.

To those who are precious.

AUTHOR'S NOTE

Detective Dave Burrows appeared in my first novel, *Red Dust*. I had no idea he was going to become such a much-loved character and it was in response to readers' enthusiasm for Dave that I chose to write more about him. Since then, Dave has appeared as a secondary character in fourteen contemporary novels, including *Broad River Station*, and five novels (set in the early 2000s), where he stars in the lead role.

Fool's Gold, *Without a Doubt*, *Red Dirt Country*, *Something to Hide* and *Rising Dust* are my novels that feature Detective Dave Burrows as he begins his career.

In these novels, set in the late 1990s and early 2000s, Dave is married to his first wife, Melinda, a paediatric nurse, and they're having troubles balancing their careers and family life. No spoilers here because if you've read my contemporary rural novels, you'll know that Dave and Melinda separate and Dave is currently very happily married to his second wife, Kim.

Dave is one of my favourite characters and I hope he will become one of yours, too.

PROLOGUE

2011

'I've told you, Alice, I haven't touched anything! What can I do to make you believe me?' Kyle's voice was pleading as he looked over at his wife, but she wouldn't return his gaze.

Her arms were crossed tightly across her chest as she stared out the car window at the Mount Gambier country. The paddocks of tall grass rippling in the wind were passing at a hundred and ten kilometres an hour.

'Alice?'

This time she turned to him, her blue eyes flat and cold, no trace of their usual sparkle.

Kyle drew a breath as he remembered the words from his mother: *Never get between a Sharpe and their money, son. There's some truth in their last name.*

'You've been skimming money from the bank accounts,' Alice snapped. 'Dad told me all about it.'

At a glance, Kyle could see heat flooding her cheeks. She was fuming, and he knew he had two options: he could deny all knowledge, calmly and quietly, or he could get angry.

'Look in my briefcase. The statements are there, along with all the reconciliations. There's nothing amiss. Oliver's got this wrong.' His words were firm and quiet, but anger pulsed through him as he said his father-in-law's name.

Oliver Sharpe was an interfering, obnoxious man who thought he knew better than everyone about everything, and Kyle didn't like or trust him one bit. He had only ever seen the old man's aggression aimed at others, but now here it was, coming at him. He shouldn't have been surprised.

'I don't believe you. Dad doesn't make mistakes like this.' She shifted in her seat to look straight at him. 'A hundred grand? In six months? The whole time we've been married!'

'And as a senior accounts officer I'd like to think I don't make mistakes either. If you believe him,' Kyle snapped, pushing his foot down on the accelerator, 'why are you here with me, going to the accountant? There must be some doubt in your mind.' He rearranged his face and softened his voice, with difficulty. 'I'd hope there's doubt in your mind. After all, I *am* your husband—I'd like to think you trust me.' The hurt was real.

'Do you think I *want* this to be true?' Her voice held an accusation, while her long fingernails tapped on the edge of the window. 'No, I *want* to go to the accountant, I *want* to hear that this is all a big misunderstanding. I *want* to go home. I *want* things to be the way they were when we brought you into the business.' She paused. 'The trouble is, I don't think that's going to happen.'

Gripping the steering wheel tighter, Kyle could see all his hard work, the long hours on the tractor, the countless times he'd bitten his tongue to get on Oliver's good side, being snatched away by the opinion of a person he didn't even know. The accountant was paid by Oliver, instructed by Oliver—if he wanted Kyle out of the business, that's exactly what would happen.

Everything was going wrong. His whole life was coming to a grinding halt over a stupid misunderstanding.

'Kyle, slow down!'

'What?'

Alice's voice broke through the waves of anger that were overtaking Kyle's mind.

'You're going too fast. Look!' His wife nodded frantically towards the speedo.

He looked down. One hundred and twenty.

Lifting his foot slightly, the ute slowed. Kyle dragged in a deep breath. 'Look, Alice . . .'

'No, Kyle, I don't want to talk about it.' She held up her hand in a stop sign. 'I want to get to Foster & Foster and see what Hannah has to tell me.'

'Oh yeah? And what about what *I* want? I'm your husband, don't I get a say in any of this?' The red-hot angry words shot out of him before he could stop them.

'I don't think you're in a position to have a say.'

His knuckles were white. This wasn't how it was supposed to go. Glancing in the rear-view mirror, he saw a vehicle coming up behind them, the indicator on as if they were going to overtake. His eyes flicked back to the landscape in front; large, fat-trunked trees lined the road leading to the corner not far ahead.

The morning was foggy and dew was glistening in the pale light as the sun tried to force its rays through the heavy, lead-grey cloud.

The white Nissan X-Trail pulled out.

'Really?'

There was no way the driver behind should be passing on this stretch of road. Kyle's instinct was to lift his foot from the accelerator, but he didn't. Instead, he pushed it down harder and felt the ute jump away as the turbo kicked in.

'What are you doing now?' Alice's tone was a mix of exasperation and angst.

'This bloke needs a lesson on how to drive.'

'Kyle! Don't.'

Clearly the driver realised there was a problem, because he pulled back in behind Kyle.

'Shouldn't try to pass when you can't see what's coming up, idiot,' he muttered, once again glancing to the front.

On the wide, sweeping bend was a large tree and around the corner, Kyle knew, the road opened up into a long stretch of bitumen, where the guy behind would be able to pass. He pushed his foot down a bit harder.

'Stop it. Slow down. Please, Kyle.' This time there was fear in his wife's voice. 'Don't be stupid.'

He ignored her, his eyes flicking between the road ahead and the ute behind them. The Nissan was still in the left lane. Good. He took a couple of breaths.

'This is crazy,' Alice said softly. 'Come on, slow down.'

'How about you grab all the information from the back seat and look at it, Alice. You'll see for yourself then.' Lifting his foot, the vehicle slowed.

Alice cast a worried look towards him. 'Okay.' She twisted around in the seat and reached behind her.

'Every cent is accounted for.' He watched her in the mirror as she did as he asked.

Not able to reach, Alice undid her seatbelt, grabbed the paperwork and sat back down in one quick, fluid motion.

'You'll see *now*,' Kyle said, the word coming from him more loudly than intended.

'It's not going to matter what I think,' she said tightly, as she studied the reconciliations. 'If Dad has found something amiss . . .'

'But I haven't stolen anything!' He banged the steering wheel hard with his fist, and the ute jumped away as he pushed his foot down once more. 'I haven't!' His face was warm from the anger that was radiating through him, and his fist throbbed a little from hitting the wheel.

She looked up from the printed pages.

'Kyle!'

'What?' The word snapped out of him.

'The corner! It's . . .' His wife reached out to yank his arm but didn't connect, because with one quick movement, Kyle had pulled the steering wheel to the left, throwing the ute to the side. A wheel hit a pothole and the vehicle bounced, throwing them together, and Alice's arm bounced off Kyle's as he held the wheel.

A loud, high-pitched shriek emerged from Alice, just as the left-hand side nose of the ute hit the gum tree.

Glass shattered.

Metal tore.

When Kyle's head hit the steering wheel, he couldn't hear Alice's screams anymore.

CHAPTER 1

2021

Dave climbed out of the police-issue vehicle and looked at the house.

A loose sheet of tin lifted in the breeze, and the verandah sagged at one end. Deep cracks ran through the cement path leading to the front steps, and black ants ran busily in and out of the crevices.

Derelict and uninhabited, Dave thought. *Lonely.*

Ducking under the overgrown bougainvillea bush and taking the few steps to the door, Dave raised his hand to knock on the splintered wood.

The noise echoed around the large stone house. Then, nothing.

'You in there, Joel? It's Dave Burrows, Barker Police.' Moving over to the dirty windows, he cupped his hands to peer inside, but all he could see in the darkness was a lone couch with a throw sheet over it and screwed-up newspapers scattered across the floor.

He walked along the verandah, his boots grinding in the dirt, looking in each window.

Nothing.

'Joel Hammond? I'm here to check in on you. Make sure you understand your parole conditions. Dave Burrows from Barker Police,' he called again.

'Oh yeah? Why's that?'

At the corner of the house, a small, wiry man with shaggy hair stood with a shovel in his hand.

Dave smiled. 'Joel Hammond?'

'Yeah.'

'Good to meet you. I'm Dave Burrows—'

'From Barker Police. Yeah, I heard. What can I do you for?'

'I got a note from my colleagues in Adelaide, saying you were being released and heading back up this way. Thought I'd drop in and say g'day. Let you know if you need anything, I'm around.'

Joel didn't answer, he just stared at Dave, raised the shovel and drove the tip into the dirt, in the same spot repeatedly.

'You got back out here all right?'

'Yeah.'

'And no trouble?'

'Look, I don't know what you know, or what you've been told, but I'm not here to cause trouble. Or take it from anyone else. I've just come back home.' Joel glanced around and leaned the shovel against the house. He took a couple of steps towards Dave before he spoke again.

'Not that there's anyone here to make it a home anymore. But I've done my time. I just want to get on with things without any interference from anyone.' He paused and looked steadily at Dave. 'I've already lost nine years of my life for a crime I didn't commit, so how about you get on your white horse and fuck off to where you came from. I don't need anybody's help.'

Dave had to give it to the man, he sounded sincere, while also angry. 'Look, I understand your mistrust of the police. And, sure thing, I'll head off now, but I'm here to keep the peace in Barker, and if you get hassled, I want to know. Like you said, you've done your time. I'm not saying it's going to happen, but it's only fair you know, there've been a few rumblings around the place.

'The Douglas family knew you were coming back, and Steve was stirring up a bit of trouble at the pub last Friday night. I just wanted you to know. Look, I'll leave you my details. Any problems, just get in contact.' Dave nodded and dug in his wallet for his card, before holding it out to the man. 'And just a reminder—don't forget to report in once a week at the station. That way I won't have to come looking for you.'

Joel Hammond didn't move, so Dave placed the card on the nearest windowsill and turned away.

⁓

'How'd you go?' Jack asked from behind the mountain of paperwork on his desk at the police station.

'Pretty stand-offish,' Dave said as he took his jacket off and hung it behind the door. 'I can understand why, though—the bloke's just spent nine years in jail. Being a copper, I'd be the last person he'd want to see. Might've thought I was coming to give him a hard time.'

'He should've been pleased at the heads up, especially if Steve Douglas wants to make trouble.'

'I bet he hoped he'd just slip back under the radar. The fact the town knows already and it's hardly been twenty-four hours isn't a good sign.'

'Don't know why you'd be surprised that word Joel is back has spread so quickly. This is Barker we're talking about here.' Jack took a new form from the pile in front of him, glanced at it, and signed near the bottom. 'Did you find out anything more about him?'

Shaking his head, Dave sat down and wiggled the mouse next to his computer to wake the screen. 'He didn't offer anything except that he was innocent.'

'Of fraud? A crim saying they're innocent? Gosh, there's a surprise!' Jack's tone was as dry as the paint on the walls.

'Who's innocent of fraud?' Kim stood in the doorway holding a plastic cake carrier. 'Joel Hammond?'

Both men broke into a grin and Jack got up quickly to take the container from her.

'Smoko on wheels. Cheers, Kim,' Jack said as he lifted the lid. 'Look, Dave. Chocolate mud cake.'

'One of my faves.' Dave stepped over and put his arm around his wife, dropping a kiss on her head. 'Thanks, honey.'

'You're welcome,' Kim said as she sat in Dave's chair. 'Were you talking about Joel?'

'Hmm,' Dave nodded. 'I went and saw him today. Community policing and all that.'

'Such a shame. He was a nice boy at school.'

Dave glanced at Joel Hammond's file, open on his desk. 'How did you know him at school?' he asked. 'You wouldn't have been there together.'

Kim shook her head. 'No, not in the same year, but I was a prefect in Year 12 and he was in primary school then. I can't remember what year, but he was a little-y. Big brown eyes and freckles. A bit of a clown. Always teasing and playing jokes. Then as he grew up, he used to come into the roadhouse all the time. Just a genuine, nice guy. Quietly spoken and polite.'

'Who defrauded his employer,' Jack said around the cake in his mouth. 'This is really good, Kim.'

Kim raised a shoulder. 'Hmm, well, that was what the jury decided, wasn't it?'

'You think there was some doubt? What makes you say that?' Dave frowned a little as he looked at her.

'Answering a question with a question. So typical of you, Dave! And what can I say?' Kim chided. 'I wasn't on the jury, so I don't have all the evidence or the information they would have had.'

Raising his eyebrows at his wife, he gave a slight shake of his head. 'That's my girl, always making sure that everyone gets a fair hearing!'

She cut a piece of the cake and handed it to him with a sunny smile. 'Seriously, though,' she continued, 'I found it hard to believe—I never thought there was a reason for him to do it.'

'Do what exactly?' Jack asked. 'I wasn't here then, so I only know what I've read on the file—that's he defrauded his employer to the tune of two hundred and fifty thousand by getting cheques signed and depositing them in his own bank account.'

'Yeah,' said Dave, 'it was back in the days before EFT was used. The stock and wool cheques would be piled up on the desk of the finance manager and he'd go through and sign each cheque. He didn't know who or what he was signing for—he trusted the people below him. And think about this: it was a large stock firm with heaps of cheques being written. He might've had to sign two or three hundred cheques a day. Joel put the cheques with his name on them in the middle of the pile and the finance manager signed away.' Dave shook his head. 'It's so easy and obvious now to see how it all happened, but he got away with it for a couple of years.'

'Hold on,' Jack said. 'Joel was put away for defrauding a company, not the Douglas family. What's their connection to all this?'

'Ah well, that's another story,' Kim said, making herself comfortable on the chair in between the two desks. 'Joel was dating Maggie Douglas when they were teenagers. Max and Paula were quite strict with their daughter. Well, the boys too, but not as much. There were a few times the three

Douglas boys went out and got drunk and caused havoc around the town, and I didn't hear of any repercussions.

'Now let's remember that Max Douglas is the minister at the Baptist church. So the story is that Maggie slipped out the window one night to meet Joel. They went to the grain silos on the edge of town. You know how there're ladders to climb up the side? Well, they were climbing to the top when she slipped and fell. She was only sixteen, so all this happened quite a while ago now.' Kim paused. 'The first thing the parents knew about it was the police knocking on their door. They thought she was tucked up in bed, when in reality she was in the morgue at the hospital.

'Joel was already being questioned, because he'd raised the alarm. He was completely innocent of what happened, but the family made it so hard for him, he had to leave town.' Kim gave a sad smile. 'The whole incident was horrible for everyone.'

Jack's eyes narrowed. 'How did the coppers know for sure he didn't have something to do with her fall?'

'I don't know, Jack.' Kim fixed him with a look a mother might give her insolent child. 'But they must have been certain, because there weren't any charges laid. Nothing more than a tragic accident. But the family couldn't understand why he was walking away when they'd lost their daughter.' She paused. 'I can't remember if Joel was even at the top of the silos as Maggie went up. It's a long time ago now. I wasn't involved with either of the families, except when they came into the roadhouse, so I only heard what was on the street and there was plenty of talk, let me tell you.' She shrugged. 'You know me, I don't take any notice of gossip unless I know it to be true.'

'What did the Douglases do to make it so difficult for Joel to stay?' Jack pressed.

'Honestly, I can't remember all the details. I just know that he left town and went to work in Adelaide, then the next thing I read was that he was on trial for fraud.'

There was silence then, as Jack leaned forwards to cut himself another piece of cake. 'That's all pretty terrible,' he said finally.

'The Douglases never recovered from Maggie's death,' Kim said. 'As you wouldn't from the death of a child.' She stopped for a moment and took a breath, and Dave knew she was remembering her sister, whose only son had been murdered. It was the first case Dave had investigated in Barker, and Kim had been the reason he'd come here to live.

Graham had been run over by a stampeding mob of cattle. Trampled to death. The police were never able to prove Dave's theory, but he was sure that the cattle had been spooked by men Graham owed money to. Perhaps they'd cracked a whip or let out a yell—however they'd done it, they'd been clever and covered their tracks. It was the one murder he had never been able to solve.

Graham's parents had become shells of the people they once were, and eventually they sold the farm and moved away, no longer able to bear being on the land where their son died.

The only good thing to come out of that case was that Dave and Kim had reconnected years—decades—after their short-lived teenage summer romance. A summer romance neither of them had ever forgotten, despite their lives taking them in different directions.

Dave reached out and touched Kim's arm as he remembered walking into the roadhouse and seeing her for the first time in more than ten years. Her hundred-watt smile had been enough to make him fall head over heels in love with her again. If he'd ever fallen out of love with her; he doubted he had.

'So, all that aside,' she said, glancing at him, 'my question would be why would he have wanted to steal that money? His family was comfortable. He never wanted for anything when he was growing up. Joel always drove the nicest cars and dressed in fashionable clothes when he came back here. Not that he came home often. But people ran into him in the city and he used to meet his parents halfway, in Clare, instead of coming to Barker.' Kim frowned. 'It must have been so hard for the poor man, not being able to come back to his family home.' She sighed. 'For a while the Douglas family made life very uncomfortable for Joel and his parents, and it was easier for him to leave than stay. Such a sacrifice.'

'Where was he working?' Jack asked.

Dave picked up the file and tossed it towards him. 'Have a read, if you want. It's only a personnel file, nothing about the investigation in there. We can order that if need be. But he was in Adelaide at the head office of Stockomatic. Like Elders and Nutrien today, but a smaller company. They went bankrupt a few years ago.' Dave leaned back in his chair, putting his hands behind his head.

'I'm not surprised, given the way their finance manager checked things,' Jack scoffed.

'Joel's mum and dad were lovely people,' Kim said. 'Generous. Always used to donate at the annual P and C fundraiser and to the church, and Verity gave whatever food she had left over from the market garden to the old folks home at the hospital. They never wanted any recognition. The town is poorer without them; they've both passed on now.'

'Wait on,' Jack said. 'Joel hasn't got any family here? There's no one at all left? Why would he come back?'

Kim shook her head. 'From what I know he's alone in the world now. His parents died . . . oh, must be four or five years ago, and they didn't have any other children. Poor Joel was still in prison when they passed. I remember there was talk about him not being at the funeral. The father went first, then she did. Only six or eight months apart. Dave, you must remember that?' She looked at him. 'Billy and Verity Hammond.'

Dave nodded slightly before turning to Jack. 'Often people who get out of jail go back to what's familiar. The house he's in is where he grew up; it would feel safe to him. After being in prison all that time, safety would be very important to Joel.' To Kim, he said, 'I remember them vaguely. I never had anything to do with them really—they must've been law-abiding citizens.'

16

Dave gave her a gentle wink and Kim's smile was sad as she answered.

'They were. Very much so. That's why Joel being caught up with a fraud charge doesn't make any sense to me.'

Dave harrumphed. 'Why does anyone do anything? I've met enough crims to know they don't need to come from—' he used his fingers to act as quotation marks '—a "bad" family to break the law. If the court convicted him, then it was proved beyond reasonable doubt. That's all I know. What I don't want to happen here is the town taking revenge against a bloke who's done his time in jail and was cleared of any wrongdoing in an accident.' He shook his head. 'Some people just seem to have horrible luck, don't they? I mean, look at this case. His girlfriend dead and he ends up in jail—two completely different situations.'

'Yeah, you're right,' Kim said, standing up. 'Anyhow, I've got other meals to cook for Catering Angels. Poor old Mrs Hunter had a fall and her daughter called asking me to cook up a week's worth of meals for her, so I'd best get on.'

'Barker's own meals on wheels,' Dave said with a gentle smile. 'Okey-doke, honey. I'll see you at home.'

Kim looked at Dave. 'Maybe I'll drop some food off to Joel.'

Not able to help himself, Dave laughed. 'Of course, you will. I never doubted it.'

Jack looked up from the file he'd been flicking through and waited until Kim left.

'Nine years,' he said.

'Nine years, what?' Dave asked, reaching for another slice of cake.

'Don't you think that's a long time to go away for a white-collar crime?'

Dave stopped chewing. Jack was dead right.

CHAPTER 2

Emma Cameron took a swig of wine and held the glass over her head as she danced. Around her, her friends bumped bodies as they swayed and bounced in time to the music on her verandah.

This was how she forgot the accident. Drinking, partying, working. Blocking out any remnants of the noise: the screams, the tearing metal, the blaring sirens.

This was also how she forgot her divorce.

Jacqui slung an arm around Emma's shoulders and together they belted out 'D-I-V-O-R-C-E' along with Tammy Wynette.

On the wide cement-based verandah was a balloon structure: pinks, yellows and oranges interwoven with chiffon and silk. The balloon vagina had been Jacqui's idea. 'It's a divorce party,' she'd said with the usual wicked gleam in her eye. 'You know, the start of a new life. Leave the entertainment with me, I'll fix it!'

Emma had been hesitant, knowing that her friend would turn up with something crazy—and she had. Now, Jacqui was insisting that the two of them and Maddy, all recent divorcees, be 'rebirthed' by pushing themselves through the balloon vagina.

God almighty, Emma thought. *What is this?*

Through blurry eyes she could see the moon reflecting off the roof of the machinery shed. The noise of their whoops and the music was bouncing off the line of hills behind the house before being swallowed up by the darkness.

'Woo-hoo!' screamed Maddy as she pushed her way through the birth-canal balloons and came out the other side.

Jacqui, who was in charge of the next step—the 'baptism'—grabbed a bottle of champagne and poured it over Maddy's head. The liquid spilled on the cement and splashed up around their feet.

Emma waited her turn, watching the crowd gathered around the front, waiting to welcome the newly rebirthed divorcees into the brand-new scary world of singledom.

Maddy was now dripping with champagne and it was Emma's turn. Putting her wine glass down and hands out in front, she pushed her way past the rubber-smelling balloons and soft, shiny material. There were tears on her cheeks but she refused to dwell. Her new title was 'divorcee'. The email confirmation had arrived last week. She and Phil were finally finished.

Thank god. Even though it made her sad. Thank god.

Yesterday her brother had sent her a text message, a meme: *My life didn't go according to plan and that's okay.*

Guessing she might feel like that at some stage in the future, she'd sent back a thumbs up, but the words didn't resonate with her now.

Emma felt hands reaching in to pull her through the final couple of steps of the balloon vagina, and suddenly she emerged into the new world. Raising her arms, she let out a squeal of joy. Or was it pain?

'Yes!'

The three women put their arms around each other while the rest of the party-goers threw confetti and streamers over them.

All three were done. Rebirthed. They were finished with the past and starting anew.

As the women broke apart, someone put another drink in her hand and the music changed to an upbeat nineties song. Emma was pulled up to dance by a man she'd gone to school with, and willingly let herself be pushed around the dance floor, all the while moving in time to the beat. Her farmhand Matt was leaning against the wall, beer in hand, talking to a couple of blokes and they locked eyes. He tipped his beer towards her in a form of salute. She smiled and closed her eyes and she twirled around and around. Maybe she'd ask Matt to dance later. He'd always looked like he was light on his feet ... Especially if there was a cow chasing him!

Maddy handed her another drink as she danced past, and Emma's vision started to get blurry.

Finished. The word kept running through her head. Then another: *Done.*

Yes, they were, and that was good. She and Phil could have never worked. Emma didn't know why she'd thought they could.

But now she was single. Alone. And who was she now that her past life was gone?

~

The thumping headache made itself known before Emma opened her eyes. Her tongue was stuck to the roof of her mouth, and she didn't want to smell her own rank breath. The sunlight was bright even through her closed eyelids, and she threw a hand up to cover her eyes.

'Ugh.' Emma tested parts of her body for pain. Rolling over, but keeping her eyes closed, she reached for the glass of water she always kept alongside her bed. Empty. 'Bugger,' she whispered.

Taking her time, she got up and went to the ensuite and drank straight from the tap, letting the cold water dribble over her tongue before gulping greedily. The headache was throbbing.

Switching the tap off, she rummaged in the vanity drawer for Panadol. Or preferably something stronger. The crumpled packet she found held only one tablet. That would have to do for now. She swallowed it and stuck her head under the tap again, gulping more water before gingerly climbing back into her bed. Pulling the doona around her tightly, she reached down to switch on the electric blanket. Her naked body was freezing as well as hurting.

Closing her eyes again, Emma lay there waiting for the Panadol to kick in, hoping that if she didn't move, the pain might go away.

She couldn't help but think how strange it was—even after eighteen months—to be sleeping alone. Emma had assumed that once Phil left, over time she would get used to the left side of the bed being empty, but she hadn't. Even after all these months she still woke in the middle of the night to silence, and when she stretched her hand out to feel his body and warmth, all it met was a cold, empty sheet.

Hugging the pillow to her, she breathed deeply, trying not to allow the anxiety to overwhelm her. Her stomach felt as if a cold lump had settled at the bottom, and within her heart was a gnawing hurt that didn't stop.

Emma hadn't known that heartache was an actual physical thing until she realised she was going to be divorced at forty. That wasn't how her life was supposed to play out.

She'd wanted children, people to love and care for. A home.

She had a home, but it was empty of everything else. No children. No husband.

A tear leaked out from behind her closed eyes and she frowned gingerly. These thoughts needed to stop right now, otherwise she might never stop crying. There was no place for a pity party because the sadness would only grow and grow until emotions threatened to overwhelm her.

When Emma thought about Phil, she knew that some part of her would always love him—but only like a brother.

23

No, not even that. A distant cousin. They hadn't been friends before they were a couple, and they hadn't spent long getting to know each other before they got married . . .

'No!' The word came out too loudly and reverberated around her head. A painful groan and a couple of breaths later, she muttered, much more softly, 'Stop it, Emma. Just stop it.'

Throwing back the covers, and ignoring the pain in her head, she padded out to the kitchen and switched on the kettle.

Her living room was full of half-empty bottles, dirty wine glasses and beer cans. Confetti covered the floor, and in the corner stood the balloon vagina, which at the time had seemed like a fun and crazy thing to do.

Now all it seemed to represent was her loneliness.

She had a vague recollection of the party moving inside as the night had gone on and the damp, cold air settled around them. Maddy had insisted the vagina come inside too.

'In case she gets cold,' she'd said, her face worried, clutching her wine glass.

Sighing, Emma couldn't face the clean-up just yet. Instead, she grabbed a glass of water and sucked it down before making herself a strong coffee and walking out onto the verandah, knocking over an empty beer bottle as she went.

'Shit!' Looking around, she saw more bottles scattered.

She hoped her girlfriends would come back out this morning to help her clean up. At that thought, another foggy memory sprang into her mind: the bus they'd hired coming to get everyone about 3 a.m., though she was a little fuzzy on the time. What Emma did remember was leaning against the door frame waving everyone goodbye and telling them all how much she loved them.

She was a loving drunk, not a fighting one.

The grey July clouds were scurrying across the sky, as dark and moody as she felt this morning. In contrast, the paddock at the front of the house was green with the barley crop that was just about at the start of jointing mode, when nodules formed at the main stem. Emma called it the untidy stage. The plants were long and straggly, and the leaves fell all over the place, rather than standing strong and tall as they would when they were older.

Sitting in the swinging chair her friends had bought her for Christmas, she gently pushed off with her foot and sipped her coffee. The Panadol must have kicked in a little, she realised, because her head didn't hurt as much as it had half an hour ago.

Looking out across the paddock, she felt a sense of satisfaction. When Phil left, she hadn't been sure she would be able to manage everything. Even though he hadn't worked on the farm, he'd usually been home earlier than she had, so he'd cooked, done the washing and cleaning—all the things she loathed. He certainly had been a good house husband. Phil had done the accounts for the farm too, but he'd rarely got his hands dirty. Farming just wasn't his thing, so she had employed Matt and together they had kept the place going.

For a moment she looked at her hands and thought about Phil's. They were white and his fingers long and thin. Inside hands. Ones that had never seen physical work. Whereas her dad's—and Matt's—were tanned and had ingrained dust and grease in the little cracks. They were hands like hers.

Deception Creek had been her father's farm, and his father's before that, and she loved it fiercely. Thankfully, Phil had understood that he didn't have any claim on her heritage. His accountancy work had taken him in to his Barker office every day, while Emma and Matt had worked tirelessly to put the crops in and look after the few cattle they had.

Emma felt a wet nose on her foot and looked down to see her Kelpie, Cash, looking at her with his large brown eyes. It was as if he knew she was hurting.

'What's up there, Cash?' she asked, reaching to rub his nose. He let out a quiet whine and flopped down under the chair. As she rubbed his belly with her foot, he let out a contented sigh and closed his eyes.

If only all men were as easy to please as Cash.

That had been Phil's problem: farm life was too quiet for him. He'd wanted to spend more time in town—in Adelaide—and a farming lifestyle didn't lend itself to that.

She would never forget their last fight.

'Are you coming with me or not?' he'd asked. 'It's *The Boy from Oz*! I booked the tickets months ago. You said you'd come.'

Emma had shaken her head. 'You didn't tell me the date! And I can't. I've got the seed cleaner coming tomorrow.

26

I've had it booked since before harvest. I can't cancel on him now, it'll put the rest of his program out with all the other farmers around the place.'

'This is fucked, Emma,' he'd snapped, his eyes bulging as he glared at her. 'This can't go on. You're completely married to the farm. Not me. We never go anywhere together; I might as well be single.' He'd stomped into the bedroom to pack.

The anger that had flared through her had been swift and ferocious. Phil not understanding her business had been a constant theme since they'd married eight years before. He was always getting angry when she couldn't make an event he'd planned—but never told her about. Then he'd go partying in Adelaide without her and posting photos of himself with women she didn't know.

But that wasn't the only thing wrong with their relationship, she'd known that in that final argument. She couldn't remember the last time they'd had sex. He had tried to initiate love-making three or so months earlier, but she'd turned away, having only finished three weeks of seeding that night. Then she'd tried a month later, and he'd turned away. That had been unusual. She'd wondered if he was getting his needs met elsewhere, but she hadn't had the energy to have the conversation.

And without the intimacy of love-making and with the busyness of her work, they'd stopped talking.

Then, as she'd watched him walk away, Emma had understood there was nothing between them anymore. As familiar as she was with his face and the landscape of his body, the thought of spending another eight years together was no more appealing than yet another Christmas visit from his parents. Or aphids eating her barley crop.

'Well, maybe you should be single, then.' She'd bitten out the words before she could stop them.

'What?' Phil had stopped midstride and turned to look at her, just as she drew in a gasp of horror.

Had she really said it aloud? She may have thought it often over the past twelve months but she'd never actually said it to Phil's face. Once something like that was said, it couldn't be taken back.

'Nothing. Sorry. I'm just frustrated, that's all. I do want to go with you, I do. But you know as well as I do that there're some things I just can't put off, and this is one of them.'

As Phil had stood looking at her, she'd noticed a myriad of emotions cross his face, but relief had seemed to be the strongest. 'You know what?' he'd finally said. 'You're right. I think we'd be better off apart. You're married to this godforsaken farm, and I have a life to live. I'll pack up and move into town.' He'd glared at her again. 'Maybe you should remember that at some stage you're going to be here alone on Deception Creek, which takes up your whole life, and I bet you'll wish you'd made a different decision.'

By later that afternoon, there had been nothing of his left at the house, and only a cloud of dust hanging in the still air over the driveway to show he'd ever been there.

That had been eighteen months ago.

A small sob escaped her, and Cash lifted his head to look at her.

'It's okay,' Emma told him. 'I'll be okay. I always am.' She picked up her coffee cup and got off the swing, before heading back inside.

The stench of alcohol hit her, and she wrinkled her nose. The cleaning shouldn't be put off any longer, but instead, Emma went into the office and switched on the computer.

Facebook came up and let her know she was tagged in nine-plus photos. She and Jacqui, clearly drunk, smiling and red-cheeked. The three of them—Maddy, Jacqui and Emma—arms around each other, toasting the newly divorced Emma. Separate photos of all three emerging reborn from the balloons and with champagne being poured over their heads.

For god's sake. Here she was at forty and acting like a teenager. Her father would probably roll over in his grave if he could see these. Her mother certainly would. She could almost hear her saying '*Now, Emma*' in the disapproving tone Emma remembered so well. Still, she had to admit, when she'd come home to work on the farm ten years ago, her mum's tone had softened towards her, glad that her daughter had come back to where she belonged.

Still scrolling through her timeline, she saw more photos of the night from other friends who'd been there. Everyone had had a good time, there was no doubting it.

Stopping to glance at the picture of her surrounded by pink balloons, an ad flashed into her timeline.

HelloSingles.

A dating site.

She squeezed her eyes shut and let out a breath. Blinking open, the ad was still in front of her.

Against her better judgement, she clicked on the link and was taken through to a page where she could create an account.

'Don't be stupid,' she whispered. 'You're hungover and lonely. Don't do this.'

Minimising the screen, Emma indecisively got up from her chair, then sat back down again. Her hand hovered over the mouse.

Click.

The website flashed back up.

Click.

Minimised.

The phone rang and she jumped. Looking at the screen, she saw it was Maddy.

'How's the head?' Emma asked her friend.

Maddy groaned. 'I'm too old for this shit.'

'Ha! You're the youngest out of all of us. So, times that by a bit and imagine how the rest of us are feeling.'

Giving a throaty laugh, Maddy said, 'I'm trying not to. The night was awesome though, despite me feeling like crap. My head . . .'

'Yeah, I know. Mine's the same. But you're right, it was a great night. Thanks for everything.'

'Is there much to clean up? I was thinking about coming out to help you, but I don't think I should drive yet.'

Emma walked into the lounge room, then out onto the verandah and looked again. Really there were just a lot of bottles to take to the tip and glasses to wash.

'Nah, don't worry about it. I'll be fine with it.'

Walking through the house, she went into the kitchen and opened the fridge. 'I think I need bacon and eggs for breakfast, though.'

'Good idea. I might head to the cafe and see if they'll cook me a bacon-and-egg burger.'

'Heard from Jacqui?'

'Nah, knowing her she won't be up until later.'

Maddy paused for a moment and Emma could feel there was something big coming.

'Now, look, I know you're not going to like this, but my cousin Paul is coming to visit Mum and Dad for a few days next—'

'No.'

'Hey! You don't even know what I was going to say.' Maddy sounded hurt, but Emma knew better.

'Yes, I do. You were going to play cupid. Just don't, Maddy. I'm fine. Okay?' Her tone was firm.

'But—'

'The answer's no. It's not up for discussion.'

Clearly sensing she wasn't going to get anywhere, Maddy changed the subject. 'What are you going to do once you've cleaned up?'

'Probably go back to bed.' Emma gave a rueful laugh. 'I wish. I've got to get a mob of cattle in for calf marking tomorrow. But I don't need to do that until later. Hopefully I'll feel a bit better by then.'

'Why don't you get Matt to do it? There's a band playing at the pub this afternoon . . .'

'Maddy, if I don't see another glass of wine forever, it won't bother me.'

'Yeah, yeah, yeah, until next time.' She paused. 'Still, I don't think I need any more for a few days either.'

Emma couldn't help herself: she giggled, knowing Maddy was right. Over the past year, they'd all said that at some point.

'I'll see how I feel later and text you, okay?'

'Sounds like a plan. Talk to you then.'

They hung up and Emma pulled the bacon and eggs out of the fridge and switched the kettle on again. She thought about Maddy's offer to set her up, and cringed. It just wasn't something she could do. But maybe . . . The singles website popped into her head again. Was there a difference between a set-up from a friend and the computer?

No was the answer. But was she really ready for the whole town to know she wanted a partner? Which wouldn't be able to be avoided if she signed up with HelloSingles.

Putting the bacon in the sizzling pan, she went back into the office and brought up the dating website again, looking at it a bit longer this time.

CHAPTER 3

Joel swung the axe down and felt the satisfaction of the branch jarring against his hands before it gave way. He was physically fit from all the exercise he'd done while in prison, so the rotten tree was no match for him.

He'd spent hours every day in his cell doing sit-ups, squats and push-ups. And he'd spent years dreaming of what it would be like when he could be outside again as a free man. Feel the sun and wind on his skin and the rewards of hard, physical work.

Looking over at the house, he felt a twinge of sadness. His mother had been incredibly house proud. Since her death—and his father's—their home had fallen into disrepair. It wasn't surprising, really, considering no one had lived in it for four years, but it still made him pause.

Joel dropped the axe and rubbed his hands over his arms, feeling the goosebumps appear; they came every time he thought about his parents.

Were they a sign his parents were close by? The same thing had happened when he'd pushed open the door for the first time, three days ago. His childhood home was dark and dusty, but the sense of his parents was strong. He thought he'd heard his mum's laughter from the bathroom, had a strange feeling that she would be cleaning, which of course she wasn't. In that moment, his head knew what his heart didn't want to accept.

The feeling made him sag a little, grief pulling at his chest. His hands clenched into fists and he dragged in a couple of deep breaths as he imagined his mum turning around with a smile to welcome him.

Instead, he'd wrinkled his nose at the smell. Mould had overtaken the bathroom and a hive of bees in the eaves had given the house a sweet, musty smell, which permeated through the ceiling and down into the bathroom, where a few dead bees lay scattered near the vanity.

Joel had gone outside to investigate how entrenched the bees were. His mother had loved having them around, because they pollinated her veggie garden. Joel's memories of bees weren't quite as nice, though. As a child he remembered walking barefoot across the lawns and getting stung. He remembered his dad removing the sting with tweezers then using the laundry whitener, Bluo, to stop the pain. His foot stayed blue for days where his dad had dabbed it on.

As he'd stared at the bees, he'd decided that his mum would have loved them there, and so, seeing as the workers had taken no notice of him since he'd arrived, he decided they could stay.

Over the past three days, he had worked tirelessly to return the house to some sense of order, and as he looked at the garden now, he knew his parents would be happy. There was still work to do, but it was a good start. He wiped his brow, then picked up the axe and swung it again. What else was there to do? Job hunting wasn't an option yet. There was enough money to live on from the inheritance from his parents; the amount in the bank account was more than he would ever need, for sure.

He was going to be one of the lucky ones. It was common knowledge that convicted crims found it hard to get work after they were released. And anyway, he had enough to do here for a while.

The inside of the house was another issue; there was so much to do to return it to its former glory, but the sponge and dishwashing liquid under the sink—where his mother had always kept it—had been enough to get him started.

The visit from the copper the previous day had made it fairly clear that Joel wasn't going to be welcomed back into the community easily. He'd expected as much. Country towns had long memories and a penchant for bearing grudges.

He swallowed hard, trying to keep the anger at bay. He'd been treated unfairly in so many ways, but his mother had always put things in perspective.

'Darling,' she'd say, when he was low and desperate to come back to Barker. 'Your comfort isn't the most important thing. You *will* come out of this stronger and then, and only then, will you be able to make a difference to people who have been in the same situation you have.'

For now, he would keep to himself and hope for a bit of peace. Maybe in time, he *could* help others.

Joel dragged the branch away to the pile he'd started and hoisted it onto the top, before taking the matches from his pocket and lighting one. Squatting down, he held the flame to the dry leaves at the bottom of the pile and watched as it flicked and flashed around the fuel and finally took hold.

The orange flames flared towards the sky, sending sparks flying upwards. Some people might feel burdened by all the work that needed to be done on this three-hectare block on the edge of town, but he didn't. He was grateful.

Grateful for somewhere to live. Grateful to smell the air and be outside. Grateful to be home.

Last night he'd woken in the early hours of the morning, still believing he was in prison. The noises filtering through the darkness, though, didn't make sense. The creaks and bangs were loud as the wind moved around the walls and windows, and for a moment he'd thought it was someone trying to get into his cell. Then, realising where he was, Joel had smiled and rolled over, hoping for sleep again.

It hadn't come. Instead, he'd got up and turned on the light, and examined all the family photos that hung on the wall. No one had been around to take them down.

His parents smiled at him in faded colour on their wedding day. Then, as he moved along, he saw himself in the obligatory school photos, his six-year-old self smiling through missing front teeth.

Then there was the Christmas he'd turned twelve and been given a motorbike, and later when he'd turned thirteen and his dad's Rotary friend Mr Cameron had brought him an orphaned lamb to raise. Their daughter Emma already had too many, Mr Cameron had said.

Maggie, too, was in a photo with him, from only a few months before she died. Eating lunch with his family, smiling and laughing. No one had ever smiled as much as Maggie had. And no one could have known that bright, fun life would be snuffed out so soon. The photo, taken while they sat at the kitchen table, was too much of a stark reminder of the fragility of life and the guilt he—they—would forever feel, now that Maggie wasn't here.

Joel had wanted to save her, he really had.

His heart kicked up a notch as he thought back to that night, saw the moon shining on her blonde hair as she put one hand on the ladder and glanced down at him.

'Come on, 'fraidy cat,' she'd said.

With his mouth dry, he hadn't been able to answer her.

'Hello? Hellloooo?'

Jolted from the memories, Joel looked to where the voice was coming from. He wasn't expecting any visitors and they were not welcome.

'Hello? Joel, is that you?'

A grey-haired woman in a floral skirt and sensible-looking navy jumper walked around the corner, and Joel dropped the axe. The woman was holding a plate draped with a tea-towel, and a soft breeze brought the aroma of freshly baked biscuits.

'Mrs Kerby?' he asked as he was instantly thrust back into his parents' bright yellow kitchen, Mrs Kerby sitting at one end of the table, his mother at the other end. Cups and a tea pot in front of them and talking nineteen to the dozen. His father had always found something very important in the shed that needed attending to when Mrs Kerby visited.

'Ah, it *is* you. I thought maybe the squatters had moved in.' The old woman came to stop in front of him and her gaze raked over his face. 'So, you're back?'

'Yeah.' Joel nodded, unsure what else to say. He hadn't seen his mother's friend in . . . well, he wasn't sure how long.

'Good to see you here. The old place needs a clean-up.' She looked around. 'Your mother would be devastated if she saw the garden looking like this.'

Joel followed her gaze. The fruit trees needed to be thoroughly pruned and fertilised, while the veggie garden beds that his mum had so lovingly tended were overgrown with self-seeded tomato bushes and weeds as high as his waist.

'Mmm, she would.' The words felt as if they were sticking in his throat. He hadn't spoken to anyone except law-enforcement people for so long, he'd forgotten how to make conversation.

'Well, lad, I guess this is a good job for you, then. I mowed the grass for a while but it was too much for me. Biscuit? I cooked these before I realised a squatter could have moved in.'

Joel nodded uncertainly. 'Thank you.' He lifted the tea-towel and took one. He managed to eat the biscuit in two bites, it tasted so good, and then he pushed the fire with his foot and grabbed the rake, heaping piles of leaves onto the blaze.

Dark, heavy smoke flowed from the stack, like signals being sent across the land.

Mrs Kerby leaned against the fence and looked at him. 'You okay now? Go all right in there?' she asked. 'Wasn't too bad?'

Looking at her, Joel tried to work out what she was asking. Prison was a fucked-up joint. Prisoners could be the lowest of the low, fighting between their own factions. Trying to bribe guards. A place where everyone wanted more: more food, more time outside, more phone privileges.

He shrugged.

'No one,' she started, then paused. 'No one, uh, hurt—'

'No.' The word pushed out of him like carbonated drink from a shaken bottle.

'Good. Good. That was always your mother's biggest worry. That you'd be . . . damaged when you got out.'

Damaged? He was more than that. He couldn't spend nine years in jail for a crime he didn't commit and come out as he'd gone in. 'I can't remember who I was before.' As he said the words, he saw a look he couldn't name cross his neighbour's face.

There was silence except for the crackling of the flames.

'No,' she finally said, 'I don't suppose you can.' Mrs Kerby leaned down and threw a stick on the fire before looking back over at her house. 'Well, you'd better come to dinner tonight,' she said. 'I'll cook a roast. I'm sure it's been a long time since you've had a home-cooked meal. Will lamb be all right?'

Not giving him a chance to answer, Mrs Kerby walked out of the yard without a backwards glance.

Fear swirled in Joel's stomach. What would he talk about? Were his manners still okay? What was he supposed to take?

His fear morphed into resentment. He shouldn't have to feel like this.

BP—as he had come to call Before Prison—he'd been an articulate, social, content man. A bloke who enjoyed a beer at the pub with his mates and was comfortable in a restaurant or at the movies or theatre. Now, he couldn't think of a worse place to be, surrounded by people, pushing and shoving. Just thinking about the noise made him want to put his hands over his ears.

The commotion in prison was loud, constant and echo-y. Joel craved silence.

It was part of the reason he'd come home.

Barker was a quiet, sleepy town.

The only problem was the place held too many regrets for him and grudges from others, and he wasn't sure he'd be able to keep them all at bay.

And if he couldn't? He didn't know what might happen. Especially if he came across the Douglas family or, in particular, Steve. He'd had it in for Joel, even before Maggie died.

⁓

The fire had died down to a glow of coals, and there wasn't any more fuel.

Joel knew he couldn't put off a trip into town any longer. He'd seen a mouse run across the kitchen floor when he'd drunk his black coffee for lunch, and knew he needed traps.

He also had to take something to Mrs Kerby's house for dinner tonight. Chocolates or wine or . . . something! It had been so long since he had set foot in the local store, he had no idea what they would have or what would be appropriate.

In the garage was his father's car: a fifteen-year-old Toyota Camry, not driven for years.

Joel didn't know if his parents had still been driving at the end of their lives, just as he didn't know where they were buried in the cemetery—a visit there was on the top of his list of things to do, once he'd sorted out the house and yard—or what their last few weeks of life had been like. Maybe he'd hear about that tonight.

Collecting the keys from inside the kitchen cupboard, he went out into the garage, wondering if he would even remember how to drive. When he'd lived in Adelaide, he'd caught public transport; the only time he'd used his BMW 3 Series 335i was when he'd driven to Clare to see his parents.

And what a stir that had caused. People walking down the street had stopped to watch the bright red car roll down the road and come to a stop. They'd seen a good-looking, professional young man get out, lock it and stroll casually to the cafe where he'd booked a table for lunch.

People had whispered behind their hands, perhaps wondering who he was, if he was someone famous, and he had suppressed a smile.

They had been heady days, despite the knot of guilt in his stomach that had never seemed to go away.

Maggie.

His breath caught in his throat as he looked at the Camry. Nothing like the BMW he'd had before all this had happened. Still, his life was nothing like it had been, and having to get back in a car was just another fear he would need to face.

Yesterday, he'd found his dad's battery charger in the shed, and hooked it up. Putting the key in the ignition, he held his breath, waiting to see if the battery was charged enough to start the car. The engine slowly and sluggishly turned over, before gathering momentum and sparking to life.

Excellent, one hurdle down.

Patting his pocket, Joel felt to make sure he had his wallet.

In the driver's seat, foot on the brake, he shifted the gear stick into reverse and checked his mirrors. Then he backed out.

Pushing down gingerly on the accelerator, Joel took off slowly down the road. As he drove, getting used to the motion of the vehicle, he lost the frown and anxiety. A smile lit up his face as a feeling of freedom blossomed within him.

Instead of going to the supermarket, he flicked his indicator on to turn onto the road that went past the school, then the footy oval and the pool. He drove the perimeter of the town and marvelled at how it hadn't changed. There were a few newer, more modern houses built on blocks that he remembered being empty, but the rest was the same, even down to the old steel rocket-shaped slippery dip in the Lions Park. How many times had he burned his skin on that, sliding down in the middle of summer?

At the school, he wanted to park and look in, but he didn't want to draw attention to himself, so he slowed and looked over the fence as the car crawled by. He saw the classroom he and Maggie had shared through Year 11; the oval where they had sat and talked during recess and lunch; the toilet block where Steve Douglas had cornered him one day and threatened him with a beating if he didn't stay away from Maggie.

There hadn't been a reason given, just the threat.

He drove on, staying away from the railway line and the silos. It didn't take long to circumnavigate Barker, and within a few minutes he found himself back in the main street and parked in front of the IGA.

Unsurprisingly, the street was just as he had hoped: empty. He grabbed his list from the passenger's seat, yanked open the door and quickly walked into the shop.

A young girl stood behind the counter, twirling her hair and watching TV. She didn't even look his way. When he'd stacked shelves here all those years ago, his boss had always said he needed to smile and greet the customers. Still, he didn't mind, happy to be invisible.

Collecting a trolley, he started to search the shelves for the few things he needed: washing powder, soap, deodorant.

'And what the hell are you doing here?'

Joel jumped and his fingers tightened around the handle of the trolley. He looked up and saw Lynette Kindler, dressed in the IGA uniform, staring at him. Her neck was flushed, and she glared at him as if he were an apparition.

He tried to smile, then looked away and kept searching the shelves.

She took a step closer to him.

'Joel? I mean it, what are you doing here? What made you think you could come back?'

'It's my home.' He turned his shoulder away from her.

'Not anymore it's not. Not once Maggie was killed. The town doesn't want you here.'

Finding his mouth dry, Joel tried to swallow. 'It's a free country,' he finally managed.

'So? You gave up your right to live here when she died. What about *her* life? You stole that. Do you think we want the likes of you around here, with our kids?'

Lynette had never been a pretty girl at school, but with the sneer on her face, and leathery skin and deep wrinkles from sun damage, she was downright ugly, Joel decided.

'I'm staying.'

'Well.' She put her hands on her hips and glared at him. 'Don't say you haven't been warned.'

'Warned about what?'

Another woman, this one with curly blonde hair falling below her shoulders, had stepped into the aisle. Joel couldn't remember her name but he recognised her face: it was open and kind, and she flashed a smile at him, which faded when her eyes cast across to Lynette.

'Warned about what, Lynette?' There was steel in this woman's voice, a sort of cool disregard that made Joel want to run and hide behind her for a moment.

Lynette flicked her head and stared defiantly at her. 'None of your business, Kim. Just keep out of it. This is between Maggie's family and friends and this arse-wipe.'

Joel looked down as embarrassment flooded through him. How dare she humiliate him like that? Did they really think he didn't care about what had happened to Maggie?

Did they really think he didn't have nightmares about that night? Surely they understood he missed her as much as they did.

A bubble of sadness mixed with anger started in the pit of his stomach. A whirling noise in his mind stopped him from hearing anything thing else as he stared hotly at the cruel woman who was making accusations about something she couldn't possibly know anything about. His eye twitched and he knew he had to leave before something flicked inside him.

He started to silently chant: *Don't react, don't react, don't react*.

'Get out of here, Lynette. Go back to the job you're supposed to be doing. Show me you're not as small-minded as I think you are.' Kim's voice filtered through the mist inside his head.

Lynette tossed her hair. 'He's not welcome here, Kim, and you'd do well to remember that. Wouldn't want to see you have to choose sides now, would we? Your husband being the local copper and all.'

She pushed past them both and left the aisle. All was quiet again.

Joel breathed a sigh of relief and looked at the woman called Kim. He thought he remembered her now.

'Joel?' Her voice was kind and soft, like her face. 'I'm Kim. I'm not sure if you remember me. I run the roadhouse, have done for years; you used to come in and get hot chips on Saturday morning after sport. I was a bit older than you at school.'

Memories started to come back. The smell of chips and onions cooking. The gold pay-phone in the corner of the roadhouse he sometimes used to call Maggie.

'Hi,' he said. He knew he should thank her for her words to Lynette, but he didn't know how.

'Sorry about that. Lynette's always been a hothead. I guess you remember that from school.' Kim paused and leaned forwards. 'You need to know, Joel, that her opinion isn't everyone's.'

He shrugged. 'It is what it is.'

'How are you settling back in?' she asked. 'Do you need anything? I'd be happy to help.'

Shaking his head, Joel looked down. 'Got to get on,' he said and threw a couple of things he didn't need into the trolley before pushing it away from her.

He tried to remember Kim. He thought she'd always been nice.

Lynette, on the other hand, had briefly dated one of Joel's mates and had always been a bit mean. Cruel even. Were they married now? he wondered. He hoped not, for his mate's sake; no one deserved to get stuck with the cold, heartless Lynette. The girl who had always had a sour look on her face and had no empathy. He remembered someone had called her 'the rottweiler' once, because she was always jumping down someone's throat. The name suited her.

She had always worn her hair pulled tightly away from her face in a short ponytail, highlighting her snub nose and lips, which seemed to be in a permanent pout.

As the memories came thick and fast, the walls of the supermarket started to press in on top of him and his breath came more quickly. The red haze of humiliation and resentment descended again at the memory of Lynette's words. His chest felt tight and, breathing hard, he knew he had to get out of there, now.

Letting the shopping list fall from his hands, Joel turned and shoved past Kim, running through the aisles to the glass doors. He pulled instead of pushing and let out a half groan of helplessness and anger when the door didn't open.

Out in the street, Joel tried to slow his breathing as he bent over, clamping one hand over his mouth to stop himself from crying out. A few seconds later, the other searched his pocket for the keys of the car. Finally, he yanked open the door and tumbled inside.

His hands shaking, Joel tried to get the key into the ignition. It took three goes before he finally inserted it and started the car.

Quickly, he backed out and drove home.

Home to where it was safe.

Home to where there wasn't any noise.

Home to where he could be himself.

CHAPTER 4

'God, Dave, it was awful. You should have seen the look
on Joel's face. Like someone had stabbed him in the heart.'
Kim heaved the shopping bags up onto the bench and put
her hand to her chest. 'Then he ran like an animal let out
of a cage.'

'It's going to be hard,' Dave said.

'I tell you, if I could smack that woman . . .' Kim said,
her voice shaking in anger. 'What gives her the right to
carry on like that? I mean, he's only just arrived back!
Surely our town isn't so small-minded.'

Dave put his hands on her shoulders. 'Calm down, honey.
It'll be all right.'

'All right? How can it? She was so horrible to poor Joel.
If the rest of the townspeople are going to be like that, then
he's in for some kind of hell!'

'I've got no doubt. And he would have felt embarrassed,
but it's not the end of the world. I'm sure he won't have

expected a warm welcome.' He bent down and kissed the back of her neck. 'I know you have a kind heart and you hate seeing people put down and hurt, but this is one fight Joel is going to have to fight himself.' Dave paused. 'With us there if need be.'

'Us?'

'The coppers. I'm not going to let anything get out of control in Barker. We'll be watching the whole situation very carefully.'

Kim turned around and put her arms around Dave, leaning into his chest. 'I would have liked to have thought we were much more inclusive.'

'Grief and anger always bring the worst out in everyone, especially when there's someone who can be blamed.' He tightened his arms around her. 'And ex-cons have a notoriously hard time once they get out of prison. Joel's lucky to have a house to go to. Lots don't. Some don't even have families.' He paused. 'Ex-cons get given a small amount of money, and unless they have family or somewhere to go, most of them end up in shelters their first month or so out.'

Kim pulled back, looking appalled. 'I'd never thought . . .'

Dave knew that by tomorrow morning Kim would probably have organised to feed and house as many ex-crims as she could, her heart was so big.

'It's pretty hard to find a job when you've got a record. And imagine being confined for so long, getting your three meals a day, not having to worry about paying bills or anything, just trying to stay out of everyone's way and keep alive, then suddenly being thrust out into a world you don't know anything about anymore,' he said. 'Think about how much the world has changed in the nine years that Joel's been inside. You know, technology, the internet, all that sort of thing, let alone his parents dying. Life on the outside will be a huge adjustment for him.'

'I know, I know,' Kim said, shaking her head. 'That poor man, and then stupid Lynette, who would have no idea.' Dave saw her rub her hands over her upper arms in a comforting action she always did when she was upset. 'Don't these poor people have someone to help them come back into society? Surely the government can't just toss them out and expect them to be okay.'

Dave went to the fridge and pulled out a beer. 'Yeah, they get case workers assigned to them, but that's only if they stay in the city. Joel will be on his own up here.' He pulled the top off and took a sip.

Kim grabbed a knife and an onion and started to chop it. 'Well, I bought his shopping for him. Obviously he needed it, so I'll drop the bags around after I've made a couple of meals for him.'

Putting the beer down, Dave looked in the shopping bags. 'Have you got anything in the freezer?' he asked. 'From Catering Angels?' He was proud that Kim had started her own catering business. The locals now called her when their family members were too sick or unable to look after themselves. Dave knew that Kim didn't just provide food, she provided company and conversation as she dropped each meal off to lonely people. Her empathy was just one of the things he loved about her.

Cocking her head to the side, still dicing, she said, 'Hmm, I think I do. Probably only curries and casseroles, though.'

'Come on,' Dave said, tipping the rest of the beer down the sink. 'Grab them and let's go and pay him a visit.'

Joel was sitting on the bathroom floor, his arms wrapped around his knees, when he heard the sound of an engine pull up outside.

He froze.

Don't let it be Steve Douglas, he thought. *Not yet. Just give me some time.*

Maybe it was Mrs Kerby wanting to know why he hadn't turned up for dinner. He hadn't let her know he wasn't coming. He couldn't. There was too much bitterness and animosity running through his body, too many tears trying to force their way to the surface.

Heavy footsteps sounded on the porch, and then there was a loud knock.

'Joel, it's Dave Burrows, Barker Police.'

Dragging in a deep breath, Joel closed his eyes and tried to relax his quivering shoulders. He recognised the voice. Why was the copper here now?

Joel hadn't cried since Maggie had died. He had always felt too numb. But since he'd returned to Barker, he'd found himself on the verge many times.

'Mate, can you let us in?' Dave called again. 'Got a few things for you.'

He tried to call out, 'Coming,' but the word got stuck in his mouth. Instead, he slowly brought his body off the cold lino and walked towards the door.

His hand touched the doorknob and he left it there for a moment, taking a few more steadying breaths. From the corner of his eye, he saw a shadow pass by the window.

Cupped hands and a female face stared in. Joel recognised the woman from the IGA. Opening the door, he stood back to let them in.

'G'day, mate, just got a few things for you.' Dave held up the shopping bags and walked through the doorway. Kim followed, an esky in her hand.

'Hello, Joel,' she said with a soft smile.

Still unable to say anything, Joel closed the door. He remembered Lynette had said something about her being a copper's wife.

'Kitchen through here?' Dave asked, following the passageway.

'Ah, yeah. Right at the end.'

Following them, he watched as Dave put the bags on the bench and Kim set the esky on the floor. She opened it and took out five containers.

Joel blinked. 'What?' he asked, looking confused.

'Joel, I'm so sorry that Lynette Douglas said what she did to you today. It was horrible, and uncalled for.'

'Douglas?' Joel was confused.

Kim paused for a moment, looking baffled. 'Oh, Douglas is her married name. She married Steve Douglas.'

'Oh.' Not Ben. Well, he got off lucky, didn't he? But Lynette had married one of Maggie's brothers—that explained her hatred towards him. And Steve, of all the brothers. What must life be like for her?

A short silence stretched out between them until Kim rushed on. 'You left your list, so I bought what you needed. And,' she indicated the containers, 'there's food here. Enough for a few days, hopefully. I'll bring some more—'

'You didn't need to,' Joel stuttered, overwhelmed at their kindness. It had been a long time since anyone had shown him any compassion. He didn't know how to accept it.

'We wanted to. Didn't we, Dave?'

Dave nodded. 'How are you settling in?' he asked. 'Everything okay?'

Joel looked around and then waved his hand to the outside. 'Got a bit more cleaning up to do.'

Dave walked to the kitchen window and looked out. Joel watched him nervously. Was he going to ping him for burning the leaves? Suddenly he wasn't sure if he was even allowed to light a fire.

'How much land have you got there?' Dave asked. 'Looks like there's a great veggie patch. Bloody big one.'

'Um, five acres.' Joel voice was soft. 'Mum used to grow lots of veggies. She loved the garden.' Without warning, a lump appeared in his throat, quickly followed by goose-bumps. He gazed out the window too, expecting to see her working in the garden.

It was empty.

'I like a bit of gardening myself, but I just don't seem to get a lot of time.' Dave turned to face Joel, who stood cemented to the floor near the bench, staring outside.

'Joel,' Kim said, 'shall I put these in the freezer for you?'

'Thanks.' He pulled one of the shopping bags towards him and looked in. Everything he had written on his list was there, plus a few more things: chocolate and a loaf of bread. There was what appeared to be a homemade cake in a container too.

Dave turned back to look out of the window. 'Want a hand to shift that log onto the fire?' he asked. 'It's too big for just you, I'd reckon.'

Slowly answering, Joel said, 'Yes.' Then, 'Thanks,' as if he'd just remembered his manners.

The two men went outside, and Joel stirred the fire up with the shovel.

Dave threw a few medium-size logs on the coals, then they went to drag the branch over.

'I've got a beer in the car,' Dave said as he brushed his hands off. 'Want one?'

'I don't drink anymore,' Joel said. He looked away so Dave couldn't see the pain in his eyes as he answered. Even though he hadn't been drinking when Maggie died, he hadn't ever wanted to touch another drop. Life was too uncertain, too fragile. He was used to the ridicule, so he braced himself.

Dave just nodded and walked over to the closest veggie garden bed. 'My mum used to be a bit of a gardener as well,' he said. 'Except she mostly grew flowers.'

'Mine didn't see any point in growing something you couldn't use.' It was the longest sentence Joel had spoken since he got out of prison. The words felt foreign on his tongue.

'Well, that makes sense. We had trouble growing too much out of Northam, where I grew up. The heat was intense during summer. Everything had to be hardy.' He turned to look at Joel. 'What do you think you're going to do now?'

'Clean up around here,' he replied, looking around.

'What about work?'

Turning away, Joel hunched his shoulders over. 'It's going to be hard with a record. But I've got enough to live on for a while.' He glanced over at the tall man. He realised anyone could work out this bloke was a copper, without knowing. Dave was above six foot and solid. Joel's dad would have said he was built like a brick shithouse. '*No wind going to blow that bugger over!*' His hands were work-hardened and his flecked-grey hair suggested he was in his fifties. Joel looked into his face as Dave answered him.

'Yeah, mate, it will be. You're going to have some tough times in the next while. You know that you've got to report to the station once a week?'

The steel-blue eyes were kind, but Joel imagined they could turn hard and icy if something made Dave angry.

A strong gust of wind caused the flames to jump towards the men. Joel didn't move, just held out his hands to keep them warm and nodded.

Dave took a step back then moved closer again.

'I've got a two IC there. Jack Higgins. He's a good bloke. If I'm not there, you'll be okay with him.'

'Right.'

'Can you tell me what happened with Lynette Douglas today?'

Raising one shoulder in a shrug, Joel said, 'Doesn't matter. She must have her reasons.'

'I'm sure she does, but I'm in charge of keeping the peace in this town and I'll be doing just that. What happened?'

Joel turned to him and forced himself to look Dave in the eye. 'Why're you doing this? You don't know me, or anything about me.'

'Nope, you're right, but like you said to me the other day, you've done the time. Everyone deserves a second chance. And I like quiet and peaceful towns.' Dave grinned. 'Look, I'm very aware that you've been in jail, just as everyone else is, and it doesn't mean I won't come down on you like a ton of bricks if you stuff up on your bail or do something illegal, but until then . . .' The words hung in the air.

Joel was silent.

Dave leaned against a gum tree and waited.

'She said the town didn't want me back,' Joel finally said.

'Right. That all?'

'Something about me being an arse-wipe. I stopped listening after that.' Joel looked away so his humiliation didn't show.

'That had to hurt a bit?'

'They can think what they like.' Joël took a breath, then spread his hands around to indicate the land, a defiant look on his face. 'But this is mine now. It used to be my home. It still . . .' He stopped. When he spoke again, his voice was strong and steady. 'It still is. I'm not going anywhere.'

CHAPTER 5

The cattle bellowed loudly, stopping to turn around and look for their calves, as Emma hunted them across the paddock and through the gate, into the yards.

Opening her ute door, she tumbled out quickly, grabbing her poly pipe that doubled as a cattle prodder from the back.

Cash was chained to the tray, dancing around, desperate to be let into the action, but she hushed him.

'If you get off, the cattle will double back over the top of me while they're chasing you and I won't be able to get them into the yards. Stay there.' She jogged up behind the cattle, calling out, 'Hop in, hop in, hop in,' as she banged the poly pipe on the ground for effect. 'Get in there!'

One mum turned around and looked at Emma as if she might charge at her, but Emma took no notice other than to take a couple more steps towards her and bring the poly pipe down heavily on her rump. The cow sniffed at a calf who was passing her and then trotted towards the opening of the yards.

'Hup, hup!' Emma called again, this time pushing a couple of calves forwards. Their legs were thin and stick-like, and one was knuckled over on her hocks. Both looked as if they were only a day or so old and weren't quite as strong as the calves born earlier.

A cow with milk leaking from her teats left the mob and came back with a bellow so loud, Emma could feel it reverberate from the ground up through her feet to her chest. The cow sniffed around the calf, then when she realised it wasn't hers she ran towards the mob again, searching, calling for her calf.

Pushing the two smaller calves into the yard, Emma slammed the iron gates shut and chained them together with a satisfied sigh. Getting the cows into the yards without them trying to turn around and get back out was no mean feat, especially when they had their bubs with them.

Her father had always taught her that, no matter what, the cattle had to go into the yards on the first go. If they doubled back and got away, they'd be harder to get in next time. Enjoying the cold and the grey skies, Emma ran her fingers over the chain on the gate. She could almost hear her father's instructions from when she was a child. '*Quick, Emma! Up behind them. Call out to them. Let the buggers know you're there so they don't turn around.*'

She looked up at the sky and wished that her parents could see her now—that they could see these cattle, see the improvements she had made to the farm and her plans for the future, to know that she was continuing what they had built, what her grandparents and great-grandparents had started.

Hanging her hands over the rails, she leaned against the gate and assessed the stock. The calves were good, strong sturdy animals with sound structure. Her dad would have been proud of them. He was the one who had introduced her to Nick and Sarah Moyle's Pathfinder Stud, where she'd bought her bulls for the past eight years. They produced good 'doers', and she'd always enjoyed the trip to Naracoorte for the bull sale. Her calves were sought after by feedlotters and always brought her good prices.

Emma had toyed with the idea of trying to finish the stock off for butchers herself, but her land didn't lend itself to that—it was too dry, with unreliable rainfall and not enough feed at the right times.

Nodding her head in satisfaction, she turned away and focused on the paddock where she'd last seen Matt, looking out for his familiar form. Raking her eyes across the stony land, she could just pick out the reflection of the sun shining on the silver bullbar, near the trough. He must be cleaning it.

Her phone dinged and she reached into her top pocket, flicking open the cover to look at the screen. She expected to see Jacqui's name; she was due to send through the details of a wine tour they were going on in a few weeks.

At the same time she realised the message wasn't from Jacqui, she became aware it wasn't the normal tone for WhatsApp either.

You have one new match.

Emma looked up. Her heart gave a thump and started to beat a little too fast.

Cash was still leaning over the side of the tray, his tongue lolling out in a happy fashion. The cattle were still in the yards. The sky was still grey. Everything was still the same as it had been two seconds ago, but now the dating site had told her a man was interested in her profile.

Somehow, that changed everything. Or at least it felt like it did.

Her fingers itched to open the app. Instead, she slowly put the phone back in her pocket and pulled open the door. She patted Cash's head, letting her fingers run down his soft ears. 'You're a good mate, aren't you?' she said.

Getting into the ute, she picked up the mic of the two-way. She had work to do. 'On channel, Matt?' she asked.

Static silence filled the ute, so she shoved the gear stick into first and drove closer to the yards and swung around next to the calf crush that Matt had set up earlier.

'On channel, Matt?' She tried again, looking to where she'd seen the ute.

This time he answered.

'Cattle are in. I'll set up and start drafting,' she told him. 'How far away are you?'

'Just finished fixing the trough in South Two. About ten minutes.'

Emma nodded, then gave a rueful smile as she realised he couldn't see her. 'Good-oh. Reckon I'll be ready by then.'

Hanging up the mic, she gathered the tags from the passenger's seat and got out and dumped them on the large steel bench that ran along the edge of the yards near the crush, before taking the rest of the equipment out of the back.

She filled a bucket with water from the tank near the loading ramp, then tipped in disinfectant and set it down next to the tagging pliers, ear markers and elastrators.

Laying out the tags from one to fifty, she then opened a container full of green castrating rings. The little male calves weren't going to have their balls for much longer.

'Oi!'

Emma jumped as Matt came into her line of sight. He was striding towards her, his gait as familiar as the blue Levi's jeans, red shirt and boots he wore most days. His dirty, oily Akubra was pushed down hard on his head so the wind couldn't shift it, and she could see herself reflected in his sunglasses.

Suddenly self-conscious, she ran her fingers through her tangled curls and gave him a quick smile.

'I didn't hear you,' she called, waving her hand towards the cattle. 'So noisy!' She walked up to him, by the tray of his ute, so they could talk.

'Want me to draft?'

'No, I will. Can you make sure that crush is okay, and then when I've got some of the calves into a pen by themselves, you can get them down the raceway.'

Matt nodded and turned to fossick through his toolbox just as her phone dinged again.

Her face flamed as Matt's hand stilled and his head whipped around to look at her. It was just a quick glance before he went back to his toolbox and grabbed a can of lithium grease, but it was enough to make her stomach drop.

Why had he done that?

Shit, shit, shit! she thought. Was this dinging noise the same one everyone had with HelloSingles? Was that why Matt was looking at her so curiously? Did he know what that noise meant? Why was it that the cattle had decided to fall quiet at that exact moment?

Oh my god! Another thought dropped into her head. What if Matt was on there too? Was that how he knew the notification noise? What if they got a match? How embarrassing would that be? The boss and the workman hooking up on HelloSingles. Still, at least she knew they'd have some similar interests.

Heat radiated from her as she turned away. She knew Matt was single, but that was all. He'd answered her ad in the *Stock Journal*, along with two other blokes and three women. As much as she'd wanted to employ a woman, none of them had had Matt's experience in station country.

He'd cut his teeth on a sheep property out of Port Augusta, where the feed was salt and blue bush and stones littered the surface of the earth. Then he'd moved to northern New South Wales and finished up at Barker, working for her. Matt was the model employee, and she had never given any thought to his personal life. All she knew was he turned up on time to work, did more than she asked or expected and left at night to head back into Barker.

As far as she knew, he'd always been single. He'd never once talked of an ex, and they talked a lot during their long days. Well, it was more like Emma talked and Matt listened.

And that was why Phil had taken a serious dislike to Matt.

It had been in one of her vulnerable moments that she'd asked Matt to come to the divorce party and she'd been even more surprised when he'd answered yes.

Emma glanced at him. Matt was opening the crush and stood up, just as she looked over. He had a strange look on his face and Emma looked away quickly . . . just as her phone dinged again.

The urge to race home and delete her profile was overwhelming. What on earth had she been thinking? She couldn't bear it if everyone knew she was a sad and lonely middle-aged women who was looking for a mate.

Her mum would have said something like: *'Don't worry, love. Someone will turn up when you least expect it.'*

Maybe, but Emma never went anywhere to meet anyone she didn't already know. Everything she'd read had said that online was the 'new' way to meet people. Even with that knowledge, there was a part of her that really didn't want anyone to know what she was doing. No one she knew had met anyone through a dating website.

Pushing the embarrassment aside, with her poly pipe in hand, Emma opened a gate into the yard and walked confidently through the large animals. A calf sniffed her leg and the mum reeled around, fixing her eyes on Emma as if she were going to eat her for breakfast. A quick but firm tap of the poly pipe on her nose turned her away again.

Opening the gate into the round yard, she herded ten cows in and pushed them out into another pen, away from their calves.

Another quick glance saw Matt busy with his side of things. She took the phone out of her pocket, glanced at the screen and felt her stomach fizz with excitement, trepidation and horror.

Four matches now.

God!

Turning the phone to silent, she put it away and concentrated on what she had to do.

The calves, bewildered and wondering why they were by themselves in a pen, called out loudly, foam forming at the edge of their mouths as their constant cries dried out their mouths.

Directing the calves into a small forcing yard, Emma pushed them up the raceway, towards the crush. She made sure she was in close behind them, like her father had taught her. These little buggers were known to kick, and they couldn't hurt too much if she was right behind them. The sore and bruised shin bones came from when she'd stood too far away and the calf managed to connect with the full force of its leg extension and hoof.

'Yup!' Emma yelled loudly, indicating for Matt to start, while she went back to draft the next few, happily forgetting all about the matches on her phone.

~

The sun had just begun to sink, and an icy chill was coming over the land as Emma and Matt pushed the last of the cattle into a paddock with fresh feed. The cows, heads down, munched contently, forgetting for a moment that they didn't know where their babies were, while the calves ran to each cow, trying to get their head near the udder. A quick sniff and the cow either let the calf drink, or sent it on its way to keep looking with a swift kick.

As they started to mother up, the noise abated, and Emma leaned against the ute with a smile on her face.

'Good job done, that one,' she said to Matt. 'Thanks for your help.'

'Wouldn't have wanted them to be any bigger, little buggers,' he said. 'Got a cracker of a kick for my trouble.' He rolled up the leg of his jeans to show her the bruise that was beginning to turn a deep purple.

Emma bent down to look and saw there was a large egg-shaped swelling as well. 'Ooh, that looks pretty sore. They're mongrels for that,' she said, forgetting her previous embarrassment. 'You'd better ice it when you get home.'

'She'll be right,' Matt said in his slow drawl. 'Beer?' He held one that he'd taken from the fridge on the back seat and held it out to her. 'Hair of the dog after the party and all.'

'I won't say no.' She reached for it as her phone vibrated against her breast. The noise was almost inaudible, but not quite. It was enough for Matt to look down.

Shit! She shouldn't have taken the beer. What would have been much more sensible was going home and deleting her profile straight away.

'It was a good party, wasn't it?' Emma said quickly, trying to distract him.

Matt held her gaze for a moment before letting a smile cross his face. 'Thanks for the invite, boss,' he said. 'You were right, your girls know how to throw a good party.'

Holding up the beer in a cheers, she ripped the top off and casually took out her phone. Taking a sip, she swiped up and gasped.

'Oh no! I've forgotten I'm supposed to be at the Remote Rural Women's board meeting,' she lied. 'Crap, I'd better go.' She turned to get into the ute. 'Thanks for the beer and the help. Sorry, I've got to run. We need to find an arid-pastures specialist to come and talk to the board, so we're discussing that tonight.'

Matt took a swallow of his beer and held up his hand to say goodnight. 'I know a bloke. Rick Morris knows a shitload about arid pastures. I met him when I was working in New South.'

Emma wanted to stop and ask him more—Matt knew so many people and so much about arid farming—but she couldn't tonight. 'Thanks for the info. I'll google him when I get home. See you in the morning.'

She turned the key and took off quickly. The ute was bouncing down the road as she looked in the rear-view mirror to see Matt standing, his legs apart and arms crossed and his beer resting on his chest, watching her leave.

~

Pulling the ute up near Cash's dog cage, Emma let him off the back and went to the bin to scoop out his dinner.

What she really wanted to do was get into the house, pour herself a glass of wine and look at the profiles of the men the site had matched her with. Or delete her profile. She wasn't sure which.

Cash danced around her feet as she filled up his water container and checked the chooks. There were three eggs. Well, that was one normal thing.

'Come on, mate,' she called to Cash and opened the door to his cage, waiting for him to jump in. Then she groaned as the strange expression on Matt's face came to her. 'What the hell?' she said to Cash as he jumped up into the kennel. Burying her head in his soft coat, she closed her eyes and breathed in his doggy scent. Cash gave a little whine and Emma realised she was holding him too tight. 'Sorry, sorry,' she said quietly and let him go, and he immediately started to wolf down the pellets.

'Night, my friend,' she said, reaching in to give him one last pat. As she did, another memory flashed into her mind, of her last dog, a border collie, lying still and cold on the ground where this cage stood now. Phil had baulked at the price of a dog cage on legs, lifted high off the ground, but Emma had sworn she would never lose another dog to a snake bite and had bought it anyway. After that there'd been a few nights where there hadn't been many words spoken, but it hadn't been his money she was spending, so she hadn't cared. A good dog was worth two workmen.

With one last pat she shut the door, sliding the bolt across before heading over to the house.

The faintest prickles of stars were beginning to shine through as she walked inside. She placed her phone and notebook on the bench and then opened the fridge door, trying not to notice how quiet the house was.

How lonely the house was.

Even before Phil had left, it had felt like this. Why was the silence and solitude bothering her now? Pouring a glass of wine, she looked at the phone lying silent on the bench, wondering what it held for her, if anything. With a deep breath, and a long swallow of wine, she sat down and opened the screen.

You have five new matches.

She tapped, and a familiar face flashed onto her screen, causing Emma to drop the phone in horror.

'*What?!*' She slammed down her glass and tried to find the settings to delete her profile.

'Oh my god, no,' she moaned. 'Where's delete?' In her hurry she accidentally flicked out of the site and into her emails.

'For fuck's sake!'

Adrenalin made her hands shake. How could this have happened? How could these bastards have made her very first match her ex-husband?

CHAPTER 6

'Emma?' Jacqui's voice came down the phone. 'Are you all right? You sound . . . weird.'

Turning the wine glass, which held her fourth pour, Emma answered, 'Fine. I'm just fine. How are you?' She felt oddly out of her body, as if something terrible had happened to someone she knew, not to her.

Is it really that awful? the practical side of her brain asked. *Surely this has happened to other people.*

I don't care if it's happened to other people! her emotional side screamed. *This is awful!*

'Ooh, I'm not convinced about that,' Jacqui said. 'Come on, 'fess up. What's going on?'

'Oh god!' Emma wailed.

This time her friend sounded alarmed. 'What is it, Em? Talk to me.'

'Phil . . . Phil and I. Um, we just got . . . got, um . . . We just got matched on a dating app.' Emma looked down at her still-shaking hands.

In the hour since she'd finally managed to calm down enough to work out how to delete her profile, scenarios had run through her head.

Option one: Phil leaving the office and heading to the pub for his two after-work beers, telling everyone what had happened. 'Mate, you wouldn't believe it! That ex-missus of mine? She's on HelloSingles!'

Option two: Phil posting a screenshot to Facebook with an eyeroll emoji.

Option three: Well, she couldn't think of another one right now because Jacqui was barking with laughter.

Somewhere deep inside her brain, Emma recognised that Phil had put himself on HelloSingles too, but . . . Jacqui's voice interrupted her thoughts.

'You're kidding me?'

'No. I'm not. It's not really fu—' she broke off as embarrassment flooded through her again.

'Oh, come on! Yes, it is!' Jacqui let out another peal of laughter.

Emma stayed silent until her friend stopped.

'Okay, okay.' Jacqui took an audible breath but Emma could still hear the laughter in her tone. 'I'll admit, that was very unfortunate, but . . .'

Taking another swig of wine, words shot from Emma. 'Unfortunate! There's a shitload of other words I could use.' She dropped her head into her hand. 'Ugh,' she said quietly.

Jacqui sighed. 'Sorry, Em. Do you want me to come out?'

'No, it's fine. I just—' She let out another heavy sigh. 'I can't believe it.'

'Has he got in contact?'

'Of course not. There's no way he would. He's probably as horrified as I am.' Emma ran her fingers through her hair, wishing she could do something useful rather than sit here and complain. But she couldn't make her brain work. There were things to do: reconcile the bank account and update the farm diary with today's activities, for two. Matt's wages and superannuation must be just about due.

'Look, the algorithms will have matched you both and sent the suggestion to you. How interesting is it that Phil is on there too? He's not going to get in contact because it will be as embarrassing for him as it is for you, like you said.'

Emma was silent for a moment. 'I know,' she said quietly.

'On the bright side,' Jacqui said as she smothered another giggle, 'at least it wasn't only you and Phil who thought you were well matched!'

'Not for long, we weren't.' Emma, reflecting on the absurdity of her life right now, let a bubble of laughter escape. 'What the actual hell?' she asked Jacqui as she gave another snort.

'There we go! That's more like it. You know, it's really not that bad.' She paused. 'And by the way,' she asked in an accusatory tone, 'how come you're on there and you haven't told us?'

Emma stood up and walked to the fridge, hoping something would materialise into her hand for dinner; preferably something she didn't have to cook.

Why did she always think standing in front of the fridge would make food appear when there was nothing in there in the first place?

'I did it Sunday morning,' she admitted.

Jacqui let out a low whistle. 'What, with a hangover and all?'

'Yeah, well, I clearly didn't know what I was doing. I was probably still drunk. You're all a bad influence on me.'

'Ha, you reckon we were the ones pouring all that wine down your neck, do you?' She laughed again. 'Mm, well, I can see how you'd think that.'

Outside, the clouds crossed the sky, hiding the moon and plunging the house into darkness. Emma hadn't even turned on a light since she'd arrived home, choosing to sit in the murky dark and stare at the screen of her phone, hoping by some miracle she had misread the notification.

She reached across and turned on the light, blinking as the kitchen lit up. Deciding that bacon and eggs were going to be enough for dinner, Emma got out the frying pan and lit the stove as she talked.

'I don't even know why I did it.'

'Ah well, I guess if you've had enough to drink, anything can happen.'

The bacon sizzled as Emma cracked a couple of eggs on the side of the frying pan and took out a plate. 'Hmm, don't I know it.'

There was a pause. 'Are you really okay? You seem a bit low.'

'I'm not sure,' she admitted after a moment. 'I'm not sure.'

'What is it?'

'I'm a bit lonely, that's all. Everything else is fine. And you know, it might not have anything to do with the divorce. Let's not forget I live half an hour out of town and the only person I see in a day is Matt, and perhaps the postie if I meet him down at the mailbox. If I'm lucky a salesman or stock agent calls in, and even they don't cold call as often now.'

'Yeah, I can imagine it would get lonely.' There was another pause. 'I don't suppose . . . Oh, hi.' Jacqui's voice sounded muffled and then she came back on the line clearly. 'Em, I've got to go, someone has just arrived. I'll talk to you tomorrow, okay?'

'Have fun!' Emma put excitement into her voice. 'Don't do anything I wouldn't.'

She put the phone down on the counter, wondering what the 'I don't suppose' had been leading to, hoping it wasn't going to be the suggestion of another set-up. She didn't seem so desperate that her friends needed to do that, did she?

Taking her plate to the lounge, she sat down and ate as she watched the news. One good thing about being by herself, she mused as she wiped her fingers on her jeans, was that she could eat what she liked, when she liked, where she liked.

Her thoughts flicked back to the HelloSingles app and the other men who'd been matched with her. She hadn't even looked at their profiles before deleting everything. Perhaps . . . She shook her head. *Don't be ridiculous!* she thought. *Take a teaspoon of cement and harden up. You're fine here, just as you are.*

And she *was* fine. She knew she was. The house just felt very . . . empty. And she just felt very . . . numb.

Glancing at the clock, she saw that it was only 7.15 p.m. Her bed was calling, but she didn't want the nightmares that filled the darkness in the early hours of the morning. They only brought the smell of burning rubber, the sound of the woman's screams, her own fruitless attempts to pull her from the wreck.

Emma finished her dinner, washed the plate and frying pan and then stretched out under a blanket, ready for another night of restless, broken sleep on the couch.

The sun rose gently, and Emma watched the pinks and golds spread across the sky from the verandah.

Cash was at her feet and she absent-mindedly patted him with one hand while sipping her coffee, enjoying her favourite part of the day.

From the paddocks, she could hear the occasional bellow from a cow and, further in the distance, a tractor. Her neighbour was spraying early today.

The cool air touched her cheeks and she closed her eyes, breathing in the delicious, moist-smelling air. Really, there was no better place than her farm. Deception Creek's soil ran through her veins and she knew she wouldn't, couldn't, live anywhere else.

Her father used to say, '*If you've got dirt in your veins you can't wash it out.*' That's what Emma had, she knew. The rich, red dirt of the mid north of South Australia ran through her. The smell of cattle shit, rain on dry earth and freshly cut hay were her breath, and the gum trees and creeks that crisscrossed the land were her map.

Deception Creek had a history of bushrangers and cattle duffers. The hills that lined the horizon had hidden a group of thieves for ten years, back in the late 1800s. The story, which still echoed around the Hoppers' pub walls, was that there had been about ten men who knew those hills so well that they could disappear at any given moment. Like when the local police turned up wanting to arrest them for the theft of thirty cattle, or nine goats, or even harassing a woman as she'd hung clothes on the line at the homestead.

Emma had traipsed through the hills and along Deception Creek and found the occasional horseshoe or rusted knife in the dirt or at the back of a cave, and she'd loved knowing she was stepping on a part of history no one really knew that much about. But most of all, she loved that it was her home, bought by her great-grandfather three generations ago.

Putting her cup down, she got up and with a burst of energy jumped off the verandah and jogged across to her ute. Cash gave a bark and followed her, leaping into the back tray before she got there.

'Just you and me, buddy,' Emma said as she scratched his ears and got in. 'Think that's safest, don't you?'

Cash gave a small bark.

'Yeah, yeah, I know Matt's here too. Couldn't do this without him,' she said with a smile as she saw a cloud of dust rise into the morning sky. 'Look, here he comes now.'

Switching the radio on to the ABC, she listened as the Rural Report talked about the weather and grain-market futures, making a note in her diary of the day's prices.

Matt pulled up next to her and gave her a grin as he took his travel mug from the holder and had a sip.

'Morning, boss,' he said.

'Did you hear how high these grain prices are?' Emma exclaimed, waving her notebook.

Matt raised his eyebrows with a nod. 'Sure did.'

'Look, I've worked out . . .' She looked down at the phone in her hand and tapped the calculator app. A few sums later, she said, with wonder, 'You know, Matt, I could get the last part of the loan on the farm paid off if harvest comes off the way we think it could.'

'Well, that'd be an achievement,' he said. He paused as a magpie came in to land on the branches above them and warbled loudly. When it stopped, he had a half smile on his face. 'Actually, that's more than an achievement, Emma. That's freakin' awesome.'

Emma looked down at the screen again and checked the figures, then let out a laugh.

'I might have done it,' she said, her eyes shining. 'Geez, Matt, you know how hard it was for me to get that debt below a million, and now we might actually clear it once and for all!'

'You're a legend, Emma,' Matt said. 'You've had a lot of blood, sweat and tears since you came back, and look at you now.' He scratched his head and turned his gaze towards her. 'But I'm not here to give you a big head. Do anything interesting last night?'

Emma felt like a bucket of cold water had been thrown over her as she remembered the dings from the HelloSingles site. She ignored her discomfort. 'No, just me, dinner and a wine,' she said. 'Oh and the TV! You?'

'Sounds like we had pretty similar nights.' He held her eyes for a moment. 'Anyway,' he leaned back against the seat of the car and stretched, 'I better get on. There's a fair bit of work to do.'

Still chuckling, Emma put her phone up on the dash. 'You're right. I'm going to check the cows and calves we marked yesterday, make sure they've mothered up okay. Where are you headed?'

'I'll move that mob out in the back paddock closer to the yards so we can mark them in the next week or so.'

'Great.' Emma flashed another smile and started the engine. 'I've got to head into town after I've done that, so I'll catch you towards the end of the day. If not, tomorrow morning.'

Matt nodded. 'See you then.'

To get to the paddock, Emma had to wind her way down into a creek, and past an outcrop of native pine trees and granite, before the road took her along the fence line to the gate.

Putting her window down, she inhaled the still-cold air and watched the diamond dew drops that hung on the leaves sparkle in the sun as she drove across the landscape, quiet but for the occasional bellow of a cow.

As she arrived at the gate, she could see that some of the cows were out grazing, while the others were sitting, legs tucked under their large stomachs, chewing their cud. Pulling up, Emma watched the calves. None were worse for wear after their experience yesterday. A couple put their heads in the air and sniffed, before taking a few tentative steps towards her.

Turning the engine off, she shushed Cash and waited, a smile of pure pleasure on her face.

She knew that, curious as to what the large white, noisy thing was in their paddock, the calves would take a couple of steps forwards, then back, before coming closer and closer. A brave one sniffed the tyre and Emma slowly hung her arm out of the window, waiting.

Finally, she felt the tickle of hairs and a wet nose on her skin as a calf sniffed her, then tried to nibble her hand. The roughness of the tongue reminded her of the cat she'd had when she first came back to the farm. A black cat with green eyes, called Jinx, who had slept on her bed to keep her company through the night terrors. The same nightmare over and over of watching a car smash into a tree on a bend and being first on the scene.

She'd given up her job as an agronomist after that, not wanting to be on the road so much. The bloodied body of the woman—Alice, her name had been—was imprinted on

Emma's mind, and nothing she did could erase that image. Nor of the flames that had erupted while Emma had held Alice's hand.

The driver, Kyle, hadn't been hurt. He'd been so lucky, the ambos had told him. The ute had only just clipped the tree on the passenger's side. He'd lost his memory of the crash, but Emma remembered all too well yelling at him to help her try to pull Alice out. All he'd been able to manage was to stare at her dumbly. Though with the grief and torment that would have followed him ever since, Emma wasn't sure if 'lucky' was the right word. She suspected he wished he'd died in the accident with his wife.

Without warning, Cash gave a whine and the calf jumped back, spooked. He scattered the others who were coming closer and they all took off with a bellow, their tails in the air, upsetting the mums as they went. Within seconds the whole mob were crying out to each other to find their baby or mother and the cows were chasing after the calves.

Emma laughed as Cash started to bark loudly, unable to control his excitement. He ran from one side of the ute to the other as it rocked under his pacing.

Starting the engine, Emma drove off, circumnavigating the paddock before ending up at the trough. Algae was starting to grow, so she grabbed a screwdriver and brush, undid the bung, and with long sweeping motions scrubbed the cement walls and base before letting fresh water flow back in.

The email Kyle had sent her last week played on her mind. They'd stayed in contact, because they'd both been through trauma and had supported each other for a while.

I'm going okay. Back at work again. The time off for the anniversary of Alice's death was needed, but I think I'm back on track now. How're things on the farm? I hope you're having a good season. Might be up your way in the next few months. Would be nice to catch up if you were around.

The anniversary of the crash was the only time they communicated now. Early on, they'd emailed every month or so, but then Kyle had moved interstate and Emma had buried herself in work. Phil hadn't liked them emailing back and forth, either. Just as he hadn't liked her working closely with Matt.

It was nice not to have to hide the emails anymore.

'Come on, Cash,' she said, throwing the brush in the back of the ute. 'Town time. I might get myself a decent coffee while I'm there.'

Cash cocked his ears and put his paw on her arm as she went to get into the ute. Emma stopped and patted his head. 'You can't come with me,' she said. 'Not this time. I won't have room.' Pausing before putting her forehead to Cash's, she whispered, 'I freaking hope I don't see Phil. What a fiasco!'

CHAPTER 7

Trees lined both sides of the main street of Barker, their large black seed pods hanging menacingly from the drooping branches over the wide footpaths. Emma didn't know the name of the tree, but she couldn't imagine Barker without them. A few cars were parked in front of the post office, and others in the shade. Not that it was hot; it was more from habit, Emma knew. The forty-plus-degree days in summer made Barker locals find any piece of shade they could to stop their cars from being blistering hot when they got back in, though it didn't stop them from burning their hands on the steering wheel or the backs of their legs on the vinyl.

Emma sighed contentedly. Nothing in Barker changed, and that's what she loved about the town. It was small and safe. You could bank on Barker being sleepy and quiet.

She turned the wheel and parked in front of the IGA.

'Emma!' a voice called out and she looked over her shoulder.

Zara Ellison, the local journalist, was bouncing over the road towards her, and Emma felt herself smiling. She'd met Zara a few months ago when she wrote a story on female farmers. Emma had featured on the front of the *Farming Journal* along with Cash and her ute. The article had come out not long after she and Phil had separated, and Emma had appreciated the boost to her confidence.

'Hi, Zara. How're you going?' Emma asked, grabbing her handbag from the seat and slamming the door shut.

'Pretty slow at the moment, but I'm finding things to do. How about you? Any feedback from the story I did?'

Laughing, Emma ran her fingers through her hair and nodded. 'Yeah, a few old friends from school friended me on Facebook and some of the agronomists I used to work with before I came home messaged me as well. It was nice to hear from them.'

'Good. I had a great response from the readers about the whole story. So many women wrote in and said they were glad we'd highlighted how many successful female farmers there are out there.'

'How's Jack?' Emma asked as she stepped towards the kerb.

'Good,' Zara replied, nodding. 'He's stuck in the office with paperwork today, so he tells me, but that could change in an instant.'

'Of course.' A car she didn't know drove slowly down the main street and Emma looked at it curiously. 'Someone's got visitors?'

Zara followed her gaze. 'Oh no, that's Joel Hammond. He got out of jail a little while ago and has come back home. You'd almost have to know him, wouldn't you?'

Emma felt the surprise flow through her. 'Oh, Joel? Yeah, of course! I haven't thought of him in years. He used to come and work in the shearing shed at Deception Creek when he was a kid. I seem to remember he got into trouble with the police, didn't he?'

Zara gave her the rundown, and then said, 'Poor bugger. I don't think he's feeling especially welcome.'

Emma shook her head. 'Why's that—because he's been in jail?' She rolled her eyes. 'That'd be right. God, there are some small-minded people in this town.'

'I think it's more because of Maggie Douglas.'

Emma remembered. 'Ah, yes. So, so sad. But her death was such a long time ago. Surely people have got better things to think about than dredging up the past? Anyway, it was an accident. Nothing to do with Joel. He just happened to be there.'

'Yeah, the police ruled it an accident, but the family, from all accounts, is pretty upset he's back. It'd be pretty hard to get over that sort of thing. Still, Joel hasn't got any family here either. It would be tough on both sides.'

Emma nodded. She knew only too well how lonely it could be. 'It must be awful to come back to your home town and feel like you don't belong,' she said wistfully.

Zara reached out and put her hand on Emma's arm. 'You miss your parents.'

Unbidden, a lump found its way into Emma's throat, and she swallowed. 'Yeah, I do. It's hard to accept they've gone. And so close together. I'm sure Dad died of a broken heart after Mum went.'

It made her heart ache to think about the day her dad found her mum clutching at her chest in the chook pen.

'I've heard of that happening, when people have been together for that long. My great-aunty and uncle died within a couple of weeks of each other.' Zara looked off into the distance. 'I can't imagine loving someone that much, can you? I'd be really sad if Jack died, but I like life too. My brother Will would have rather been alive. So would have Dad. I think we need to live life to the fullest.'

Forcing herself to laugh, Emma said, 'Yes, well, liking life seems a good reason for not dying. Anyway . . .' She looked off towards the cemetery at the end of the road. 'Dad faded away after Mum, until one morning he just didn't get up.' She crossed her arms, trying to hold the sadness inside her chest. 'It's not like they were that old. Seventy isn't old anymore, is it?'

'You're absolutely right there. The older I get, the more I realise that people I used to think were old were actually pretty young!'

Emma laughed. 'I know what you mean. Hey, I'd better get on. I've got a fair bit to do today. I'll see you around, okay?'

They said their goodbyes, and then Emma went through the sliding doors into the supermarket, looking down at her list as she pushed the trolley.

'Oh, sorry,' a male voice said as she rounded the corner into the cleaning aisle and bumped into another trolley.

'No, it was me,' Emma said looking up, startled. 'I wasn't looking where I was going. My fault. Oh. Joel?'

The man froze, and it seemed to Emma that he had to force his eyes to meet hers.

'Yeah,' he answered cautiously.

'It's me, Emma Cameron. From Deception Creek. Our parents were friends. You used to come out and rouse-about when you were in high school. I was older than you, just by a little.'

'Oh. Yeah. Hi.' His shoulders twitched.

Emma watched as his gaze slid away from her and searched the shop as if looking for a way to escape.

'Have you got a bit of cleaning up to do?' she asked, indicating the scrubbing brushes and cleaning products in his trolley.

'Yeah. Bit to do.' He swallowed and went to move past her. 'House is in a bit of a state. I better . . .' His eyes flicked towards the counter.

'It's good to see you, Joel. I guess the house probably feels a bit empty for you. I know mine does, since both my parents died and I got divorced.'

Joel's eyes flicked back to her, and she detected a small amount of interest in them before he shut down again and spoke in a monotone. 'All good. Thanks. Got to . . .' He indicated he had to leave, and she stepped back.

'Take care,' Emma said, picking up a packet of sponges and tossing them into her trolley.

The next aisle was canned food, and she worked her way back to the fridge, where she took out a one-litre bottle of milk and then checked her list again.

'I saw you talking to him.'

Emma looked up. 'Oh, hi, Lynette. You're working here today?'

'I work most days. And I saw you talking to him.'

'Sorry?' Emma did a double-take. Lynette's face was red with anger, and her lips were pursed in a snarl. 'What's wrong?'

'I saw you talking to him. Joel Hammond. You won't want to do that, Emma. Don't try to pick that friendship up again.'

'What?' Emma wrinkled her forehead, trying to understand the woman's anger. 'Oh.' Annoyance flashed through her. 'Last time I looked, Lynette, it's a free country. I don't see any problem with me having a chat to Joel.' She went to move on, but Lynette blocked her path. Emma eyeballed her. 'And I'm not really sure why that should bother you.'

'It's obvious, isn't it?'

Emma gave her a curious smile. 'Perhaps to you.'

'We don't want him here! Steve and me, the whole family—we don't want a reminder every day that Maggie isn't here anymore. We don't want to see him walking down the street, breathing air, when Maggie is lying in the cemetery because of him!'

Emma thought carefully about what to say. She didn't want to antagonise Lynette any more, but she needed to be clear that what she was saying wasn't okay.

'I would have thought that every person in the Douglas family wakes up every day and knows that Maggie isn't here with them,' she said carefully. 'Having Joel back isn't going to make that any different.'

Lynette took a step towards her. 'Seeing him breathing will hurt that family. God, haven't they been through enough?' The tip of her nose was shiny, while her eyes were narrowed and filled with anger.

'Okay.' Emma held up her hands. 'I'm not arguing with you over hurt I can't understand, but I don't think trying to run Joel out of town is going to do anything worthwhile. Maybe he'll decide he doesn't like it here and leave anyway. Look, I've got to go.'

'We'll make sure he does,' Lynette said. 'And if you side with him, you'll be sorry.'

Emma stared at the woman, wondering at this rage-filled overreaction. Lynette hadn't been part of the Douglas family when Maggie died. And it was so many years ago. But there wasn't any point in continuing to talk to her, so Emma gave her a nod and went to the checkout, hoping that Joel was well and truly out of the store.

~

Lynette's breath was hot and angry as she gulped air into her lungs. Steve, the youngest of the three Douglas brothers, had ranted and raged when he'd found out Joel Hammond was coming back. He'd even rung the detective in town to demand that he stop him returning.

Of course, Steve was used to people doing his bidding. He was the principal at the Barker Area School, and if he wasn't telling his teachers what to do, it was the students. And he wanted Joel out of town, now.

For Lynette, just seeing Joel and knowing the anger that it brought Steve, made her want to lash out and hit him. She loved her husband dearly, as she did his family, and having this . . . scumbag back in town was going to hurt them more than anyone could realise, she just knew it.

Her father-in-law was the minister in the town's Baptist Church, but although Max always preached forgiveness, Lynette wasn't sure that Steve had it in him to be as generous.

Last night at dinner, the whole family had been together, discussing his return.

Paula and Max had hardly eaten, just kept pushing the dinner Lynette had cooked for them around on their plates.

Lynette had reached out to Paula, putting her hand on her arm. 'What can I do to help you?' she'd asked quietly.

Paula had smiled sadly and covered her hand with her own. 'There is nothing, dear. Nothing at all. We can't bring her back. And this was God's will. We don't have to understand why.'

Max had cleared his throat. 'Paula's right,' he agreed. 'Forgiveness is important—God asks that of us. Joel is back and there isn't any reason for him not to be here. Wherever he's living won't change the fact that Maggie's gone. Just let bygones be bygones.'

'What?' Steve had blustered. 'You can't be serious? There's no way he should be allowed to live in Barker!'

'Why not?' Sam had asked. 'Mate, it's a free country and he's living in his parents' house. His house now.'

'He's a convicted criminal,' Lynette had said.

Andrew, the middle brother, had shrugged. 'Not of Maggie's death, he's not.' He'd paused. 'Do you even know what he was put in jail for?'

They'd all looked at each other.

'I don't, for one,' Andrew said. He got out his phone and tapped on the Google app, but Paula stopped him.

'Don't,' she said. 'Just don't. I can't stand to have this conversation. Let's leave Joel to his own devices. As God is our witness and judge, to run him out of town is not ours to do. Let's make a decision now.' She eyed everyone at the table. 'If we see him, we'll just cross to the other side of the street, unless we get put in a position where we have to talk to him and then we'll be polite.'

'That's what God would expect us to do,' Max agreed. 'We're not his judge.'

Lynette watched his jaw work up and down as he spoke, knowing he meant what he was saying despite the pain it caused him to speak the words.

Sam had taken a deep breath. 'No matter your thoughts on God,' he said quietly, making it clear he didn't share his parents' belief, 'Joel was cleared by the police. He had nothing to do with Maggie's death. We need to trust them.' He let out a sigh. 'Look, Andrew and I gave him a hard time when it first happened, Steve, but it's in the past now. We're never going to forget Maggie, and I miss her just as much as you do. But, mate, holding onto this anger you've got . . . well, it's not healthy.'

Steve stood up with such force he pushed his chair over. 'I can't believe you all!' he shouted.

Lynette froze and looked down at the table. She'd known this would happen. A quick glance showed three empty vodka cans where Steve had been sitting.

'His life shouldn't be easy! He's taken Maggie's. Joel should always be reminded of what he's done. Not just to her.' He'd paused, and Lynette had watched him walk around behind everyone and touch their shoulder as he said their names.

'Because of what he's done to you, Mum. To you, Dad, Sam, Andrew.' He touched his own shoulder. 'To me. We all loved her. And we need to protect the town's children. Who's to say he won't try to befriend one of them and do something similar.'

Lynette had gulped back tears. She knew exactly what Maggie's death had done to Steve. It had broken him. His desire to be a teacher, then a principal, had been borne out of his desire to protect children. He'd told her that on their first date.

In the years since, Steve's behaviour had made it clear that protecting children was more important than protecting adults.

His anger simmering below the surface could boil over at any moment, and now, as she stood in the bright sunlight, Lynette knew she had to hatch some kind of plan to get Joel Hammond to leave town. For everyone's sake.

CHAPTER 8

Emma couldn't get the bewildered look on Joel's face out of her mind as she loaded the dog food into the ute.

'Cheers, Janey.' She waved to the girl on the forklift, and reversed out of the car park, testing her steering and brakes. The heavy load, which included large drums of chemicals for spraying the wheat crop, made for a sensitive steering wheel. Even though the accident she'd witnessed hadn't been her fault, the fear that crept into her nightmares made Emma extra cautious when driving.

As she headed towards the council offices where she had to register her new tractor, Emma decided to take a detour past the Hammond house. When she was in high school, she often used to stop and buy some of Mrs Hammond's fruit and veggies for her mum—turning up during lunchtime with a ten-dollar note clutched in her hand—but she hadn't been past in years. She remembered how the garden had been filled to overflowing with fruit trees, vegetable plants and herbs. Mrs Hammond would beckon her to come inside the gate, place a box in her hand and guide her through.

Growing on the front verandah had been a large, spiky bougainvillea along with pots of camellias, which Mrs Hammond had told her once were the only plants she grew that didn't serve a purpose.

'The trees, Emma,' Mrs Hammond would say, 'are for the birds' nests. They flower and give life to bees too.'

Emma had loved to wander around absorbed in the wildness of the garden. Tomatoes, peas, beans, broccoli, cauliflower, capsicums—Mrs Hammond grew it all. She would take Emma's hand and show her how to tell if a vegetable was ripe and ready for picking.

'Smell this,' Mrs Hammond would say as she thrust a bunch of basil under her nose. 'Now, not all farming men would like what you can make with this basil, but a lovely pesto would make great use of it.'

Emma would giggle, knowing her dad was a meat-and-three-veg man. Whatever pesto was, she wouldn't be seeing it at their kitchen table. Still, she would put it carefully in the box and take it home to her mother.

After she had picked her fill, Emma would take the precious produce back to school and then, later, carry it on the bus home.

Emma's father had done something similar with Joel, guiding him through the procedures of the shearing shed when he'd come out to rouse about. He'd shown him when to sweep the belly of the ewe away, or the crutch of the wether, and how to throw a fleece and not to drop the broom.

But even with Joel spending time at the farm over the school holidays and her at his house, they'd never really crossed paths. A couple of years' age difference seemed so big back then. It wasn't now.

Turning the corner, she drove down the familiar street a few blocks away from the school and slowed as she approached the house. She hadn't given much thought to Joel over the years since they'd left school, and though she'd felt sad when she learned that Mrs Hammond had passed away, she'd been out of town and hadn't made the effort to come back for the funeral—they hadn't been that close, she told herself. Verity Hammond was the nice lady who had sold her fruit and vegetables and taught her about plants and insects. Though, Emma had admitted to her mum at the time of Mrs Hammond's death that perhaps it was the lessons she had learned in that garden that had prompted her to become an agronomist. During those times with Mrs Hammond, Emma had developed a love of insects and plants, which led to her wanting to know more about how they could work together in harmony.

'Ah, Emma,' Mrs Hammond would say, 'aphids are a pest, that's right, but we don't need chemicals to get rid of them. Here.' She would mix a little Epsom salts and liquid soap in water and hand Emma the spray bottle. 'Just a little on the leaves. And don't forget to spray underneath the foliage too.'

Ironically, it was this early training that led Emma to study agromony, which in turn changed all thoughts of working in sync and organically on the land. *Kill the bad insects and fill the soil with synthetic fertilisers so we can grow the biggest, highest-yielding crops we can*, she was told, all the while ignoring the fact they were killing the good insects and worms in the process.

And as much as she loved organically grown food and good cultures within the soil, Emma had worked out quickly that organic farming wasn't feasible in large-scale cropping enterprises. So, she'd accepted what the industry was and got on with advising farmers what chemicals to spray and types of grain to grow.

The jolt she felt on seeing the familiar house startled her. The overgrown bougainvillea waved its fronds wildly in the breeze and threatened to scratch anyone who walked past the white fence, now faded and peeling.

Then she saw Joel. He was outside, up a ladder on the verandah. At first she thought he was cleaning out the gutters, but then she realised he was scrubbing the walls.

'What?' she said aloud, and then she saw the trails of yellow leaking down the wall. 'Oh no, what imbecile would do that?'

Which little bugger had egged the Hammond house?

And then she knew, and anger flared inside her. What right did anyone have to do this to him? From the outside, it seemed like Joel had come home just wanting to live the quiet life.

A small voice popped into her head and she recognised it as her dad's: '*Back the underdog like all good Aussies, Em.*'

She wanted to laugh, but it was absurd. This had nothing to do with any underdog. This was about a family who were badly hurt, victimising a man who'd been cleared of any wrongdoing in their daughter's death.

Still, if it was one of the Douglases who had done this, by anyone's standards it seemed too juvenile for them.

Kids, perhaps.

Lynette was angry enough to do something stupid, she thought. *But to what good?*

Lifting her foot off the accelerator, Emma wanted to stop and help Joel, but she didn't really have a reason. And what had he been in jail for? She couldn't quite remember. Something white collar, she was almost sure . . . But maybe it wasn't.

All her instincts told her told stop and help, to offer support. That's what her mum and dad would want her to do. But she didn't want to interfere. Or get involved with something that wasn't anything to do with her.

Speeding up again, Emma kept on driving.

Joan put her head in through Dave's office door. 'Mrs Kerby is on the phone,' she said.

Dave frowned, trying to place the name.

'She lives opposite Joel Hammond,' Joan clarified.

'Ah.' Dave paused before picking up the phone, wondering what the call was about. 'Dave Burrows, Mrs Kerby. How can I help you?'

'Hello, Mr Burrows. Are you the right person to talk to?' she asked. 'I've never had to call the police before.'

From her tone, Dave could tell she was nervous. And perhaps a little frightened. 'I'm sure I can help you. If I can't, I'll point you in the right direction,' he said. 'And call me Dave. What's bothering you, Mrs Kerby?'

There was silence.

'Hello? Mrs Kerby, are you still there?'

'Yes. Ah, yes . . . yes, I am. I'm not sure what to do. My neighbour, Joel Hammond. Someone has thrown eggs at his house. It doesn't sound like much, I realise, but there was a terrible mess on the walls this morning.'

Dave closed his eyes and let a heavy breath out through his nose. 'Right. Did you see who did it?'

'No, I didn't. But I can see him on the front verandah scrubbing the mess off now. The naughty little beggars must have used at least two dozen eggs. Such a waste, let alone anything else.'

Glancing at his watch, he saw it was only late morning. It would have happened last night, while it was dark, he was sure. Gutless pricks.

'Did you notice it when you got up this morning?'

'I only realised something was wrong when I saw Joel out on the verandah. I got the binoculars out to see what he was doing. I like to check on him, you see.'

'Why do you do that?'

'His mother and I were good friends. I feel a responsibility towards him. And I'm pretty sure he doesn't have many friends.'

'That's very kind,' Dave answered, picturing a woman wielding binoculars, and wondering if he was dealing with a garden-variety busybody. 'Did you hear anything unusual last night?'

'Well, I woke up in the early hours, thinking something had disturbed my sleep, but I couldn't tell you what it was. It was very quiet.'

'No vehicles or voices? Dogs barking, perhaps?'

'I don't remember any noises. But I am positive something woke me. By the time I was alert enough, everything was quiet.'

'Right. And . . .' Dave paused as he scribbled down a couple of notes. 'And why have you called us?'

'I'm sure Joel won't.' Mrs Kerby sounded definite. 'He doesn't like the police very much.'

'Why's that?'

She scoffed down the line. 'You actually have to ask that, Mr Burrows?'

'My name's Dave,' he corrected her gently. 'And I have to ask these questions in case there's something else I'm missing here.'

There was another long silence as Dave let her think over his question.

Then she sighed and started to speak. 'I don't know the full story, but Verity—his mum—always swore he was innocent of the fraud charge. She was adamant. And, look,

I do always believe where there's smoke there's fire and a parent will always stand up for their child, so I was never sure if she was wearing rose-coloured glasses or if she had reason to believe what Joel told her.' She hesitated. 'I have to admit I never asked.'

She was quiet again, and Dave let her think through what she wanted to say next. So many people became uncomfortable with silences, that they had to rush to fill them. Often that's where the best information came from.

'You know, Joel changed after young Maggie Douglas died. Like anyone would, I guess—such a tragedy to be involved in. He became withdrawn and locked himself in his room for weeks on end. Looked like the walking dead for a long time afterwards. In fact, a couple of times I wondered if he was right in the head. And if he wasn't . . . Well, who knows what he might have done?'

Dave was writing as quickly as he could, then spun his chair around to the computer and brought up Google.

'What can you tell me about Maggie Douglas's death?' he asked.

'She fell from the silo one night. Joel was there. I understand they'd been going out for a few months . . .' Her voice trailed off. 'I used to look after Maggie when she was a young one. I have to admit I was surprised when they started seeing each other, but then Maggie was always wanting someone to love her, and Joel was kind and considerate. They'd always been friends.'

'And you think he was involved?'

'Oh, not that he caused it, rather that he was there when it happened. Poor boy. He really was put through the wringer by the police during those first few days after Maggie died. Interviews at home, then at the station.' She paused. 'The nice policeman who used to be here . . . Oh, now what was his name. Granger? I think that's right. He called in detectives—from Adelaide, of all places. It didn't seem right to bring strangers in.'

Dave didn't see any reason to point out that was protocol. Instead, he asked another question. 'So, you knew Maggie quite well?'

'Well, yes, I suppose I did. But I hadn't been minding Maggie since she was twelve or thirteen, so a few years had gone by without much contact with her or the family.

'And Joel . . . I wish Verity were here to explain all of this to you. All the jail and charges. I was there as a friend, but . . . She never said much.' Mrs Kerby's tone lowered and she let out a deep, sad sigh. 'I have to admit I never asked, because I didn't want to be seen as nosy. I always thought Verity would talk to me if she wanted to.'

'That's okay,' Dave said calmly. 'Look, I'll come out shortly and see Joel, then I'll pop across to you, if you're going to be home?'

'I'll be here,' she said.

'Good. I'll see you soon.' He replaced the phone, feeling surprising sympathy towards Joel. The bloke was a crim, he reminded himself. That was the long and the short of it.

Maybe Kim's innate empathy was beginning to rub off on him, after all this time.

He typed into Google: *Joel Hammond and Maggie Douglas*. The search engine came up with Joel's charges, photos of the car driving away from the courthouse and a story. Dave sent it to print, and then scrolled down until he saw a faded school photo of a girl with braces. Her hair was pulled back into a ponytail and fastened with a blue ribbon. Underneath was the caption: *Violent death for teen Margaret Douglas*.

Dave shook his head, his dislike of the media stirring in him. To him, violent meant someone had used physical force to deliberately hurt another person. From what he could understand, that wasn't correct in this case. Maggie's death had been ruled an accident. He could only imagine how Maggie's parents felt when they'd seen that caption.

He clicked on the link and started to read.

> Margaret Hayley Douglas, sixteen, died on Saturday while climbing the Barker silos. It is alleged she and boyfriend Joel Hammond were aiming to reach the viewing balcony when she slipped, lost her grip and fell eighty metres to her death.
>
> Her father and local minister for the Baptist Church, Max Douglas, spoke publicly for the first time today.
>
> 'Maggie was a bright girl, with much potential and a bright future in front of her,' he read from a statement. 'Our family is devastated at her loss and hope that the police will do everything in their power to find out how such a tragic event could occur.'
>
> Hammond is helping police with their enquiries.

There wasn't much to go on there, so Dave snatched his keys from the desk and grabbed his jacket from the back of the chair. 'Joan,' he said to their secretary as he stepped out into the front office, 'you've been here for years—'

Without giving him the opportunity to finish his sentence, she burst out laughing. 'Calling me a fossil now, are you, Dave?'

Grinning at her, he thought again how steady she was and how the office wouldn't run without her. Joan took her work and herself seriously, and it wasn't often her sense of humour shone through. And just like Kim, she was a wealth of knowledge on all things that had happened in Barker over the years before he arrived.

'I wouldn't dare,' he said, then he asked, 'Can you remember much about when Maggie Douglas died?'

Pushing her glasses up onto her forehead, Joan smoothed her grey hair back and looked at him, her face changing from smiling to grim.

'It was awful. The ambulance sirens woke us at about 11 p.m.—I remember, even now, because it's so unusual for Barker to have a siren unless it's the fire siren at the station alerting all the volunteers they need to come to the truck.

'I knew something dreadful had happened, but it wasn't until the next morning, when I went to church, that we heard about poor Maggie.'

'It was talked about at church?'

'Of course!' Joan's eyebrows shot up in surprise. 'Have you forgotten that Max is our minister? He couldn't take the sermon that day. Too distraught.'

'Ah, right. Sorry, I wasn't thinking.' Dave wouldn't admit that all churches were much of a muchness to him.

'Maggie's death was the talk of the town. We prayed for the family for a long time afterwards.'

Dave nodded.

'Her family were so upset—not thinking clearly. One of the brothers, Sam—' She broke off, thinking. 'Yes, I'm sure it was Sam who went around and stood in front of Joel's family home and screamed obscenities at them. The police were called that day. I'm sure it wasn't the only time, but I wasn't working here then, so I couldn't tell you exactly. I guess the reports would be in the archive room, still.

'Then they got that detective in from Adelaide, and Steve, I think it was, or maybe Andrew—one of the brothers anyhow—nearly assaulted him when he went to tell the whole family that it was an accident. Poor fellow. He took off out of town as soon as the case was finished. Didn't like the country style of communication, apparently.' She took a sip of her tea and looked over the rim at Dave.

'And the police were sure Joel didn't kill Maggie?' Dave asked.

'You know as well as I do, Dave, that they would have taken that boy, locked him up and thrown away the key if there was just an iota of guilt there. The police were sure. But the Douglases were just as sure that Joel had killed her.' Joan stopped and closed her eyes for a moment. 'For a while at least. Max and Paula finally came to terms with the fact that it was an accident and so did Andrew and

Sam. Only Steve has hung onto the belief that Joel was responsible. And the anger.'

'Was there any history of him hurting her?'

'Steve? Oh no. I never heard him even raise his voice to her. He doted on Maggie.'

'No, Joel. Had he been caught giving her a clip around the ears, or a fat lip or anything like that?'

Joan shook her head. 'Everyone who knew him said he was a gentle boy. Wouldn't hurt a fly. Still, I guess you can never be sure what happens in the middle of the night when there are only two people around. And one isn't around any longer to answer any questions.'

Her last words sounded slightly sinister.

'You think he pushed her?'

'I don't think anyone can ever know for sure. But the police didn't have any doubts, and that's good enough for me.' She paused, watching him. 'Why all the questions, Dave? What are you thinking?'

'I'm just trying to understand the history here. Sounds like someone's given Joel's place a once over.'

'This town has a long memory.'

'As does every small town—or rather the people who live in them.' He stopped and harrumphed a bit and frowned. 'Okay, what I'm trying to understand is why the Douglases were so hell bent on the idea that Joel killed her. You're telling me that there's no previous record of assault, that he's a kind bloke. Is there any sense in their accusations, or was it purely that they needed someone to blame and Joel was the easiest target?'

Joan was nodding as Dave spoke. 'A little of both, I believe. She was the only girl among the boys, the apple of everyone in that family's eye. The boys always protected her at school and out and about, and the parents—well, they'd tried for a long time to have a little girl. After three boisterous boys, Maggie was very welcome. To lose her was like throwing a firecracker into the house—it was bound to explode.'

'Happy home?'

That brought Joan pause. 'Well . . .' She drew out the word. 'I would assume so. On the surface, yes, I would say so. The boys were always polite, if a bit scruffy, but they are boys, you know.' She gave a shrug. 'I think Paula may have had a little trouble controlling them. Like I said, boys—and country boys at that.'

Dave pursed his lips and went to speak as the door opened.

'Hello, hello,' Jack said as the door banged behind him. His eyes landed on Dave's jacket. 'Going somewhere?'

'Yeah, taking a little drive. Hi, Zara.'

Zara, who was holding Jack's hand, smiled. 'Hello, Dave. Hi, Joan.'

Dave could tell she wanted to ask where he was going but knew better than to ask. Zara was one journalist he liked—mostly because she was Jack's girlfriend and she'd helped him out of a few tight spots when the regular lines of enquiry weren't getting the job done, but also because she was ethical and didn't report anything but facts she could substantiate.

'Zara, I'm pleased you're here,' he said. 'You'd know the Douglas brothers?'

'Yep. Oh well, actually, I know Steve and Sam. I haven't met the other one. He works away in the mines, apparently. A fly-in–fly-out bloke.'

'Sam—what does he do?'

'He's a farm consultant. Works out of Port Pirie.'

'But lives here?'

Zara shook her head. 'Nope, but comes back to visit often.'

'Considering how feral they could be when they were younger, the boys have turned out very well. Their parents would have to be proud,' Joan said. 'Especially Steve. I hear so many people saying what a great principal he is. The school runs without a hitch and he seems to really love the kids and want what's best for them.'

'Hmm, okay, that's good info. Thanks.' Dave nodded to Zara. 'What are you up to, Jack?'

'Just need to get something for Zara, then I'm all yours if you need any help?' Jack keyed in the code to get behind the counter and opened the door.

'Yeah, I think you should come along.'

'Righto.' Holding the door open so Zara could follow him through, he said, 'Two minutes.'

Dave nodded. 'I can wait.' He looked over at Zara, who was glancing around the police station as if hoping a story might jump out at her.

'Haven't seen you for a while, Zara,' he said. 'What are you working on?'

Zara put her bag down and opened it. 'Check this out,' she said and held out a glossy pamphlet that had a microphone and the words *Crime Stories* emblazoned across it. 'I've started investigating interesting unsolved crimes and talking about them on my podcast.'

'Have you now?' Dave asked in a dry tone. 'So, you're going to be a thorn in my side again?'

Zara had the good grace to give him a wry smile. 'Not yet. The one I'm investigating at the moment is a woman who walked out of a house in Murray Bridge and never came home. The family are desperate to know what happened to her.'

'I'm sure they are. Aren't you working for the *Farming Journal* anymore?'

'Yeah, I still am. Just doing this in my spare time. It's really interesting, but heart-breaking. I'd never really understood the grief families go through when they don't have an answer. Whether it's a body or an indication that their loved one is alive.'

With a sigh, Dave nodded. 'Yep, it's shit,' he said honestly. 'I had a case once where the woman left and the family put a missing person's report out on her. She went into a cop shop in another state, told the blokes in there she was fine but she didn't want to go back to her family and they weren't to look for her.

'The parents and the husband were really shocked, but after a while—months, if not years—they concluded that they were happy they knew she was alive and okay. Still heartbroken, of course, that she didn't want them to contact her.'

'God,' Zara said.

Joan swivelled in her chair. 'There are some people who are just so selfish,' she said.

'It can be a lot more complicated than that, Joan,' Dave said.

Jack came back and handed his computer to Zara. 'Thanks, sweetheart. I'll see you when I get home.'

Zara gave him a quick kiss on the lips. 'See you all later.'

Outside, the late morning light was pale, although the sky was a vivid blue. A few cotton-wool clouds drifted by, the wind for once gentle, the temperature pleasant.

'Where are we off to?' Jack asked.

'Joel Hammond's house had eggs thrown at it last night. His neighbour rang to report it. You haven't met him yet. Time you did.'

'Eggs? Kids, was it? I would have thought graffiti or something more might have been the go rather than just eggs.'

Shrugging, Dave said, 'Who knows?'

It was a short drive across the railway track to Joel's house, but Dave circled down along the line and stopped at the old railway station, which had long been abandoned.

They sat there looking at the tall cement structure of the two silos until finally Jack said, 'This isn't Joel's house.'

'You're a funny bloke,' Dave answered.

'So . . .'

'This is where Maggie Douglas died. I'm trying to get a sense of what happened back then, if there is more to Steve Douglas's anger towards him.' He indicated to the silos. 'It's a long way to fall.'

Jack looked up. 'How tall are they?'

'I have no idea. The coroner indicated Maggie fell approximately eighty to ninety metres.'

'She had no chance. It's a wonder they had a body to work with at all.'

They fell silent as they looked up at the great cement structures outlined against the sky. The silos were huge constructions, with cylinder-shaped holding capacity. Tin on the flat roof, round caps on the top, with windows on either side.

'I can see why the cops would have had questions,' Jack finally said. 'So many options to kill someone here. Joel could have gone up in front and stamped on her hands, causing her to fall. Perhaps he actually prised her fingers from the ladder. Imagine a dark night, no moon. Everything silent except for them talking or laughing or whatever they did. Maybe Joel dared her to climb up.'

'See there,' Dave pointed to the edge of the silo where large bolts stuck out. 'Looks like they removed the ladder. I guess that happened after Maggie died. And, yeah, you're right. Everything you've mentioned could have happened. It's the sort of crime someone could get away with.'

'Zara did a story on these last year,' Jack said. 'I don't quite remember but something about some controversy when the grain handlers didn't open them for harvest. It meant the farmers had to cart their grain to towns further away.'

'That's never good. Longer trips make it harder to keep the grain away from the headers.'

'Yeah, and rumour has it they aren't going to open this year either.'

Dave looked up and tried to imagine what Maggie would have done when she realised she was going to fall.

'She would have screamed,' he said to Jack.

'Maybe, maybe not. Depends on if she was pushed, if she accidentally fell or she let herself fall.'

Dave nodded thoughtfully and looked to see how close the houses were. There was an empty, ramshackle building, which had served as the butter factory in years gone by, and next to that was the bowling club.

Dave pointed to the houses that adjoined the club. 'What do you think? One hundred metres from here to there?'

'Not much more.'

'If she did scream, they would've heard her. Barker is completely silent at night. A passing car at best.'

'Except for the drunks walking home on a Friday or Saturday.'

Turning in a circle, slowly, Dave took everything in. The empty railway shed, where a gust of wind caused a piece of tin to bang loudly against the rusting walls, while the stone train station lay empty. Rubbish blew against the doors and leaves skittered along the ground, making a scraping noise as they went.

'It's a pretty lonely stretch of the town, when you think about it,' Jack said quietly. 'Anything could have happened out here that night, and no one except Joel Hammond knows the truth.'

CHAPTER 9

The *For Sale* sign on the empty block next to the Hammond house dug into the earth, the weeds growing wild and untamed. They looked out of place now that Joel had started to clean up the garden. Across the road was Mrs Kerby's tidy house, and then the road stretched into a long line of vacant blocks. It was a development that had never got off the ground, nor had there been the population to use them.

The street was empty of people, and as Dave checked the area for anything untoward, he realised, more than he had before, that this was a silent, isolated street of just two occupants. If something happened out here, only two people, if that, would hear or see it.

Galahs were perched on the powerlines and on a few of the gum trees in Joel's backyard. Dave could hear them tearing at the leaves. Some of the debris floated down, landing softly on the tightly packed gravel path.

Dave looked on the ground for footprints or car tracks, anything to indicate that someone had stopped last night and hurled eggs at the wall.

'Any sign whether they came on foot or in a vehicle?' he asked across the bonnet to Jack.

'Nothing. I guess they could have walked on the footpath, but even though it's gravel, there aren't any prints.'

Dave assessed the house and noted where Joel had been cleaning. There were fresh spots among the dust that coated the house wall.

'Pretty easy to walk in here without anyone seeing, in the middle of the night. Even Mrs Kerby has to sleep at some stage.'

Jack's eyes strayed across to the road. 'She might just like a good chinwag. I reckon it could get lonely out here, and we're not even out of town.'

'Eight streets back from the main drag,' Dave said. Frustration filtered through him, and with a deep breath, he went over and rapped on the door.

'I'm busy.' Joel's voice came from Dave's left. He was holding a hose and looked like he was about to wash down the wall.

His gaze fell to Jack. 'Who are you?'

'G'day, Joel,' Dave said. 'You remember I told you about my offsider, Jack Higgins. Jack, this is Joel Hammond.'

'Good to meet you,' Jack said.

As Joel nodded, Dave noticed he still hadn't brushed his hair—it stuck out from his head like steel wool. His dirty clothes hung from him, scarecrow-like, but despite his wild-looking appearance, his blue eyes shone brightly and his face was beginning to lose the haunted, hunted look Dave had seen in other ex-crims.

'Sorry about this.' Dave indicated the wall. 'Something like this wouldn't normally happen here.'

Joel shrugged. 'Doesn't matter.'

'It matters to me. I don't like this type of behaviour in my town.'

'Can't stop 'em if you don't know who it was.'

Dave harrumphed. 'Do you know?'

'How did you find out?'

'Your neighbour cares about you.'

'Might've known she'd do that.' He looked across the road and waved at Mrs Kerby's house. 'She'll be watching from the house there somewhere.'

Despite the harsh tone, Dave could see that he was grateful Mrs Kerby had kept an eye out.

'So, who do you think might have done this?' Dave asked again.

'Could be anyone. Anyone who thinks I killed Maggie. Kids who are too scared but intrigued by an ex-crim.'

Dave chewed the inside of his lip and nodded thoughtfully.

'Nothing to do with the fraud charge, then?'

Joel looked surprised. 'Ah ... I don't ...' He shrugged as his eyes darted around.

'It could be, then?'

'I've got no idea.' Joel turned the hose on. The water hit the wall with a thump, making Dave raise his voice to be heard.

'You were found guilty,' he persisted. 'Was anyone around here, in Barker, affected by what you did?'

Joel stilled, then slowly turned the hose off and looked Dave straight in the eye. 'Being found guilty and *being guilty* are two different things.'

For once, Dave didn't know what to say.

Jack filled the gap. 'Did you hear anything strange or unusual last night?'

The water bounced off the wall and hit Joel in the face, running down his cheeks like a rush of tears.

'Like what? The wind. That's all.' He turned to Jack. 'Oh yeah, and a mopoke owl calling out.' He glared at Jack. 'Whoever did this wasn't going to knock on the door and announce themselves.'

Dave watched Joel as the man talked more than he had when he'd first arrived back in Barker only a few days ago. There was a fight in Joel he hadn't seen before, and as much as he was glad, he knew that fight could boil over. He also knew why Joel had spent five years in jail for a white-collar crime, and had an extra four added on. It wasn't because he couldn't handle his fists.

'When did you realise this had happened?'

'Not long after I got up.'

'Is there any other damage?' Dave asked.

Joel shook his head. 'Not that I've found.'

Dave turned and stared back at the street. 'What did the shells look like when you found them?'

Both Jack and Joel looked curiously at him.

'What do you mean?' Joel finally asked.

'The egg shells. Were they crushed or cracked into a few pieces?'

Joel looked around as if the shells were still on the ground, but he'd already removed them.

'I think they were crushed.' He glanced towards the side of the house. 'They're in the bin there.'

Dave took a few long steps to where the bin was sitting alongside the wall and opened it. 'Got your phone, Jack?'

At his shoulder, Jack reached in to the bin and took a few photos of the eggs, then put the lid down.

'They're crushed,' he said.

'Right. That means whoever it was came onto the verandah and pushed them into your wall rather than throwing them from the street, which would explain why you didn't hear anything thudding as they hit the side of the house.'

'I sleep pretty well.'

'But you would've woken to a noise, I'm sure.' Dave knew that Joel couldn't have done all that time in the slammer without learning how to wake at any noise, no matter how quiet.

'I usually do. I didn't hear anything last night.'

Dave looked at Jack, then around them.

'Worth dusting for fingerprints on the wall and gate, do you think?' he asked Jack.

'Can do. Except everything's been cleaned down.'

'Don't worry about it,' Joel broke in. 'It doesn't matter. It happened. Let's just move on.'

Dave frowned. 'I don't want to do that, Joel. I'm the one who has to keep control in Barker, and if this type of thing is going on, there needs to be a stop put to it straightaway.'

'I'm not pressing charges, so you can't do that.' Joel turned the hose back on and started to rinse the wall.

Blowing a breath out in frustration, Dave knew he was right. Unless Joel wanted to do something, his hands were tied.

'Make sure you ring me if anything like this happens again.'

'I won't.'

'You're happy to let whoever is doing this get away with it?'

'For the moment.' Joel turned his back on them.

Jack and Dave exchanged a glance before Dave shrugged and walked over the road to Mrs Kerby's house, Jack falling into step behind him.

'I've got the kettle on,' Mrs Kerby said as they set foot on the steps leading to her front door. 'What would you like—tea or coffee?'

'Tea would be great,' Dave answered. 'I'm Dave Burrows.'

'Greta Kerby. And you, young man?' Greta led them into the kitchen, where a freshly baked cake and cups were set out on the table.

'I'll have a tea too, thanks. I'm Jack Higgins.'

'This is such an awful business,' she tutted as she moved around the room, boiling the kettle and putting tea leaves in the silver pot. 'His mother would be so upset to think someone had defaced her home like that.'

'What can you tell me about the family, Mrs Kerby?' Dave asked and took out his notebook. He assumed the lady was in her late seventies or early eighties, and though he could tell she'd been tall, her body now was stooped and her movements slow. Her eyes still sparkled, though, showing her mind was active.

'They were a lovely family. Just the one child. Although they would have liked more, it just didn't seem to happen for them. And Verity and Billy both doted on that boy. You know, I did think they might have spoiled him too much, but if they did, he kept his feet on the ground. Wasn't a bragger. A nice boy. Helpful and polite.'

She poured the hot water into the tea pot and brought it over to the table.

'Just let it draw a little,' she said, before cutting two big slices of cake and placing them on side plates. 'Here. It's past morning-tea time. You must be hungry.'

Jack grinned. 'Thanks very much. It looks delicious.'

'Well, thank you, young man. I don't have anyone to cook for anymore, so I enjoy it when I'm able to.' Greta looked pleased as she pulled out a seat so she could sit down.

'Your family aren't here, Greta?' Jack asked.

'Oh no, no. They come and visit as often as they can, but my son is in finance in Sydney and my daughter lives in Brisbane with her young family. It's hard for them to get away often.' Her voice sounded wistful. 'The street is fairly lonely with just the two of us here, but I get out enough for it not to bother me too much.'

'Do you remember much about Maggie? She spent time over the road, didn't she?' Dave asked. 'And you said you looked after her when she was a kid?'

'You know, it's so long ago I can't quite recall.' Her eyes flicked to Joel's house before she picked up the tea pot to pour. Her hands were shaking slightly. In interviewing a younger person, Dave may have seen that as nerves or the fact they were lying. It wasn't as simple with an older person. Although he had to admit, he didn't think Greta was telling him everything. 'I know Verity told me that Joel had a girlfriend, and she and Billy found it cute. But Maggie's family didn't like it at all. Thought she shouldn't have a boyfriend at her age. They wanted to focus on her last years at school. They thought Joel was a distraction, I remember Verity telling me.'

'Ah, that old maxim of kids needing to focus on their study,' Dave said encouragingly, while he wrote *Parents didn't like her having a boyfriend* in his notebook. *Controlling?* He focused on Mrs Kerby while keeping an eye on Jack. He'd straightened at the comment about Maggie's parents too.

'Yes. And see, they were Baptists. Such traditionalists, the Baptists are. They didn't want their daughter gallivanting around at night with a boy. Probably wouldn't have mattered who the boy was,' Mrs Kerby said with a slight shrug of her stooped shoulders and an inflection in her tone. 'Their rules seemed to be very strict. If Joel and

Maggie were at the house, then one of Joel's parents had to be there. She wasn't allowed to go otherwise.'

'They were protective of her.' Dave underlined the word *Controlling*.

'I would say to a fault, but who am I to judge? Every man knows his business best. Now,' Mrs Kerby leaned forwards, 'when I worked for Mr and Mrs Douglas for a time, as a housekeeper-cum-babysitter—though I guess babysitter isn't the right word for a teenager, but I was there when she came home from school and made sure she did her homework and that kind of thing—I had exacting instructions about who I was able to let into the house after school and what she was able to do when she'd finished her homework. None of it was what I would perceive as odd, but it was strict.'

'And what did you see when you were at their house looking after Maggie?'

Greta took a slow sip of tea, seeming to think carefully about her words. 'I would say the same thing: the whole family looked out for that girl, the brothers included. They were very rigid in their routine and . . . I think that's about all there is to say about that.' As a full stop to her sentence, she put her cup down with a slight bang.

Dave wanted to raise his eyebrows, but he kept his face impassive. He didn't like the sound of these parents much. 'And what did Maggie think about this strictness?'

'She accepted it as normal. That's what it is, isn't it, Mr . . . I mean, Dave. Whatever happens inside your own home is normal to you, because you don't know any different.'

120

Jack brushed some crumbs from his notebook and nodded. 'That's very true,' he agreed, before he made another note.

'Maggie didn't rebel?'

Greta shook her head. 'Not that I saw in the home. She was very compliant.'

'Do you think the Douglas family have it in for Joel, then?'

'It's hard to say. I don't have a lot to do with the family anymore. They certainly did blame him for Maggie's death. How relevant that is in their thinking now, well, you'd have to ask them. And, if they did, surely you'd understand that?'

'Not really,' Jack answered before Dave could. 'He was cleared by the police of having any involvement with her death. It doesn't seem plausible they would hold a grudge for this long.'

Dave wanted to drag him outside and shake him. Of course it was plausible! There wasn't any 'normal' thought process when it came to losing a child, regardless of how it happened. When his daughter Bec was very small she had been shot by a criminal who was hell bent on taking Dave down. Although she hadn't died, he felt as if he'd lost her in the moment the gun had been fired; his marriage had been over and then he hadn't been allowed access to his children for some time after that. There was no rhyme or reason to the pain and anguish that followed. Or his behaviour.

'Oh now, Jack,' Greta chided, 'that's a simplistic view. If Maggie hadn't been with Joel, she would still be alive.'

Jack finished his mouthful and spoke. 'Surely you don't believe that. She might have climbed up the silos anyway. I would have thought *theirs* was a simplistic view,' he said gently. 'If indeed that's still their way of thinking. We know it's Steve's.'

'I understand how you would,' Greta said, nodding. 'But this is Barker, and small towns have long memories. And, sometimes, small minds.'

'Why did you stop working for the Douglases?' Dave asked, with a frown at Jack. 'Did they decide Maggie was too old to need you there?'

Mrs Kerby's mouth went into a thin line and a look of defiance crossed her face. 'They didn't like my lifestyle.'

There was a beat of silence and Dave fought the urge to glance across at Jack.

'Could you expand on that?' Jack asked.

'Well, dear, after my husband and I divorced when the children were very young, I found love again. But not in the way this small town approved of. My partner was a lovely woman, and once they found out that Sally and I were lovers, Mrs Douglas sacked me.'

The silence at that comment was broken only by the distant bark of a dog and the chainsaw that had been in periodic use since Dave and Jack had left Joel's house.

'I see,' Dave said heavily. 'I'm sorry you had to go through that.'

'Pfft,' Mrs Kerby said with a flick of her hand. 'As I said before: this is a small town with small minds. If Sally and I had been concerned about what people thought of us we would have moved. But my dear,' she leaned forwards with a smile that told both men that she didn't care what anyone thought, 'if Sally was still alive, God rest her soul, she would say exactly as I have.' She sat back in her chair and raised her tea cup just a fraction.

Dave wanted to laugh at the clear unspoken 'fuck you' in her words and gestures.

'Is there anything else you can tell us about Joel, or Maggie, or any of the Douglases that could help us?' Dave asked.

'Well,' she hesitated. 'I don't know if this is anything, but just before I finished up working for the Douglases, Maggie complained of having trouble sleeping. When I asked her if there was anything troubling her, she said she was having nightmares, but that's all she'd say.'

'You think there was something else?' Dave asked, leaning forwards.

After a long moment, Greta shook her head. 'I couldn't say.'

Jack was frowning as he got into the car. 'There's something strange about this,' he said.

'What are you thinking?' Dave asked.

'I can't put my finger on it, but I'm not liking the strictness of the family. That just seems weird. Almost obsessive.'

'Not necessarily back then,' Dave said as he started the car and pulled out into the street. 'Don't forget, it's quite a few years ago—twenty . . . what, nine? Yeah? Things were different back then. I mean, it wasn't quite "Come home when the streetlights come on", but it was close.'

'But that's what I mean. Most kids would've been allowed to do just that, especially in a small country town, way back when. Maggie wasn't,' Jack said. 'I still feel there's something odd about the situation.'

'Good,' Dave said. 'Trust your gut. I've always told you that. What are you going to do to work out what it is?'

'I'd like to pull the file on Maggie Douglas and check out if there've been any arrests or complaints made against any of the family—the brothers, all of them.'

'Righto, you do that. Good idea. Although if Steve is a school principal, you'll probably not find anything on him. Still, it's worth checking. And I reckon I'd better start going through that fraud file to see if there was someone around here who Joel upset.'

'There is one other thing that's bothering me,' Jack said.

'Which is?'

'Egging a house. It seems pretty petty to me. Not done by someone who's holding a lifelong grudge. More like kids who've heard he's back in town and don't know half the story, much less the truth. Or, like Joel suggested, an inquisitive teenager.'

'I agree.'

'So . . .'

'We keep an eye on Joel's house. We might even do a couple of patrols during the evening and early morning. But I believe that whoever did that isn't going to cause us too many problems. It'll be someone like Lynette Douglas we're going to need to look out for.' He paused. 'She's an angry woman, isn't she?'

'Yep,' Jack agreed. 'Do you think she could give us any information?'

Dave pondered this as he drove. 'We could certainly go and have a yarn, but I don't want to stir the Douglases up unless we have to. I've got a bad feeling this could get out of hand very quickly if we do.'

'We've got a responsibility to all involved here.'

'We do.'

'But . . .'

Dave turned to look at Jack. 'But what?'

Jack paused, and then said, 'What if it turns out that Maggie's death wasn't an accident? What if it was murder?'

CHAPTER 10

1992

Maggie swung her school bag over her shoulder and smiled at Joel.

'Coming? I'm going to the pool.'

'I told you, I can't. I've got a ton of homework to do.' He avoided her gaze, knowing she would be pouting.

'Come on, you promised me you wouldn't leave me by myself. Not with . . .'

'I know!' snapped Joel. 'But . . .' He took a breath and tried to control his temper. This boyfriend–girlfriend thing was a lot more tiring that he'd expected. 'Maggie, why don't you come back to mine? Mum will have the aircon on. I know it's not the same as going to the pool, but . . .'

Maggie wiped her brow. 'It's revoltingly hot. I can't believe this is the fifth day above forty. I hate the heat and water is cool.' She put her hand out to open the iron gate and jumped back. 'Shit! That's hot.'

Joel fought the urge to roll his eyes and bumped the gate with his school bag. 'You should know that. You've lived here for a few years.'

As they walked down the footpath together, Maggie slipped her hand into his. 'This is fun,' she said. 'Pretending and all.'

Joel glanced around and saw the school bus driver watching them, a half grin playing around her mouth. He assumed she couldn't wait to get home and ring a friend to tell them what she'd seen. Great: more gossip. He'd already been warned off by one of Maggie's brothers and he was half expecting a phone call or visit from Maggie's father. Everyone in town knew how much of a short leash the family kept Maggie on.

'Joel?' Maggie squeezed his hand, and he refocused on her.

'What?'

'It's fun.'

'Um, yeah. It is. So, are you coming home with me or what? I have to start my maths study. We've got a test in a few days and I can't fail it.'

'You should come to the pool and cool off first. Then we can go back to your place. It's easier to study when you're cool.' A cloud crossed her face. 'Your house is much nicer than mine.'

Joel looked down at her and felt his heart squeeze. He had promised her he wouldn't leave her alone. But he also had this maths test to study for. He was a straight-A student now, but he didn't want his marks to drop; the uni course he wanted to apply for looked at all of the year eleven and twelve grades, not just the final exam results.

'Come on,' Maggie cajoled. 'It'll be fun. We don't have to stay long. Just enough to cool down. Then the aircon can keep us cool! I think Greta's on pool duty; we might be able to con her into giving us a free ice cream.'

'I'll have to run home and get my bathers,' he said. 'And you don't have to con anyone for anything. I'll buy the ice creams. I've got the money.' Warmth shot through him as he watched her face come alive with pleasure.

'You've always got money! You'll have to teach me to budget the way you do. I've got no idea.'

Joel shrugged. 'I work. You're not allowed to. Hard for you to save when they divvy out pocket money weekly rather than letting you out into the real world and showing you what has to happen.'

'I'd like to work. That'd get me out of the house a bit more.' She twirled around dreamily. 'Perhaps I could be a hairdresser or someone who does make-up for weddings.'

'Maybe to begin with you could stack shelves, like I do. You've got to study to do those other things. You'll have to work on your folks,' Joel said. 'Or just go out and get a job and then tell them. They're not going to say no if you do that.' He stopped and looked down at her. 'They wouldn't want to lose face in town. Might lose church members!'

Maggie bumped him with her elbow. 'Hmm, maybe you're right.' She gave a brilliant smile and started to walk again. 'Anyway, I've got my bathers in my bag,' Maggie said. 'And it's hot, so let's go!'

Half an hour later, they arrived at the pool and Joel handed over the entry fee for both of them.

Greta pushed back his money. 'Your folks bought a season ticket,' she said with a smile, then focused on Maggie. 'It's been a while since I saw you, young lady. How are you keeping?'

Maggie put her bag in the locker next to the office. 'I'm fine, thanks, Greta. Just doing what I normally do.'

'And how are your folks? And those brothers of yours?'

'Just the same.'

Joel watched as Maggie forced a smile onto her face at the mention of her family. She was like a caged animal, he'd decided. Pushing at the boundaries to be let out and explore the world on her own. To be her own person. Someone who wasn't recognised only by her last name and what her parents did for a job. The stigma of being a minister's daughter weighed on her in a way that didn't seem to extend to her brothers.

Joel knew that last weekend, Sam and Steve had been at the park knocking back scotch-and-Cokes with a group of kids from school. Not one of them was old enough to drink, but all of that seemed to have been kept from Mr and Mrs Douglas. He'd never asked if Maggie knew about it, but even if she did, he was sure she wouldn't have said anything to her mum or dad. As much as she fought the constraints of her family, she was loyal to them in a way that Joel couldn't work out. Especially to Steve. Their relationship baffled him as much as his lack of understanding of why her parents kept such a tight rein on Maggie. Oh yeah, he'd heard the story about the cousin disappearing, but that had been in a different town.

And surely it was Mr and Mrs Douglas's choice not to go to the pub every Friday night, or not to join in with any of the sporting teams around town. But to withhold it all from their daughter too?

As far as Joel knew, there was nothing in the Bible about not socialising with people outside of the church. But that was the rule they seemed to stick to. Mrs Douglas taught Sunday School and after-school Religious Education. She went to choir practice and helped at the church op shop during the week.

Mr Douglas spent hours with the adult members of the church, through Bible study and counselling people who hadn't quite taken the faith on, or needed extra support. Other times he'd be in his office preparing his sermon. On the few occasions Joel had been at the Douglas house he had heard Mr Douglas practising aloud, with all the fire and brimstone he could muster.

As far as Joel could see, it was their life and beliefs they were forcing on Maggie. He wondered what the definition of a cult was. How she'd got away with hanging out with him for as long as she had, he wasn't sure.

'Last one in is a rotten egg,' she said, bumping her fist into his arm.

'Hey! That's not fair, I've got to get changed,' he called to her back as she ran down the grassy hill and jumped into the water with a scream.

'Good to see her having some fun,' Greta said softly. 'Are you looking after her, Joel?'

'As best I can,' he replied, but he couldn't help but frown, wondering what she really meant. No one was really able to look after Maggie. She was a free soul, when no one else was watching.

CHAPTER 11

2021

Sitting at her computer, Emma opened her email and took a sip of wine while she waited for her new messages to download.

Four o'clock was a little earlier than she would normally pour herself a drink, but she'd had one at lunch with the girls and decided that another one now wouldn't hurt.

Thankfully she hadn't run into Phil when she'd driven past his office; the curtains were closed and the building looked deserted. Maybe he was in Adelaide or away. It was unusual for the secretary not to be there, though. She briefly wondered if he was leaving town—she felt sad at the thought but, at the same time, she understood why he would. He wasn't from Barker—he was a blow-in, and though he had mates, without a really good network here it was hard to make the place feel like home. He had always spent a lot of time socialising in Adelaide, so a move would make sense, she mused.

Lunch with Jacqui and Maddy at the pub—the usual when Emma was in town—had been the normal mix of laughter and news.

As a teacher at the local school, Maddy was always full of entertaining stories about what the kids had done over the past week. But Jacqui had been quiet, which was unusual; Jacqui was normally the life of the party, or lunch, or whatever they did. Her quick wit and smile kept them all on their toes.

Jacqui hadn't come back with the information on their girls' trip away to the Barossa Valley either, which was also unlike her.

The emails dinged in and Emma scanned her inbox. Her heart took a leap when she saw Phil's email address.

I have your last lot of financials ready for you to pick up. When suits you? Or I could post them back.

Emma let out a breath and leaned back in her chair. Well, obviously he was in town. And these were the last financials Phil would ever do for her. Posting would be better, but she didn't want to risk them going astray.

That's good, she told herself. We can start to move on now. She quickly typed back: *Thanks, Phil. How about Monday?* and hit the send button. HelloSingles hadn't been mentioned and, for that, Emma was grateful. Maybe they would just both pretend it never happened.

Scrolling through her emails, she stopped when she got to one from Kyle. *Strange*, she thought. *What's he want?*

Double-clicking on it, she read: *Hi Emma, I've decided to take a little more time off and head out on a road trip. The ten-year anniversary has been pretty tough. I'll be heading your way in the next few days. I'd like to catch up if you wanted to? Maybe I could take you to lunch?*

Emma's fingers hovered over the keyboard as she composed her answer. She really didn't know Kyle other than sharing a traumatic event with him.

Her vehicle had been behind them, and she'd watched as his ute strayed onto the shoulder on the corner before veering towards the tree and connecting. Her memories of managing to swerve to avoid the accident were as clear as when it had happened. Emma remembered the noise of the locked-up wheels on the gravel as she'd pulled off to the side of the road. How her fingers had shaken as she snatched up the two-way radio handset in the car and called for an ambulance, and then run back to help them.

Kyle had been out of the ute, dazed and in shock, by the time she'd got there. He'd stood staring at her as if he were frozen to the ground as Emma ran to the passenger's side of the car where a woman was trapped.

That woman was Alice.

Emma had tried to pull the door open, but it was crushed in by the tree.

She remembered screaming at Kyle, 'Help me! Help me save her,' but he hadn't been able to move.

Then she'd smelled the fuel and seen the flames.

Alice's legs had been wedged under the caved-in dash and there wasn't anything anyone could do. When Kyle had yelled, 'Watch out!' Emma hadn't left the trapped woman. How could she when the fear and terror were so strong in Alice's eyes—they'd pleaded to be saved.

'It's okay,' Emma had said over and over, 'the ambulance is on its way. We'll get you out.'

Alice had tried to speak, but blood had flowed from her mouth. No one who had been there that day needed to have a good knowledge of first aid. It had been clear Alice wasn't going to live.

The heat had become more intense, the smell of burning rubber too strong.

In the end, it had been the ambos who'd dragged Emma away. The firies hadn't got there in time, and the car—with Alice still inside—had erupted into a ball of diesel-fuelled flames.

Emma had sunk to the ground, crying.

Kyle had just stared at the car, even as he was cared for by the ambos.

The police had arrived shortly afterwards, cordoning off the road and making sure the area was safe.

Emma had sat in the back seat of the police car with a blanket around her shoulders while the coppers asked questions about what she'd seen. Then they'd kindly driven her back to her office and left her in the care of work colleagues and friends.

After that the dreams and the memories had come thick and fast, and there was nothing Emma could do to stop them. Every time she went out on the road, she shook and cried and came back a nervous wreck, and she knew it would continue.

Two months after the crash, she handed in her notice, packed up her house and drove—very carefully—back to Barker and to Deception Creek. She hadn't left since.

Then, about six months later, Kyle had contacted her. He'd said he needed to talk to someone who knew what had happened, who had experienced the same trauma. He needed her to tell him what happened, because he couldn't remember.

'I know this is strange, but I feel like we've gone through this together. If you don't want to talk, that's fine, but I thought I'd ask,' he'd said on the phone. 'And I'd like to know what happened with Alice. Was she conscious? Did she say anything, right at the end? I just don't . . .' He'd broken down, and Emma's heart had gone out to him. She knew that whatever distress talking about the accident with Kyle brought up for her, it would help bring him peace.

Her parents had encouraged her. 'You might find it helps, darling,' her mother had said as she'd put a cup of tea in front of her. 'Talking to someone who knows.'

'Why would you want to do that?' Phil had asked. They'd been dating only a few months. 'It'll just bring everything up for you again, when you're beginning to get on top of your thoughts.'

Her counsellor had agreed with her parents: 'You know, Emma, I can sit here and listen to you talk and I can offer strategies about how to deal with the emotion you're feeling, but I can't possibly understand what you're going through because I haven't been there. Try as I might, I can't talk through the realities of it.'

She'd agreed to meet Kyle in Adelaide, in a coffee shop—with Jacqui outside, in case she needed an excuse to leave.

They had talked for hours.

Kyle spoke about his grief in losing his wife. The guilt he felt because he was driving. The way Oliver Sharpe had shunned him since the accident.

'Did Alice say anything?' Kyle asked over and over. 'Surely she at least asked for me?'

Emma hadn't wanted to tell him the truth: that instead of words, blood had spilled from her mouth. That Alice's eyes had been wide with terror and she'd known exactly what was happening to her. However slowly and haltingly, Emma had spoken that truth with tenderness and pain.

Then, she'd talked of her horror and guilt at not being able to save Alice.

'I couldn't shift her,' she'd said. 'Her legs were stuck.'

'I wish I'd been more with it,' Kyle had said. 'But I . . .'

Emma had grasped his hand. 'You were in shock.'

'I don't remember,' he'd said again.

She'd talked about being questioned by the police, and how the image of the ute was stuck like super glue in her mind.

They had met two or three times a year for the first couple of years, to debrief. Gradually, this became once a year, on the anniversary of the accident.

Emma wondered what they would talk about now. She didn't want to head out for lunch only to sit through stilted conversation with long stretches of silence.

And, she had to admit, she didn't want to talk about the accident anymore. She lived with the memory of it every day—in some ways she thought Kyle was lucky to not remember anything. The number of times she wished she'd been able to erase it from her mind were too many to count. And now? Well, it was over and done with, and trying to put it aside was where she was at.

Ah, Mum, she thought. *What would you do?* She looked over at the photo of her parents above her desk and felt the familiar pang of missing them.

Her mum had been her rock. Her adviser, her friend.

As Gail smiled down at her daughter, Emma felt the tingling on her arm—she'd felt it before when she'd called out to her mother for advice. She was sure she could hear Gail's words: '*You must only do what is good for you, darling.*'

Emma ran her hand over the goosebumps that had appeared, and closed her eyes, listening hard. Did her mum have anything else to say?

A loud bang echoed through the house, and Cash jumped up from his position under the desk and let off a round of barking. Emma's eyes snapped open and her hand flew to her chest as her heart started to pound.

'You home, Emma?' called Matt.

'Jesus,' she muttered, before raising her voice. 'In the office, Matt.' She shook her head to bring her back to reality, and glanced up at the photo again. *You must only do what is good for you.*

Quickly, she typed: *Give me a yell when you're in town, Kyle. I'll see where I'm at.* She hit send, minimised the screen on the computer and swivelled in her chair as Matt walked into the office with Cash at his side.

'Mate, you'd think by his bark that this dog would eat you. He's such a bad actor!'

Emma let out a laugh and reached down to pat Cash's ears. 'I know. He'd lick you to death rather than eat you. Especially if you—' She stopped talking and scratched under Cash's chin.

The dog flattened out his ears and let his mouth hang open with pleasure. She giggled again. 'Do this,' she finished.

'Such a first-class sook,' Matt said and dropped down into a chair. He took off his hat and crossed his legs, his jeans pulling up so Emma could see his socks beneath. They were odd—one black, one blue.

She stifled a grin. 'Do you want a drink?'

'Nah, not just yet, thanks,' Matt said. 'Got a few other things to do before I head home.'

Emma noticed a glow to his cheeks, and when he took his sunglasses off, there was a white ring around his eyes. 'You're a bit burnt,' she said.

Matt rubbed his fingers over his cheeks. 'That's the trouble with overcast days; they're worse than the really hot ones. I put sun cream on too!'

'Can be. So, what's up?'

'Have you checked the wheat in the hill paddock?'

Emma shook her head. 'Not for a week or so. Have you been there?'

'Yeah. I reckon there might be a bit of rust beginning to show.'

'Bugger. Still, there was rust in the paddock next door last year, so it's not surprising. I bought some fungicide today, it's on the back of the ute. I half thought this might happen.' Emma picked up a pen and made a note in her diary.

'Okay, I'll get the sprayer out tomorrow, then.' He leaned back in his chair. 'I've been thinking. Deception Creek has got two really different types of country, hasn't it?'

Emma leaned over and dragged her notebook towards her. 'Yeah, it has. All to do with rain. The Goyder's Line runs straight through the middle of this place, and the areas where we grow the crops have a few more inches of rain than the back of the place. Deception Creek itself is almost the dividing line.'

'Yeah, so, I've been thinking about the back half. You know you were talking about wanting an arid-pastures specialist and I told you about Rick?'

'Mmm.'

'He did a trial of saltbush a bit further north than here, and it worked. They planted medic clovers in between the rows of saltbush so the sheep didn't get too thirsty from the salt they were eating.' He handed over an envelope he was holding. 'There're some photos in there for you to have a look at.'

Emma withdrew the printed images and flicked through them.

'I guess you've noticed that in the crab holes, the feed skips away quicker than it does on a flat surface?' Matt asked as he scooted his chair closer and tapped on one of the photos.

Emma felt his knee bump hers and then stay there while he continued to talk.

'With our type of country here, heavy rain sheets off rather than soaking in.'

'Yeah, but in the crab holes the water lies in the puddle and sort of harvests it, so the moisture stays there longer. Then the grasses get away and hold on longer because there's more moisture.'

'And that's what he's done here. See these furrows?'

Emma looked at where his finger was pointing and saw a small germination of plants within a deep furrow between the foot-high saltbush plants. The seedlings were strong compared to the smaller versions on nearby flatter ground.

'That makes sense.' She spun around to her computer and typed into Google, *Saltbush properties for feed*, and hit the enter button.

An article from *FarmOnline National* came up, and Emma skim-read about a new variety of saltbush that had become a stop-gap for feed when seasons were dry. The bush had increased wool production on some farms by twenty-five percent.

'Sounds pretty good. I wonder why I haven't heard about this,' Emma said, still reading. 'This article is from 2018 and it's already been adopted in Western Australia. I don't remember seeing anything about it in any of the farming magazines I've read.'

'Want to come for a drive? I think I've got the perfect spot for you to trial this if you wanted to.'

'Sure.' Emma was out of her chair with excitement fizzing through her before she could stop herself. 'Take a beer?'

Matt stopped putting his hat on, and Emma could almost hear the wheels turning. 'Ah, go on then! Twisted my arm.'

Emma collected two beer cans each from the fridge and followed Matt out to the ute.

A cool breeze was blowing, and she looked up at the sky. It was clear blue, and it wouldn't be long before the sun slipped below the horizon, throwing pinks and golds onto the hills and making them glow.

Climbing in beside Matt, Emma handed him a beer. 'Tell me more about this Rick bloke,' she said as the engine rumbled to life and Cash let out a bark from the back of the ute.

'I think the first thing to know about Rick is his need to understand the soil he's working with. That's his catchcry. If he can do that, then he can help his clients improve their productivity through what they plant.'

'He's an agro as well?' Emma racked her brains to see if she had come across him in her work.

'Yeah, based in Queensland, so not someone you would know, I don't think. He's got his own business.'

'Right.'

'He's helped a heap of station owners improve their carrying capacity. He's a top-shelf fella.'

Matt swung the ute towards the northern part of the station. Emma took in the familiar landscape out the window. She liked the way Matt drove, his hands steady as he kept the wheels on the narrow track that wound along the summit of the ranges before curling down among small crevices and gullies. She felt safe with him.

The creek, for which the property was named, was deep and lined with rocks of all sizes, as well as gumtree roots gouging through the purple gravel in the creek bed.

Amid the stony hills, covered in bushes and long golden grasses, Emma felt contentment. This was her place and she loved it.

'Okay. Here's where we're looking at.' Matt indicated a stretch of flat land at the edge of the boundary fence. 'It's low-lying enough that the water will lie here until it soaks in. And over there,' he pointed to the clump of native pine trees, 'there's shelter from the trees as well as what the saltbush would offer.'

Emma sat back and surveyed the land. She could see what he was saying. 'So, a trial, you think?'

Matt nodded and took another sip of his beer. 'I really want this for you, Emma,' he said, swinging his gaze around to her. His brown eyes held hers. 'It's important that we get this land as productive as possible, especially considering the way climate change is affecting the weather and rainfall in this country. You know we're getting drier years than in the past, and I think this is going to be our new norm.'

Emma nodded agreement, and as she did, felt a weight lift from her shoulders. She took a sip of beer. 'Do you know, I'm so glad to have you with me on the farm. I often feel like I have to tackle this sort of thing all by myself, and it's huge! Well, it feels huge.'

In the back of the ute, Cash gave a sigh and flopped down to sleep. Emma got out, taking her beer with her, leaned against the bull bar and assessed the plot Matt was suggesting.

Matt came around to the front of the ute too and clinked his beer can to hers. 'I'm always around if you need me,' he said.

Emma smiled. She really had struck gold when Matt had applied for the job. 'I'll need to do a bit of research and I'll talk to the Remote Rural Women's Board about it. See if we can apply for a grant to bring Rick across. But it certainly sounds interesting.'

'You don't need a grant. He's coming to visit me next month. He'll hold an information day if I ask him to.' Matt grinned and gave his eyebrows a little wiggle.

Emma turned to look at him, curiosity on her face. 'Mate of yours?'

'In a roundabout way. He's my uncle.'

Emma raised the can to her mouth, watching him silently for a few long moments.

'Really? You're a dark horse.'

He met her eye, and held it. 'There's a lot you don't know about me.'

CHAPTER 12

1992

Joel grasped Maggie's hands as her feet found his shoulders under the water.

With a mighty push he heaved himself off the bottom of the pool and heard Maggie let out a scream of delight as she erupted into the air and then dove under the water.

Wiping his face, he put his head to the side to shake the water from his ears and looked for Maggie, who had just burst through the surface with a smile on her face.

'That was awesome,' she gushed. 'Let's do it ag—'

'Maggie!' A voice cut through the laughter and splashing of all the kids in the pool, and Joel watched as Maggie's head swung quickly towards the entrance.

A tall figure was approaching the pool edge.

'Oh no,' she muttered and started to swim towards him.

Joel followed her quickly.

'Maggie, you were told to come straight home from school.' Her brother, Steve, towered above them both. 'Mum's worried about you. I've been sent to find you.'

'I'm fine. I'm with Joel.' Maggie crossed her arms over her chest and stayed just a little away from the pool's side.

'You should have come home. That was what was asked of you and now I've had to come looking for you.' Her brother looked down at Maggie from the grass, his eyes never leaving hers. 'Come on, you know I've got better things to do than this. Let's go.'

Maggie looked away and didn't move.

'Steve, I'll make sure she gets back okay,' Joel said, putting his hands on the edge and heaving himself out of the water before standing up in front of Steve.

He was the same height as Steve, but not as muscly. And Joel was four years younger.

The two teenagers eyed each other.

'That's kind of you to offer,' he said. 'But—'

'Mum's not home anyway,' Maggie broke in. 'It's Tuesday and she's at CWA and then choir practice.'

'You're right, but she rang to check in. You weren't there and now here I am.' He sounded annoyed. 'Maggie, this is the third time in as many weeks. You know the rules. It just mucks all of us around if we don't do what we're supposed to. Come on, let's go.' Steve turned around as if there wasn't any discussion to be had.

Maggie's hand went to her mouth, and she shook her head. Joel thought he saw tears in her eyes, but when he looked again he wasn't sure.

'Mate, I promise I'll get her home safely.' Joel took a step towards the brother. 'We'll finish up here and have a shower in the change rooms and I'll walk her home. We won't be much longer 'cause I've got a test to study for.'

'Thanks for the offer.' Steve gave him a cold stare. 'But I'll wait. I bet she's got homework to do too.' He turned to Maggie, who had swum down to the ladder and was climbing out. 'Haven't you, Mags?'

She didn't answer but grabbed her towel from the ground and wrapped it tightly around her body.

Joel, uncertain what to do, followed her. 'You don't have to go,' he told her. 'You can come and have dinner with us.'

'Yes, I do. I shouldn't have convinced you to bring me down here.' The resignation in her voice was clear. 'It wasn't fair when you had a test coming up. I'll see you at school tomorrow.' Maggie disappeared into the change rooms without looking back.

Steve, who had followed Maggie's every movement until she disappeared into the dressing room, went back to the entrance to wait, ignoring Joel. Joel saw Steve acknowledge Greta with a smile, but she only gave a nod in return.

Without thinking, Joel jogged up to the boys' change rooms, which backed onto the girls' rooms, and spoke quietly through the wall.

'You all right, Maggie?' he asked. 'I can wait if you want me to.'

There was silence, and then Maggie stuck her head over the partition. Joel jumped and looked around, making sure there weren't any boys in stages of undress.

'What are you doing?' he hissed. 'You can't do that!'

She didn't smile.

'Don't worry about waiting,' she said. 'Steve won't let you walk with us. Sorry about this.'

'What's going on?'

'It's because of Hattie.' She shrugged. 'That's the way it is.'

Joel looked carefully at her face. Her usually flashing eyes were dead, and she was biting her fingernails.

'And it's around this time of year she disappeared, so Mum gets more upset.'

'Okay,' he said, but he made sure she could hear the uncertainty in his voice.

'I'll be fine. See you at school tomorrow.'

She disappeared, back over the other side.

A movement behind Joel made him turn around. Steve was looking at him from the doorway. Ignoring him, Joel grabbed his towel and went into the shower cubicle. A few moments later he heard her say goodbye to Greta and Steve's Torana fired up. The engine revved a couple of times before taking off in a spray of gravel.

'Wanker,' he muttered.

Joel turned on the taps in the shower, then stripped off and got under, letting the water run over his face. He couldn't shake the feeling that something really wrong had just happened, but he couldn't work out what it was. Maggie had changed the moment she heard Steve's voice. The tension in her body had been obvious. Was it just because she knew she had to go home? She'd escaped and been herself for a few hours, but then she got caught.

Towelling himself dry, Joel got dressed, threw his bag over his shoulder and went outside, shielding his eyes against the bright sunlight.

'See you later, Mrs Kerby,' he said to Greta as he left the pool.

'Joel, have you got a moment?' Greta beckoned him over. 'How's your mother? I haven't seen her for a few days.'

'She's fine. Busy with the garden, that's all. And Dad's away.'

'Ah, right. I thought it was odd I hadn't seen her.' She paused. 'You're good friends with Maggie, I see?'

He nodded.

'How do you think she is at the moment?'

Taking a beat to answer, he wondered if there was more to her question. 'Fine. I just see her at school mostly.'

'Good, good. She's a lovely girl.'

Joel didn't answer. He wasn't sure where this was going. He knew that the Douglases had sacked Greta; Maggie had told him. And why. Maybe Greta was now looking for something she could use against the family, which in turn would hurt Maggie. Well, he wasn't going to be the one who got his friend into trouble.

'I'd better go,' he said and grabbed his bike from the stand before she could ask him anything more. 'See you round.'

CHAPTER 13

2021

Jack pushed open the front door and smelled garlic and onions. There was soft music playing from the kitchen, and he felt a rush of warmth run through him.

There was something to be said for living with the woman you loved. And Zara was just that. The woman he loved.

'I'm home,' he called as he took off his boots and jacket and hung it on the hat rack, closing the door behind him.

Zara appeared in the hallway, smiling. 'Hey you,' she said, going to kiss him. 'You good?'

He put his arms around her waist and drew her to him. 'Much better now,' he said as he found her lips.

'Uh-uh.' Zara wriggled out from his grasp. 'I'm cooking and I don't want it to burn.'

Quickly Jack grabbed her waist and pulled her to him again. 'It'll wait.' He felt her relax under his hands as he kissed her long and hard before letting her go. 'Dinner tastes pretty good to me,' he said with a wicked grin.

Zara laughed and gave him a soft slap on the arm. 'Idiot,' she said affectionately, before running back into the kitchen. 'Lamb shanks in red wine and golden syrup,' she told him before he could ask.

'Yeah, well, I could get used to that,' Jack said, nodding approvingly.

'Your turn to cook tomorrow night. I'm going to be late.'

Jack took a beer from the fridge and pulled out the bar stool at the bench. 'I can do that. What are you up to?'

'Last counselling session.'

'Oh yeah, I forgot. Sorry.' He looked at her and thought how much she had changed over the past year. She'd gone from an angry woman who was running from her grief and trauma by working hard and pushing everyone in her life away, to a happy, free person who balanced her life. 'We should go out to dinner to celebrate.'

'You're not going to get away with avoiding cooking that easily,' she said as she opened the oven and put the baking tray inside. She leaned over and gave him another kiss. 'Anyway, I'd rather spend it with just you.'

Jack noticed her empty wine glass. 'Do you want another one?'

Zara shook her head. 'Lachie needs me to finish a story tonight, so I'd better not.'

'Lachie's a slave driver,' Jack said. 'What's the story?'

'There're some rumblings about the government wanting to introduce a new Pastoral Act,' she said. 'I want to ring Emma Cameron and see if she can give me a comment for the story and then I'll be able to get it through to Lachie tonight.'

'Do you want to do that now? I can watch this.' He nodded to the oven.

'I'll only be a few moments,' she said.

'Go on.'

He took another sip of his beer as Zara headed into the office. He flicked through Facebook on his phone, then Instagram, stopping only to like a couple of photos his sister had posted of his niece and nephew. He let out a soft groan as he remembered that he'd promised to take them to the Adelaide Royal Show next school holidays. Had he really promised to take the two little ferals to a sugar-infested, hyperactive event?

Shit, he had!

Putting down his beer, he went around the kitchen counter and opened the oven door a crack to check the shanks. A puff of heat hit his face, along with the lamb and garlic smell. His stomach rumbled.

Zara laughed loudly from the office. 'Can I quote you on that?' she asked. The answer must have been yes, because Zara asked if Emma was sure.

Jack picked up his beer and wiped the condensation away, thinking back to the file he'd started to read today on Maggie Douglas.

Emma Cameron had been one of the people interviewed in the aftermath of Maggie's death. Jack hadn't come across her before but he knew her name. Her ex-husband had been Jack's accountant for the past couple of years. Phil seemed like a nice enough bloke, perhaps a bit boring though.

Zara was smiling as she stepped back into the kitchen. 'All done and filed.' She came up and put her arms around Jack's neck. 'So, I'm all yours now.'

'Gotta be happy with that,' Jack said, slipping his arms around her waist again. 'What was Emma's quote?'

'Just about how the Act is outdated. One of the things that bothers most of the pastoralists is that public access roads often go straight through their properties, which can cause all sorts of biosecurity problems, let alone people driving through places unannounced.'

'Who keeps the roads up?'

'That's another reason to update the Act. No one seems to know. Graziers mostly do it themselves because they need to get trucks in and out, but they're public roads, with the public driving on them. In theory it's the government's responsibility.' She gave him a kiss then reached for the tea-towel and turned away. 'How was your day, my love?'

'Interesting.' Jack sat at the bench while Zara pulled out some potatoes and started to peel them. 'Can I ask what you know about Emma Cameron?'

Zara raised her eyebrows. 'Not a lot. I interviewed her a few issues back, but before that, not much.'

'What can you tell me about her?'

'Hmm, agro. Came home about ten years ago. Both parents are dead, so she works the family farm. Split with husband, oh, I don't know, a year ago? That article I did was the female farmer story. I interviewed her and few other women for it.'

'Yeah, I remember. You didn't go to school with her here?'

'No, she's a fair bit older than me. That's why I don't know her very well.'

'Right.'

Jack tapped his fingers on the bench.

Zara smiled and put her hands over his. 'Did you know that Dave does that when he's thinking?'

'What?' Jack looked at her.

She squeezed his fingers. 'When he's thinking, he taps his fingers on the desk or bench or wherever he is. You've started to do it too.'

'I didn't realise,' Jack said, grinning.

Zara went out of the kitchen and came back with her laptop. 'I don't know what you're looking for, but the easiest thing is to google her.'

'I don't know what I'm looking for either.'

Zara typed in *Emma Cameron, farmer, Barker, South Australia* and scanned the screen. 'Facebook profile, LinkedIn profile. Insta and Twitter. There you go: she's on every social media site you can think of.' She scrolled down. 'Oh.' She fell silent as she started to read. 'Shit, I didn't know any of this. Did you?'

She turned the computer around and let Jack scan the article.

Jack read aloud. '*Emma Cameron was the first on site. The female passenger died on impact, while the male driver was treated at the scene.*' He looked for a date: *2011*. 'When did you say she came back to Barker?'

'Ten years ago.'

'About the same time as this,' Jack said.

'Can you tell me why you want to know?'

'Chatham House Rules.'

Zara nodded her understanding. This was one thing that had come out during her counselling. She wanted to be able to help Jack but she wanted the stories at the same time. So she and Jack had come up with a compromise. When they spoke under Chatham House Rules, neither of them could use the information for their work.

'I read the file on Maggie Douglas's death today, and Emma gave a statement to the police as part of the investigation.'

'She would have been at school with Joel.'

'Emma's older, but not much.'

Zara turned back to the computer. 'You know, she said that she left agronomy because she didn't like being on the road much. That could be why. I don't know how I'd go if I came across an accident like that.' She pulled the computer closer and, after examining the photo, pointed to the passenger side. 'Looks like they only just clipped the tree.'

Jack went around and stood behind her. 'No damage to any other part of the car,' he mused. 'No names of the deceased or injured. Can you try to find them?'

Zara made a few taps on the keyboard and looked down at the list of options that had come up. 'Hmm, no. Can't see . . . Nope.'

'I'll check it out tomorrow.'

'Can I ask why Emma gave a statement?'

'She was staying at a friend's house that night, only a couple of streets from the scene. Looks like the coppers back then did a door-knock to see if anyone had heard anything. You know, a scream or a cry.'

'And did they?'

He looked at Zara. 'No. No one heard anything.' Jack paused. 'Maggie would have had to have screamed.'

Zara was quiet as she took in what he said. 'I guess it was late in the evening.'

'What she did say was that Joel used to help out on the farm during the school holidays. He hated it when any of the animals were hurt or died.' Jack watched as Zara continued to google. 'Do you remember anything about Maggie?'

'How old do you think I am?' Zara asked with a laugh. 'No, in all seriousness, I didn't know her at all. And to be perfectly honest, I didn't even know that someone had died on the silos until I went to do a story out there very early in my career and saw a plaque on the silo. It's a generational thing, I guess. In time people stop talking about it.'

Jack ran his hands through his hair, frustrated.

'Why, what's bothering you?' Zara asked, turning away from the laptop to fill a pot with water and put the potatoes on to boil.

'There's something not right about the outcome of that case, I'm sure of it.'

Zara whipped her head around and stared at him. 'What? You think Joel had something to do with it?'

'I don't know. The parents seemed too strict to the point of silliness.'

'They're church-going people. A minister, to boot. I wouldn't be surprised at anything they did.' She wiped her hands on the tea-towel. 'They're a strange family. Keep to themselves mostly, and the boys—well, they're personable enough, but . . . Oh, I don't know. Not friendly. Except Steve. He's always got a smile and says g'day.'

'Who are their friends?'

'Only people inside the church, I think.' She stopped and thought. 'I . . . hmm. I don't think I've really seen them out at all, now I'm focusing on them. I know Lynette—she's married to Steve, the youngest brother. She does a few hours at the IGA every day.'

'Are the sons church-goers as well?'

'I don't know about the ones who live away from here, but Steve, I don't think so.' She paused. 'Joan would know. Max Douglas is the minister of her church. Baptists, I think.'

Jack opened another beer and offered Zara a glass. She shook her head.

'See, all of this just feels off,' he said.

'But why? I'm not seeing where you're going here.'

'It's the close-knit nature of the family. Sounds like they didn't need anyone else except themselves.'

'Some families seem to be like that. Like couples who just like hanging out with each other, perhaps because they're content in each other's company.'

The oven timer dinged and Zara checked inside while Jack poured the water out of the potatoes and started to mash them.

'Yep, you're right.' He bumped her hip with his. 'Like us.'

'But we still like to socialise with other people too.'

'I know we do.'

He put a couple of heaped spoonfuls of the potato on each plate while Zara dished up the lamb shanks and hit the microwave start button to cook the beans.

'I'm still not sure what you're thinking here,' she said.

Jack grabbed cutlery from the drawer and looked at her. 'I'm not either. All I know is that what's written in that report is not all that happened. I just can't work out how I know that.'

CHAPTER 14

Dave leaned back in his chair and ran his hands over his tired eyes. It was dark outside, and Jack had long since left the station.

He should have been home by now too, but the file on Maggie Douglas's death had drawn him in and he hadn't stopped reading until he'd reached the end.

There was a lot of concerning information in there, and Dave was astounded that the police hadn't investigated further.

'Accidental Death' was the result given. But after everything Dave had read, that finding just didn't seem right.

On the surface it did. A young girl falling from a silo with no other outside influence.

But not if you read between the lines. That's where things got a little murkier. Jack's intuition was spot on, and Dave agreed. He just couldn't put his finger on what it was. Perhaps it was because Joel Hammond had been with her and his account of what had happened was a bit blurry. Joel would have been in shock, and Dave had noted that the statement was taken the very night of the accident, by the local blokes. Surely the coppers would have thought to go back and clarify his statement after the event?

The detective from Adelaide hadn't done that.

His phone beeped with a text message. *You okay, honey?*

He glanced at his watch and saw that it was nearly 8 p.m. *Sorry, sorry. Got caught up. On my way home now.*

Dave shrugged into his jacket, and then locked the office. Out on the street, he made a slight detour and walked the extra block towards the silo.

A pale moonlight bathed the quiet streets of Barker and lights shone on each corner, illuminating the footpath. His boots clicked on the cement and he tucked his hands in his pockets to keep them from the chill.

The silos stood outlined against the darkened sky, seeming more sinister in the night than during the daylight. Moonlight danced off the few narrow windows at the top. But for the occasional pigeon cooing, the night was silent.

Leaning against a streetlight pole, Dave tried to imagine what had happened that night. And he asked himself why it was so important to know the truth this long after Maggie's death. Would it change anything?

Should he just let Steve and Lynette work it out with Joel? Or maybe he could speak with Max and Paula to see if they had any lingering doubts and anger towards Joel. Perhaps the parents were sending Steve on their behalf.

Deep down, Dave knew that if he had absolute evidence he could place in front of the Douglas family, then the harassment would have to stop.

He also knew that if petty incidents like the egging of the house kept up, he would have to do something. If these rumblings went on, it wouldn't take long for the town to divide itself three ways: pro Douglas, pro Joel Hammond, and those who didn't care either way.

Just as Dave was contemplating going to have a chat to Paula and Max Douglas to try to find a reasonable way forwards, the sound of stones being kicked startled him and he turned to see Joel Hammond walking towards him.

'Funny time to be out for a walk,' Dave said as Joel stopped in front of him.

He had his hands in the pockets of a long dark coat, and a dark beanie on his head. Dave could see how he would easily fade into the darkness.

'Could say the same for you.'

Dave indicated towards the silos. 'Can't be good memories for you here.'

'Nah.'

Dave stayed silent, the puffs of his breath visible in the cold night air.

The two men stood next to each other, silent, looking at the brooding dark shades in the sky.

'Want to tell me about it?' Dave finally asked.

Silence stretched out between them until a mopoke call broke it.

'Maybe,' Joel answered quietly. 'Sometime. But not tonight.'

'I've read the file and have a few questions.'

Joel turned to Dave. 'Mate, she's been dead for a long time. The questions can wait until daytime, don't you think? I'm not going anywhere.'

'Of course they can,' Dave answered softly. 'You know where I am. You've got to turn up tomorrow for a check-in anyway.'

'I know.'

'Catch you tomorrow, then.'

Dave left Joel still staring at the silos.

As he walked towards home, he thought about Max Douglas's statement.

Max Douglas: I checked on Maggie at ten p.m. She was still working at her desk and said she'd be going to bed in the next ten minutes or so. When I walked past her doorway next, the light was off.

Senior Sergeant Cummings: Her door was open?

MD: No, there wasn't any light coming from the gap underneath the door.

SSC: I see. And you were sure she was in bed?

MD: There wasn't any reason to think otherwise. I'd never caught her sneaking out of the house before. I assumed she'd turned off her light and gone straight to bed.

SSC: Maggie wasn't a rebellious child?

MD: No. Not at all.

SSC: Why do you think she chose that night to go out?

MD: *She'd started to become friendly with this . . . boy.*
Joel Hammond. I'm sure he suggested they meet.

SSC: *But you don't have confirmation of that?*

MD: *No. You don't seem to understand. Sneaking*
around is out of character for her. Someone must
have put the idea into her head. She wouldn't have
had it herself. Or at least she wouldn't have acted
on it. Maggie knew our rules.

SSC: *Which were?'*

MD: *Bed by 10.30 p.m. at the latest. Maggie wasn't*
to leave the house after dark by herself. They'd
been the rules since she was a little girl.

SSC: *Tell me about her friends.*

MD: *Well, there was this Joel she'd started spending*
time with. Neither Paula nor I were happy about
that, but I guess you've got to give your kids space
as they grow, don't you? Still, we thought she was
too young to be tying herself to one person. One
boy. But we allowed them to have a certain amount
of time together.

SSC: *And female friends?*

MD: *Yes, Maggie had a couple of good friends, but*
neither of them spent a lot of time here. They saw
each other mainly at school and talked on the phone.

SSC: *I'll need you to give their names to the constable*
after the interview. Did Maggie play any sport?

MD: *No.*

SSC: *Was there a reason for that?*

MD: *Maggie wasn't interested in sports and her mother and I didn't think that the sports uniforms were, ah, suitable attire for a young woman.*

SSC: *Did Joel ever come to your house?*

MD: *Only a few times and only when a family member was in the house. If Paula and I aren't there, usually one of the boys is. Maggie was rarely on her own.*

SSC: *Was that a conscious decision on your behalf? I believe Maggie was sixteen.*

MD: *Her cousin disappeared on the way home from school one day. In broad daylight. Hattie was only ten. We were always concerned for Maggie's safety.*

Dave knew that Senior Sergeant Cummings would have made a note to look up the file on the cousin, but what he kept turning over in his mind was the fact that Cummings barely questioned Max Douglas any further about not leaving Maggie home alone. Because the Senior Sergeant was right. She had been sixteen; not a child.

~

'So, what I see,' Dave said to Kim as she put his dinner in the microwave to heat up, 'is a girl who was being smothered. Isolated. Kept away from her friends. And in this day and age, that would be classed as abuse.'

'People have different ways of bringing their kids up, honey. You know that. And if her cousin disappeared in broad daylight and was never found, I'd say that was a very good reason to be acting the way they were. They would have been petrified something would happen to her. That type of trauma shapes a person.' Dave looked at Kim as she stood with her arms crossed, leaning against the counter. She had her hair piled up into a knot on her head, with a few strands falling around her face.

He got up and went over to her, putting his hands on her shoulders and rubbing his thumbs along her collarbone.

'You're gorgeous.'

Kim smiled up at him and shook her head gently. 'That's not what we're talking about.'

'I know, but I had to tell you.' He leaned down and kissed her before taking his hands away and sighing. 'Can you tell me anything about the family that's going to help me here?'

'You know what I think?' she said. 'I think that it doesn't matter what happened. The fact is, Maggie is dead. Her death was ruled an accident. Joel is back in town and he's the one who is alive and who deserves to be able to put all this behind him. I'm not saying that the Douglas family's feelings don't matter, because they do, but—'

'I agree with you, honey,' Dave broke in. 'But I can't do that if someone in the town is going to cause Joel problems and upset the harmony we have here. Next thing there'll be fights, and who knows what. I can't have that.'

'Dave.' Kim laid a calming hand on his arm. 'Are you getting a bit ahead of yourself? Do you think you should just sit back and see how this plays out? If you're worried about the egging . . . well, it's so childlike, I can't think any of the Douglases are behind it. It's not like someone has set fire to the house or—'

'God, don't say that! It might happen.' He took a sip of beer. 'What about Lynette Douglas? You were pretty upset with her the other day.'

'She's a hothead,' Kim said, dismissively.

'And that's the type of person who'll cause trouble.' Dave gave a short, sharp nod, as if he were putting a full stop on the end of his sentence.

The microwave beeped. Kim took out the plate and placed it with some cutlery in front of Dave, who was sitting back at the bench.

'What's being aimed at Joel—whether it's verbal abuse from Lynette or from any of the Douglases, or eggs thrown by kids—well, it isn't founded. If it's kids being little shits, then they need a lesson on how to treat people. If it is the family . . .' He held up his hands and sighed. 'I don't quite know how I'm going to deal with that yet, but, again, they can't treat someone like a leper and let it affect the town. That's just the way it is.' Dave picked up his knife and fork. 'Did I ever tell you about the case I worked up the north of WA?'

'Which one, sweetie? You did a few.'

'Old Bob Holden, a bloke I used to partner with, and I had to go and find out who was stealing stock from an Aboriginal station called Spinifex Downs. There was a fair bit of racism still going on, and back then towns often only had one copper. Boogarin was just like that. One copper.

Imagine if racial tensions got out of hand and there was only one bloke in town trying to control an angry mob. This bloke, Glen King, his name was, he couldn't see what was in front of his nose because he was worried his town was going to erupt with the crap that was going on between these couple of whitefellas and a few blokes from Spinifex Downs. He was shit-scared he was going to lose control of the town.'

'But, honey . . .'

'No, I know it sounds mad and it won't happen here, but I have to be on top of this. And Jack does too. We can't let any tensions fester between Joel and whoever wants to run him out of town.' He raised his eyebrows. 'Which, I might add, Lynette has already alluded to doing. Having direct evidence we can present to the Douglases will put a stop to it.'

Kim raised her hands in a calming way. 'It's okay, I get it. But you're very worked up about a case from a long time ago, which is unlike you. What else is going on?'

'It affects the present day.' Dave speared a piece of meat and rubbed it through the gravy.

'I don't believe that's all.'

Dave took his time in answering. 'They've called this an accidental death. I don't believe it was.'

Kim gasped. 'You think Joel killed her?'

'No, I don't think that either.'

'Then what?'

Dave slowly looked at her, his face serious. 'Perhaps something far worse.'

CHAPTER 15

Standing in front of Phil's office was causing Emma's stomach to flip-flop like it hadn't done in ages.

The deathly silence on the street wasn't helping.

Come on, she told herself. *It's okay.*

Before she could take the first step forwards, the door yanked open and Phil stood in the frame. 'Coming in or not?'

Emma jumped back, then put a smile on her face. 'Of course, I was just gathering my thoughts.'

Without answering, her ex-husband turned and went back into his office, leaving her standing on the steps. Quickly, she followed him, nodding to Natasha, Phil's secretary, as she went.

Not sure if she should go into Phil's office, she stood in the doorway and waited to be invited in.

Phil frowned when he sat down at his desk. 'I don't need to ask twice, do I?'

Adjusting her handbag, Emma swallowed and walked in, taking the chair opposite his desk.

'The financials are done, and I've lodged your tax return with the ATO,' Phil started as he picked up the bundle of pages. 'You've got a bit of tax to pay, and I'd recommend your new accountant adjusts the percentage of Pay As You Go tax upwards, so Deception Creek Holdings doesn't get so large a tax bill next year.'

'How much is it?' Emma asked.

Phil named an eye-watering amount. 'Still, it's not unexpected considering you've been paying off the loan, which has decreased your interest payments, and you sold off the last of the sheep.'

'Yes, only cattle now.'

'Which in turn made a lot of income.' He pushed some pages over. 'You can sign here.'

'Hang on a moment,' Emma said. 'Let me read it all first.'

Phil leaned back in his chair, sadness playing around his eyes. 'Don't you trust me now that I'm not married to you? You would've signed before.'

Pen in hand, Emma stopped. He was right. 'It's not that,' she said quietly. 'I have to understand this myself. You're not there to explain this sort of thing to me anymore.'

Silence filled the room as Emma looked through the pages and asked a couple of questions, which Phil explained clearly.

Finally, she signed and gave the pages back. Phil stamped them and handed over her copy.

Emma stood up. 'Thanks . . .' Her voice trailed off. What was she supposed to say now?

'How'd you go on HelloSingles?'

Heat shot to Emma's face. 'That's not really any of your business.'

Phil got up and came around the desk to perch on the corner. 'You know, Emma, I thought you didn't want the intimacy of a relationship. That you were happy with the farm. You must've changed your mind to put yourself out there.' He stopped and looked down. 'I wish the intimacy could have been between you and me.'

Fiddling with the straps on her handbag, Emma tried to speak and was surprised to find a lump in her throat. 'I know, Phil. I'm sad we didn't work out too.'

They looked at each other for a long moment, then Emma turned towards the door. 'Thanks for everything, Phil,' she said. 'I'll see myself out.'

'You pushed me away. I kept trying and trying and you kept pushing me away. But now you're obviously craving what you thought you weren't.'

Taking a breath, Emma said, 'I'm not craving anything, Phil. I'm perfectly happy out there by myself. I'm sorry you got caught up in the HelloSingles thing. I don't think either of us expected that.'

There was a silence between them, and Emma wondered how you could be in love with someone, make love to them, share every detail of your life with them, and suddenly not feel anything for them. She realised she knew nothing about Phil's life now; if he had a new girlfriend, or if he still went to the pub on Friday night for a beer.

The thought made her sad, but at the same time, it didn't bother her what Phil was doing or who he was spending time with.

'I'm sorry it didn't work between us, Phil,' she said again softly.

'I am too. We didn't work because you're too immersed in Deception Creek, Emma. I know we had our differences, but I couldn't compete with the farm. That land is first for you. It's everything.'

Even though the words were harsh, Emma heard the pain behind them. The regret behind them.

'I hope if you find someone new, that you remember what I'm saying now. Because you deserve to be happy, but so do I.'

Emma nodded. 'Well, thanks for the advice.'

'I'm leaving town.' He scratched at his beard.

She drew in a deep breath. That was new. But not unexpected.

'When?'

'Next week. Natasha and I will pack up the office and move everything to Adelaide. I've got the office being offered for rent.'

Realisation filtered through.

'Natasha is going to Adelaide with you?'

'Yeah. She was a big support when we split up.' He looked at her, and Emma knew he was trying to see if she was hurt.

She wasn't, but a strange sensation suffused her stomach. Regret and melancholy. They had been good together for a while, but not good enough.

'I know, I know, I was on HelloSingles too, but I'd forgotten to take my profile down.'

After a couple of shallow breaths, Emma smiled. 'Well, that's wonderful news, Phil. Congratulations. I'm glad you've found the contentment *you* were craving. I hope you'll be very happy together.'

'I guess we'll see where it goes.' Phil nodded and stood, holding out his hand. 'Your new accountant can get in contact if they have any questions.'

Nodding, Emma put her hand in his. Then she leaned forwards and put her arms around him. 'Good luck, Phil.'

He stood frozen for a moment, then gave her an awkward one-armed hug. 'You too.'

The music coming from the jukebox was pounding when Emma pushed open the door. Jimmy Barnes belted out 'Working Class Man' as three young blokes stood in front of the screen feeding coins into the slots and choosing the next few songs.

'Emma! Here!'

She looked over and saw a table in the dining room where Maddy and Jacqui were sitting. She made a drinking sign with a hand, but the girls shook their heads and indicated they had a bottle of wine and three glasses.

'Hey!' She leaned over and kissed them both before flopping into a chair. 'God, I'm glad to be finished for the day. I'm exhausted.'

'You'll need this, then.' Maddy filled her glass to the top.

'Pisshead,' Emma said affectionately.

'Pot, kettle,' Jacqui replied.

They laughed as they looked at each other. Emma registered that Jacqui was looking strained, but she was too tired to ask what was up just now.

Emma took a sip and closed her eyes as she felt her body start to relax.

'What have you been doing, Em?' Jacqui asked as she picked up the menu.

Emma opened her eyes and leaned forwards. 'Okay. Gossip Central. Phil has a new girlfriend and they're moving to Adelaide next week.'

From the silence at the table, Emma realised they knew already.

'You knew and didn't tell me?'

'Only heard yesterday. The real-estate agent is leasing it out and they rang asking if we wanted to take the office over because it's bigger than ours,' Jacqui said. 'I haven't had a chance to tell you.'

Emma took another chug of wine. 'Oh.' It was the only thing she could think to say. Then she frowned. 'You don't think it would've been good to know before I walked in to see him today? Forewarned is forearmed and all that?' She put the glass down with a bang.

Jacqui raised her eyebrows. 'Sorry, Em. I didn't know you were going to see him today. If I had, I would have rung you.'

'Ah well,' Emma slumped down. 'It doesn't matter, does it? What's done is done.'

'He's always been a bit strange.'

Emma opened her mouth, but nothing came out. She knew Maddy was trying to comfort her, but she didn't want to hear Phil bagged out.

'Yeah, sorry, but he was, Em. Something to do with all those figures he surrounded himself with, I reckon.' Jacqui put her glass down and smiled to take the sting out of her words.

'You didn't like him?'

'It didn't matter what we thought, it was you who mattered. Then you saw sense, so it's all good!' Jacqui lifted a shoulder in a half-shrug.

Emma wanted to jump to Phil's defence, but she realised her friends were right. He had been slightly odd; his sense of humour could be off at times and he was a bit socially awkward. But she'd loved him for a little while.

She looked at the faces of two of her best friends and again felt her body relax. The girls who had her back no matter what. How she loved them.

'Hey,' Maddy leaned forwards this time, 'what do you know about that Matt who works for you, Em? He's a bit cute.'

Letting out a laugh, Emma said, 'Where did that come from?'

'I saw him at the pub the other night with a woman about his age. Pretty glam she was too. Not from around here.'

'What night was this?' A funny feeling she didn't recognise welled up in her stomach.

'Hmm, must've been on Saturday night. All frocked up, with heels on.'

'I don't know much about his personal life,' Emma said shortly. 'And I don't want to. He works for me. So long as he turns up on time and does his job, what he gets up to in his free time is his business. And,' she looked at both of her friends, a half-smile on her face, 'I don't care.'

Maddy laughed. 'Oh, come on, he's a bit of eye candy. Haven't you noticed the way he looks at you? I saw him the night of the party. It was like he was lusting—'

'Oh, stop it!' Emma said firmly. 'Don't be ridiculous. What has got into you tonight? Men on the brain.'

'Well, I'd start watching, just in case.'

'Sounds like he's got a woman, so he doesn't need me.'

Jacqui broke in. 'What ended up happening with HelloSingles? Have you got any hot dates to tell us about?'

Emma held the glass to her cheeks as a burning feeling rose in them. 'Phil made a comment about that today. But it was okay, he wasn't horrible or anything. It's just so embarrassing.'

Jacqui and Maddy groaned in unison.

'What'd he say?' Jacqui wanted to know.

'Nothing much, really. Just made sure I knew that he knew. Anyway, I've got other news.'

'What's that?'

'Kyle is coming to Barker.'

Both girls stared at her. 'Kyle?'

'Yeah. He said he found the anniversary a bit harder this year, so he was taking some time off and getting on the road. Having a holiday. He's coming here.'

Jacqui narrowed her eyes. 'Why?'

'I don't know. I think he just needs to get away from everything. He's going to the Flinders Ranges to have a look around, so it's not too much out of his way to turn up here.'

'When's he coming?' Maddy asked.

'On the weekend.'

Jacqui took a sip of her drink. 'How do you feel about that? Do you really want to talk about it more? What else would you talk about instead?'

Emma gave a little huff. 'I don't know. We'll just have to find other things to chat about.' She paused. 'But he might need to; even with all the information I've given him, he still doesn't remember the accident, and that's how we've always talked. I guess we'll just see how it goes.'

The silence around the table told Emma that the girls really weren't sure about what was happening here. And how could they be? None of them had experienced what she and Kyle had. She didn't see his visit as strange like they did. In fact, there was a part of her that was looking forward to seeing him.

'Should we order?' Emma asked.

The girls grabbed the menus and chose, then Jacqui went to the counter.

Maddy leaned forwards. 'You didn't answer the question about HelloSingles. Have you had any interest?'

Emma twirled her glass around and then helped herself to a refill from the bottle. 'I took my profile down.' She sighed. 'It's really confronting putting yourself out there when you're in a small town and the net isn't that wide.'

'Em, that's how people meet people now. There's nothing to be ashamed of. It seems like there're heaps of people that internet dating works for. And maybe you should open the net a bit wider. The drive to Adelaide's only four hours, you know.'

'I know,' she said quietly. She nodded, trying to choose her words well. 'I'm just not sure that's me. Yet. Maybe in time.'

'Anyway,' Maddy smiled like the cat who had the cream, 'I think you should look closer to home.'

'What?'

'Matt! I promise, he's interested.'

'Yeah, yeah. He's only worked for me for years and . . .'

'Until last year, you were married,' Maddy pointed out.

Jacqui smiled as she sat back down at the table.

'What did I miss?'

'We're going to have to have a conversation about getting Emma to realise that Matt's got the hots for her. And if that doesn't work, we'll have to convince her that putting herself on a dating site is perfectly okay,' Maddy said.

'Matt has nothing to do with this,' Emma said. 'And I'm happy the way I am. I'll find someone in time, so let's just leave it and talk about something else. And we need to set the date for this weekend away in the Barossa. I want something to look forward to.'

CHAPTER 16

1992

Joel stirred and stretched, opening his eyes in the dark.

What had woken him?

Crack!

He threw back the covers and got up to look through the window. Pulling back the curtains, he saw a shadowy figure outside. It waved at him and beckoned him to come outside.

His watch read 11.25 p.m. On a Wednesday night. What the hell was Maggie doing out now?

Fear trickled through his stomach as he pulled on his jeans and fossicked around to find a shirt. Was she all right?

The door creaked as he opened it. He stopped, listening, hoping his parents didn't hear.

What was going on?

His feet were silent on the verandah and then suddenly wet from the dew as he went down the steps and to the bush where Maggie was hidden.

'Are you okay?' he asked, grabbing her upper arms and making her look at him.

'I'm *wonderful*!' she slurred as she put her arm behind his neck. 'Come on, let's go for a walk. It's a *beautiful* night.'

'Wait, Maggie, you're drunk. What's going on? Where'd you get—' Joel tried to back away from her but she held on tightly. He quickly realised she needed him to help her keep upright. 'Shit.' He looked around, trying to work out what to do. Wake his parents to help him? Try to get Maggie home?

'Let's walk. We can look at the stars.'

With a desperate glance at his house, he sighed. He didn't see any other option. 'Where to?'

'How 'bout the oval.' She started to stagger down the street towards the school, still hanging on to Joel, which in turn made him follow.

'I'm not sure this is a good idea, Mags,' he said as he walked alongside her stumbling frame.

'I don't care. They won't find me there. Gotta go to the oval.'

'Okay, okay, we can go there.' He looked over at Mrs Kerby's house and was grateful to see that the lights were out. 'But you need to be quieter.'

'I don't want to be quiet!' She raised her voice and let go of him, turning in a circle, her face skywards. 'I want to be *heard*. Seen.'

Joel frantically looked around, glad there was no one else on his street except for Mrs Kerby across the road—and he was pretty sure she was a little deaf.

Even though Maggie's words were loud across the silent town, there didn't seem to be any movement anywhere.

'I know, I know,' he said calmly. 'But let's do that when the town's already awake, hey? Old Mrs Kerby'll have your guts for garters 'cause you've scared her. Or worse.' He took Maggie's arm and guided her into the darkness so no one would see them if they did look out from their windows.

'Look at them,' she said, pointing up to the sky. 'They're so beautiful. Don't you think they're beautiful, Joel? They're so . . . starry.'

'Yep, they're beautiful, all right.' He kept his voice low and calm. 'Do your folks know you're out?'

Maggie laughed harshly. 'Don't be stupid! I snuck out. I've done it before.'

'I know.'

As they walked, their footsteps seemed to echo loudly in the darkness. Joel kept glancing around. He knew he'd be dead if Mr Douglas came looking for Maggie.

'Yeah. I love being out in the dark. Where I can be free and no one tells me what to do.' She stopped, and made him do the same. 'I hate them,' she said suddenly, gripping Joel's arm.

He tried not to flinch as her nails dug into his skin. 'Why, Maggie? You keep saying this stuff, but *why*? I've got to be able to help somehow, don't I? So, tell me.'

Tears spilled from her eyes. 'No one can help me.' Her voice trailed off. 'No one.' She abruptly sat down on the grassy footpath.

He joined her, putting his arm around her and letting her cry on his shoulder as anger flooded through him. 'I want to, Maggie. You've got to let me.'

Her sobbing got louder.

'You asked me to pretend to be your boyfriend, so I am. And I want to act like that, which means helping you. Why can't you talk to me?'

Maggie looked up, her cheeks smeared with tears. She searched his eyes and then leaned forwards, pushing her lips onto his. They were moist and soft and she tasted like alcohol. Joel closed his eyes and left his lips on hers. Then he pulled back and looked at her.

Maggie pushed herself onto him, making him fall backwards onto the grass. She started to take her arms out of the sleeves of her shirt.

'Shit, what're you doing?' Joel tried to get out from under her. 'Maggie! Don't do that.'

She straddled him and took her shirt off, revealing her soft white skin and pure white bra.

'Touch me,' she said, grabbing his hands and putting them on her breasts.

He snatched them away as if she were on fire.

'No! Stop it, Maggie. What the fuck are you doing? We're mates. Or have you forgotten?'

'Don't you want me?' she asked, her eyes wide. Quickly she covered her breasts with her hands and looked for her shirt. 'Why don't you want me?'

'Ah . . .' Joel's eyes were everywhere but her face. 'Um.'

She scrambled off him and curled into the foetal position on the ground and started to sob, her hands over her head. 'Why?'

'Because we're friends and I don't want to stuff it up.' He looked at her lying on the ground, pulling at her hair.

'I'm so ugly,' she wept.

'What? No, you're not, you're really pretty. But we're mates, Maggie. That's all. That doesn't mean I don't think you're beautiful.'

Maggie sat up, her eyes red. 'Kiss me, then.'

Joel stilled. 'Um . . .'

'Go on.' She shut her eyes and waited.

Joel looked around again, then leaned forwards, touched his lips to hers and then pulled back. 'Come on,' he said before she could speak. 'I'd better get you home. I really don't want your dad coming looking for you, do you?'

Maggie wept harder. 'I don't want to go home. Can't I stay with you?'

Joel saw desperation in her face. He wanted to take her home and put her to sleep in the spare room, but the thought of Mr Douglas coming to find her was too frightening.

'I don't think so.'

Maggie rounded on him. 'I hate you!' she spat and brought her small fists down on to his chest. 'I really, really hate you.'

She staggered to her feet and stumbled off into the darkness.

CHAPTER 17

2021

'Joel, it's me, Kim. I've got some food for you.' She knocked on the door for the second time.

'He's gone out,' a voice called from across the road.

Kim turned and saw Mrs Kerby out on her front step with a teapot and cup on the table next to her.

'Hello, Mrs Kerby, how are you?' Kim asked, leaving her basket on the verandah and walking across the road.

'I'm well, thank you. And yourself?'

'Great, thanks. Isn't it a beautiful day?' She glanced up to the clear blue sky.

'Farmers will be needing some rain soon.'

'The crops I've seen on the road are looking quite nice.'

'At a thirsty stage, so they are.'

'Do you know when Joel will be back?'

'He left in the car this morning, but I don't know where he went, so, no. He keeps to himself.'

'Can't say I blame him. Must be nice having a bit of company back over the road, though. You've been out here by yourself for a long time.'

'Would you like a cup of tea?' Mrs Kerby asked, just as a familiar vehicle drove down the road.

Kim turned at the noise and waved at Zara, who pulled to a halt next to her and leaned out of the driver's window.

'Hello, what are you up to?' Zara asked and waved across at the elderly lady.

'Just dropping some food off to Joel,' Kim replied, stepping up to the car.

Zara grinned. 'Should have known that's what you were doing.'

'You busy?'

'Nah, just finished a story for the *Farming Journal*. Waiting to see what Lachie has for me next.'

'I'm going to have a cuppa here, want to join me?' Kim raised her eyebrows a little, her back still to Mrs Kerby.

Zara stared at Kim, then looked across at Mrs Kerby. 'Who's the oldie?' she asked.

'Mrs Kerby. I'm about to get to know her better than I do now.'

'What are you up to, Kim Burrows?' Zara turned the car off and opened the door.

'We'd love a cuppa, Mrs Kerby,' Kim called out. 'Do you know Zara Ellison? I'm sure you'd know her family.'

'Oh yes. Your family's on Roeberry Glen, aren't they? Your mother is seeing the doctor?'

Zara took the couple of steps up onto the verandah and smiled, holding out her hand. 'Yes, that's my family. Mum is still out there on the farm.'

'Brave woman, that one. Sorry for your loss. Your brother and father. Gosh, there's been some tragedy around Barker of late.' She brushed a bit of lint from her jumper and looked at them.

Kim nodded her agreement. 'I think we could all do with a very calm couple of years, don't you, Mrs Kerby?'

'I'll heat up the kettle again. And call me Greta.' She picked up the pot of tea and went back inside, while Kim and Zara drew chairs around the table.

Zara looked suspiciously at Kim, her eyes full of questions.

'Wait and see,' Kim said with a grin, then leaned back in her chair. She raised her voice so Greta could hear her inside. 'Joel has done such a big clean-up since he got home. When I first came around only a day or so after he got back, the weeds were taller than the fence, all the garden beds were overgrown and the trees were blocking out most of the sun. He's given those gums a serious haircut!'

'He's been planting things in the veggie garden, as well,' Greta said as she brought out the pot and two more cups. 'That needs to rest for a moment or two.' She went back inside and came back with a plate of biscuits.

'You're giving Kim a run for her money, Greta. She's an amazing cook as well.'

'I like cooking for people, just as I'm sure you do.' She nodded towards Kim. 'It's nice having Joel back across the road. I take him a few treats now and then,' she said, sitting back down.

'I bet he appreciates that. He wouldn't have had anything nice in prison, I'm sure.'

Greta looked across the road. 'He seems like he's settling back in, even with the silly people who threw eggs at his house.' There was silence while she took a sip of her tea. 'His mother worried about him in jail. She'd be glad he was home, making the place look respectable again.'

'Such a worrying time for everyone,' Kim said.

'The old wives' tale of bad luck running in families was certainly right here.'

'You were friends with Verity?'

'Yes, I was. I liked her very much. She was a wonderful neighbour.'

Kim picked up her cup and blew on the hot liquid. 'I can't understand how such a nice bloke got caught up in fraud. Just seems unreal, doesn't it?'

'Sure does.'

'Do you know what happened?'

'Not enough to be able to make any comment,' Greta said firmly.

'But you know something?' Zara asked.

Kim glanced over at Zara and saw that her journalist instincts had kicked in. *Good*, she thought. It was what she'd hoped for.

'Verity and I were friends, I told you that. I'm not going blabbing to anyone willy-nilly, you know.'

Feeling a buzz of excitement, Kim realised that Mrs Kerby knew a lot more than she had previously let on.

'I just find it odd that his family was so well-to-do and yet he was caught stealing money,' Kim said carefully and gave a rueful smile. 'It doesn't make sense.'

'No, I agree. His mother never believed he did it.'

'That's what she said? He didn't do it?'

Greta paused a moment in thought and then said, 'Actually, she'd come over here some afternoons after she'd spoken to him on the phone. They only got one call a week, you see, and never for very long, so she'd be a bit upset. Sometimes we'd have a glass of sherry, and other times, nothing at all.

'Then she'd say, "He was set up, Greta, but we can't prove it." I never probed or asked anything more. I just listened and tried to support her. There didn't seem to be anything more I could do.'

'Did you believe her?' asked Kim.

'Like I said to that nice Mr Burrows, I think where there's smoke there's fire, but who knows? Only Joel knows the god's-honest truth.'

Zara leaned forwards and put her cup on the table. 'Poor Joel. It seems like the world is against him a bit. He'll wish he didn't come home.'

'Oh, I don't think so, dear. There's enough to keep him occupied what with the garden and all. I'm sure he worries about what people think of him, though. Always been that way inclined.' She waved her hand towards the main street.

'If the townspeople would be gentle with him, they'd find they had a wonderful ally. He's a very loyal man.'

'I've met him a couple of times. He seems quite shell-shocked,' Kim said. 'I wonder if anyone from Barker ever visited him in prison?'

'Verity and Billy used to go as regularly as they could. I don't know about any of the other family members, or even friends. I went once, but he wouldn't see me. Embarrassed, no doubt. Still, he knew I was thinking of him.'

'Prisons are horrible places,' Zara put in. 'I've been to a few, and if you can keep away from them, then it's a good idea to.'

Mrs Kerby looked at Zara. 'What do you do?'

'I'm a journalist. I write about agriculture and the like for the *Farming Journal.*'

Greta sat for a moment, her fingers rolling and unrolling the edge of the table cloth. She looked as if she were a woman carrying a heavy burden.

Kim went to say something, but Zara shook her head slightly.

'A journalist, you say?'

'Yes. I've worked on a lot of investigative stories as well as all the farming ones.'

'It's a job you like?'

'I love it,' Zara said simply.

'Ah.'

Kim put her cup on the table and poured everyone another round.

'I have one thing I was going to give to Mr Burrows,' Greta said slowly. 'I've had it a long time. Verity gave it to me before she died—I wasn't sure why, but now I wonder if it might be helpful to . . .'

She looked from Zara to Kim. 'Mrs Burrows,' she said, 'would you give it to him?'

'Of course. What is it?' Kim could see the excited tension in Zara's body—that of a reporter about to get a scoop.

'I'll get it for you.'

After Mrs Kerby went inside, Zara looked at Kim and whispered, 'You're up to something.'

Kim nodded. Keeping her voice low, she said, 'I want to know what happened with that fraud charge.'

'Why?'

'I don't know. I just think there's enough of a cloud hanging over it that it's worth looking into.'

'Have you talked to Dave about this? Don't you remember how much trouble you got into when you posted bail for Essie last year?'

Kim nodded, remembering the woman who had been arrested for accepting drugs through the post. There had been more to that story than the Federal Police believed, so Dave had started to investigate—until Kim had posted bail for Essie, and Dave had been taken off the case. Oh, he'd been angry with her for a little while, but both of them knew she'd do it all over again. Because of her actions, Essie had been brought home and reunited with her granddaughter, instead of languishing in jail.

Kim gave her a look and said softly, 'We're just going to have to be careful with how we go about this then, aren't we?'

'She knows something, I can tell,' Zara said. 'It's in the way she holds back.'

The door pushed open and Greta was back with a foolscap book. 'Here it is. Verity kept every newspaper article there was, I think.' She handed bulging pages across to Kim. 'You never know, you girls might find something of interest in there for you as well.'

Kim opened it and stared at the first headline: *Corruption Charges Filed Against Financial Officer of Stockomatic.*

She turned the page to the next headline: *Joel Hammond Charged with Thirty-Two Fraud Offences.*

Kim put her hand to her chest as she imagined how Verity and Billy would have felt when they read these. Their only son being plastered over the front pages of the newspapers for something so untoward.

'Ah.'

'Yes, very confronting headlines, aren't they?' Greta said, rubbing her hands along her arms. 'They upset Verity quite a bit.'

'What about her husband?'

'See, I never really knew what he was thinking. He didn't talk about Joel much. Think it hurt too much, him being a respected community member, in Rotary and all.'

'And you're alone?' Kim asked gently.

'My Sally died a couple of years back. I've been by myself since.'

'You must be lonely at times.'

Greta nodded. 'Sometimes. I didn't think I'd find love again. Especially not with Sally.' She shrugged. 'So I was blessed to have the time I did with her. I don't suppose anyone can know what the future holds. Sally and I had thirty lovely years together. It was a blow when she died. Still . . .' Greta smiled miserably. 'Death will come to all of us in time.'

Silence fell around the table. Kim looked at Zara out of the corner of her eye and could see that she was swallowing hard trying to control her emotions.

'Isn't that the truth,' Zara said softly.

Kim leaned over and touched Zara's arm. 'But we have each other.' She looked at Greta. 'Us girls can stick together.'

'And that's a lovely way to be,' Greta said, nodding.

'Did Sally know Verity too?' Zara asked.

'Oh yes, we three would sit around chatting until the cows came home! We all enjoyed each other's company. Billy, on the other hand . . . well, poor love . . . he would come over sometimes, but not often. I think our lifestyle was confronting for him.'

Kim could well believe that; a country town back in the 1980s. Stigma could be a dreadful thing. She was surprised she hadn't heard about Greta and Sally before now.

'I guess we'd better get on,' Kim said, putting her empty cup down. 'It's been so lovely to get to know you a little better, Greta. You make sure you come and visit me when you're passing.'

'Greta,' said Zara, putting her arm on Kim's to stop her from standing, 'you said there might be something in the scrapbook that would interest us.' She looked the older woman in the eye. 'Can you tell me what that might be?'

Greta answered Kim first. 'I'd like that, Kim.' She paused and tapped the scrapbook, looking at Zara. 'When Verity gave me that, she said that there might come a time when something useful would come from it. I think she knew Joel would have trouble if he came back here to live; she must've thought there was something in here to make his life easier when he returned. I've read through everything in the past week and can't see anything, but I'm sure Mr Burrows, or maybe you, would know how to do that much better than me.'

Zara nodded. 'I'll have a look-see.'

Greta looked relieved.

'His name's Dave,' Kim said after a moment's silence. 'I don't think I've ever heard him called Mr Burrows. And we'll make sure he gets it.'

'Thank you.'

After they had said their goodbyes, Kim and Zara walked out together.

'Want to come to my place?' Kim asked quietly.

Zara showed the hint of a smile. 'Of course I do.'

~

'I can't believe we're doing this without telling Dave.' But Zara was smiling as she said it. 'He'll be wild with me, and I've worked so hard to gain his trust.'

Kim put her hands on her hips and peered at Zara over her glasses. 'Greta said *we* might find something in here, not just Dave. I'll make sure the book gets to him, but he won't be home until later, and I don't have time to go down to the station. Do you?' A half-smile was on her face. 'It would be silly for us not to dig a little deeper first.'

'Well, on your head be it! If he catches us, I'll tell him you led me astray.'

'As if he's going to believe that.' Kim gave a small laugh, then turned serious. 'See, Dave is focused on the Douglases causing Joel problems—but I think there's more to it than that. That fraud charge never sat well with me. Let's see if there's something that doesn't add up.' She paused. 'Maybe I'm wrong, but we should just have a look. Plus, you might get a story.'

Kim positioned the book between them and turned the page.

> It has been alleged that Stockomatic Finance Officer, Joel Hammond, has defrauded the company of more than two hundred and fifty thousand dollars, spending the money on new cars, personal expenses and shares.
>
> Fraud Detective, Harry Maddow, said the activity had taken place over two years in an extremely sophisticated operation.
>
> The CEO for Stockomatic issued a statement saying the company lawyers were investigating, but

he intended to see that Mr Hammond was charged with as many counts of fraud as can be proven.

Mr Hammond maintains his innocence.

Kim turned to the next page.

CHAPTER 18

Exclusive Interview with Joel Hammond

by Bob Elder

The gates clang behind me as I walk into Port Augusta Prison. It's a long drive from Adelaide down the Port Wakefield highway, with endless farming land, large gum trees and salt lakes covering the countryside.

As I pull into the car park, the constant grumble of the large trucks travelling east–west is present, along with the stream of caravans, their drivers completing the lap around Australia or wanting to conquer the wildness of the Nullarbor Plain.

The prison, surrounded by high fences topped with razor wire, sits in the shadow of the Flinders Ranges. While galahs screech overhead and shed the nearby gum trees, the sun is hot and relentless, the sky a long plain of blue nothingness.

Visitors must sign in and wait to be escorted to a room, where guards can listen to our conversations. The noise is of steel on steel, clanking; and of yelling, from both the inmates and the guards.

I'm here to see Joel Hammond.

Hammond was convicted of fraud, having stolen two hundred and fifty thousand dollars from stock firm Stockomatic while in the position of Finance Officer.

Having consistently denied the charges, Hammond wrote to me asking for my help, insisting he'd been set up by an unnamed person. This is his opportunity to tell his side of the story.

Today is a non-contact visit, so we face each other across a table. I'm unable to take any recording devices in with me, only a note pad and pen, which I have to prove I have taken with me and not left in the possession of the inmate.

You might think these restrictions excessive for a white-collar criminal. However, Hammond isn't innocent in all of this. Four months ago, he assaulted two prisoners, leaving both close to death, resulting in his sentence being extended.

Hammond accepts the extra charges and time for the assault, but he is clear he will not accept the fraud charges.

I can see that during Hammond's time here—five months now—he has been working out. Although his face is pale and he looks in need of a few hours in the sun, he is fit and strong.

My first question is: why did he invite me?

Softly spoken, he answers, 'Because you always find the truth.'

'And what is the truth?' I ask.

'That I'm not guilty.'

We discuss the case, his sentence—five years, plus the extra four for grievous bodily harm—and how the fraud was achieved.

In the half-hour I am there, I can see he clearly believes his own story.

Stockomatic buys and sells sheep, cattle, goats and other livestock. The company also supplies farmers with the chemicals and merchandise they require to successfully run their farms. The company acts on behalf of the vendor to sell their animals, for a commission. The stock agent then sources a market, organises the sale and transportation and, once the sale is complete, the buyer pays Stockomatic, where the money is held in trust to pay the farmer.

Cheques are written out and signed by the Finance Manager.

This is where the fraud occurred.

Cheques were made out in Hammond's name. They were slipped into the pile of legitimate payments to be made, and the Finance Manager signed them, not cross-referencing the name and amount on the cheque to the sales made by the stock agents.

'Cross-referencing by the Finance Manager isn't required,' Hammond says. 'By the time the cheques land on his desk, all checks and balances should have been completed. It wasn't his job to do the cross-referencing. People below him do this.'

'The cheques were in your name,' I counter. 'They couldn't have been deposited in an account that wasn't opened by you. That was brought up in the trial.'

'Yes, but it wasn't proven that I opened the bank account.'

'How do you explain that?'

'I can't.'

'And how,' I ask, 'do you explain the car you bought? The cash to buy this car didn't come out of any of your other bank accounts, yet the amount paid for the car was transferred out of the account you say you didn't open, with the funds going to the car dealership in Adelaide.'

'I was given the car as part of my work package.'

'By who?'

'The company. The keys were left on my desk on the day I started there.'

'You understand that your side of the story seems very far-fetched and hasn't been collaborated by any of the Stockomatic employees,' I put to Hammond.

This is where things become interesting.

'Perhaps,' Hammond tells me in a considered tone, 'perhaps, there is a reason for that.'

The half-hour I have with Hammond finishes at that moment, the guard telling me my time is up and I must leave.

> I will be investigating this case over the next few
> weeks to see if I can uncover anything that might
> throw more clarity on the situation. Stay tuned.

Zara looked at Kim and then quickly flicked through the rest of the pages. There wasn't another story written by Bob Elder.

Without saying a word, Zara took out her phone and googled the journalist's name.

'Do you know of him?' Kim asked.

'No. And it doesn't look like I'll get to. See here, he had a stroke.' She turned the phone around for Kim to see. 'Just a short note from the paper he worked for, saying he was in hospital care but wasn't expected to regain consciousness.'

'How old was he?'

Zara scanned the article. 'Doesn't say . . . Oh yeah, here. Sixty-three. I might ask Lachie if he knows of him and where he is now.'

'Might've passed on, by the sounds of it. When was that? Eight years ago?'

'Well, Joel went into prison nine years ago and it said he did the interview . . .' She flicked back to the article. 'He'd been in jail five months when Bob went to visit him. So, around that time. Just reading his bio, he investigated quite a few cases where the inmate said they were innocent, and he managed to get them exonerated.'

Kim crossed her arms. 'If Joel got hold of that bloke, he must have been hoping the same thing would happen for him. It's unlikely he would have contacted Bob Elder if he wasn't innocent.'

'I'd agree with that. It's a wonder another journalist didn't pick it up and have a go. These types of investigations can take a journalist from a mediocre career to working with the top editors on national newspapers.'

Kim looked at Zara with a smile. 'I guess there's nothing stopping you from looking into it, then.'

'I guess not,' Zara said slowly, the cogs turning in her mind. The case was from a long time ago. How would she track down all the people who were involved? Some could be dead. Would Joel talk to her? He hadn't given any indication he wanted to be acquitted now. Had he given up on it?

There were so many questions running through Zara's mind that she didn't hear Kim's next question to her.

Only when Kim leaned over and tapped her long, red fingernail on the page did Zara look up.

'What?'

'He didn't ask who the other person involved could have been.'

'The journo? No, he didn't. I think that would have been one of my first questions. A starting point. Still . . .' She thought about how she would have done it. 'There's every chance he did ask but didn't print it in the story; he wouldn't have wanted to alert whoever it was. And it would've been too early to print the name—he would've had to have had hard evidence to do that.'

'What do you think?' Kim said. 'Will you have a go?'

'It's very interesting, isn't it?' Zara nodded, contemplating what she'd just read. 'Maybe if I could talk to one of Bob Elder's old colleagues, I might be able to access his notes and start looking into it without talking to Joel to begin with. I wonder if his notebooks are still around. He would've handwritten everything back then.' She looked at her friend. 'Are you going to tell Dave?'

Kim smiled. 'I'm going to give him the book and tell him you were with me when I got it. He can work it out from there.'

Zara rolled her eyes. 'Of course he'll work it out.'

'I'm sure he will. No secrets in our relationship.'

'Better get on and get cracking then, hadn't I?'

'Yep, you'd better.' Kim opened the freezer and looked at how many meals she had left. 'And I had better get on with the cooking. I've got four orders for Catering Angels tonight and I'll have to get them delivered too.'

'Is the business still going well?' Zara asked, getting off the stool.

'Flat strap. There're always people who need help with their meals. The new manager I've got in the roadhouse is very good. I hardly go there anymore to check on her.'

'Do you need a hand delivering the meals tonight?'

Kim shook her head. 'No, it's all pretty easy, thanks. Gina Hunter has gone to have a baby in Port Augusta, so I'll drop a few meals in so she doesn't have to cook when she gets back. Mr Mavel is in hospital, so Mrs Mavel needs a couple of meals, and so does the Smythe family. I think Gordon Smythe is struggling since his wife went to Adelaide to settle in their daughter at school. He's got the other three kids at home—three under five and trying to run the garage too; he doesn't know if he's Arthur or Martha! I don't know, if I had kids I'd be teaching them to cook and clean, but there're still a few out there who just don't know how.'

'A long time ago, my brother and I used to joke about what would happen if Mum died first—Dad didn't know where the fridge was, let alone the washing machine or how to use it! If there is a silver lining to his death, that's it. I would have been living out there being his housemaid.' Zara rolled her eyes.

Kim laughed. 'Surely not. Hopefully, he would have tried to learn.'

'I don't think he would have! Anyway, it doesn't matter. Mum's still out there going great guns, so I don't have to worry.'

'What's she up to?'

'They finished seeding about a month ago and now they've moved on to crutching. I was out there the other day and somehow she'd got James in the sheep yards. I don't know how she managed that, but hell it was funny. He looked very out of place.'

'The things we do for love.' Kim smiled.

'All right!' Zara clapped her hands together and grabbed her phone. 'I'm taking some photos of this story and then I'd better get on and make some moves on this.'

CHAPTER 19

Emma frowned at the unknown number as her phone vibrated in her hand.

'I hate it when I get these,' she said to Matt. 'I'm never sure if it's important or just a telemarketer.' She sent it to message bank and put the phone back in her pocket.

'Probably a telemarketer,' Matt agreed.

'Right, so where are we at? I've taken four samples from these GPS points.' She pointed at the map on the iPad that sat on the dash of her ute. 'And you've got them from these six sites?'

Matt leaned across and tapped the screen. 'Here, here and here.' He pointed to the first three and then to another three. 'Rick will test the soil and get a bit of an understanding of what's going on before we start seeding the saltbush.' He paused. 'I thought you were going to talk to the RRW Board about this before you did anything.'

'I decided we'd just start. It doesn't look like I've got another meeting with them for a month or so. I sent an email asking if anyone was interested in getting together beforehand and no one got back to me, so let's just get on with it.'

'Righto. I'll get these bagged up and posted across to him.'

'Nothing else we have to do?'

'Not yet,' Matt said as he packed the sample bags in a box. He then climbed out and put the box in the back of the ute before giving Cash a pat.

As Emma watched him stare out over the land, she couldn't help but think how well his jeans fitted. Then she mentally slapped herself. *Maddy's put stupid ideas into your head*, she thought. She focused again, and climbed out of the ute. 'Penny for your thoughts.'

Matt moved to stand next to her and then gazed back at the hills and across to the plains. The expression on his face was hard to read, but he seemed suddenly indecisive.

'Come on, Matt, it's not like you not to talk.' She gave him a gentle elbow to the ribs. 'What's on your mind?' She patted Cash and waited.

'We're a bit short on water here, don't you think? Especially since you've got the cattle now. They drink a shit load.'

'Yeah, I put building a couple more dams into the budget this year, but I haven't been able to get an earthmover here yet. I've been ringing around but every other bloody farmer this side of Goyder's Line has had the same idea.'

'Got any ideas where you want to put them?'

'I thought I'd wait on their advice. Digging dams is the earthmovers' business, so I figured they should know the best spots. They've got the machines that measure the height and fall of the land, so that way we wouldn't be guessing with the runoff.'

Matt nodded.

'But you've got an idea of where you'd put one?' she asked him.

'See here.' He pointed out to the ranges, ran his finger down the horizon.

Emma couldn't work out what he was looking at. 'No.'

Matt moved to stand behind her, pointing his finger over her shoulder. Emma got a whiff of his aftershave and blinked a couple of times before she focused on the tip of his finger and where on the hills he was indicating.

'There's a gully here.' He traced the outline in the air, all the way to where it opened out onto the flats and ran towards the creek. 'If you're going to plant this saltbush here, then this would be a great spot to put a dam. You wouldn't have to pump water, except into the troughs that you'll put into each paddock you're going to fence off. You could build the dam right at the bottom of the hill. I don't reckon you need the earth moving fella to tell you that this is a natural catchment.'

Squinting, Emma could see what he was talking about. She went to the ute and got out the binoculars and re-focused on the spot.

'Yeah, and if we put contour banks in here, that would slow the flow of the water down so we wouldn't get too much erosion,' she said, excitement flitting through her stomach.

'I thought that too.' Matt stood back with his arms crossed and feet spread as if he were planted into the ground. Dressed in Wrangler jeans and a thick cotton shirt, Matt looked every bit the farmer and the passion on his face showed Emma how much he loved Deception Creek.

'Trouble is,' Emma said, 'I'm hoping to get the farm paid off this harvest, like I told you.' She flashed him a smile. 'I really don't want to spend too much money just yet. I want to know what I'm going to get crop-wise before I make too many commitments.'

'Fair call. But you don't want to get lumbered with a tax problem either. All earth works and water catchments are tax deductible.'

'If it's not the banks trying to attack the bank account, it's the government. You're screwed either way.'

Matt grinned, and Emma noticed how his eyes crinkled when he smiled.

Stop it, you idiot! she scolded herself.

'Emma,' Matt turned to her. 'I don't suppose . . .'

Her phone rang again. Looking at the screen, she saw an unknown number. Again.

'Hang on, I'd better get it, just in case there's something wrong,' Emma said and walked away a little. 'Hello?'

'Hi, Emma,' a male voice said. 'It's Kyle.'

'Kyle, hi! I didn't realise it was you; you've got your number blocked.' She looked back at the ute and saw Matt kick the ground as if he were frustrated, turn away and walk down the flat to the creek.

'I've arrived in the bustling metropolis of Barker,' Kyle said. 'It's bigger than I thought it would be.'

She laughed. 'I don't think that can be right. There's only one pub.'

'True. There's supposed to be a pub on every corner of every country town, isn't there?'

'Apparently so. Not here in Barker, though. Where are you staying?'

'I was hoping you could recommend somewhere.'

'Oh, you haven't booked anything?'

'Not at this stage. I didn't think it would be difficult to find something. Maybe I could crash with you?'

Emma's eyebrows shot up and she took a couple of backwards steps without thinking. Surely he was joking.

'Ah . . . maybe try the caravan park. There won't be anything too flash there, but it'll be comfortable.'

'Oh yeah, I saw that on the way in. I'll do that. Would you be free to catch up for dinner tonight?'

Emma glanced at her watch. 'It's pretty short notice. I wasn't expecting you until tomorrow and I've got a fair bit on in the morning. How about tomorrow night? That be okay?'

'Sure,' he said after a moment. 'No problem. That sounds fine. Tomorrow it is.'

'No worries. You'd better text me your number so I can send you a message when I'm on my way to town.'

'Okay, will do.' Silence. 'I'll see you tomorrow.'

Emma put the phone back in her pocket and once again eyed the site where Matt had suggested. How much water would it run and how big could she make it, she wondered. If they dug it deep, unlike some of the other potholes on Deception Creek, the evaporation during summer wouldn't be too bad.

A mob of galahs flew over, and Emma realised the sun was beginning to sink. How had the day got away from her again?

Matt was walking back carrying a couple of pieces of wire, which he threw in the back of the ute.

'You were going to say?' Emma said.

'Sorry?'

'Just before the phone rang, you said, "I don't suppose you're . . ." You don't suppose I'm what? Was it about the dam?'

'Got no idea what I was going to say,' Matt said, suddenly standoffish.

Emma frowned, but all she could do was nod and say, 'Okay.'

As she headed towards the ute she looked at her watch.

'Shit! Sorry, Matt, I've probably held you up. The day's just got away, hasn't it? Come on, I'll run you back to your ute so you can get into town.' She slammed the ute door, and Matt got in beside her. 'Got any plans for tonight?' She thought back to the comment the girls had made at lunch—how he'd been out with a woman who wore heels. *Did he like heels?* she wondered.

'Might head to the pub for a feed,' Matt said. 'I'll be a little late in the morning 'cause I'll get those samples posted off, but it shouldn't be much past smoko.'

It was on the tip of her tongue to ask if he was going with anyone. Instead, she took her lead from him and kept the conversation work-focused. 'I'll be right to start putting those strainer posts in since we got the tractor out to the fence line today.' She put the ute into gear and turned towards the homestead.

'I finished that spraying for the rust too,' Matt said.

'Can you write when you finished it, in my diary?' She indicated the book on the dash. 'I'll need to update that on the computer when I get back, with the batch number and chemical.'

Matt took the diary and flicked to the right page, before jotting down a couple of notes. He took his own notebook out of his pocket and Emma could see he was adding in the extra details she'd asked for.

His muscles flexed in his forearm as he wrote, and Emma looked away—just in time to swerve away from a roo who was hopping across their path towards the creek.

Matt fell against her with the force of the turn and Emma let out a small cry. 'Shit, sorry,' she said, getting the ute back under control. Without warning, her breath caught, and she couldn't find any more air.

She tried to bring the car to a standstill and get out, but her hands and feet wouldn't obey what her brain was saying.

'Uh,' she clutched at her chest and tried to take another breath; and another, but she couldn't find the oxygen she needed.

'Emma?' Matt looked at her and grabbed the park brake, bringing the ute to a shuddering stop before it stalled. 'Emma, it's okay, you need to breathe.' He grabbed both of her hands and made her look at him. 'Breathe in,' he said slowly. 'Breathe out.'

Emma closed her eyes and concentrated on his voice, trying to catch her breath. Her heart was thundering with fright while her brain screamed: *breathe, breathe, breathe*.

Every breath was constricted, and she couldn't get enough inside her body to slow the fear of suffocation.

'That's it, slowly does it.' Matt's voice calmed her.

Slowly, slowly, the thudding in her chest slowed and she managed to take a small breath, then a larger one. After a few more moments, her eyes opened and she looked straight into his concerned gaze.

'You okay?' Matt didn't let go of her, just kept his eyes intently on her.

'Ah, yeah, sorry,' Emma said through jagged breaths. She disentangled one of her hands and pressed it to her chest as air began to filter into her lungs. She felt Matt push his fingers into her wrist to feel her pulse.

'Geez, your heart's going a million miles an hour. What happened there?' he asked.

'Yeah. Yep, I'm okay. Sorry. Just a bit of a panic attack. I've had them before, but it's been a long time. Sorry to throw you around like that.'

Matt regarded her quietly, as if waiting for her to tell him more.

'I witnessed a really bad car accident,' she explained quickly. 'I get really freaked out when things go wrong in cars.

'That bloke I was just talking to . . . his wife was the one who was killed in the accident, and sometimes we catch up, 'cause we're the only two who understand what we've been through.' She swallowed.

'Ah, Em,' Matt said. 'That's pretty rough. Do you want me to drive?' He rubbed his thumb over the back of her hand.

'No, no, all good.' She gave him a quick glance and her breath caught in her throat and she couldn't take her eyes from his. 'Straight back on the horse and all that.'

Slowly, after what seemed an age of charged silence between them, Matt leaned towards her and touched his lips to hers.

CHAPTER 20

Jack slammed the report down on Dave's desk and crossed his arms. 'There's absolutely nothing in that file to suggest that Joel had anything to do with Maggie Douglas's death. What's Steve and Lynette's problem?'

'The family weren't privy to what's in this report,' Dave said mildly. 'And it's up to us to find other evidence we can put in front of them to prove it. You're getting yourself emotionally involved, Jack.'

'I'm going to talk to Joel. Do you want to come?'

'Nope, I'm going to leave this to you,' Dave answered. 'I've got a few things on the go here.'

Jack stopped. 'You sure? You've got a rapport going with him. He'll probably trust you more.'

'Perfectly sure.' Dave slid his glasses down to the end of his nose and looked at Jack like a principal looking at a student. 'I've told him you're a good fella. Just make sure you maintain a professional distance, okay?'

'Oh well, that's helpful. If he believes you. Okay.' Jack didn't need to be told twice. He grabbed his jacket. 'I'm going to walk there, get my thoughts in order. See you later.'

'Hmm,' Dave was clearly already lost in the new file he'd requested.

Jack shrugged into his jacket, checked for his notebook and pen and then left the police station. Halfway to the Hammond house, he thought he should have rung to check that Joel was home, but then he realised that Joel didn't have a landline and probably hadn't yet bought a mobile.

He wouldn't have anyone to put into the contacts.

As Jack turned the corner, he heard shouting. Quickly he picked up his pace to a jog and headed towards Joel's house, where he saw Steve Douglas planted on the footpath, his body rigid.

'You're a mongrel,' Steve yelled at Joel, who stood inside the front door, silhouetted behind the glass frame. 'You killed her. How can you show your face around here? Haven't you got any shame?'

'Hey!' hollered Jack, still jogging. 'Hey! What's going on here?'

'Shame?' exploded Joel. 'You've got no idea what I live with every—'

'Oi!' Jack called again as he picked up his pace. 'Cut that out.'

Steve Douglas swung around. 'Good. I'm glad you've showed up. You can come and do what you blokes, who call yourself coppers, should've done in the first place.'

'And what's that, Steve?' Jack asked calmly as he finally stood in front of the angry man, trying not to show he was puffing from the run.

'Arrest him for murder and get him out of town. I want him gone from here.'

Jack got his breathing under control and looked at Steve. His eyes were bulging and his cheeks were red. The vein in his neck stood out as he yelled the word 'murder'.

'Right, Mr Douglas,' Jack said sternly. 'That's enough. No matter what you believe, the report stated that Mr Hammond here was not responsible for your sister's death. I'm sorry, they're the facts. Now, if you have evidence to contradict this, then by all means we'd be happy to hear about it down at the station, but this isn't the way to make yourself heard—or endear yourself to the police.

'Can I remind you, sir, that you're the principal of the local school. Kids and their parents look up to you, and acting like this is not setting anything like a good example.'

Steve's chest was heaving as he seemed to ignore Jack's firm words and took a step around him, until he was on the path that led to the front door.

'I wouldn't do that if I were you,' Jack said loudly. 'Go home, Steve, and I'll come and talk to you later.'

The man didn't react, just continued to stare at the front door as if he could open it through sheer willpower.

'Now!' Jack barked out the word, and this time Steve swung around and looked at him. 'Go on. Head home,' he instructed. 'I'll come and find you later.'

With a roar of anger, Steve backtracked, storming off to his car, leaving the kerb with a squeal of tyres.

Jack stood watching the tail-lights of the car and smelling the rubber left behind on the road.

The door opened and Joel stood there, looking shaken. His hair was wild, sticking out as if he'd been woken suddenly.

'All right, mate?' Jack asked, taking the steps two at time and landing on the verandah with a thump.

'Yeah. Fine.' The words came out of Joel like a piece of elastic snapping, and Jack could feel the anger radiating from him.

'Can I come in?'

'If you need to.'

'I think we should have a bit of a chat, don't you?'

Joel shrugged and turned, walking down the passageway. Jack followed him through to the kitchen and sat down while Joel slumped at the table.

'They've got no idea,' Joel said softly. 'None.'

'About?'

'What I go through every day. Every night. I see her falling in my dreams . . .' He broke off and rubbed his hands over his face. 'I can't talk about it.'

'When did Steve turn up?' Jack asked.

'About ten minutes before you did, I suppose. I thought Mrs Kerby must've called you.'

'Nope, I was coming to talk to you anyway.'

'Right.'

'What did he want?'

'You heard everything. Bit of a broken record, Steve is.'

Jack tapped his fingers on the table, then leaned forwards. 'Yeah, I can see that he's pretty upset. Maggie's death obviously affected him deeply.'

'Maybe.'

Jack saw defeat in the man sagged in front of him. Joel's fingers were dirty and bruised from the constant yard work, and his clothes were tattered. He looked like a drifter who was trying to put down roots, as uncomfortable as that was.

And a bully was causing him angst. Jack narrowed his eyes, angry. 'Can you tell me what happened that night, Joel? Not what I've read in the report; everything in your words. From your memory.'

'No, I don't want to talk about it at all,' Joel said, twisting his shirt around his fingers. 'I still have nightmares when I think about it.'

'I understand, Joel, I do, but this is getting out of hand and neither Dave nor I want you—or the people living in this town—living under these conditions. There's hurt on both sides, so let's see what we can do to ease that and live harmoniously together. I'm guessing you're not going to leave Barker, and Steve and the rest of the family have lived here for years, so they won't either. You both need to work through this. I'm worried that something worse could happen to you if we leave it any longer.'

Joel got up silently and left the room. Jack wasn't sure whether to follow him or stay put, so he sat where he was and listened to the footsteps on the wooden floorboards towards the front of the house.

Finally, they came closer again and Joel reappeared, now with a book in his hand. He held it up.

'My maths book. I had a test the day Maggie died,' he said quietly. 'I'd been trying to study for it for weeks but Maggie kept turning up, trying to get me to come to the pool with her, hang out.'

Joel put the book on the table in front of Jack. Jack didn't open it, but let Joel keep talking.

'Same thing happened that day. I needed to go home. I was trying to get into accountancy at uni and it was an important test.' He shook his head as he sat down. 'It never seemed to matter to Maggie. If she needed me, she turned up looking for me.'

'Did you mind that?'

'Not really. It was nice to be wanted.' He drew in a breath and then started to talk very fast, as if he'd been wanting to get this off his chest for a long time. 'Maggie asked me to pretend I was her boyfriend. That was about five months before she died. I didn't really know why she did that. I would've liked to be her real boyfriend, but I was scared that we wouldn't be friends if we broke up.

'I always wanted her to be around, and I liked her company, so I said I'd pretend, that was all. I told her that really clearly.' He nodded to the exercise book. 'She drew in the front page.'

Jack opened it and saw bold writing: *Maggie loves Joel*, with a love heart drawn around their names. The indentation of the writing went through to the next page, and Jack fought the urge to trace his fingers over it.

After having read and heard so much about Maggie over the past few days, to see something she'd written, her handwriting, sent a chill up Jack's spine. It was a reality check, a reminder that this wasn't just a decades-old case; he was dealing with real people who had known Maggie, who had loved her. People who had experienced her smile and laughter, her tears and pain. All the parts of her.

'I didn't know she'd done that until after she died. I found it the day after.' Joel leaned his chin on his palms and stared out the window as he spoke. 'We spent a lot of time together. We'd sit together during recess and lunch, I'd walk her home from school and sometimes we'd study together. Always at my place, never at hers. I went to her place just twice, and it wasn't very nice. The atmosphere was . . . sterile.'

'Was there a reason for that, do you think?'

'Maggie hated going home. Her parents were tyrants, and she didn't like the rest of her family much. But she always toed the line, did what they wanted. She understood they were frightened for her safety after what happened to her cousin.' He paused and his eyes found Jack's. He gave a shake of his head. 'She had her ways of making sure she had freedom, though.'

'How so?'

Joel talked on as if he hadn't heard Jack's question. 'Oh yeah. See, Maggie was a bit cheeky. Devilish, maybe. She'd sneak out at night and be back before they even realised. She only did it a few times and whenever she came around to my place—it was the thrill of being free.' Joel paused a moment before he continued, his voice different. 'Then something changed. She wouldn't let me leave her by herself when we were out or even at my place. She made me promise never to leave her alone, which I thought was really weird, but she'd never tell me why. And there may not have even been a reason. She just used to say, "I just don't want to be without you," then she'd grin up at me.' He rubbed his hands together as he spoke, and looked out the kitchen window, lost in memories.

'Maggie was short—didn't even come up to my shoulders—so you can imagine her looking up at me with those eyes made my heart want to stop.' He stood up and went to the window and put his hand over his chest as if his heart were hurting. 'I begged her to tell me how to help her, but she couldn't. Or didn't. I never knew which.'

'Did she drink?'

Joel spun around and looked at Jack. 'Why do you ask that?'

'I've read the autopsy report. The alcohol content in her blood was high. Now, this is information her parents wouldn't have known; it wasn't in the police report, just the autopsy. She'd been drinking only hours before she died. Did you get her the booze?'

'Me? No. She stole it out of her parents' cabinet.' Joel spread his hands out. 'That's what I was told by Maggie. If it was true, though, it was a wonder they never noticed. They were basically teetotallers, hardly had any alcohol in the house. And they kept on eye on everything she did. I heard later that she was buying it from the pub. I don't know why they would've sold it to her knowing she was underage. The publican would have recognised her. I guess I'm not one hundred percent certain which is true.'

'How did you hear that?'

'I heard Mum and Dad talking one night. Mr Douglas must have gone down to the pub and given them a blast. It caused a bit of a stir at the time.'

Jack made a note to follow this up.

'Did you realise Maggie was drunk that night?'

'Yeah. Yeah, I did. She wasn't as smashed as she'd been the night before, though.'

'The night before?'

'The night before she died. She turned up and threw stones at my window, wanted me to go out with her. But she was really drunk and upset.' He swallowed but continued on. 'Maggie took off after we had a bit of a tiff, but I caught up with her and managed to get her home. I had to leave her at her window because I couldn't get her in without her parents hearing. She was always a loud drunk. And she'd been crying.'

'Was there a reason for that?'

Joel flushed and turned away for a moment, then looked back at Jack. 'She wanted me to kiss her and I wouldn't. That made her think she wasn't attractive, which wasn't true. Maggie was beautiful. Sad and broken, but beautiful. I've thought about this for years and years. I think it was the way her parents kept her locked up the way they did. Maggie didn't seem to know what she wanted. And

I couldn't save her.' His voice broke a little, and Jack got up and poured a glass of water from the tap.

'Come and sit down,' Jack said, setting the glass down on the table. 'What did you have to save her from?'

'Herself!' Joel said a little forcefully. 'She was miserable, but then there were times she'd be happy and fun to be around. Then sad all over again. It was a cycle.'

Jack wrote down *cycle* and looked at it for a few moments. 'Joel, could you tell when these sad times were going to happen? Was there a pattern?'

Pursing his lips, Joel sat at the table and took a sip from the glass. 'I don't know.' He let out a loud groan and thumped the table. 'I was only a kid too! I didn't know to look for those sort of things.'

'Mate, you can't change what's happened. There's no way you could have known anything about Maggie's psychological state of mind. You looked after her. She was lucky to have you.'

'It doesn't feel like that,' Joel muttered.

Jack watched Joel's bent head. He didn't want to ask the next question, but he knew he had to. What he wanted to do was give the bloke a hug. Offer some support. How could he make Joel realise that he'd done more for Maggie than most?

Sighing softly, Jack knew he couldn't do that. Not yet. First, he had to get to the other end.

'Going back to the drinking. Had you had a few that night too?'

'No. She always turned up here already drunk.'

'Okay, so you didn't drink together?'

Joel shook his head. 'Never. We were both underage. The blokes used to take the piss out of me 'cause I wouldn't drink, but I had a goal and that was to get into uni. I didn't have any distractions other than Maggie.'

Jack wrote that down too, then thought about the dark walk to the silos from the Hammond home. 'That night, Joel, it was cold. Why did you end up at the silos?'

'Maggie wanted to go there.' His linked his fingers together and Jack saw his knuckles turn white. 'She always wanted to do something crazy when she'd had a few! And Maggie . . . well, she was hard to say no to.'

'You didn't want to go?'

'I didn't mind. But she was never as much fun when she was drunk as when she was sober, and I was always shit-scared her dad would find us together. I tried to stop her. Tried to stop her from going up.'

Jack nodded. 'I read that in the report.'

'But she wouldn't have it. She had to get up to the lookout area. I kept saying, "No, Mags, you've had too much to drink. Not tonight. We'll come back tomorrow." But she wouldn't have it. I even grabbed her a couple of times to stop her getting to the ladder; you know, on her upper arms. But the last time . . . The last time she was too quick for me. Twisted away and was up there before I could stop her.' He swallowed. '"Look at me," she kept saying. "Look at me, I'm free up here. I'm free." Then she fell.'

Jack let the silence go on for a while, so Joel could gather himself. Finally, he said, 'Joel, you say she fell. Did you see her fall? And did she scream, like she was frightened?'

'When I saw her, she looked like she was flying towards me. Her arms were outstretched—it was like she had wings. And she was smiling. Her hair, it was streaming back towards the stars.' His voice cracked again, and this time the tears arrived. 'There wasn't any noise until she hit the ground.'

Jack didn't want to press, but again, he knew he had to. 'Did you actually see her fall?'

Joel put his hands over his eyes, trying to stop his tears.

'I'm sorry to make you relive this, mate. I really am. But did you see her fall?'

Not able to speak, Joel shook his head. 'I . . . I looked up and she was already in the air.'

'Do you think she could have jumped?'

Pounding his fists gently on the table, Joel looked like he wanted to run away. 'I've gone over and over and over this every single day since it happened. There was no reason for Maggie to kill herself. Yeah, she had overpowering parents, but that was it. She was happy. Loved. We had fun. Uh—' He broke off and put his head on his arms and sobbed.

Somehow through the tears, a word appeared.

'No.'

'No, you don't think she jumped?'

'No, she didn't jump.'

CHAPTER 21

As he stepped onto the footpath outside Joel's house, Jack pulled out his phone. 'Dave, can you come and pick me up in the patrol car?'

'What's up?'

'We need to go and have a chat with Steve Douglas. He's been at Joel Hammond's place.' Giving Dave a quick rundown, Jack finished with, 'I think we should go and ask him why he wants Joel run out of town. Other than the obvious.'

'Right-oh. I'll be there shortly,' Dave answered.

As Jack waited on the street, he turned over everything Joel had told him, pressure-testing the information for holes and untruths. He couldn't see any. The man had no reason to lie, as far as Jack could see. Joel had been cleared, and Maggie's death classed as an accident.

At the same time, Jack couldn't see why the Douglases

would lie either. Sure, they were a strange, close-knit family, but they weren't even there the night Maggie died.

Jack saw Dave come around the corner and pull up next to the kerb.

'Interesting times, mate,' Dave said as he got in.

'Steve's got a bit of an angry streak to him,' Jack said, clipping his seatbelt. 'But so has Joel. He looked like he was about ready to have a go at Steve if he got any closer. The door was shut but I could see through the glass, the way he was standing. Like a bull ready for a charge if he took one step over his safe line.'

'Joel's got form, don't forget. That's why he got those extra four years in prison. He just about killed a couple of blokes. What was he going to do to Steve? Punch him?'

'Fly out the door and do something, anyway.'

'Shit,' Dave muttered. 'I don't want this getting violent.'

'I think it's already there.'

'Mmm, then we'll have to head it off at the pass. Did you get anything useful out of Joel?'

'He told me about the night Maggie died. He's sure she fell. And she didn't scream.'

'You didn't run the suicide theory?'

'He said she didn't have a reason.'

'What do you think?'

'I think I haven't got anything that says "beyond reasonable doubt", but I know there's something else—I just haven't found it yet.'

'Okay. You take the lead since you were there this morning, not me.'

'If you think so.'

'I didn't get to tell you this morning, but yesterday Kim brought me a book that Verity Hammond gave Greta Kerby before she died. It's full of newspaper articles she collected during Joel's trial.'

Jack turned to look at him. 'Why has Greta got that?' He stopped. 'Actually, the better question is, how did Kim come into possession of something so important?'

Dave gave a dry laugh. 'You know Kim. Turns out she and Zara had a cup of tea with Greta yesterday.'

'Oh, did they now? Zara didn't mention it. Am I right in guessing they're stirring things up?'

'I haven't been told for sure, but you and I know exactly how this will play out, don't we? I can bet you my next pay cheque that Zara is going to chase down the mention of someone else being involved.'

'Someone else?'

'That's what one of the newspaper articles says.'

'Excellent,' Jack said with a groan, and Dave laughed.

'You've got to be impressed with the ingenuity of our women,' he said. 'And the fact they love to help us.'

'The Esme Watsons of Barker,' Jack said with an eye roll.

'You're a braver man than me to make that comment within town boundaries! You know they've got spies everywhere, don't you?'

Despite himself, Jack laughed. 'We wouldn't be without them.'

'You're dead right there.'

Dave pulled up at a T-junction and let a couple of cars go by before he turned down Cooper Street and headed for the house Steve Douglas lived in.

'You know, Steve's highly regarded around town, especially being the school principal,' Jack said thoughtfully. 'He hasn't got any priors, and this is the first time I've ever seen him unhinged. He must've really been affected by Maggie's death.'

'Loss is a strange beast. No one ever experiences it the same way, especially with a death of someone so young.'

'Don't you feel that Steve is acting outside his personality, though? He's known to be methodical and a great leader. Zara told me the school has won lots of awards since he took over. She wrote about it a while back.'

'Like I said, loss is a strange beast. I don't think I'd ever like to try to predict how someone will act, even this long after a death. A violent one at that.'

Pulling the car over to the kerb, Dave shut off the engine.

Lynette Douglas was in the garden, her thick mousey-blonde hair pulled back into a short ponytail and her shape hidden beneath a baggy, long-sleeved shirt.

'Looks like you're up, mate,' Dave said.

'Wish me luck,' he muttered. 'Hi, Lynette,' Jack said as he got out of the car. 'Nice afternoon for garden work.'

Lynette stood up and crossed her arms. 'What can I do for you both?' she asked, glancing towards the house.

'I told Steve I'd come by and have a chat with him.'

'He's in the shower. He's got a Lions Club meeting tonight.'

'That's okay, we can wait.' He smiled as Dave came to stand next to him. 'What's happening in the Lions Club at the moment?'

'I think they're working out how to raise money to fix up the Lions Park on the edge of town. It needs a bit of a tidy up.'

'He spends a lot of time helping out the community, doesn't he, your Steve?' Dave said, nodding. 'We need men like him to make the town go round.'

'Steve likes helping out around Barker. He's lived here for so long, he knows what it takes to make the town work,' Lynette agreed.

'Is Steve going okay?' Jack asked. 'Not under any pressure, is he?'

Lynette shrugged. 'If you don't count Joel Hammond, then, no, not that I'm aware of.'

'No concerns at school?'

'I haven't heard of anything. What's this all about?'

'Just trying to get a picture of Steve's life. He hasn't started taking any medication that would make him act a little differently?'

Staring at him, Lynette frowned. 'Why would you ask that?' Her tone had changed, her voice softer as she looked at the ground.

'Ah, well, I saw him having a bit of an altercation with Joel Hammond today and I thought it was really out of character. I wanted to check he was okay. Seemed very peculiar, that's all.'

Her head flew up and suddenly her eyes began to flash. She took a step towards the two men. 'See, this is why Joel

229

Hammond needs to leave. Him being here drives people to do things they normally wouldn't.' Her voice faded into a high begging. 'Can't you make him go?'

Jack put his hands in his pockets and rocked back on his heels, regarding Lynette. 'You don't seem to like Joel Hammond much.'

'No surprises there,' she huffed as she leaned the shovel against the wheelbarrow and bent to pull a couple of weeds from the garden bed.

'I know about the history with the Douglases, but why don't *you* like him?'

'Because my husband doesn't and that's what wives do—support their husbands.'

'Ah, so you don't actually have a reason. Only what you've been told.'

She put her hands on her hips and gave a theatrical sigh. 'Maggie died, Jack,' she said slowly, clearly trying to make her point clearer. 'It affected the whole family, but Steve in particular. I don't want him to be upset all the time, the way he has been since that man came back to live in Barker. It's been hard for all of us.'

'How's he changed since Joel came back?'

'Well, he's always felt Maggie's death. The anniversary, her birthday and so on, they're all hard on him. But this is different.'

'How so?'

She paused, then Lynette's hand flew up to her throat and she took a moment to answer. 'He's not sleeping. I hear him up at all hours of the night and then find him asleep on the couch in the morning.' She rubbed her upper arm and tugged at her sleeve. 'He's agitated and touchy . . .' Her voice trailed off. 'Drinking more. I don't know, his behaviour is hard to pinpoint. And, yes, that's the medication you're talking about. Joel Hammond being here. *Him* being here is a constant reminder to Steve and his whole family that Maggie isn't anymore.'

'Yeah, I've heard you say that before,' Dave said calmly, 'but I'm wondering why Joel is the problem. I'm sure you have photographs in the house that are also a constant reminder. Other memories too. Can you help me understand?'

The door slammed, and Jack and Dave looked over to see Steve coming from the house, his hair wet.

Lynette went to him and put her hand on his arm. 'They're wanting to talk to you.'

Steve shook her hand off and fixed his gaze on Jack. 'Did you get rid of him?'

'Get rid of him? What?' Lynette asked, her eyes flicking back and forth between the men. 'What do you . . .'

Steve rounded on her, towering over her as he spoke sharply. 'I went to talk to him, Lynette. See if I could make him see sense and move on.'

Jack watched as Lynette let her breath out with a whoosh. She rubbed her arm again.

'Maybe we could go inside and have a chat,' Dave suggested as a couple of people came out onto the street to see what was happening.

'Yeah, good idea,' Lynette said, pulling off her gloves and walking quickly towards the front door to hold it open. Jack watched her glance around at the neighbouring houses, and he wondered, was it just that she didn't want the public's attention, or was it something else?

The men followed, and Jack took out his notebook as he walked.

When they were settled at the kitchen table, Jack said, 'I'd really like to understand why you want Joel Hammond to leave Barker.'

Steve paced the floor as he spoke, casting an imposing figure above the others seated at the table. He was a large man, Jack realised. Larger up close than the man he saw from a distance, walking down the street or stopping to talk and laugh with school parents. 'Every time I see him, I want to kill him. Not that I should be saying that to you, but I think of what he did to my sister and I can't understand why he didn't go to jail.'

'Can you help me understand what he did?'

'My god!' The words exploded from Steve. 'How did you get to become a cop? Are you that *stupid*?'

Jack forced his face to be still, and Dave cleared his throat as a not-so-subtle reminder that he was there.

'There's no need for that type of insulting behaviour, Mr Douglas,' Dave said firmly. 'What we are trying to do is—'

Lynette broke in over the top of him. 'Steve's right,' she said quickly. 'Joel was encouraging Maggie to do things that—'

'Shut up, woman!' Steve growled. He savagely pulled a chair out and sat down close to Jack and leaned towards him, within an inch of his face.

Breathing heavily, Steve seemed to wrestle with himself.

'Mr Douglas,' Dave warned.

Finally, Steve spoke in bullet-like words. 'He. Raped. Her.'

Silence.

'Could you repeat that?' Jack asked, making sure his eyes didn't flick to Dave.

'Yeah, you haven't been told that bit, have you?' he sneered, leaning back. 'He had his way with her. Maggie told me. Turned up at my bedroom door, sobbing her heart out, saying that he'd hurt her.' The words pushed from his mouth as if he'd never said them before.

Jack focused on Steve and hoped that Dave was watching Lynette's reaction; had she known this?

'I see. When was this?'

'A couple of months before she died.'

The veins stood out in Steve's forehead and fury radiated from him. He sat completely still, staring at Jack.

Dave leaned forwards and spoke softly. 'And how did you help her, Steve?'

Lynette got up from the table and started to pace the room, fiddling with her clothes. As Jack's eyes left Steve to watch her, he realised that this wasn't news to her. And it went a long way to explaining her bitterness towards Joel.

If it was true.

'*Help her?* What could I do? I wanted to go to the police, but she wouldn't let me. Everything I suggested, she refused. Begged me not to. I couldn't do anything.' Steve stood up from the table. 'That's why he shouldn't be here, among our children. I'm here to protect children. It's my job. Joel

Hammond is a rapist and a thief and he has no place here in Barker. He's been in jail for god's sake!'

'Did you tell your parents?'

'No. Maggie pleaded with me not to. Neither of us wanted to upset them; they were so protective of Maggie as it was.' He shook his head and looked down at the table, all the fight seemingly gone. 'It was bad enough that our cousin had never been found, but to have this happen as well. To another beautiful, innocent soul . . .' He spread his hands out. 'It beggared belief.'

Jack wrote down the last sentence Steve spoke and underlined a couple of words.

Lynette sat back down again, and Jack's attention returned to her as she pushed her sleeves up and ran her fingers through her hair.

'Did you know this, Lynette?' he asked.

'Yes. Why do you think I've been so vocal about him leaving town? There are children here to think of.'

Jack nodded. There was nothing in Joel Hammond's file to suggest he had indecently assaulted Maggie or any child. He wasn't a paedophile. Jack could understand Steve and Lynette's fear, but it was unsubstantiated, as much of their argument was.

'How did you find out?' Jack asked Lynette.

'Steve told me after we got married.' Her voice seemed high and strained.

Dave spoke quietly to them both. 'So, why not come to the police and tell us? This is a serious allegation—it's certainly the first we've heard of it. There's nothing in the report that suggests a sexual assault. We can't help you if we don't know.'

Jack nodded in agreement, carefully watching their reaction.

Steve's body seemed to deflate further, and he hung his head. 'I don't know. I don't suppose there's anything that can be done now, is there? I mean, Maggie isn't here. You can't get any evidence. And I'm the only one she told. That . . . that *mongrel* over there won't admit anything.'

'And it would drag your parents into something they don't need at their age,' Lynette said, turning to Jack and Dave. 'If there isn't anything you can do now to convict him, you have to make sure he leaves town.' She narrowed her eyes. 'He *has* to go.'

~

Out in the car, Jack threw his notebook on the dash and let out a loud sigh. 'What the fuck?' he said. 'I didn't see that coming. I thought there was more to this case, but I didn't think it was *that*.'

Dave started the car, not answering.

Jack kept talking. 'Surely it can't be true. And, if it is, I can't believe I missed it.' Jack turned to look at Dave. 'Have we read Joel wrong?'

'Do you believe Steve?'

Jack stopped and looked at Dave. 'You don't?'

'I don't know. Stranger things have happened, I guess, but . . .' He raised one shoulder. 'Never assume, remember?'

Nodding, Jack went back to the first lesson Dave ever taught him: check everything and don't assume what you're being told is the truth. Or a lie.

As they drove down the main street, Jack's mind whirled. He noticed Dave flick a hand to wave to a couple of people on the street before he turned into the station car park.

Silence rang out between them as Dave shut off the engine and opened his door. Glancing over at Jack, he said, 'We have an obligation to look into this.' He slammed the door and went inside.

Jack groaned and pushed his head back into the headrest, thinking, then he got out of the car and followed Dave.

Dave was already at his desk reading the file on Maggie Douglas. 'Yeah,' he finally said, tapping a spot. He passed the file over to Jack. 'The autopsy report. There isn't any visible sign of rape. Now, two months before she died is probably too long ago to actually be able to know this, but there's nothing here that indicates she was raped in the weeks leading up to her death. And when I say raped, I mean forced trauma.'

Jack grabbed at the file and turned it around so he could read it. 'But there were clear signs of sexual activity.'

'Yes.'

'Joel denies even kissing her. Was too frightened to lose her friendship.' He looked up. 'Who else could she have been sleeping with?'

They were both quiet, their brains racing with possibilities.

'We know Maggie was sneaking out,' Dave said slowly. 'And any other time, she was either with Joel, or her family.'

'Yeah, but we also know she'd go to Joel's when she was away from home. Let's not forget either, that Maggie tried it on with him once.' Jack stopped and flicked through the file, as if searching for an answer. Finally he put it down and looked at Dave. 'I don't believe she was promiscuous.'

'I agree with that.' Dave's phone rang and he grabbed it out of his pocket as if he were pleased at the distraction. 'Hey, Kim. How's it going?'

As Dave chatted to his wife, Jack flicked through the statements in the Maggie Douglas case, skim-reading each one to see if he had missed anything earlier.

There were statements from the Douglas family— Max and Paula, Sam, Andrew and Steve—as well as Joel Hammond, Billy and Verity Hammond, Emma Cameron, Greta Kerby, Maggie's teachers and friends, and a few people who had lived across the road from the silos at the time of Maggie's death.

Jack looked up suddenly, just as he heard Dave tell Kim that he and Jack would be at the pub in twenty minutes, but his focus was on the file. 'Hey, are any of these teachers still in town?' He read out their names.

'I don't recognise any of them.'

'We should see if we can speak to them again. They might've seen something they didn't mention because they didn't think it mattered. Schools are a melting pot of emotions and hormones, and whoever Maggie was sleeping with might have been at the school. Maybe it was a teacher, which is why no one knows anything about it?'

He didn't hear Dave's answer as he bent his head back down and kept reading.

'Ready?' Dave's voice broke his focus. He looked up.

'Sorry?'

'We've got to go and meet the girls.' Then, when Jack looked at him blankly, he added, 'That was Kim. She's with Zara at the pub, and we're going to meet them. Now.'

'Right.' Distracted, Jack looked back down at the pages and frowned. 'You go. I'll catch up.'

'Hey, Jack?'

'Hmm?'

'This is a cold case. Zara will have my nuts if you don't come with me. That file will still be here tomorrow.'

'I can feel we're close,' Jack exclaimed.

Dave nodded. 'And pubs are also a great source of information. Let's go.'

CHAPTER 22

'Two chardonnays, please, Hopper,' Zara said, waving her card near the EFTPOS machine. 'Gee, it's busy tonight.'

'Just how I like it, love,' Hopper said as he grabbed the wine out of the fridge and poured two. 'How's life with you? I haven't seen you for a while.'

'I got back from Adelaide today. Had to go down for work.'

'You must do some kilometres. Don't you get sick of flitting here and there? Surely it's time you stayed in one place for a while?'

'What, and get boring? I don't think so! That's not me.'

Hopper sighed. 'I know it's not, but that young copper of yours might get tired of you not being home.'

Zara grinned and leaned in closer. 'I'll tell you a secret.'

The old man's eyes sparkled. 'What might that be?'

'I think he likes it when I'm not there. Gets the TV remote all to himself.'

Hopper let out a laugh. 'Well, I hope you're right, missy. I don't want you in here crying all over my bar if you're not.'

'I promise I won't.' She winked and took the two glasses back to the table that Kim had reserved in the corner next to the fire.

The warmth had made Kim's cheeks glow and she looked relaxed as she stared into the fire. Zara nudged her friend with her foot to get her attention, before handing her the glass of wine.

'Cheers,' Zara said as she sat down with a sigh. 'I'm buggered.'

'Cheers to you. It's all that driving you do.'

'Ah, don't you start! Hopper's just told me Jack's going to find someone else if I don't stay home.'

Kim giggled. 'Nice to know he cares.'

'They broke the mould when they made him, that's for sure!'

'How'd you get on in Adelaide?'

'All good. Lachie and I went out to lunch and talked about the new layout of the mag they're going to trial next month and I caught up with a few people, but nothing too exciting. Except . . .' Zara smiled and sat up a bit straighter. 'The most interesting thing that came out of lunch was that Lachie used to know Bob Elder.'

Kim's glass stopped halfway to her mouth. 'Seriously?'

'Uh-huh! So, I've got an introduction to his widow in the next couple of days.'

'Oh Zara, you have to go back to Adelaide again?'

'No, that's the best bit!' She felt a hand on her shoulder and then lips on her head.

'What's the best bit?' Jack asked her. 'Hey, you.'

'Hey, yourself.' She raised her mouth for a kiss.

'God, you lot are sickening,' a voice called out from the bar.

Dave laughed. 'That's why you're here by yourself, Hampy,' he called back to the unmarried shearer sitting at the bar.

Laughter from the bar surrounded them as the men sat down.

Jack took Zara's hand and held it under the table, before speaking to Kim. 'I hear you got a gift,' he said.

'Gift?' Kim looked confused. 'No,' she said slowly, 'it's not my birthday.'

'From Greta Kerby.'

'Oh yeah!' Kim let out a laugh and leaned towards Jack. 'I did. Or rather, *we* did.' She looked across at Zara and winked. 'The scrapbook. Now isn't it an interesting piece of literature.'

'I don't know, I haven't seen it yet.' He looked at Dave pointedly. 'I'm still waiting.'

'I think you've got enough on your hands at the moment,' Dave scoffed.

Dave turned to Zara. 'He's reminding me of you when you pick up the scent of a story. Head down and focused. What have you done to him? I've never known him to be so dedicated before.'

'Now, this is all my good influence. You owe me,' she said, raising her glass to Dave.

'Oi, I can hear you all, you know,' Jack said, good-naturedly.

They all laughed.

'Hmm, head down and focused. I'd love to ask what you've got your nose into,' Zara said to Jack, 'but I don't suppose I'd get an answer.'

'No, I don't suppose you would. Where's the menu?'

There was a sudden noise outside, and all four looked through the window.

Lynette and Steve Douglas were right outside. Steve looked angry, his hand holding tightly to Lynette's arm as she stumbled.

'What's going on . . .' Jack started, just as Lynette brought her hand down onto Steve's arm, trying to twist out of his grasp but failing as he dragged her out of view.

'I'll be back in a sec,' Jack said and pushed his chair aside, eyes on the window.

'Jack.' Zara half stood and put her hand on his arm.

'He's right,' Dave said as they watched Jack leave the warmth of the pub.

~

Outside, the air was cold and the street was empty. Jack walked around the corner looking for the couple. He soon heard the sounds of a scuffle at the back of the pub.

Steve had Lynette pressed up against the wall, his body crushed into hers. Jack couldn't be sure if they were making out or something more sinister.

'Everything all right?' he asked.

Steve's head whipped around and he moved away from Lynette as if he'd been stung. 'Fine,' he answered, straightening his jacket. 'Isn't it, love?'

Lynette stayed pressed against the wall, staring up at her husband.

'Isn't it, love?' Steve said again, his voice loaded.

'Uh, yeah. Fine.' Lynette pushed herself away from the wall and stumbled as she tried to stand upright.

'I'll just get her home,' Steve said, taking his wife's arm and pulling her in the direction of their place.

Jack nodded and watched them leave, Lynette walking unsteadily beside Steve.

～

'All okay,' Jack said, sitting back down at the table. 'I'm starving. What have you all decided on?'

As he looked at the menu, Zara slipped her hand onto his knee underneath the table.

He looked over at her and smiled as he squeezed it.

'Um, I'm not sure if you're quite done yet,' Kim said in a low voice, gesturing to the doorway.

Lynette stood framed against the darkness, wobbling back and forth, searching the room. She locked eyes with Jack and immediately weaved her way, unsteadily, to their table, where she fixed a glassy-eyed stare at them.

'If it isn't the fearsome foursome,' she said sarcastically, holding onto the back of Kim's chair for support. 'All having dinner and pretending that nothing's wrong outside your little world. Why aren't you running Joel Hammond out of town?'

Kim and Zara looked at each other, while Dave smiled. 'We're having some dinner, Lynette,' he said quietly. 'Might be best if you head back home, hey? Steve still out there?'

'Don't reckon I'll be doing that. Not for a while.' She moved around the table and grabbed Dave's upper arm.

Jack quickly moved towards his friend and boss, just as Kim gave a small gasp. Zara stood up, but Jack grasped her hand and pulled her back into her seat, seeing that Dave had the situation under control.

Dave held up his hands as Lynette leaned forwards and almost toppled into him. 'Steady there, Lynette,' he said, helping her to stay upright. 'Why don't you want to go home?'

''Cause he's angry that Joel Hammond's here.' She spoke as if Dave were simple. 'So angry. You've got to get him to leave so life can go back to normal.' Her unfocused stare went from Dave to the rest of the table. 'Can you please . . .' She was pleading, but she seemed unable to finish her sentence.

'Look, you've had a bit to drink tonight, so how about heading back to your house. Why don't I drive you?' Dave offered.

'I don't drink,' Lynette said, pulling her jacket tightly around her despite the heat from the fire. 'I don't drink, don't smoke, don't do anything that might cause a fuss. That's the way the Douglas family is; they don't like being the centre of attention.'

Dave stood and tried to take her arm, but she pulled back. 'Well, I think it's time to leave, if you don't want to cause a scene.'

Lynette turned to Kim and Zara. 'And here's Mother Teresa and her sidekick. How about you both stop making his life easy by giving him meals and whatever else you're doing.'

'Hey—' Zara said, but Jack stood and stepped between the women.

'Come on, Lynette,' he said. 'I'll help you home. That's the best place for you tonight.' He tried to guide her towards the door, but she slapped him away.

Hopper came out from behind the bar. 'Now what's going . . .'

Dave shot him a look and he retreated quickly.

'Keep your filthy hands off me,' Lynette said fiercely. 'You just stay away!' She brought her hands up to ward him off. 'You've got no idea what's good for me!'

Kim stood up. 'Come on, Lynette,' she said in a no-nonsense tone. 'Let's go.' Kim put her arm around Lynette's shoulders and led her outside. Jack went to follow, but Dave shook his head.

'Leave her be. I don't think an authority figure is going to help with this, and Kim's pretty good at looking after herself. Let's order. Knowing Kim, she won't be long.'

Jack looked out the window and watched as Kim spoke to Lynette with her usual mix of sympathy and seriousness; she simply had a way of getting people to open up to her.

'What're you having?' Dave asked, pulling out his wallet. Jack refocused and looked at the menu, then at Zara.

'Steak or parmi? What are you going to have, Zara?'

'Um.' Zara looked at the menu. 'I think I've lost my appetite.'

'Hey, don't let something like this upset you. It happens all the time,' Jack said. He turned to Dave. 'I'll have the chicken parmi.'

'Oh, make that two,' Zara said, still looking towards the window.

Dave nodded and left the table.

Zara got up and made to walk to the window, but Jack stopped her. 'Are you sure we shouldn't go out with them?' she asked him.

'Yeah, I am. Don't worry, I'm watching and so is Dave. Kim won't come to any trouble out there. So, how was Adelaide?'

'Good.'

Jack could see she was having trouble concentrating.

'Look, here she comes. Told you she'd be right.' Jack nodded towards the door where Kim was entering, her face solemn.

She took her seat quietly and gave a small smile. 'Crisis averted.'

Zara reached over and squeezed Kim's hand.

Dave returned with another round of drinks. He put his hand on Kim's shoulder and squeezed. 'Good job, honey.'

Kim took a sip of wine, and Jack saw her hands were shaking. Turning to Dave, Kim said, 'Lynette said you went to see Steve today.'

Dave didn't answer, just looked at her as if to say, *You know I can't answer that.*

'Did you see the bruise on the back of her hand?'

Dave and Jack looked at each other.

'Maybe it wasn't out by then,' Kim continued. 'She told me it was from having a canular inserted yesterday. Some type of transfusion.' Kim paused. 'Is Lynette sick, that you know of?'

'Geez, you're asking the wrong person,' Dave said. 'I have no idea. She certainly didn't mention anything this morning and I didn't see a bruise. What was she supposed to have a transfusion for?'

'She wouldn't say.' Kim looked around the table thoughtfully before she continued. 'You know, Lynette has put on weight in the last little while and seems a bit angry with the world. Without gossiping, I'd almost say the puffiness of her face is a bit steroid-y.'

The men looked confused, but realisation spread over Zara's face. 'You think she has cancer?'

Kim raised her shoulders. 'I have no idea. Everything I've just said is an observation.'

'But she was drunk,' Jack said.

'Maybe not. Medication could leave her unsteady, seemingly out of it.'

Jack felt a fizz in his stomach. 'Yeah, strong meds. Like opioids.'

CHAPTER 23

'I'm worried about you,' Emma said to Jacqui. 'You're not yourself.' Emma poured a glass of wine and settled in to the swing seat on the verandah to watch the sunset. The layers of gold were slowly turning into rich pinks and reds, silhouetting the few clouds that lined the horizon. Putting the phone on speaker, she sat it on her lap.

'Honestly, Em, I'm okay.' Jacqui paused. 'There's just a few things going on at the moment that I'm not sure how to deal with.'

Emma heard the tension in her friend's voice, and her heart hurt for her. 'A problem shared is a problem halved,' she said softly. 'Let me help, Jac.'

There was a sniff, then a sob. 'I'm so ashamed,' Jacqui cried suddenly. 'So ashamed. I'm an idiot!'

Emma waited her out, taking a sip and pushing the swing chair off with her foot. It rocked her gently while Jacqui got herself under control.

'I've been blackmailed.'

Emma stopped the swing while she tried to understand what Jacqui had uttered. 'What do you mean?'

'I've been talking to a guy online and . . . I sent him some nudes.'

'What?' Emma couldn't believe what she'd just heard. This was clever, smart Jacqui; a teacher who knew all about technology and online behaviour. She taught kids how to avoid this sort of thing at school! 'Oh no.' Emma saw exactly where this was going.

'I can't believe I was so stupid. I hear about this sort of thing all the time.'

'Where's he posted them?'

'He hasn't done it yet. Well, not that I know of.' She dragged in an unsteady breath. 'He's demanding money not to post them on social media.'

Emma was silent, not sure how to respond. Finally, she asked, 'How much?'

'Ten grand.'

'Shit!' She put her wine down and got up to pace the verandah. 'We've got to go to the police. They'll be able to stop this, surely.'

'He said not to—' A cry escaped her. 'I'd rather pay.'

'No, no, no! That's how they keep getting away with it,' Emma exclaimed. 'You know that, Jac. We have to go to the police.'

'I don't know how many copies he's made or what might happen if the police get involved. God,' Jacqui wailed, 'I'm a school teacher. Imagine what this will do to my career if anyone sees them!' Her sobbing was ugly, and Emma desperately wanted to make the hurt stop, but she didn't know how to.

'Jac,' she said. 'Jacqui, you need to listen to me. There isn't a choice here. We need to go and see the police, no matter what he's threatened you with. They can't be allowed to do this to people—and you're reacting this way because you're frightened.' Emma tried to imagine the fear Jacqui was feeling. The consequences of this were huge, as was the humiliation.

'No! We can't! Em, you know that once something goes up online it's there forever, no matter what. I can't risk—'

'He's playing on your vulnerability, Jac. You have to report it. Even if it's only so he doesn't do it to someone else. I'll come with you. How—' She stopped, not sure if she should ask the question. 'Which site? How did you meet him?'

Emma could imagine her friend wiping her tears away and chewing the inside of her cheek, the way she always did when she was worried.

'On Bundle.'

Emma's heart sank. 'Is that the one where all his information can disappear and he can't be traced?'

'Yeah.'

'Are you still talking to him?'

'Only when he contacts me. He keeps sending messages about the money.'

Cash got up from under the chair and went to Emma, as if he were feeling her distress. He pushed his nose into her hand and whined softly.

'Has he given you a deadline?' Emma asked.

'Not yet.'

'Right, I'm coming into town tomorrow, and we're going to see Jack Higgins. In the meantime, you'd better take some screenshots. You need proof of what's going on.' She paused. 'Will you do that?'

'You've got no idea how distressing and embarrassing this is, Em,' Jac said softly. 'None.'

'I'm trying to, Jac. But you're right. It's a bit like the accident for me. Until you've been through it, you can't understand.' Emma didn't know what to say after that. The thought of someone posting nudes of her for the whole world to see was enough to make her feel ill. 'We'll sort it out, Jac, I promise. I'll be alongside you all the way.'

The silence was broken by a sniff and then, 'Thanks, Em. Thank you.'

Emma could hear the heavy relief in her friend's voice. She ended the call and stared at nothing. Cash whined again and the noise broke into her thoughts. She leaned down and put her nose to his, patting him softly, glad for the warmth and comfort.

'Geez, Cash,' she said quietly. 'What the hell?'

Cash looked up at her, expectant.

'This is so, so wrong.'

Emma's phone beeped with a message: *Can you grab some more vaccine and calf marking rings when you're in town next?*

Matt. Heat flooded through Emma as she remembered his lips on hers.

And the reaction when the kiss ended.

They'd both pulled away and looked at each other, horrified.

'Sorry,' he'd muttered, moving over as close to the passenger's door as he could be.

'No, it was me,' she said. 'I'm sorry.' She'd looked straight ahead and driven back to the sheds. 'Not thinking straight.'

Matt had got out without a word and left Deception Creek quickly. Emma had stayed in the ute staring after the cloud of dust. How had that even happened? They couldn't! They had to work together.

All the emotions of longing, loneliness and horror were rolled into one as she'd slowly got out of the ute and walked to the house, Cash on her heels.

His lips had been warm and the kiss sweet, she realised, before squeezing her eyes shut to black out the memories.

Her friends had a lot to answer for; she would never have seen Matt in that light if it hadn't been for them.

And she could never see him like that again. *We have to work together*, she repeated over and over.

But she couldn't help but think of the easy comfort between them. Their conversations and similarities. Their friendship.

Yep, can do, she texted back and then threw the phone on the seat beside her.

Cash put his paws up and looked at her.

'Ah no,' she said. 'You're not getting up . . .'

Jumping onto the swing chair, Cash put his nose to her cheek, leaving a cold, wet spot, and then flopped down with a sigh, his chin on her leg.

'Yep. Good to know you take notice of me,' Emma said, her hand automatically patting him.

Her phone lit up with another message.

Kyle, this time. He'd been in town a couple of days and they still hadn't caught up.

I'm about to order dinner at the pub, if there's any chance you're passing by.

Emma looked at her hands—they were dry and filthy from the day's fencing. Dirt was wedged under her finger-nails, and a couple of bloody cuts crossed her arm where the wire had scratched her.

Being tired and a little sunburnt, what should happen was a shower and bed.

She knew from her nightly routine of standing in front of the fridge that there was nothing there to eat. Still, if she went in to see Kyle, she could get a decent feed and drop by Jacqui's place on the way home.

Before she could change her mind, she sent a message back: *Have a drink and I'll see you in an hour.*

~

Emma nervously tugged at her shirt and then put on her jacket. It had been a few years since she'd seen Kyle, and right at that moment she wasn't sure she wanted to see him at all.

The pub looked busy for just gone six o'clock. As she climbed out of the ute and slammed the door shut, Emma caught sight of Joel Hammond sitting on the bench outside the deli, drinking a takeaway coffee.

Emma was surprised; she thought he'd been keeping to himself. Walking over, she smiled. 'Hello,' she said. 'What are you doing here?'

'Mrs Kerby needed a few things, so I brought her down,' he said, glancing over his shoulder. He rubbed one hand along his leg and swapped the coffee over so he could repeat the action. 'I'm still waiting for her to finish the shopping.'

Nerves. Emma knew all about that.

'Well, I'll catch you later,' she said, unsure what else to say.

Joel nodded, clearly just as reluctant to engage in chitchat.

Kyle was sitting at the end of the bar. His face split into a big smile when he saw her. Getting up, he met her halfway across the floor and kissed her cheek.

'It's good to see you,' he said.

'Let's sit,' she said hurriedly, suddenly conscious there were some people watching them. There would be gossip and innuendo before the night was finished.

With Barker's love of gossip, however, she wondered why she'd never heard anything more about Matt's mystery woman.

'What'll you have?' Kyle asked, flashing a gold credit card at Hopper.

'Just a lemon squash.'

'That's not much fun. Surely you can have one?'

She shook her head. 'I had one before I came in. I hate driving if I've had anything to drink. I thought you would have as well.'

'Yeah, you're right.' Kyle's smile faded. 'Sorry, I didn't realise you had to drive. I'm used to being in the city where I can catch an Uber any time.'

Hopper came over and looked at Kyle, waiting for his order.

'Emma,' Hopper said to her. 'Busy on the farm?'

'Always, Hopper, you know that.'

'A lemon squash and another beer, thanks, mate,' Kyle said.

Hopper narrowed his eyes slightly as he served up the drinks. He brought the EFTPOS machine over, and Kyle waved his card somewhere near it then turned to Emma, ignoring the barman, so Emma smiled and thanked Hopper.

'Tell me what you've been up to. You look amazing, by the way. What's happening with the farm?'

Emma talked about the fencing she and Matt had done that day and the saltbush trial they were organising.

'I'd be lost without Matt,' she said. 'He's so clued on and got the brawn I don't have. And he's always thinking about how to improve things.' As she said it, she realised it was true. Deception Creek without Matt would be like a bar without beer. He was part of the landscape.

Kyle frowned. 'Sounds like he's almost too good to be true. Have you checked to make sure he's not a con man?'

Emma laughed. 'Matt's been with me for six years. He's not a con man. He's a very steady, stable bloke who I can rely on.'

'Ah well, you've got to be careful, though. Even the most trustworthy types can screw you over.'

'Speaking from experience?' Emma wrinkled her brow, wondering what type of story she was going to hear.

'No, no. I only know what I read in the papers. Sounds like there're some terrible people out there doing anything for a buck, trying to get their hands on innocent people's money.' He took a sip of his beer. 'What they need to do is get a job and earn money for themselves. It seems to me there's not too many who earn an honest living.'

Feeling a rant coming on, Emma changed the subject. 'What about you? You said you needed some time away?'

Kyle looked down at the bar and wiped away the ring of condensation his beer had left.

'Yeah, it was a bit tough.' He seemed to sink into himself for a little while, then he looked up. 'But now I'm travelling a bit, it's easier. I'm busy, and though I never really forget, I don't dwell on the accident as much anymore, but missing Alice never goes away. It's like I have . . . I don't know . . . a permanent hole in my chest. I still miss Alice, though.'

'I don't suppose you'll ever stop loving the woman you married,' Emma said quietly. 'You've never found anyone else?'

Kyle shook his head. 'No. I don't think I want to. Alice was pretty special.' His voice trailed off as he looked towards the window. An unreadable expression passed over his face and a frown settled on his handsome features. Kyle shifted the chair to make sure he faced away from the window and was a little closer to Emma.

Following his gaze, Emma saw Joel and Mrs Kerby pass by, and she wasn't the only one. The bar's noise dropped, just for a moment, then people started to talk again.

Emma's thoughts quickly returned to Alice as a memory of her begging eyes and blood-filled mouth came to her. She blinked.

'Don't you get lonely?'

'Oh look, don't get me wrong, I'd love to have someone in my life and, yeah, I do get lonely. I've had a couple of goes at meeting women, but they never seem to live up to how I remember Alice.' He shrugged. 'I think I'm destined to be alone.'

'No one should be alone forever,' Emma said. The idea of becoming a lonely old woman frightened her beyond belief. She pushed the feelings away and refocused.

The crowd in the pub got noisier as the sport came on the news. The Adelaide Crows had lost their last three matches and the coach was being interviewed about their poor performance.

'He needs the boot,' someone said, above the clinks of glasses.

'You watch, the whole club will come out in support of him over the next week, then he'll be sacked within two weeks.'

'Yeah, that's what seems to happen,' Hopper agreed. He walked past Emma and Kyle. 'Another round?'

Kyle drained the last of his beer and nodded. 'Cheers, mate.'

'Have you heard from Alice's family?' Emma asked while Hopper poured the drinks.

Scoffing, Kyle turned to look at her. 'Only from the lawyers early on in the piece telling me never to contact the family again.'

'That's really sad. I'd hoped they would change their minds. Surely sitting down and talking about a person you all loved would be nice for everyone. You'd have memories to share.'

Hopper put the drinks in front of them and Kyle took out his card.

'It's my turn,' Emma said.

'It's not often I get to go out to dinner with a gorgeous lady,' he said. 'I'll get them.'

Gorgeous? Emma thought, looking at her work-weary hands. *I don't think so.*

'Come on,' she said. 'It's a bit noisy in here. Let's go through to the dining room.'

When they were settled at a table, Kyle smiled and handed her a menu. 'What about you, Emma? You've been divorced for a while now. Any blokes on the horizon?'

Giving a little laugh, Emma shook her head, pretending she didn't feel the soft pressure of Matt's lips on hers. 'Not a skerrick.'

'I don't understand why. You're intelligent and pretty. Got a great career.'

'I think the word is over-qualified,' she said with a grin. 'At least, that's how I like to look at it.'

'Yeah, well, I can understand some blokes being intimidated by you, for sure. You're successful in a man's world.'

Taking a sip of her drink, Emma gave a harsh laugh. 'If you ask my ex, I'm married to the farm. Not at all interested in anything else.' She put the glass down. 'That's a myth, by the way. Agriculture isn't a man's world anymore,' she clarified. 'There are heaps of women in all sections of the industry nowadays.'

Kyle seemed to ignore her last statement. 'Maybe you just didn't have the right person to want to spend time with.'

Emma shrugged. Perhaps Kyle had a point there. She and Phil hadn't shared common interests.

'I don't know,' Emma hedged. 'But whatever the issue is, farming is more than a full-time job and it takes up every bit of time I have. I've worked really hard and I'm hoping by the end of harvest I can pay the farm off. That's something none of the generations before have managed to do and I'm not going to stuff it up in any way.' She leaned back in her seat. 'See, when Mum and Dad died, they left Deception Creek with a debt, and even though most farms have loans, it wasn't how I wanted to run my business. I'm happy enough to borrow for the yearly operating costs, but I don't want to have a liability over my head that a couple of bad seasons or higher interest rates might cause problems through a large core debt. To pay off that sort of debt means I have to work my arse off. You know the sort of loan that's been there since the farm was purchased.'

'But you lost your marriage in the process.'

Emma was speechless for a moment, but she saw sympathy in his gaze. 'Yeah, I guess you're right, I did. But that was my choice.'

'It must be hard to love your career that much and not have someone to share that with.'

Taking another sip of squash, Emma pushed away the image of Matt laughing with her in the cattle yards. His strong hands holding hers as she struggled to breathe and then his gentle kiss. 'Hmm.'

'However,' Kyle smiled, 'you achieved what you wanted to, so all power to you!' He raised his glass to her.

'I don't think I've ever celebrated that, you know.' She raised her glass too, with a large smile. 'Here's to Deception Creek.'

'To Deception Creek,' Kyle echoed.

Emma glanced at her watch. 'I've got to go and see a friend tonight, so we'd better order.'

Kyle jumped up. 'What would you like?'

Emma quickly scanned the menu. 'Steak and veggies with mushroom sauce, I think. Thanks, Kyle.'

Watching Kyle walk towards the bar to order, she realised he'd got even better looking with age. His hair was now salt-and-pepper grey, but he looked fit and trim. And he filled out his jeans nicely.

Her phone dinged with a message from Jacqui: *Hey, don't worry about coming around. I'm going to bed. If I'm sleeping, I'm not thinking or feeling. I'll see you after school instead.*

Emma scrunched up her lips as she read the message. She really wanted to see Jacqui tonight, just to make sure she was okay. Still, it didn't look like she had a choice now.

Okay, sleep well xx

'Sorry about this. I'm not sure what's going on.'

Emma heard Kyle's voice and looked over. He was looking at his card, confused.

'What's up?' she asked when she walked over.

'Bloody card isn't working. Don't know what's wrong. It was working when I bought the drinks. Maybe the line to the bank is down.'

'I don't think so,' Hopper said in his no-nonsense tone. 'It's working for everyone else.'

'It's okay,' Emma said digging her purse out. 'You can get the next dinner.'

'What? No. I'll use my other card.'

Emma nudged him out of the way. 'It's fine. Cards can often be temperamental, I find.'

She paid and they went back to their table, but Emma stayed standing.

'So sorry,' Kyle said, his face red with embarrassment, but Emma waved his apology away.

'It happens.' She put her glass on the table. 'I'll be back in a sec,' she said, nodding towards the bathrooms.

'Sure.'

Hopper came out from behind the bar as she went over to the small passageway.

'Be careful of that one, Emma,' Hopper said as he met her in the doorway. 'I've seen his kind before.'

CHAPTER 24

Zara looked at the list of questions she had for Joel and made two more notes before stuffing her notebook into her handbag and heading out the door.

Jack was in the kitchen making a coffee, shirtless. She could see his muscles working as he poured the water into a cup and then stirred in some milk.

'Back soon, sweetie,' she said. 'Did you want me to bring you anything?'

'No, I think we're okay. We've got enough for dinner tonight.' He glanced at his watch. 'Shit, I'd better get a move on or I'll be late.'

'Looking pretty good to me right there, Mr Hot Pants. Think you should just stay a house husband and get around shirtless all day,' Zara said, hoisting her bag over her shoulder. She went into the kitchen and jumped up to sit on the bench.

Jack spun around and pulled a stripper pose. 'All yours, baby!'

Zara leaned forwards and caught his arm, pulling him towards her. 'Mmm, I wish we both had time,' she said, putting her lips on his. 'I'm going to talk to Joel Hammond.'

Jack's expression changed to stern. 'You be careful, then. If Steve Douglas turns up, make sure you leave.'

Zara nodded.

'You won't, will you? I know you. Ring me straightaway if he does. I'm not joking, Zara. There's every opportunity for things to go pear-shaped here.'

'I know, sweetie,' she said soothingly. 'I saw that last night. I'll see you later.' She gave him another kiss, jumped down from the bench and let herself out of the house.

The heavy grey clouds hung menacingly low in the sky, while the spattering of rain was just enough to wet the pavement.

On the drive to Joel's, she thought about Lachie's approach to interviewing. 'Make sure you get to speak to them in person, if you can,' he always said. 'Over the phone's never the same. You can get so much more out of them when you're right in front of them.'

Joel was dressed in a thick jumper and weatherproof jacket, and was digging in one of the veggie gardens when she arrived. At his feet were punnets upon punnets of seedlings and bags of fertiliser.

'Hi, Joel,' she called out. 'I'm Zara Ellison from the *Farming Journal*. Have you got time for a chat?'

Joel looked up and his face immediately clouded over at the words *Farming Journal*. 'I haven't got anything to say to any journalists.'

'I'd like to talk to you about Bob Elder,' she said.

Joel straightened up. 'He's dead. Not much to talk about there.'

'That's why I'm here. I want to help you. Maybe pick up where he left off.'

Joel narrowed his eyes and put down the shovel. He kicked the dirt over a capsicum plant he'd just put in the ground and walked towards her. 'Why would you do that?' he asked.

'Would you like me to?' she said.

He regarded her for a moment, then turned away. 'It's in the past now. There's no point. Better off just to leave it.'

'What, you don't want to be exonerated?'

'No chance of that.'

'Look, Joel.' Zara put her bag over her shoulder. 'Could we just have a chat out of the rain? I've done a bit of research on Bob Elder and, from what I understand, you wouldn't have gone to him if you were guilty.'

Zara didn't wait for an answer but went over to the verandah and sat on the edge, waiting to see if Joel would follow her.

Instead, he grabbed a punnet of corn and dug into the rich soil, carefully taking each seedling out and placing it in the ground before gently covering it.

Zara got out her phone and brought up the photo she'd taken of the article Bob had written. Without looking up at Joel, she started to read from it: '*Having consistently denied the charges, Hammond wrote to me asking for my help, insisting he'd been set up by an unnamed person. This is his opportunity to tell his side of the story.*'

'Now,' she continued, looking over to Joel, 'I've investigated Bob Elder. He had a pretty good track record for sniffing out the truth. If there was a cloud hanging over a case, he'd solve it and have the right person brought to justice.

'The way I see it is, you wouldn't have gone to him if you were guilty, because he would have found you out. You've always maintained you didn't take the money. So, let's have a look into it. You obviously talked to him a bit, because he wrote the first piece of the article.'

Joel nodded. 'Yeah. He came and saw me in jail. Was allowed to visit for half an hour.' The bitterness in his voice was clear. 'Half a bloody hour. Can't tell anyone anything in that time.'

'But you told him enough to get him interested.'

'Yeah. He was keen. Trouble was, visiting times were over almost before they started. And he never came back.'

'When did you hear he'd died?'

'Not for ages. A good couple of months, I reckon. I'd written to him and he'd never answered. Finally, a letter came from his office saying he wouldn't be able to help me because he'd passed away.' He looked at Zara and then came over and sat next to her. Taking off his hat, he brushed the droplets away from his face and stared back out over his garden. 'I hoped someone else would take my story on, but there was no one in his league and the paper never offered to follow it up.'

'I'm not of the calibre of Bob Elder,' Zara said, 'but I've been involved with some investigative journalism. Do you want me to look into your case? It will mean dragging up the past and answering a lot of questions. The end result could be very good for you, though.'

Joel shrugged. 'I don't see the point. I'm a free man now. It won't matter if I'm cleared of the charge or not. My life's already buggered up and I'll always be viewed with some sort of suspicion. Having the charges overturned won't change people's opinions now.'

Zara chose her words carefully. 'What if whoever did this to you has done it to someone else? What if that person is in jail too? You've got the opportunity to stop it from happening to anyone else.'

Joel looked at her. It was clear that the thought hadn't ever entered his head. 'Okay,' he said slowly.

'I've got an appointment to see Bob's wife tomorrow. I'm going to ask if she's got any of his old notes, from when he went to see you, or from his investigation. Are you okay with me doing that?'

'It was nearly nine years ago.'

'Journos keep everything. I know, I do it; you never can be sure when you might need a piece of information again. I've got no doubt he would have made notes on your case. He may well have interviewed other people in preparation. The question will be if his wife has kept them.'

Joel looked over at her with what seemed a cross between desperation and excitement. 'Do you really think this is possible?'

'I don't know,' she answered honestly. 'A lot will depend on what information I can find and if people are still around and willing to talk. Alive would be very helpful.' She flashed him a smile, hoping he would smile back. Humour got people to loosen up and trust her. 'But almost every criminal makes a mistake, and if one was made in your case, there's a good chance I'll be able to find that mistake.' Zara paused. 'Although I need to make it clear that I can't promise anything. But I'll be doing the best I can.'

The wind blew through the trees and made the tin roof creak. Joel looked up at the sky and seemed to be contemplating what she'd just said.

'Okay,' he finally answered. 'Okay. Let's have a go.'

Zara took a deep breath in through her nose and closed her eyes. She wanted to scream out, *Yes!*

'I've got some questions for you, if you're prepared to answer them.'

'All right.' He kicked his heel against the edge of the verandah and then clenched his fists.

'Do you want to get used to the idea first?' Zara asked, sensing his nervousness. 'I can wait. It's been like this for nine years already; a few more days won't make much difference.' She didn't mean what she was saying, though. She wanted to be on the trail immediately, but she had to make sure Joel felt comfortable with everything she did.

'Nah, it's okay. Let's just do it.' He stood up. 'Do you want to come inside?'

'Wherever you're most relaxed.'

He looked from Zara to the front door, then back out over the garden. 'Come over and sit with me while I plant. I like being outside.'

'Sure.'

Picking up a couple of punnets and indicating for Zara to do the same, Joel went back to the garden bed while Zara put the hood of her rain jacket over her head and did as she was asked.

'You're planting heaps here,' she said.

'Mum used to be sort of a market gardener. I thought I'd try the same thing, since it's going to be pretty hard to get a job.'

'Getting exonerated should help with that.'

'Maybe. But it won't give me back the nine years of my life I lost or undo the changes that jail made to me. It won't take away the fact I couldn't go to Mum's funeral, or Dad's, or spend any time with them in the last few years of their lives.' He was quiet, then, as he dug furiously in the dirt. Eventually he started to speak again, the passion rising in his voice with each word. 'See, what was taken away from me, Zara, was more than my reputation or anything like that. It was my life. I'd already lost my home—coming back to Barker was impossible because of Maggie and how difficult it made life for everyone back here—and then this happened!'

'Let's start at the beginning,' she said gently, passing him the beans. 'When did you start working for Stockomatic?'

'In August of 2009, and left—if you'd call it that—in 2010. The court case was late 2011 and I was in jail by 2012.'

'What was your position there?'

'Finance Officer.'

'Were there people above and below you?'

'Above. I had the lowest position in the finance department.'

'And what was your job?'

'I processed the sales.'

'You'll have to explain that to me.'

Joel sat back on his haunches after digging eight small holes with his fingers. There was some wire stretched out across the back of the veggie garden where he was going to plant the beans so they could grow upwards.

'Say a farmer sold twenty head of cattle at . . .' He shrugged. 'I don't even know what a good price is these days. Maybe eight hundred dollars. Nah, make it a thousand for round figures. I needed to see the sale contract, which was written out and signed by the stock agent and seller. That showed me there was an agreement to sell the stock. When the stock arrived at the sale yards and were sold, I got that information too—the buyer's name and what price the cattle made and details so we could charge them. I then had to process the sale—get the money paid into the seller's bank account and send out the invoice to the buyer.'

'Okay, I understand that. You were creating the invoices and paying the vendor.'

'Yep, sort of. I didn't actually make the payment. I created the cheque to be signed by the Chief Finance Manager.'

Zara scribbled quickly as her mind raced ahead. 'Okay, did you check bank accounts to see whether those payments came through?'

'Nope, that was above my pay grade. I never . . .' He stopped and looked at her to stress his words. 'I never had access to the bank account.'

'And how did the cheques get created?'

'There were two people who were able to print them. The software would pull all the payments that had to be made and print a remittance slip with a cheque on the end. Once I hit print, all the cheques that were due that week were printed and then put on the Chief Finance Manager's desk.'

'And he'd sign them?'

'Yeah, the cheques needed two signatures, so one from him and then the other would be the firm's accountant.'

'Right. And the cross-referencing—how did that happen?'

'Someone in the finance department was supposed to do that.'

'Not you?'

'Not me.'

Zara nodded and made a couple more notes while she thought of other questions.

'The finance department seemed to be quite large. How many of you were working there?'

'Five doing the same job I was, plus two managers and two accountants. It was a large business.'

'Do you know where they all are now?'

'Funnily enough, no one stayed in contact with me.' The bitter tone was clear.

Zara closed her notebook. 'When I get back from meeting Bob Elder's widow, I'll let you know what further information I have. But I've got one more question.'

Joel looked like he'd been through the wringer. His shoulders slumped.

'Do you know who did this?'

'I don't.'

Zara squinted. He'd spoken too quickly. One of her jobs as a journalist was to be able to read body language and hear untruths when they'd been told.

She was sure she'd been told a lie.

'Okay, let me rephrase that question. Who do you think did it?'

'I really don't know.'

Again, she heard the lie in his tone.

'Joel, I'm not going to be able to help you unless you tell me everything,' she said, frowning. 'What about this one: Why do you think whoever did this framed you?'

'Because I was the one who'd been there the shortest time.'

'Right. You'd be the easiest to trick?'

'Yeah. See, I reckon Stockomatic was like the mafia.'

'Why?' Zara asked quickly. 'What do you mean by that?'

'They like to own you. The company car I had? That was part of my salary package. My understanding was that the company owned it and I just drove it. That's how it would work in most businesses. But not this one. Ownership was in my name as was the invoice, but I had no idea until the court case came up. I never saw the registration papers. By then, there was no one to help me. My lawyer was a legal aid lawyer—I didn't have any money to hire a decent one because the court had frozen all my assets. I wasn't her only client and she didn't give my case the time it needed.'

The breeze brought a few heavy droplets from the trees above them, soaking through Zara's jeans. She rubbed the damp patch as she thought about the information Joel had given her.

'How can they buy a car in your name?' she wondered aloud. 'You'd have to sign paperwork for that.'

But as she said the words, she knew that with the right know-how, anything was possible.

CHAPTER 25

Emma held Jacqui's hand as they pushed open the door and walked into the police station. An older woman with tightly curled grey hair and glasses sat behind a Perspex barrier, busily typing.

Jacqui took one look at her and turned to leave, but Emma held her hand tightly and kept walking across to the counter.

'Good afternoon,' the woman said. 'How can I help you?'

Glancing at her name tag, Emma smiled. 'Hi, Joan. Could we see Jack Higgins, please?'

'Jack's not in today. Is it urgent?'

'No,' Jacqui said quickly. 'No, it's not. I can come back.' She turned as if she were about to run outside.

'Actually,' Emma spoke firmly, 'it's pretty important. Is there someone else we can . . .'

Joan nodded. 'I'll get Dave for you.' She left the counter and opened a door, letting it swing shut behind her.

'Let's just go,' Jacqui said. 'Please. I know Jack, and if he's not here, I'd rather not talk to anyone else. It's too horrible.'

'We can't let him win, Jac,' Emma said, holding her friend's hand tightly. 'We have to report this. The police are professionals, so it's not like this Dave won't be any good.'

Tears were forming in Jacqui's eyes as she looked at Emma. 'Please . . .'

The door swung open and a tall man with greying hair and clear blue eyes came out. His smile was welcoming, but his expression became concerned when he saw the tears.

'Hi, I'm Detective Dave Burrows. Looks like you'd better come through.' He used the pass hanging around his neck to open the door and usher them in. 'This way.' He turned to Joan. 'Would you get us some water, please? In here, ladies.' He pointed to the open door leading to a room where there was a table, two chairs and nothing else.

Jacqui let out a strangled sound and turned to try to leave, but Emma kept pulling her along. She wanted to cry at her friend's pain. Instead, she guided Jacqui to one of the chairs and then sat down next to her, never once letting her hand go.

Dave grabbed a chair from outside the office and brought it in, placing it opposite Jacqui.

'You've got some trouble, ladies?' Dave asked as he sat down, put his elbows on his knees and leaned towards them. 'How can I help you?'

Glancing at Jacqui, Emma made sure she could speak.

She leaned forwards. 'Are you going to tell him, Jac, or do you want me to?'

The door opened and Joan brought in a jug of water, three glasses and a box of tissues.

'Perfect. Cheers, Joan,' Dave said and pushed the tissues towards Jacqui. 'Can I ask your names, to start?'

'Jacqui.' A word finally came from her mouth. 'Jacqui Mullins.'

'And I'm Emma Cameron. Here as moral support.' She watched the policeman write down their names then look across at Jacqui.

'Can I grab your addresses and telephone numbers too?'

They both recited them.

'So, how can I help you, Jacqui? You seem very distressed.'

'I, ah, I've been really stupid.' She sniffed loudly and took a tissue. 'There's this guy. Online. I've been talking to him, thought he was really nice.' Jacqui gave a troubled moan.

Emma squeezed her hand. 'You can do this,' she said softly.

'Well, things got a bit, uh—' She glanced up at Dave and redness flooded her cheeks. She rushed on. 'Things got a bit racy and he sent me some dick pics and . . . I sent some nudes back. Now he's threatening to post them online unless I give him ten grand.'

Now the words were out, she seemed to collapse, and the tears disappeared. She swallowed hard and looked at the floor while Emma rubbed her back and looked at Dave.

'Can you stop him?' Jacqui asked as she brought her head back up to look at the man sitting opposite her. 'Can you stop him from posting them online? Please!' she begged. 'He says he's going to. You've got to . . .'

'Okay, okay,' Dave spoke quietly but with such authority that Emma knew they were in very safe hands with this man. 'Let's start at the beginning. What I can tell you is we will be doing our best to make sure that doesn't happen. But I need a bit more information first.' He leaned back in his chair and rubbed his chin. 'How did you send the photos to him?'

A couple of wobbly breaths later, Jacqui had composed herself. 'Over Bundle. There's a message service on there.'

'Right.' Dave wrote something else down, and underlined it, but Emma couldn't see what it was. 'So, from your phone?'

Jacqui nodded.

'Do you have it with you?'

'Ah, yeah.' She fumbled in her handbag and brought it out, laying it on the table in front of them. All three looked at the device as if it held nasty secrets.

'And what's this guy's name?'

'Gill.'

'Surname?'

'He never gave one.'

'Okay. What other information do you have on him? Do you know what he does for a job, where he lives, anything like that?'

Jacqui put in her passcode and tapped the camera app on her phone. 'I took screenshots of some of the messages.'

She put the phone back down on the table as if she couldn't bear to touch it.

Dave picked it up and scrolled through what was there. 'Chatty kind of bloke, isn't he? So, very little information. Jacqui,' he said, leaning forwards again, 'can I have your log-in details, please? I'll need to give these to Computer Crime ASAP and see if we can put a stop to this. Has he given you a deadline for the money?'

She shook her head. 'He just keeps asking for it.'

'Well, that's something. Let's hope that means we've got a bit of time. I'll send these screenshots to my computer and deal with it from there.'

'What will you do?' Emma wanted to know.

'I'll do a bit of digging into this bloke. See if this is his real name or a pseudonym. Then I'll get on to Computer Crimes. I can request we find out where the uploads are coming from, the IP address, that sort of thing. From that we can narrow down where he spends his time and uses the internet and so on.' He paused. 'Now, Jacqui, you haven't told him where you live, have you?'

'No.'

'So, there can't be any physical danger to you, as far as you know?'

The colour drained from Jacqui's face and her lips wobbled again. 'I . . . I don't know. I didn't think about that.'

'No phone number?'

She shook her head. 'No, we hadn't got that far. We'd really only been talking for a little while and things just got . . . um, out of hand.'

'Okay. Leave this with me and I'll give you a call when I've got some news. What do you do, Jacqui?'

'I'm a teacher.'

Dave nodded and wrote that down too.

'What does she do now?' Emma broke in. 'Does she still communicate with him, or what?'

'No.' Dave emphatically shook his head. 'No. Not at this stage. We might need you to at some point, but don't engage with him now.' Dave paused. 'Be prepared for threatening messages from him. These types escalate when they're ignored or not getting what they want.'

Jacqui gave another moan.

Dave turned and looked her in the eye. 'Jacqui, you have to disregard any communication from him until we tell you otherwise. We'll do our best to stop this as quickly as we can. Under. No. Circumstances. Unless we instruct you, are you to converse with him, okay?'

Jacqui nodded her understanding.

'Another question. What about an email address? Do you have to put one in to become active on the site? And, if you do, does this guy have access to it?'

'I don't know if he does,' Jacqui said, hopelessly. 'I've just always used the messenger function.'

'Okay.' Dave smiled gently at them. 'I have to admit, this is all a bit new to me and I've never worked anything like this before. But don't let that worry you, because the police force have people who specialise in these scenarios and I can contact them at any time; they're at the end of the phone.'

Emma smiled back at him and squeezed Jacqui's hand again.

'Thank you,' Jacqui said quietly as if all the fight had left her. 'Thank you.'

'Come on, let's get you home.'

~

Dave waited until Emma and Jacqui were out of the office and picked up the phone.

'Detective Dave Burrows here from the Barker station,' he said, when the phone was answered. 'I've a woman made a complaint regarding an online scam.'

'Detective Kate Hooper. How can I help?'

Dave explained what he'd just been told. 'I've got a few messages here that I can forward on to you.'

'Do that. What was the name again?'

'Gill. I don't know if that's first or last.' He could hear keys clicking in the background.

'He's not on our register,' Detective Hooper said, 'but that doesn't mean he hasn't used that name before and we haven't worked it back to a serial offender.'

'Is that likely?'

'Hell, yeah. Most of these fuckers who prey on the vulnerable have got form. Their MOs are similar: need money, so they find someone who's new to this and they draw them in. Doesn't matter how many warnings we put out, there will always be someone who gets caught.'

'This is going to sound like a stupid question, but they can be anywhere in the world, can't they?'

'Yep. That's the beauty of the interweb. And, look, we're talking like this Gill is a bloke, but he could actually be a woman, or a switched-on teenager who's trying to get some easy money.'

'Unbelievable,' Dave said.

'Mate, you wouldn't believe some of the shit I see in here.'

'Better you than me,' said Dave. 'I'll email this all through to you. Is there anything else I can do to help the vic at the moment?'

'You've told her not to respond?'

'Affirmative.'

'Well, there's nothing more right now. Depending on how he escalates, we might get her to exchange a few messages with him so we can track him. But,' the detective emphasised her point once more, 'make sure she doesn't respond and that she lets you know of any contact as soon as it comes through. Dealing with these parasites needs to be done when they're online so we can track 'em.'

'Righto, cheers for that, Detective Hooper.' He put the phone down and got onto Google.

He typed in 'Bundle', and as he waited for the results to load, Joan stuck her head into his office. 'I'm off,' she said.

'Okay,' he answered as he read the screen. He couldn't get in to have a look at the site without joining up. 'Strange question. Do you know anything about online dating websites?'

Joan's eyebrows hit her grey hair. 'Do you really think I would?'

Dave assessed her sensible shoes and navy slacks. 'No. You're right, of course you wouldn't.' He gave her a wicked grin. 'Still, the quietest ones are often the most surprising.'

She rolled her eyes at him. 'Whatever you think, Detective Burrows.'

'Ah, shit! My rank and surname. Now I'm in strife. Anyway, all good. Just thought I'd ask.' He looked back at the screen and clicked 'Join'. He was prompted to put in his mobile phone number, and he hesitated. The other option was logging in with Facebook or his Apple ID.

He wasn't on Facebook and he didn't know his Apple ID—that was Kim's domain.

What would happen if he put his phone number in?

'What are you actually doing?' Joan was still in the doorway, staring at him, a slight smirk on her face.

'Working out whether or not I'm going to sign up for a dating site.'

'Should I ask why?'

'Probably not, but it's not for my own benefit!'

'Good luck telling Kim about that. I'll be off before the bloodbath happens.' She paused. 'Let me know how it goes tomorrow.'

'Night, Joan,' he said and tapped his number in quickly so he didn't have time to change his mind.

The screen told him that the website was sending him a code to enter. Dave shook his head and shut down the page. He then deleted the text message as it came through. There was a reason the police department had a Computer Crimes Squad.

He tried something different. In the search engine he typed 'Gill' and was told it was part of a fish. 'For fuck's sake,' he muttered.

He thought for a minute then put the word 'Facebook' in front of Gill. This time the search came up with the profiles of two hundred and sixty-one people who had the word 'Gill' in their name. And that was only in Australia.

It would be like looking for a needle in a haystack, he decided. Especially if the person was overseas, which could be the case. Also, this was presuming that the person was using their real name. He knew that was unlikely too.

Maybe Kim could help him, like she'd done before.

As he closed the computer, he squinted, thinking hard. It never ceased to amaze him how intelligent people could get mixed up in rash and irresponsible situations. He felt for Jacqui and it certainly wasn't in his nature to judge—as a copper, he couldn't. Every person, no matter what had happened to them, deserved his help.

But to him, how someone could get caught in a web like this defied belief.

CHAPTER 26

Normally, a cloud of dust would have alerted Emma to the fact there was a car coming down her driveway, but with ten millimetres of rain overnight, she only realised she had company when Cash started to bark.

Knee-deep in barley plants, inspecting the crop, Emma looked up and frowned as she watched the unfamiliar ute slow. When the driver saw her vehicle parked at the fence, he jerked to a halt and got out.

A rush of pleasure went through Emma when she recognised Kyle; after their conversation at dinner, all her misgivings had been allayed. They'd hardly talked about the accident. Instead, Kyle had asked what type of music she liked and they'd agreed they could both like Keith Urban, but Kyle refused to think that Thelma Plum was any good at all. Emma couldn't abide Glen Campbell but liked Lady A.

In the end, they'd decided they both enjoyed The Highwaymen and Kenny Rogers, so that's who they would listen to.

Then they'd talked about books they'd read and their shared love of nature. Emma couldn't believe how easily the conversation had flowed and how much they had in common. The weight they had both felt from the accident had gone, and it was like they were meeting each other for the first time.

She leaned down and pulled out one more barley plant to check the roots, then let the plant fall back to the ground. Dusting off her hands against her jeans, she smiled and walked over to Kyle.

'How did you find me?' she asked. 'I didn't give you directions out here.'

'Hello to you too,' he said with a grin. 'I asked at the roadhouse. They were happy to draw me a mud map.'

'No secrets around here,' she said with a laugh.

'Apparently not.' He stopped and looked at her, concern on his face. 'You don't mind, do you?'

'No, it's fine. I've got time for a quick cuppa before I have to meet Matt to do a bit more fencing.'

'Ah, yes, the famous Matt. I'd like to meet him, since you spend so much time talking about him.'

Emma tried not to squirm. Was there a thread of jealousy in that comment?

'Do I?' she asked, trying to sound blasé.

'You do.'

Matt had dropped in this morning to give her the mail, and their conversation had been stilted. He hadn't stayed long, and when he'd left, she'd been surprised by the sadness that had overtaken her. Couldn't things go back to the way they'd been? She didn't want to lose their great working relationship.

Kyle nodded towards the crop. 'I don't know much about farming. What's this?'

'Barley,' she told him. 'It's doing pretty well for this time of the year, and the rain we had last night is just perfect. I was looking to make sure there weren't any insects or diseases that will cause us trouble. It's beginning to put up its flag leaf. See here?' She grabbed a plant and indicated the strong, upright, thin leaf.

'Right, and you only grow barley?'

'No, we've got wheat in as well.'

'We?'

'Sorry?'

'You said "we".'

'Oh, well, Matt's part of all this too. I guess I just include him when I'm talking, even though it's my place. Things wouldn't be the same if he wasn't here.' Again she felt the truth of her words. Deception Creek would be empty without his gravelly laughter, his conversation and his presence. That was without even recognising all the work he did.

'See,' Kyle said, 'you *do* talk about him a lot. You sure there's nothing going on between you two?'

'Absolutely positive.' Emma shoved her hands into her pockets.

Kyle stretched his hand out towards the hills. 'It's a terrific spot. The colours in the sunset last night were beautiful, with the clouds rolling in. And these gum trees. Spectacular.'

Emma looked at the wide-trunked trees with a smile. 'Oh yeah, I'd hate to think how old they are. Probably hundreds of years! In fact, there're photos of my great-grandparents standing in front of the trees that are still on the edge of the creek. You couldn't wrap your arms around the trunks, could you?'

'No, they're very large!' He walked over to the edge of the creek, on the other side of the road, and picked up some leaves. 'They seem to shed a lot, though.'

Stifling a laugh, she climbed the fence and walked across to join him. 'The cockies and galahs strip the trees. They're annoying little buggers who love to cause destruction wherever they fly.' She pointed to a deep hole in the trunk. 'They make their homes in the trees, then try to kill them by tearing the leaves off.'

'The hand that feeds you.'

'Exactly.'

A shadow passed over the sun and she looked up. A lone corella was flying across to land in the tree. 'Must know we're talking about them. Usually they're in flocks of hundreds, or at least they sound like they are.' Turning back to Kyle, she grinned. 'Tea or coffee?'

'Coffee.'

'Follow me.' She whistled to Cash. 'Get up, mate.'

Emma drove down the muddy road towards the house thinking how nice it was to have someone pop in unexpectedly. Deception Creek wasn't far out of town, but the girls rarely came out; mostly, Emma caught up with them when she went to town. The stock agent called in, but she always knew when he was coming, and once in a blue moon she'd get a cold call from a salesman.

She pulled up at the verandah, under the pepper tree, and waited until Kyle had brought his large red Ram ute to a standstill next to hers. It dwarfed her D-Max, and Emma could only imagine the fuel economy. Or lack of it.

'Big ute,' she said.

'It's a beauty, isn't it?' Kyle beamed with pride as his phone rang. He looked at the screen, then sent the call to message bank and looked back at the ute. He gave the door handle a rub with his jacket sleeve. 'I like big cars since the accident. They feel safer on the road.'

Emma nodded. 'I can understand that. Must be expensive to run, though.'

'As you'd know, you can't put a price on safety.'

'Come in.' She headed up the steps, past her swinging chair and into the kitchen, holding the screen door open for him. Inside, the wood fire pushed out heat, but she realised as she looked around that the house seemed very sterile.

There were only a few photos on the wall—with her parents at her graduation, and a couple of family Christmases. There was an aerial photo of the farm, and on the coffee table sat one of their girl group.

The bookshelf was crammed with books she hadn't had time to read in the past year—not that that ever stopped her from buying them—and the *Farming Journal* newspapers were piled up high next to her favourite chair.

'Ah, Candice Fox. Isn't she great?' Kyle was standing at the bookshelf. He pulled a paperback out and read the back-cover blurb. 'Don't think I've read this one.'

'I love her twists and turns. I rarely guess the ending.' Emma walked over and stood looking at the bookshelf with him. 'I can't read them at night, though. It has to be on a weekend afternoon, when the sun's still up.'

'I like trying to guess, but I never seem to get it right.'

'Ha! Whereas I do in other books or TV shows. I can watch *Midsomer Murders* or *Death in Paradise* and pick whodunit mostly in the first fifteen minutes.' Emma switched on the kettle and indicated for him to sit at the kitchen table.

'How do you do that?' Kyle asked in wonder. 'Half the time I spend that long getting my head around who the characters are.'

'Don't know. I just seem to have a knack for picking the baddies.'

'In real life too?'

'I haven't got anyone bad in my life, I don't think. Or, if I do, perhaps I'm not as good at picking the baddies as I thought I was.' She gave him a cheeky smile and turned as she heard footsteps on the verandah.

There was a loud rap on the door, and Matt stuck his head in.

'Oh sorry, I didn't realise you had company.'

Emma frowned. What, he'd missed the bloody great ute out the front? Of course he'd known. 'Come in,' she said. 'Cuppa? Matt, this is Kyle. I've mentioned him before.'

Matt entered and held out his hand. 'Yeah, heard about you.'

The two men shook hands, and Emma saw Kyle try not to flinch as Matt squeezed tightly.

'As I've heard about you.'

Emma put three cups on the bench and listened to the men. There was tension in both their voices.

'Don't worry about me, Em,' Matt said. Emma looked up; he rarely shortened her name. 'I'm heading out to the saltbush area. Gotta take some photos for Rick.'

He wasn't talking as awkwardly as he had been this morning.

'Oh. No worries. Whatever you need to do.'

'Kyle, you here long?' Matt asked as he took his hat off and dropped it on the table, before leaning against the bench. Emma had to give it to him, he looked very much at home. And why wouldn't he be? Matt had often come inside for smoko or a beer at the end of the day. He knew where the teaspoons and coffee were kept, just as he knew where the beer fridge was.

'I don't have any firm plans,' Kyle answered, giving Matt a friendly smile, 'so I can stay as long as I need to.' He glanced over at Emma. 'I'm hoping she's not going to want rid of my company any time soon.'

Matt's face became expressionless and he looked at Emma. As she caught his eye her stomach lurched under his direct gaze.

'Sorry, I haven't got any biscuits,' she blustered. 'I don't usually eat at smoko time.'

'Not a worry. Me either. Trying to watch the weight.' Kyle patted his flat stomach and grinned. 'It's harder to keep off as you get older.'

'I think I'm lucky with all the physical work I do, I haven't had too much of a problem yet.' Emma wanted to roll her eyes at herself. *What was she talking about?*

Cash barked at the door, and Matt went to let him inside. The dog rushed in and sniffed Kyle, then backed away from him before going to Matt for a pat. Then he took up his spot under the kitchen table.

'When will you start harvest?' Kyle asked.

Matt scoffed. 'We're a bloody long way away from that.' He picked up his hat. 'Em, I'm going to need a hand this arvo. I want to get those cattle in from the middle paddock; we've got to get those calves marked before much longer or they'll be too big.'

'Yep, I'll be around. I'll call you on the two-way.'

Matt nodded to Kyle and left, the door slamming behind him.

'Back to the harvest,' Emma said quickly before Kyle could comment on Matt's rudeness. 'Everything really depends on the finish of the season and the weather, but we usually get a start mid-November, early December. If the season end is a bit soft, then we can push it back to the middle of December.' She put one of the cups away and heaped a spoonful of coffee each into the two left.

'Do you have pod coffee?'

'Oh.' She looked up. 'No, sorry. Just instant.' She waved the Moccona jar around.

'That's fine, just thought I'd ask.' He looked around. 'That Matt seems pretty protective of you. Bossy, even. He doesn't think he actually owns the place, does he?'

Emma chose her words carefully. 'This place wouldn't run without Matt, and if he sometimes seems bossy, I'm willing to have that around because he's worth more than any workman I've ever had on the property.'

'It's just an observation,' Kyle said. He took a sip of the coffee Emma placed in front of him, and she saw a flicker in the corner of his eye at the taste. It was clear that Kyle liked the finer things in life. 'Don't you ever get frightened out here all by yourself?'

'Nope,' Emma said. 'There's nothing to be frightened about. Probably safer out here than in town.'

'Yeah, I suppose, but people would know you're out here alone. You could be an easy target.'

'I guess they would. I've never really thought about it.'

'You probably should. There could be "that one time".'

Sitting opposite him, Emma smiled. 'There could be, I suppose. But I'm not in the business of "what ifs". I feel very safe and I don't expect anything to happen. Cash is a good guard dog. He let me know you were coming today.' She eyed him inquisitively. 'You seem very distrusting of people.'

'Realistic, I think.'

Emma changed the subject. 'How are you finding the caravan park?'

'It's surprisingly nice. The units are pretty basic, but they're clean and have everything I need.' He stopped for a moment. 'Apparently, they're full for the upcoming long weekend. I'm not sure where I'm going to stay then, though.'

'That's next weekend, isn't it? Are you still going to be here? You will have been in town for a while by then.' She took out her phone and checked her diary. 'That's the weekend I'm in Clare with the girls.'

'Well, I'd planned on it. If you're not here I might need to reconsider. There's still a fair bit to see. I'd like to go over to Quorn and have a ride on that steam train I've read about.'

'Oh yeah, the Pitchi Richi Railway. That's a great ride. I did it—'

His phone rang again, and again he quickly sent it through to message bank just as a series of pings came through. They sounded like WhatsApp messages. But the last was a noise she'd heard only a few times before.

HelloSingles.

'Sorry,' he said.

'You can get that if you want to,' she said, glancing at her watch. 'I should get organised to help Matt, anyway.'

'I'll deal with them when I get back into town, just some work things. He said he didn't need you until this afternoon. We've still got a bit of time.'

'Are you still working during your time off?'

'No rest for the wicked,' he said with a grin. 'I've got a couple of clients who won't deal with anyone but me, and they're big clients, so I have to be on call for them. They pay good money and I'm happy to take it, but there're a few sacrifices involved with that.'

'I've never really understood what you do.'

'Essentially, I manage people's money.'

'Like an adviser?'

'Yeah, that's sort of it. These big clients I have won't make a move without speaking to me, which is nice but it can also be annoying when I want some time to myself.'

'That must be fairly high-pressure—I'd get scared handling other people's money.'

'Nothing to it. It's only a series on numbers on a computer screen.'

'Don't you feel responsible if something goes wrong?'

Kyle took another sip of his instant coffee. 'I don't like it when I lose money for the client, because that in turn affects me. I get paid on commission.' His phone rang again. 'Bloody hell! Sorry about this. Try to have a nice quiet cup of coffee and all hell breaks loose!' He put the phone on silent and then back in his pocket. 'Where was I?'

'Commission.'

'That's right. I get paid on commission, so I'm careful where I invest. I'm not conservative, mind you, just careful. You have to be prepared to take some risks in my business.'

Now, apparently, it was time for Emma's phone to ring.

'I do have to take this,' she said when she looked at the caller ID. 'Matt, everything okay?'

'Nah, we've got a busted boundary fence. I've got three wires strained up, but can you bring a roll of the Tyeasy wire, please?'

'Sure, I'm not far off coming out. Anything else you need?'

'Better bring the insulators for the steel posts. If the cattle are going to bust this fence open, I think we need to electrify it.'

'Righto, I'll be out shortly.'

'Catch you then.'

Emma drained her coffee cup.

'Sorry to race off,' she said, standing.

'It's fine, you're a busy working woman and I'm a bloke on holiday.' He took her hand and gave it a squeeze. 'Dinner tonight, maybe?'

A flutter of butterflies in her stomach made her say yes.

CHAPTER 27

The knock on the door echoed through the older-style house on a quiet leafy street in North Adelaide.

As Zara waited for the door to open, excitement fizzed through her and she had to stop herself from bouncing on her toes. Oh, how she hoped that Bob Elder's widow would still have his notes.

Slowly, footsteps came towards the door and finally it opened.

'Hello,' Zara smiled. 'I'm Zara. I phoned earlier.'

'Oh yes, you're the journalist, aren't you? I'm Margaret.' She opened the door wider. 'Do come in.'

Zara entered the long passageway and followed Margaret towards the back of the house.

'Sorry, I'm a little slow these days,' Margaret said.

Awards for Bob Elder lined the walls, along with photos of him with politicians and famous people, and the slow walk gave Zara time to inspect them all.

'Bob was a great journalist,' Zara said.

'Yes, he was,' Margaret replied as they came into a glass-walled room. Over the top of the roof hung branches from an old Moreton Bay fig tree, shading the room from the sun.

'What a gorgeous room,' Zara said. 'You must love spending time here.' She looked up and it was like she was sitting outside under the tree.

'I do all my writing here. It's very tranquil. I love it.'

'You write too? I'm sorry, I didn't realise. Are you a journalist as well?'

'An author. Fiction. Crime novels, mostly.'

Zara was taken aback. 'Margaret Elder? Of course! I'm so sorry I didn't put two and two together. You've written loads of novels! And I've read them all.'

Margaret inclined her head graciously. 'Twenty-five, to be precise. I hope you've enjoyed them.'

'I have! I've got them all. I would've brought them for you to sign if I'd realised. Are you still writing?'

'Oh yes, I can't imagine not writing. You would under-stand that.'

Zara smiled. 'My fingers get itchy when I'm not.'

'Mine too.' Margaret sat down and indicated for Zara to take a seat too. 'Now, how can I help you? Something about a story Bob was writing before he died?'

'Yes. Does the name Joel Hammond mean anything to you?'

Margaret put her hand up to her mouth, tapping a finger against it, as she thought. 'The name is familiar, but I can't place it.'

Zara opened her bag and found the printout of Bob's first and only story about Joel. She handed it to Margaret.

Margaret skimmed the article. 'I remember this now. This was published right before he died. I had to ask the paper to get in contact with the poor man to let him know about Bob. He'd written on several occasions, each time he sounded more frantic. I hadn't been in the right frame of mind to answer him. It was quite traumatic to lose my husband after more than fifty years.'

'I can't imagine.'

'Still, that's part of life. How can I help you with this Joel, though?'

'Most journalists keep copious notes,' Zara said. 'Was Bob one of those?'

Margaret nodded. 'He most certainly was.'

'Do you still have any of Bob's notebooks?' Zara held her breath.

'I have them all,' Margaret said. 'They weren't something I could part with. Each one holds a little piece of his soul and memory.'

'Do you think I could see them?'

'Everything is still in his office—I've never touched it. I couldn't bear to. Sometimes I go in and sit in his chair just so I can be close to him.'

Zara stayed silent, while the older lady talked.

'He used to smoke those horrible cigars of his in there, and that room still smells like it.' Margaret looked at Zara and got up. 'I'd complain until I was blue in the face and he'd still smoke away in there, no matter what

I said. And now? I'm glad the odour is entrenched in that room, because I still have something of him.'

'That's a lovely connection.'

'Well, it's a connection,' Margaret said with a wry smile. 'Even if a smelly one. Come this way. Let's see if we can find what you need.'

She led Zara into another winding passageway until they reached a door that was tightly shut.

'This is Bob's office.'

Zara sucked in her breath as she looked around the expansive room. Bookshelves lined two walls from ceiling to floor and on another was a full window. In the middle of the room sat a large desk.

'This is a dream office,' Zara told Margaret.

'Man cave, more like it,' the older woman said with a wink. 'Those chairs over there—that's where he'd sit and smoke, and when he couldn't quite get a story right, he'd stand at the window and look out on the garden until the words came.' She went in and switched on the light.

'Now, all his notebooks are on this shelf here. I don't know where you'll find the one you're looking for, but if you're an investigative journalist too, I'm sure you'll have a lovely time going through them all.'

'You don't mind me being in here?'

'Not at all. Bob would have dragged you in without a word. Neither of us could abide injustice, which is why he decided to investigate some cases further. If you're going to do that, then I'm happy for you to be here, and Bob would have been too.'

'Thank you so very much. Joel will be grateful.'

'If you help that young man, that will be thanks enough. I'll leave you to it now. If you need anything, just call.'

Alone in the office, Zara could smell the old cigar smoke as she walked over to the chairs and stood next to them.

Next, she stood at the window and then ran her fingers along the wooden desk. She imagined the journalist sitting there, typing at his computer, crafting passages and poring over trial transcripts.

People often gushed to Zara that being an investigative journalist must be *so* exciting—interviewing underworld criminals and getting the inside running from police. In actual fact, it was hard toil: reading back through reports, following up on interviews with suspects and witnesses, rehashing stories and accounts. Then, trying to link all the pieces of the jigsaw puzzle together. It wasn't so different to being a detective, really.

Standing in front of the bookshelf, she looked at the hundreds of books and wondered where to start.

Just pull a book out and read the date, she thought.

The first was from 1999—a long way off the 2012 one she was looking for. She placed it on the floor and moved on to the next one: 1998. Okay, she needed to work back the other way. Counting along twelve spines, she grabbed out what she hoped would be 2012 and was rewarded. Replacing all the others, she then sat on the floor, cross-legged, and pulled out her notebook and phone before opening the pages of the hardback journal.

Bob Elder had written in a small, neat, cursive script. Zara could see straightaway that he had been methodical and careful in how he took notes.

3 May 2012
Met with Joel Hammond. Will take on the case.
Innocent. Not telling me the whole truth. Why?
Who worked with him?
Ring and interview Managing Director.
Trial transcripts. Who testified?

The next page was dated 7 May 2012.

Met with Gordon Darker, MD. Spoke highly of JH's
work ethic when he first started the position. Was
shocked when realised what was happening.
FOM found discrepancies and went looking. Reported
to police, who took it to the AFP.
Investigator Ray Briscoe—need to interview. Prob
won't talk.
TT—see file.

Zara got up and walked around to stretch her legs and get rid of the pins and needles that had started in her feet.

TT? Trial transcript, possibly. *See file*. Looking around the room, Zara couldn't see any filing cabinets or other obvious places Bob would have stored files.

The desk—clear except for the computer on top—held three drawers on either side. Feeling like a snoop, Zara went to the right and pulled the first drawer open, revealing neatly lined-up pens, pencils and stationery.

The second drawer held telephone books and an expenses file.

The third held a box of cigars.

On the other side the top drawer was filled with mobile phone and laptop chargers. The other two drawers were empty.

Could she turn on the computer?

The door opened and Margaret came in.

'How are you getting on?'

'I've found the journal,' she said. 'TT, that would mean trial transcript?'

'I would imagine so. That sounds like his shorthand.'

'Do you know where he kept his files? The note said "*See file*".'

'The filing cabinets are downstairs in the cellar. That information will be easy to find—he always had the story he was working on at the front. Come on.'

Margaret led the way down some steps in the kitchen and opened a heavy wooden door. 'He kept everything,' she said. 'Always said he was never sure when he would need it again.'

'That's very true. It's amazing how often there are stories that link when you least expect it.'

'There you go: Bob's filing system!' Margaret waved her hand out as if she were on a game show.

'Fantastic,' replied Zara, 'thank you.' The filing cabinets— eight in total—lined one wall.

'I think that will be the one you're looking for.' Margaret pointed at the cabinet closest to the doorway.

Opening it, Zara saw a manila file labelled '*JH*'. 'Spot on.' She gave Margaret the thumbs up and extracted the half-inch-thick file. 'There we are: "*Trial transcript*".'

'Perfect.'

'Can I take these with me, or would you rather I looked at them here?'

'You can take them. Just make sure you bring them back.'

'I will,' Zara promised. 'I most certainly will.'

Four hours later, Zara pulled into the driveway of the house she and Jack shared. She stretched before turning off the car.

The door opened, and Jack stood silhouetted in the light.

'Hey, you,' he said, their standard greeting.

'Hey, you, back.' She grabbed the files and her handbag, and went over to give him a kiss. 'How was your day?'

'Not too bad. What about yours? You've got a glint in your eye that can only mean you've had some success.'

'Baby, you won't believe what I've found!' She kissed him again, and he took the files from her to carry them inside.

'What did you find?' he asked.

'The trial transcripts are probably the main thing so far. There're a few notes about some of the interviews he did and how he wanted to go about the investigation, but I haven't got too far with them. I want to read the transcript first.'

'I've got some dinner in the oven for you.'

'Thanks, sweetie, I'm a bit tired.' She dumped her handbag down and poured herself a wine. 'I'll start on this tomorrow, I think.'

'No, you won't!' Jack said with a grin. 'Open it up now and just see what the front page says.'

Grinning, Zara grabbed the file. 'You know me too well,' she said.

Charge: Imprisonment for Fraud
Year: 2012
Category: Financial / Corruption

Zara skimmed the information, which was the location, charges and judgement. She stopped at the synopsis.

One male has been sentenced following a series of investigations over a twelve-month period by the Australian Federal Police. The offender conspired to defraud his employer through an intricate money-laundering scheme.

Key Points:
In 2012, the home and bank accounts of Joel Hammond were searched and $50,000 in cash was found to be in his personal bank account, of which he claimed to have no knowledge.

Further documents seized showed that Hammond purchased a car with part of the $250,000 defrauded from his employer. There were also invoices for lavish holidays.

Sentencing:
Joel Hammond received a sentence of five years' imprisonment with a non-parole period of the same amount of time.

Zara read it all out to Jack, who had got her dinner from the oven and placed it in front of her.

'Sounds like there's a bit to go through. Nothing there about who testified against him?'

Zara closed the file and rubbed her hands over her eyes tiredly. 'There will be, but not tonight. Tonight, I want to cuddle you and go to sleep.'

'I think we can manage that,' Jack said as he squeezed her shoulder.

CHAPTER 28

Emma looked at the letter on the table and felt her heart sink.

As Matt had left that night, he'd said he'd put something on the table for her. His familiar scrawly handwriting was on the front of the envelope. She put down her lunch box and looked at the letter again.

Leaving it where it was, and opening the fridge, Emma brought out a bottle of wine and poured herself a glass before going into the office and checking her emails.

Nothing that couldn't wait, she decided.

She grabbed her dirty clothes from the day before and threw them into the washing machine, then went outside to get wood from the storage shed and lit the fire.

Back inside, the letter taunted her. Wanting to open it, but at the same time not wanting to, Emma sat at the table and took a sip of wine. Finally, she dragged it over in front of her and opened it.

With a breath, she started to read.

Dear Emma,

*I'm sure you feel as uncomfortable as I do over the inci-
dent after you nearly hit the roo. I'm sorry for kissing you.*

*This seems to have made our working relationship
strained and I don't want to cause you any discomfort.
I can sense that the whole situation does now. You won't
look me in the eye, and the last few times I've tried to
talk to you it's been hard.*

Therefore I think it's best if I resign.

*I know I'm supposed to give you two weeks' notice,
but I don't think that's going to work for either of us, so
I've taken my tools tonight. Don't worry about my last
lot of wages in lieu of leaving you early.*

*Emma, I'm really sorry to leave you in the lurch like
this, but I think it's best for both of us.*

Matt

Emma let the paper fall from her hands and stared at
it as it floated to the table.

'Shit,' she muttered, as she buried her head in her hands.
Such a stupid reaction to a panic attack. Why couldn't they
laugh it off and just get back to work?

The *Farming Journal* sat nearby on the table and she
pulled it towards her, flipping to the back.

Reading through the SITUATIONS VACANT ads, it became
very clear it wasn't going to be easy to get another employee.
There were at least nine jobs in the first column, let alone
whatever was on the next page . . . and there wasn't a single
EMPLOYMENT WANTED ad.

Maybe she should just go and talk to Matt. Tell him it was all a silly mistake. That she didn't feel that way and she wanted him to come back to work. The enormity of what Matt had done was settling on her shoulders. She couldn't run Deception Creek without him.

She got up so quickly she pushed the chair over. She had to go and talk to him. Then she stopped.

Emma realised she didn't even know where he lived in town.

~

Joel had reversed the car halfway out of the driveway when he slammed on the brakes.

'What the hell?!'

He threw open the door and scrambled around to the back of the car where Steve Douglas stood in the middle of the driveway. 'What the hell are you doing?' he yelled.

'Waiting for you.'

'Get the fuck off my land,' Joel said. 'Or I'll call the cops.'

'That's a good idea. I'd like to be here when they arrest you again.'

'Oh yeah,' Joel sneered. 'What for?'

'The rape of my sister.'

Joel was so taken aback he actually laughed. 'You think?'

'I *know*.' Steve stood with his fists clenched at his side, his eyes boring into Joel.

'Hey mate, if she was shagging someone, it wasn't me.' He thought back to the night Maggie had tried to kiss him and how quickly he'd run. Oh, he'd wanted to, but never in his wildest dreams would he have let that happen. Maggie was too precious to him.

'It couldn't have been anyone else but you. You were the only one around.' Steve moved menacingly towards Joel.

'Back the fuck off.' Joel held out his hands to ward off Steve. 'I've hurt people before and I can hurt you.'

'Just like you hurt my sister.'

Joel knew he couldn't touch Steve—his parole would go up in smoke if he did. Even with the coppers being somewhat nice to him. But Steve didn't know that.

Steve kept walking straight at Joel, staring at him, his jaw working overtime.

Joel took a step towards him, but Steve didn't stop.

'What will make you leave town?' Steve spat. 'A hundred grand? Two?'

'What!'

'I'll pay you to go. Just name your price.'

'You don't have enough cash for that. And anyway, I'm not going anywhere. This is *my* house, *my* home town.'

Out of the corner of his eye, he saw Mrs Kerby open her front door and then shut it again. He was pretty sure the cops would be here in a minute.

'Why do you want me out so much? Frightened of me, or something? Worried I know something I shouldn't?' Joel said.

Steve threw the first punch, and Joel staggered backwards. Quickly, he regained his footing and flew at the other man.

'You're not doing this,' Joel grunted as he aimed a fist into Steve's stomach. Steve fell to the ground but managed to kick his leg out and connect with Joel's, taking his legs out from under him. Joel hit the pavement.

Steve was up quicker, and he put a boot into Joel's abdomen, just as the sound of sirens became clear.

Puffing, Steve turned and ran back to his car, leaving with a squeal of tyres and Joel on the ground gasping for air and clutching at his stomach.

Greta ran out her front door. 'Oh my! Are you all right, Joel? Are you all right?' She crouched next to him and took out her hankie to hold it over his nose, trying to stop the bleeding.

'Joel, can you talk?' she asked again.

He flapped his hands around, trying to get her off him and to sit up while gathering his breath.

'Bastard,' he hissed. 'Bastard.'

The police vehicle pulled up next to the kerb and Jack tumbled out, with Dave close behind.

'What's going on?' Jack asked. 'Do you need an ambulance?'

'That bastard,' Joel managed to get out again, before dragging a breath in and wiping at his nose. 'Ugh.'

Dave helped him to his feet. 'Okay?'

Joel nodded. 'He came at me.'

'He?'

'Steve Douglas,' Greta said. 'I saw him hit Joel. Kick him, actually. Oh my god, I can't believe this is happening.' Her hands flew to her mouth. 'Your poor mother would roll over in her grave if she knew what was going on around here.'

Jack took her arm. 'Come on, Mrs Kerby. I'll get you back in the house and then we'll fix Joel up. I'll need to get a statement from you after that.'

Greta looked at Joel, who was now standing with his hand on his chest, concentrating on breathing. 'Will he be all right?'

'By the looks of it, he'll be fine. Just a few superficial scratches.'

Greta threw another look over her shoulder as Jack delivered her to the house. 'I'll be back to get your statement,' he said over his shoulder. 'And I've got some questions about the statement you gave about Maggie's death too.'

Greta gave him a startled stare. 'But that's so long ago.'

Jack nodded and left her standing on the steps to her house.

Dave was standing next to Joel with his notebook out. 'When did you notice him?'

'I was reversing out. I had to slam on the brakes so I didn't hit him. He was just standing there, looking at me through the back window. Then the mongrel offered me money to leave town.'

Dave's head jerked up. 'What? As in blackmail?' His mind spun quickly to Jacqui.

'Asked me to name my price.'

'Okay. Look, we'll need to talk to him too. But because he made the first move on you, this won't affect your parole. I'll make sure it doesn't.'

'Mrs Kerby was watching. She'll be able to tell you,' Joel said.

'I'll come back and get her statement once we've spoken to Steve,' Jack said. 'You want a lift to the hospital? Your nose looks like it's had a going over.'

Joel dabbed Mrs Kerby's hankie to his nose again and winced. 'Nothing a bag of frozen peas won't fix.'

'You sure?'

'Yeah.' Joel started to walk back to his house, but stopped and turned back to them after a couple of steps. 'You make sure he knows I'm not going anywhere. I've got every right to be here.'

Dave nodded, and then as an afterthought he asked, 'You didn't antagonise him, did you?'

'I was only responding to what he was saying.'

'Which was?'

Joel looked disgusted. 'That I raped Maggie. That sick . . . bastard. As if I would.'

Dave could see the words wanted to make Joel vomit.

'And what did you say to that?' Dave asked.

'I denied it, of course!'

'Do you know why he would have accused you of that?'

'No bloody idea.' Joel wiped at his face again and his hand came away wet with blood.

'You didn't throw anything back at him? Anything that might have upset him further?'

A slow smile spread over Joel's face. 'I asked why he wanted me out of Barker so much. If he was worried I knew something I shouldn't.'

'And do you?'

Joel looked hard at Dave. 'What I know is that it wasn't *me* who raped Maggie.'

'Why is Steve offering Joel money to leave?' Dave said. 'That's just fucking crazy.'

Jack was silent.

'You know, this whole town is getting a bit nuts,' Dave continued. 'Anyone would think there was a full moon. There must be some kind of common denominator here. Joel turns up and suddenly we're looking into the cold-case death of a sixteen-year-old girl, we've got a family all upset about him coming back, he's been in jail for something else and claims he's innocent and, to top it all off,' he gave a harsh laugh, 'we've now got a blackmail case.'

'It's not the quiet little Barker I'm used to,' Jack agreed.

'Barker and its surrounds are turning into the new Midsomer.'

'Maybe you should leave,' Jack offered with a half-smile.

'Me? How about you?'

'Everyone says the interesting stuff follows you. I'm happy with a quiet life, thanks very much.' Jack eyed Dave. 'And it was like that until you moved here.'

'Maybe I'll just retire,' Dave said. 'That'll fix the "interesting" things problem.' He pulled the patrol car into Steve and Lynette Douglas's driveway. Today the house looked as if no one was home.

'Maybe Lynette's working?'

'Maybe. Come on. Better be half-prepared for anything here, I think,' Dave said grimly.

They walked up the pathway and Dave knocked loudly on the door. 'Steve? Lynette? It's Dave Burrows. Can I have a few words, please?'

No answer. Dave pointed to the back of the house, and Jack went around the side.

'Hello?' Dave pounded on the door again.

'I'm coming!' Lynette's voice filtered through to Dave. 'What's wrong?' she asked when she finally opened the door.

'Hi, Lynette. Is Steve here?'

Her eyes flicked from the car to Dave and then to Jack as he came back to stand beside Dave.

'What's going on?'

'We just need to have a chat with your husband.'

'He's not here.' Her lips curled into a sneer. 'I don't know where he is and I'd rather you left.'

'Okay. When did he leave this morning?' Jack asked.

'I don't know.'

'Do you know where he was going, perhaps?' Dave kept his tone friendly.

'To work, I assume. That's where he normally goes.' She took a step back inside and tried to close the door, but Jack stepped closer to stop her.

'Right, and he hasn't come back here since he left to go to work this morning?'

Crossing her arms, Lynette stared at them. 'I haven't seen him since last night. He was gone when I got up this morning.'

'I see. Is that unusual?'

'No. He often goes in early.'

'Thanks. We'll try the school, then. Appreciate your help,' Jack said.

'If he comes back, would you get him to give me a call?' Dave said, handing over his card. 'It's important we speak to him.'

Lynette took the card and stared at it. 'Jesus. What's he done?' Frantically, she looked up and grabbed Dave's arm. 'What's he done?' Her voice rose.

'We just need to have a chat, as soon as he comes back.' Dave regarded her for a moment. 'Lynette, is there anything you'd like to talk to us about?'

'What? No.' Lynette retreated inside the house and started to close the door. 'Everything is just fine.'

'I'm not sure that's the case,' Jack muttered.

Dave tried again. 'Do you know if your husband has a Bundle account?'

The door clicked shut.

'Make sure you get in contact with us if we can help in any way.'

There was a sob from inside. 'No one can,' she said.

The men looked at each other and then walked away, leaving Lynette alone inside the house.

'What can we do there?' Jack asked.

'Nothing. We have nothing.'

'Do you think she knows where he is?' Jack asked when they were in the car.

'Nope. And she's worried. Whether about him or for herself, I'm not sure. Both, I reckon.' Dave's face was grim. 'Let's go and see if he's at work.'

'Nah, I'll bet he's got some claret showing somewhere. Maybe the hospital?'

'Do you want to ring them, save going if he's not there?'

Jack got out his phone and dialled the hospital's number, while Dave drove to the main street and pulled into the school.

The kids were all out playing, and Dave glanced at his watch. Mid-morning, so it must be recess time.

'You stay here,' Dave said. 'Let's not cause too much attention. I'll text you if he's here and come in then, okay?'

'Sure. Oh, good morning. It's Senior Constable Jack Higgins.'

Dave left him to it and walked quickly through the playground towards the front office, pushed open the door and smiled. 'G'day. Chasing Steve Douglas. He around?'

'We haven't seen him today,' the woman answered. 'I've been trying to call him because he had a meeting with the education department at nine. He hasn't answered.' She looked worried. 'This is so unlike him.'

Dave's phone dinged and he read the text from Jack: *He's not at the hospital. They'll ring us if he turns up.*

'How has Steve seemed over the past few days?' he asked the woman.

'Oh, much more on edge than usual. I mean, Mr Douglas is a highly strung man—always has so much going on—so it's to be expected, but the past week? He's not been himself. I'm a bit worried about him.'

315

'Could I see his office briefly?'

The woman nodded. 'It's through here.' She pointed to a door behind her, and Dave stepped around the desk. He pushed open the door and looked for anything that might indicate Steve had come back here after his altercation with Joel. There weren't any signs of blood, and the office was neat and tidy.

Dave turned to the woman.

'Would you let us know if he comes back?'

'Of course. Can I tell him what it's about?'

'Just let him know we need to speak to him.' Dave turned on his heel and left, jogging back to the car. The kids noticed him and spread out across the playground, keeping out of his way, but watching.

'Not there,' Dave said to Jack, then turned and looked down the main street, as if willing Steve to appear. 'Where else would he go?'

'Parents?'

'Good idea. Let's try there.'

There were a few people on the street watching with open curiosity as the two detectives got back into the car and drove away.

Max Douglas was coming out of the house with a bag of rubbish as they arrived. He saw them and dropped the bag.

'Oh no. What is it?' he asked in distress. 'What's happened?'

Dave and Jack walked through the open gate and up the garden path. 'We're just looking for Steve, Mr Douglas. Nothing's wrong. Have you seen him?'

'Why are you looking for him?'

Paula came out, wiping her hands on a tea-towel, and Dave watched her freeze as soon as she saw them. 'Max?' Her voice was high, uncertain.

'It's okay, love,' he told her. 'They're here for Steve.'

She relaxed. 'Oh, he'll be at home. He called in here quickly about an hour ago. I didn't see him, but I heard him.'

Max turned to look at her. 'I didn't see him.'

'No, you were at the IGA getting that lightbulb. I heard him in Maggie's room.' She looked back to Dave and Jack. 'He sometimes does that when he's feeling a bit sad. Just goes and sits in her room. I don't bother him when he's there.'

'Shouldn't he be at school?' Jack wanted to know.

'I have no idea of his schedule,' Paula said.

'Did he stay long?'

'Oh, twenty minutes perhaps. He sits on her bed and talks to her for a little bit, then he leaves.'

Dave frowned. 'Has he done that a lot over the years?'

'Ever since she died, hasn't he, Max?' She turned to look at her husband, who nodded.

'The first time I found him in there, he was curled up in her doona, sobbing his heart out. The poor lad misses her. They were so close, even though there was six years between them. Steve doted on her the moment she was born.'

'Righto,' Dave said and gave them a small smile. 'We'll head over to his house and see if we can catch up with him there.'

'Be gentle with him,' Paula said. 'He's the one who never got over Maggie's death.'

Jack was solemn when he got in the car. 'Don't go to the house. I want to go to Greta Kerby's. We need to talk to her.'

Dave looked over at him, confused. 'What's she got to do with this now?'

'I don't know for sure, but I have an idea. Trust me.'

Without a word, Dave put the car in gear.

~

Joel drove down the main street. He wouldn't have admitted it, but he was searching for Steve Douglas. This had to end once and for all.

His anger was going to overwhelm him if he didn't have it out.

In front of the hardware store, he saw Emma Cameron talking to a bloke he didn't know. He wondered if she might help him. Their families had always sort of been friends.

Putting on the blinker he pulled into a parking spot and shut off the car.

As he did so, a red ute pulled in alongside him and another man got out. He walked over and kissed Emma on the cheek.

Joel watched, thinking the man was familiar. Then his eyes narrowed.

What?

All the anger he was already feeling boiled to the surface. He reefed the car door open and almost fell from the car in his haste. 'You . . . you prick!' he yelled and ran towards Emma and the men.

He didn't have time to register the shock on their faces. He just slammed his fist into the man's face, and they both went down onto the ground.

'Joel, what are you doing?' Emma screamed as the man still standing pulled Joel from the man on the ground. 'Kyle! Are you all right?'

Struggling to get his hands released from the man's grip, Joel wrenched himself back and forth and then kicked out towards Kyle.

'What the hell?' the man who had hold of him said. 'What the fuck are you doing, dude?'

Emma was bending over Kyle now and Joel was breathing heavily. 'What are you doing here?' Joel said, gasping for air.

Kyle half sat, dabbing his fingers to his nose. 'Man, I don't know who you are, but I'm going to get you charged with assault.'

Reefing harder, Joel snarled, his eyes wide and flashing. 'You don't know who I am?'

Kyle got back to his feet with help from Emma, who stood in front of him protectively.

'Joel, are you okay? He says he doesn't know you. What on earth?'

Giving one last twist, Joel broke free from the man and took a few steps back, breathing heavily. 'You don't know me?' he asked.

Quickly, the man stepped in front of Kyle as well and held his hand out to Joel as if to ward off another attack. 'Now, mate, let's keep this civil,' he warned. 'I can call the cops if you don't settle down.'

'Call them,' Kyle spat out. 'I want him charged. This was an unprovoked attack.'

Joel stared at Kyle. Without taking his eyes from Kyle, he asked again, 'You really don't know me?'

'Never clapped eyes on you before.'

Joel rubbed his head, confused. He was sure he knew this man.

'Sorry,' he said, finally. 'Sorry.' He rushed back to his car before anyone could say anything else.

~

'You're back quickly,' Greta greeted them. She was in the front garden, cutting roses.

'I have some questions for you,' Jack said. 'About Maggie. Could you clarify a couple of things for me?'

Greta put down the roses, her mouth in a thin line. 'I can try.'

'You said in your statement that you used to look after Maggie. Where did you do that? At her house or at yours?'

'At her house.'

'Okay, and just run me through what she was like.'

Dave broke in. 'Just before you do that: how long did you look after her?'

'Three years. From when she was ten until she was thirteen. They had another housekeeper-cum-babysitter before me, so that young lass was looked after from the moment she was born until the day I left.'

'And who looked after her when you finished up?'

'Her brothers, I think.'

Dave nodded and wrote that down.

'Okay. So, Maggie—what was she like?'

'A happy little thing, when I first got there. Always smiling and laughing. As she got older, she became a bit distant and defiant. I always put it down to the fact she felt like her home was a prison.'

'Did she say that to you?'

'Ah . . .' Greta stopped to think. 'No,' she said slowly. 'That might have been my assumption.'

'So, this defiance, was there anything else that could have caused that?'

Greta seemed to be making her mind up about something.

Jack spoke gently. 'Anything you can tell us would be very useful.'

'I don't want to speak ill of the dead.'

They all waited.

'Maggie was drinking. Drinking because I think she needed to forget or dull the pain or something like that.' She paused and then opened her mouth like she wanted to say something, but didn't.

'Mrs Kerby?'

The old woman closed her eyes and took a couple of deep breaths in through her nose and then spoke.

'She never wanted to be left alone with him.' She looked Jack directly in the eye. 'With Steve.'

CHAPTER 29

'Oh my god, Steve, what happened to you?!'

Lynette ran to him as he washed his face in the laundry sink. She tried to take the washcloth from his hand, but he snatched it back and kept cleaning his face.

'Leave me alone,' he snarled.

'Steve . . .'

'That low-life prick Hammond. That's what fucking happened. I went over to have a conversation with him and he attacked me. Look at this.' He indicated his face, then pulled his shirt up to show a bruise beginning to form.

'Is that why the police were here?'

His head yanked around. 'They were here?'

'About an hour ago. They want you to call them. Dave Burrows left his card.' She paused, her voice lowered. 'They wanted to know if you have a Bundle account. What's that?'

'None of your business.' He snatched the towel off the hanger and walked into the bedroom, stripping off as he went.

'Steve, I know you hate having Joel here, but is there some way—'

Raising his hand, Steve turned and brought it down on Lynette's face. Her hand went to cover her stinging cheek. She stared up at him, her eyes wide.

'Steve,' she whispered.

'Just leave me alone. There is no possible way you could understand how much I hate Joel Hammond.'

'Darling, this isn't right. You need some help to get past this. I could—'

'You will never understand.' His words were like ice.

'Of course I understand! I'm your wife. I support you in everything you do.'

Lynette watched as her husband's face closed over and he looked at her with distaste. 'You were never my wife.' His voice was low. So low, Lynette had to strain to hear him. 'You were never my wife,' he repeated. 'You were a means to an end.'

'What?' Startled, Lynette stepped backwards. 'Steve, you're not making any sense. Maybe you were hit harder than you thought. Let me call an ambulance for you.' She went to get her phone, but he reached out and grabbed her, spinning her around until she was looking him in the face.

'Hattie was the first, but she didn't comply. Wanted to tell someone what we were doing. And really Maggie was the only one I really loved. It was her who was going to be my wife.'

Lynette felt as if she'd been slapped. Nausea gurgled in her stomach instantly. 'What do you mean? Maggie was your sister.'

'You were never able to be my true wife. I already had one. We were going to be together.' Steve rubbed his eyes as the tears started. 'We were . . .'

'Jesus, Steve. Maggie was your *sister*. You're drunk. Tell me you're drunk. This isn't true.' Lynette pulled away, and he let his hands fall to his sides. 'And Hattie? I don't understand.' She felt a strange urge to run as far as she could, but she couldn't. She needed to hear it. Hear what Steve was saying.

'Hattie was a beautiful little thing, but she couldn't hold a candle to Maggie. Then she said she wanted to tell her parents. She couldn't. Oh, it was special between us. But not so special that she couldn't be disposed of when the need arose.

'No, Maggie was the special one.' Steve was staring into the distance, living in sordid memories.

'All of this was you?' Lynette whispered. 'You killed Hattie too. And you were the one who raped Maggie?' She stared, disbelieving, at the man she loved, as everything fell into place. He had never once made his way into her bed, from the night they got married. Their single beds and separate rooms were not just because he didn't love her! It was because he had loved his sister and his cousin.

The urge to vomit was real.

Lynette thought of all the time he spent at Maggie's grave and in her bedroom at their parents' house.

She would never forget the time she'd gone into his bedroom to make his bed. As she'd pulled back the covers she had found a pair of pure white knickers and a bra on the sheets. She remembered staring at them for a long time, wondering whose they were. They were small and petite. Just like Maggie had been.

Now Lynette knew.

He'd kept trophies of her, like serial killers kept trophies of their victims.

'In what part of your twisted mind could you think this was love?' she managed to say. 'It was rape. *You raped your own sister.*'

'How *dare* you?' Steve snarled as he reached out for her neck. 'It was never rape. It was love. Always love. She loved me. Maggie wouldn't have dressed like she did when she was around me if she didn't love me.'

He looked at Lynette, but she was sure he didn't see her. His fingers tightened around her throat, and her hands flew to try to scratch them away. He was remembering his baby sister. Or perhaps it was Hattie this time.

No, his mouth was forming the word: 'Maggie.' What had he done to her? What obscene, indecent acts had he forced on her? Maybe Steve killed Maggie too, and not Joel?

Lynette felt something inside her collapse; something that would never recover.

'You're an animal,' she whispered, managing to twist away. 'An animal. Wait until your family find out. A minister of the church, no less, and the worst sin of all was coming from their own house! The police . . .' Lynette turned to run, but Steve got to her first, smashing her head into the dining table.

Lynette fell with a scream as heat ripped through her head. But as the fog descended, she heard Steve's words.

'It was love. Don't ever forget that. It was love.'

~

Jack's phone rang as they were leaving Greta's house.

'Hey, you.' Jack's mood lifted a little when he saw Zara's name on his screen.

'Jack, I've got something.'

The excitement in her voice made Jack almost forget the unbearable words Greta had just uttered.

I think he was abusing her.

'What have you got?' Jack asked.

'Do you have time to swing by home?'

He didn't even look at Dave for an answer. 'No, we're in the middle of something.'

'It's about Joel.'

'Hang on. I need to call you back in a minute.' He ended the call and waved the phone at Dave. 'Zara's got something about Joel. She's been looking into the fraud charge.'

'We need to find Steve, don't you think?'

'Yeah, we do.' He stopped as they opened the car doors and looked at his partner over the roof of the vehicle. 'But Steve has lived with this secret a long time. He doesn't know we know, so it might be better to let him calm down before we try to talk to him. Lull him into a false sense of security.'

'There's that option too,' Dave agreed. He screwed his face up in indecision. 'I don't know. The fraud thing doesn't matter as much as a child molester—a bloke who would rape his own sister—in my town. And the school principal! How do we know there aren't more victims?'

'I don't think he's hurt anybody else, do you? Sounds like just Maggie. He was obsessed with her.'

'What about his cousin. She disappeared.'

Jack felt his stomach drop. 'Yeah.'

'Makes my skin crawl, just thinking about it.'

'Fuck, I need to go home and have a shower.'

'You did well to pick up on it. I didn't. I can't believe I missed it.'

'I knew there was something that wasn't right. But I never dreamed it was that until I went back and reread Mrs Kerby's statement.'

Dave turned to him. 'But she didn't say anything specific about that, so how did you know?'

'It was what she didn't say. You've always told me to look for what's not there.'

'And what was that?'

'She was hinting at something. You know how she paused a lot, like she was considering what words to use—Greta was really careful with her choice of words. And she mentioned the brothers so often I thought there was something amiss there.'

'Bloody good job, Jack. Bloody good job,' Dave said.

'What are we doing with Zara?' Jack waited to see what Dave would say.

'Five minutes with her on our way to Steve's, and no more,' Dave finally said. 'Hopefully that will give him time to turn up back there and settle down.' He banged the dash of the car gently with his fists. 'It's new for me not to know what to do, and I don't like it.'

Jack looked over. 'Whatever happens, we're in it together.'

Zara was standing at the front gate when they arrived, and she rushed over to spread some pages out on the bonnet.

'What have you got?' Dave asked gruffly.

'Okay,' she said excitedly, 'so most of this work had already been done for me. Bob Elder was a whiz at investigation and all I had to do is put it together and talk to a few more people. So, I can't take full credit for this.'

'Hey, breathe,' Jack said, putting his hand on her back.

She flashed him a smile and drew in a deep breath. 'I've been tracing the people who worked for Stockomatic when Joel was there, and I can find all of them except one. He did the same job as Joel; in fact, they used to sit next to each other in the office. Turns out this bloke has form.'

'Form?'

'He's got a rap sheet from when he was eighteen. Got caught stealing money from the shop he was working at. Nearly a thousand dollars.'

Dave raised his eyebrows. 'Do I need to know how you found out he had a rap sheet?'

She smiled sweetly. 'Wasn't my doing. This is Bob's work. I just found them all again.'

'Wait on, wait on,' Jack said. 'How did he get a job in a finance department if he already had form?'

'That, I can't answer. I guess he managed to hide it somehow, but the fact of the matter is, he did.' She tapped a piece of paper on the bonnet. 'It's there.'

'Right, so . . .' Jack wanted to get to the bottom of this as quickly as he could.

'Okay,' Zara refocused. 'I spoke to a cop who gives me a hand sometimes and got him to do some searches for me. This guy, he's lived in a few different places. Like, five places over the past eight years. Everywhere from Queensland to Tasmania and Western Australia. Always in capital cities and always working in the finance department of whatever company he's employed by. When I started ringing the businesses he'd worked for, I saw that everywhere he's been he's left under a cloud.'

'What sort of cloud?'

'No proof of stealing money, but the business had lost money in a way they couldn't explain.'

'How did he keep getting jobs?'

'He never asked for references and, like I said, none of these businesses could prove he was stealing.' She paused. 'My guess is he falsified references to keep on getting employment. However,' Zara held up her hand, 'that is yet to be proven. It's my hypothesis.'

Dave stared at her, and Jack could see he was impressed. A glow of pride started in Jack's chest. He already knew that Zara was a top-notch journo, but he was happy whenever his peers recognised it too.

'How the hell did you work this out so quickly when

329

a heap of people looked at this case and didn't find Joel innocent?' Dave asked, crossing his arms.

Zara looked embarrassed. 'Like I said, all I've done is make the phone calls. Bob Elder had it practically finished before he died. The information I needed was all in his notes. It just needed deciphering.' She shook her hair back. 'I'd love to say that I'm brilliant at this sort of thing, and I *am* good.' She gave them a cheeky smile. 'But not so good I could solve this in a few days without some help.'

'I—' Dave broke off. 'You know, this annoys the fuck out of me. An innocent man has been put in jail and the AFP, the freaking Feds, have stuffed it up again. Along with his lawyer not doing the job by the sounds of it. He or she should have got a private investigator onto this.'

Zara shook her head. 'Legal aid lawyer,' she said. 'Never had that option, or the time to represent Joel properly. Well, that's what Bob Elder has written in his notes.'

Jack let out a sound of disgust.

'So, here,' Zara said, bringing their attention back to the pages she had spread out. 'My mate went and pulled the bank records to see if he could tell who opened the bank account the money had been paid into. It was opened in Joel's name, with his signature and his hundred-point check: driver's licence, Medicare card and passport. This bloke even had Joel's employment records.'

'Stole his identity?'

'Yep. The photos in the passport and so on *could* be Joel, but you'd have to get an expert to look at them. My hunch is that the bloke who's doing all of this has had his hair cut and grown a beard to make him look like Joel, but it's not him.' Zara turned and smiled at them both. 'And here's the clincher.'

'Oh, yeah?' Dave said.

'The account was opened in Port Augusta.'

'He's lived there?'

'Of course not! He's gone up there with all of Joel's ID because his address was still in Barker. We don't have a bank here, and Port Augusta is the closest place with a branch for this bank. He just made it look like he was here.'

All three looked at each other.

Zara raced on. 'And there's one more bit. In Perth, there was a guy charged with theft of money where this bloke also worked. He didn't go to jail because they couldn't prove it was him, but he was working for them at the same time as our guy.'

'This is all fantastic, but do you have a name? I can't chase a nameless criminal,' said Dave.

'Cole Pengilly.'

Dave rolled the name around in his mind, but it didn't ring any bells. 'This bloke is a serial fraudster. Obviously knows how to do things well.' He rolled his shoulders back and shook his head. 'Well, I guess the good thing is, you can go and tell Joel. Make sure he knows the coppers still have to investigate and prove it all beyond reasonable doubt. You can give him all the circumstantial evidence you have. Anything will give him hope at the moment.'

'Yeah, I wanted to ask you about that. It's okay?'

'I want to go through what you've got here more thoroughly, but if you're convinced that there's enough, then you were the one who went to Joel to offer your services. That's your call. I'd say yes, though. That man has been through the wringer. But Zara . . .' He closed his eyes as he thought about the revelations from Greta Kerby today. 'Make sure he understands this isn't the end of it. It'll be the fraud squad, not me and Jack, who will be taking this one. Make sure you tell him.'

'Okay, I'll go now. I wanted to check and see if he remembered a man called Cole anyway.'

'Yeah, you'd better confirm that.'

'He always said there was someone else, and I believed he knew who it was.' Zara paused. 'And there was a little note to the side of Bob's investigations that talked about the extra four years he got for grievous bodily harm. All is said was: "*Connected.*"'

'What do you make of that?' Dave looked at his watch. He was keen to get back to looking for Steve.

'I have no proof yet, but my gut feeling is, the bloke who tried to bash Joel was bringing a message to stay quiet.'

'You've done a good job, Zara,' Dave said. 'And you're probably right. There's always a way to get to an inmate if you know the system. If Cole knew how to do that, he could've got a "keep quiet" message—a threat—to Joel, no doubt.' Then he repeated what he'd said to Jack. 'But don't let it go to your head.' He grinned and patted her on the shoulder, then turned to Jack. 'Come on, Jack, we've got another mess to sort out.'

CHAPTER 30

Joel sat in the corner of his bedroom and held a bag of peas to his nose. He rocked himself gently, still confused. He was sure he'd known the man in the street. Or maybe he'd just wanted to.

Nine years had passed since he'd last seen him, and there was every chance he was different now to how he'd known him way back when.

'I'm sure it was him,' Joel whimpered. 'I'm really sure.'

But the man's face hadn't registered anything but surprise as Joel had flown at him. There hadn't been recognition or fear. Just shock. So maybe Joel did have it all wrong. That he wasn't who he thought he was.

There was a loud knock on the door, but Joel didn't move.

'Hello?' A woman's voice called out. 'Joel, are you home?'

Joel stopped rocking and listened. The tone sounded like the journalist woman. He couldn't remember her name.

'It's Zara Ellison here. I've got some news.'

'It doesn't matter anymore,' he whispered, not moving. 'It just doesn't.'

~

Kyle looked in the chemist part of the supermarket. He wanted Savlon cream and Dettol. His lips were swollen where the crazy man had hit him and he had a bit of gravel rash on his cheek from where he'd fallen. 'Crazy fucker,' he muttered as he found the items and threw them in the basket he was carrying.

Making his way to the counter, he asked, 'Have you got any roses? Or any flowers?'

'No, mate,' said the young man behind the counter, looking at his face. 'Not the sort of thing we stock. Reckon they'd go to waste around here. Anything else you need?'

Kyle frowned. 'I guess it's chocolates, then.'

His phone dinged and he looked at the screen. Quickly he tapped out a reply and put it back in his pocket.

Dinner last night had gone well with Emma and, he had to admit, he really liked her. It was the first time since Alice that he'd really liked a woman.

He wanted to go out and stay with her, but he knew it was too soon to suggest that again. The hint he'd dropped about the caravan park being full hadn't been picked up and he knew he'd have to go slowly if the end result was going to be what he wanted. Even if it meant staying a few more weeks in Barker than he'd planned.

When he'd run into her in the street today, she'd been distressed, telling him that Matt had resigned and she needed to talk to him, to change his mind. He'd seen that as an opportunity to offer his help.

Riffling through the chocolates on the shelf, he couldn't find anything even a bit fancy. Only Cadbury and Roses. He pondered the idea of taking a trip to Port Augusta, but then he realised his petrol tank was nearly empty and so he couldn't.

Kyle tried to push aside the impatience he was feeling, which had been exacerbated by Emma's refusal to let him help. Making life easier for her was something he really wanted to do and her casual comment that he didn't know much about farming, so thanks but no thanks, had made him angry.

He picked up two boxes and a card and took them to the counter, paid and went back to his car.

The caravan park wasn't far, and he could have walked, but his ute was getting a few looks around town and he always liked a bit of attention.

The diesel engine rumbled to life and he revved the engine slightly before reversing out of the angled car park.

Two people walking along the pavement glanced over at the shiny ute and then did a double-take. He smiled to himself. *Eat your heart out, grandad*, he thought as he let the clutch out quickly and shot forwards.

A police car came around the corner and Kyle had to swing the ute out of their way. Then he groaned as the flashing lights came on. 'Ah, no! Seriously?'

He flicked his indicator on and pulled over to the side of the street. This wasn't the sort of attention he liked.

'Afternoon, sir,' the young policeman—who didn't look old enough to vote—got out of the passenger's seat and walked over to him. 'Nice ute.' He looked more closely at Kyle. 'You been in a bit of action there?'

Kyle put his hand to his nose and pressed gently before nodding with a grim smile, but didn't say anything.

The young copper looked at him intently. 'Anything I can help you with, sir?'

'Ah, this is a bit older than it looks,' Kyle lied. 'Happened in another town. Just a bit of a misunderstanding.'

'I see.' He paused and let a silence fill the air. Kyle wasn't going to fill it. 'I guess you know why we pulled you over?'

'Took off a little too quickly.'

'That's right. Got your licence there?'

Kyle dug into his back pocket and took out his wallet. He checked the licence before handing it over and gave a heavy sigh.

'If you could wait there, please, sir. Perhaps I could have your keys.'

Kyle handed them over, and the young officer took them before walking back to the patrol vehicle and handing the licence in through the window. He could see an older copper pick up the mic and call in his details.

A few moments later the younger officer was back. 'I'll give you a caution today, Kyle. We don't like that sort of behaviour on our streets in Barker. Lots of young children around here. And I don't want to see you flashing any fists around here either.' He gave him a hard stare.

'Sure. Sorry, I was a little enthusiastic. I've got a date tonight.' He opted for the solidarity-in-bloke-stuff approach.

'Well, I hope your date doesn't mind a fat lip. Have a good time. At the pub?'

'Nah,' he winked. 'At her house. Never know what might happen, hey?'

The young man, whose badge said his name was Higgins, smiled thinly. 'Enjoy your evening, sir, and please do remember my words of warning.' He turned and left, but just before he got back into the car he called out, 'If you're going to date one of our local girls, and we're going to see you around a little more, I'd suggest you don't show off in that ute again.'

'Emma Cameron,' Kyle called back. 'Know her? Bit of a looker.' He liked to brag when he had a pretty woman on his arm, and he was sure Emma would fall for his charms. They always did.

Higgins nodded and the two policemen drove off.

Kyle sighed and leaned his head against the steering wheel. 'Idiot. Fucking idiot,' he muttered.

This time, he let his foot out slowly from the clutch and drove sedately back to the caravan park. In his cabin, he put the chocolates in the fridge and opened a beer. He got out his phone and tapped on the Facebook app. He wanted to friend Emma before tonight.

He searched for her name and sent her a friend request with a short note. *Looking forward to seeing you tonight* ☺. Then he pressed send.

He saw there were new messages on his dating app, but he ignored them all and zeroed in on one chat.

Where are you? he typed. Kyle could see his last three messages had gone unseen. Frowning, he closed the phone and wondered what was going on there. It was unlike her not to answer. *Don't ignore me.*

There was a knock at the door of his cabin.

'For fuck's sake,' he whispered, before opening the door with a large smile on his face. 'Mrs Devin! How are you on this beautiful day?'

'Hello, Kyle. I was calling by to see if you'd like to settle your account for this week? I had trouble with your payment last week, as you know, and I wouldn't like to see that happen again.' She looked at him as if he were the naughty boy in the classroom. 'Let's not forget it took a few goes to rectify the problem.'

This woman didn't know how to smile, and he didn't like her one bit.

'Yes, you're right, but it *was* rectified and I can only apologise for the inconvenience. Obviously the transfers between accounts didn't go through when they were supposed to.' He spread his hands out in a what-can-you-do manner and gave her a winning smile. 'But I can come to the office now, if you'd like me to. Although, I did think I'd make it through until Friday—you know, that would make it a whole week, since I paid on Friday last.' He gave her another smile, forced as it was.

'I think I'd like it if you came and paid now,' she said, turning away. 'I rest a bit easier at night knowing I haven't got any outstanding payments due.'

'Sure. Let me tidy up what I'm doing here and I'll be right up to see you.'

Shutting the door, he clenched his fist, smashing it into the pillow, wishing it were Mrs Devin's face.

The phone rang, and this time he answered it.

'Kyle, it's Alex. Got a moment?'

'Not really, Alex, I'm running out the door.' Kyle made his voice sound rushed.

'The clients want to talk to you.'

'Yes, I know and I've sent them all an email with a Zoom link for Monday morning. I'm on holiday, in case you've all forgotten, and I'm not talking to them before then.'

'They're worried they're going to miss the deal.'

'They won't. I've never missed a deal for them yet and we won't stuff this one up either.'

A long sigh came down the phone. 'What do you want me to tell them?'

'Nothing. They've got my email, so they should know that they'll see me online on Monday.' He took a sip of his beer and sat on the saggy couch. Maybe Emma could come here for dinner instead. Save him driving all the way out there and then back again. That way, he could drink.

'I'm worried they'll find another firm.'

'Alex, Alex, Alex.' Kyle lowered his voice to calm his partner. 'This is all fine and normal. Jake in particular gets jittery before a big deal goes down. Look, if it makes you feel any better, I'll send him a text message and tell him everything I've just told you.'

'Would you?'

'Will it make you feel a bit better?'

'It would. It really would.'

It was Kyle's turn to sigh. 'Fine, I'll do that.' He paused. 'Anything else?'

'Ah, no, not that I know of.'

'Good. Chat to you Monday.' He hung up without saying goodbye. Talk about being sick and tired of holding other people's hands.

Looking out the window, he saw Mrs Devin pacing back and forth outside the office, waiting for him. It didn't look like he was going to get away with not paying.

Opening the bank app on his phone, he checked the balances. *Shit.*

Things were about to implode. He had to get his hands on that extra money. He just had to.

Sending another message, he said: *You've got until tonight.*

⌒

'Well, obviously they're not here,' Dave said as they circum-navigated the house once more in the hope of seeing Steve.

They'd banged on the door and no one had answered, then Dave had tried the phone number he had for Steve, but it went unanswered.

'Do we need to put out a BOLO on him?' Jack asked.

'I've been thinking that, but we've got no reason to think he's absconded, have we? Like you said, he didn't know we were onto him, except that he gave Joel a bit of a touch up. He'll probably be expecting us to have a chat to him about that.'

'I don't know,' Jack said. 'It's pretty weird for him to disappear like he has, though. Don't you think?'

Dave thought for a few moments and then said, 'The school receptionist said he'd been skittish the past few days. I think that's worth taking note of. So, let's do one more run around the town and see what we can see, then we might organise the Be On The Lookout.'

As they drove, Dave's phone dinged with an email. He got it out to read. 'It's from Computer Crimes,' he said. 'About the blackmail Jacqui reported yesterday.'

He read aloud. *'Dear Detective Burrows, after a preliminary investigation we have found that Gill is an individual we are aware of. If you could call me, I would like to discuss the option of putting a couple of your men on this to see if we can work together to apprehend him.'*

'Right, time to get to the bottom of this,' Dave said as he rang the number provided.

'Computer Crimes. Can I help you?'

'Kate, Dave Burrows, I've got your email. Who is this low-life?'

'G'day, Dave. Thanks for calling back. He is just that. He's done this before and we've never been able to catch him in the act.'

'What, blackmailed someone?'

'Yeah, always with nudes. He's a broken record, but it's working for him. Joins a dating site, gets raunchy with someone who's a little desperate, sends a dick pic and then gets them to send something back.

'There was a report about two weeks ago from a woman who managed to get a screenshot of his request before he deleted it. See, this is the trouble with this particular site. The perp creates an account, does what he does, then when the women pay, which they invariably do because they don't want their photos up on the web and they're too embarrassed to go to the police, then he deletes his profile. Now, when he does that, all the correspondence he's had with that woman disappears.'

'Hold on, what do you mean? Surely the ones on her account stay?'

'No, everything. Every word, photo, anything they've done, goes, from both people. We're working on getting the legislation changed. It's a horrible loophole.'

'That means,' Dave said slowly, 'that people could get hurt and there's no way to find out who did it.'

'Exactly. However, we traced one woman who didn't play by his rules. He did the normal racy talk and sent his picture—which, by the way, is never his—and asked for hers. She complied, but not with what he wanted. She sent a picture of her toe!'

'What?' Dave didn't know whether to laugh or be appalled at what he was hearing.

'Got a bit of a sense of humour, that girl. As it turns out, she was slightly suspicious of him anyway, so she took screenshots of their conversations. We only found her through some fairly sophisticated IT methods. But she was talking to the same Gill who keeps popping up all over the place with depressing regularity.'

'Okay, so how do we ensure that he doesn't post these nudes of Jacqui?'

'Well, here's the interesting thing. I've been tracking him, because he's really not as clever as he thinks.'

'You know where he is situated?'

'Let's assume it's a bloke. Could be a girl but, hey, let's run with that. Anyhow, yes, he's actually holed up in your neck of the woods.'

'Jesus!' Dave glanced over at Jack, who was looking at him questioningly. 'What the fuck? I thought these mongrels operated from overseas.'

'Not this one. Seems he's going into your public library and using the free internet there.'

'It can't be that easy?'

'Sometimes it's like taking candy from a baby. They get too cocky. And other days you want to punch someone. But we still have to catch him in the act.'

Jack turned the corner and drove past the school, but other than that the kids were now in their lessons, nothing had changed there.

'Okay, well, what's your plan? There's only two of us at this station and we're on something else that's urgent.'

'Plan is to set him up. Get him online while we're monitoring him, and you be there for the take.'

'Okay, like I said, we don't have extra resources. As soon as we apprehend our POI I'll be in touch to get it organised.'

'That's fine, but I don't want him moving on before we get a crack at him. You okay if I organise some bods to head up there? We can tidy this bloke up fairly quickly that way.'

'Yeah, fine by me. I'm not precious about these things. Send 'em up. I'd rather he was off the streets too. Thanks, Kate, I really appreciate you helping me with this. I was feeling a bit out of my depth.'

'No drama. They'll be up today. I've got spare blokes, and we want this guy.'

'Do you need me to put you in touch with Jacqui?'

'I've got her details from the file you sent through. I'll ring her if you're under the pump.'

'Sure. Cheers.'

Dave hung up and blew out a breath. 'Okay, they reckon we've got the bloke here in Barker. And now they're sending up a team to set him up to take him down.'

Jack nodded. 'Good. But I think we need to find Steve. This is beginning to worry me. You can only hide in Barker if you want to.'

'His car was still at the house, wasn't it?'

'Yeah.'

'Righto, let's put out a BOLO and—'

From underneath the car, the ground shook, followed by the noise of an explosion.

'What the—?' Dave's head swivelled to see a plume of black smoke behind him.

Another blast, and this time it seemed to Dave that the world seemed to shake and spin, before little pieces of ash and brick rained down on him.

People came out of their houses and screamed as they saw the volcano of smoke above the town. Some started running and others held back, clutching their children to them, glued to the scene.

'Go, go, go!' he yelled to Jack.

CHAPTER 31

Joel heard the blast and dragged himself from the corner and walked outside. Black smoke billowed into the sky a few streets away from him. Another blast and he felt the ground rumble under his feet, and he knew that the smoke was closer than it looked. That's when he started to run.

The third explosion made the windows rattle in the houses as he ran past them. He wasn't the only one around. People were coming out of their homes, out onto the street and standing, watching, calling to each other.

Across the town, he heard sirens. Police.

He thought they'd need the fire trucks too.

Maybe the ambulance.

Suddenly, he was in front of the house that was on fire. Flames were licking up around the walls and black smoke was billowing from shattered windows. He had no idea whose house it was, but he knew someone could be inside.

'Is anyone in there?' he called to the people on the other side of the street, who stood by helplessly when he got there. 'What are you going to do? Just stand there?' He wanted to shake them. 'Is there anyone inside?'

One woman held her hand up as if to say she didn't know, while another man ran across the street.

'Lynette and Steve Douglas live here. Lynette's probably home.'

Joel didn't stop to think. He ran to the door and pushed it in, holding his hand up against the heat.

'Mate, you're mad!' someone yelled out.

'Hello!' Joel screamed against the fire and flames. 'Hello?' He scouted quickly through the kitchen, trying not to breathe in smoke, then his foot caught on something and he tumbled over. Through the thick smoke, he made out the outline of a body on the floor, not moving.

Lynette.

Joel grabbed her arms and started to drag her out. There was a muffled blast from the back of the house and Joel saw the fire in the roof spread like someone had used a fire lighter to get it going.

He was just about out the door when the stove exploded. Feeling shards pierce his back, he knew he had to keep going, to get out before the rest of the house blew up. Hands reached for him, dragging them both out of the flames.

Someone took Lynette from him and he could hear more sirens. An ambulance.

'Joel? Joel! Talk to me!' The journalist was at his side. Zara. He could hear her talking but he wasn't sure if it was to him or not.

Then, Jack was there. Joel saw him look at the woman with an expression he couldn't work out, so he closed his eyes.

'No, Joel!' she yelled at him and slapped his face. 'Stay with me. You'll be okay. You're going to be fine.'

'Don't,' he muttered, trying to raise his hand. What the hell was that about? His cheek stung. Then he felt her press something to his side, and he realised he must be bleeding.

'I'm fine,' he said, although it was an effort to talk. 'I can't feel anything, so I must be.'

'Joel.' Zara was close to his face. 'Joel, I have good news. I've found a way to prove your innocence.'

His fuzzy brain tried to comprehend what she was telling him. What? Why was she saying this now? There were houses to save, and people too.

'I don't know if Steve was in there,' he muttered.

'Joel, are you listening? A bloke call Cole Pengilly is the thief. They're going to reopen the investigation. We're going to try to clear your name.'

'Cole?' Anger and energy spread through Joel's body. 'It *was* him,' he spat, trying to sit up. Heavy hands on his shoulders pushed him down.

'Joel?' Suddenly, Jack was talking to him. 'We know you didn't hurt Maggie. It was Steve. He was abusing her, raping her. We know her death had nothing to do with you.'

'Maggie?' Joel was sure he was dreaming now. He must be hallucinating. Maybe he'd lost blood.

'Out of the way, please.' The ambulance officers came through and started to pack Joel's wounds with gauze. One barked instructions at the other and the third officer set up a drip.

There were tears on Zara's cheeks. She stayed at Joel's head, talking to him. 'Joel, do you understand?' she said. 'We know you're innocent!'

It took all of Joel's effort, but he raised his hand. 'Thank you.' But he had no idea who he was thanking. Everyone was blurry. Nothing but a fuzzy movement of colour.

'We need to move him, now,' the officer in charge said. They hoisted the stretcher up into the back of the ambulance.

Zara watched in disbelief as they drove away, their sirens blaring. As she looked around, she realised that the fire-fighters were aiming the water on the houses next door to the Douglas property, trying to save them, and another ambulance was leaving too.

Jack had left her and gone to direct people, keeping them away, while the other emergency-services crews did their jobs.

'Come on, Zara.' Kim had found her. 'Let's move.'

'He knows,' Zara whispered. 'I got to tell him.'

'Up you get, let's get you across the street.' Kim helped Zara stand and wrapped a blanket around her shoulders as they walked a safe distance away from the fire.

Across the road, she could see the charred remains of what was once a home.

CHAPTER 32

'Steve Douglas is dead,' Dave told Jack, four hours later. 'They found his body in the house. Reckon he set it alight.'

Jack nodded.

'We need to talk to Lynette,' Dave said. 'Doc said she's come around and we can. You up to it?'

'I have to be,' Jack replied.

'She's just down the hall.'

They were both quiet for a while. Then Jack spoke. 'Do we tell her?' He sighed. 'We don't even know if it's true.'

Dave looked at him sadly. 'Yes, we do.'

'But does she have to know if she doesn't already? Surely we don't need to cause her any more grief? Not after today. I mean ... Ah, Jesus.' Jack dropped his head.

'Let's just see how it plays out.'

A doctor appeared at the door, wiping his tired eyes. 'She's okay. We haven't told her about her husband. You or the family can do that.'

Dave nodded. 'Any news on Joel Hammond?'

'They've taken him to Port Augusta. He was too badly injured for us to care for him here. I'd say it's touch and go. A little more go than touch.'

'Fuck!' The word burst from Jack like a bullet. 'Where's the fairness in that?'

Dave put a comforting hand on his shoulder and left it there. 'Thanks, mate,' he said to the doctor.

'What the hell happened here tonight?' The doctor held his hands out, clearly needing an explanation.

'We're trying to get to the bottom of it.'

'Well, good luck. I left the city thinking country life was going to be peaceful.' He walked away without saying goodbye.

'You all right?' Dave asked Jack.

Jack's jaw was clenched, and he didn't know how to open it again without crying. A couple more bites down and he finally could breathe. 'No, this is fucked.'

'Yep, it is. Ready?'

'Yeah. Let's get it over with.'

Lynette was lying in the bed, small and pale, hooked up to monitors that were giving off soft, reassuring beeps. Her eyes were shut, but when Dave closed the door with a click, she opened them.

'Hey, Lynette. How are you feeling?' Dave stood near the bed, while Jack got out his notebook and, with hands covered in black soot, started to record her words.

'Okay. Better. I can breathe a bit better.'

'That's a nasty cut on your head. How did you get that?' Dave asked gently.

'I can't tell you.' Tears filled her eyes and she tried to use her hand to wipe her nose, but it was weighed down by a cannula and she couldn't raise it high enough.

Dragging over a chair, Dave sat next to the bed. 'Is there anyone you want us to call for you?'

'No.'

Not allowing his reaction to show, Dave asked again. 'Family?'

She shook her head. 'Steve is . . .'

'I'm sorry, Lynette. Steve perished in the fire.'

'He started it,' she said, with very little emotion.

Dave paused for a moment to check that Jack was recording what was being said.

'The fire? Tell me how you know that.'

'I woke up and I heard him sloshing the petrol around. I tried to move, but my head hurt too much. Then, I felt heat. There were orange and blue lights from the flames.'

'Okay.' He passed her a tissue and she took it with her free hand. 'Why do you think he did that?'

'He wanted to kill me.' Her voice rose slightly, and one of the machines beeped slightly faster.

'Okay,' Dave repeated calmly. 'Just relax. You're safe here. Steve can't hurt you.' It took a couple of moments for the machine to return to normal, and then he tried again. 'Why did he want to kill you?'

'He told me. He told me his secret. He was a filthy, filthy animal!' There was pure hatred in her voice. 'He tried to

say it was love, but it wasn't. It was plain incest, that's all.'
She burst into noisy sobs, and this time a nurse came in.

She adjusted a monitor and spoke softly to Lynette before
leaving again.

'Incest? With . . .' Dave let the word hang in the air, not
wanting to put words in her mouth.

'Maggie. He raped Maggie. Said it was love and they
were going to be married.' She stopped as if she couldn't
bear the words. 'And it wasn't just once. I think it went
on for a long time.' Lynette struggled to sit up and look at
Dave. 'It wasn't just Maggie,' she said. 'It was Hattie too.'

Dave let out the breath he was holding and looked at Jack.

Barker's dirty little secret, out in the open.

~

'I can't believe it,' Kim said, with her hand covering her
mouth. 'That's . . . Oh.'

'Yeah.' Dave looked as exhausted as he felt, and he had
one more bombshell to drop. 'Joel saved Lynette and lost
his own life in the process.' He stared at Kim, hoping she
would tell him everything that had happened in the past
twenty-four hours was a nightmare.

This time tears filled Kim's eyes. 'Oh no.'

She couldn't tell him that.

For once, Dave didn't have any comforting words. There
was nothing that could possibly be said to make anything
better. Barker would be a changed town after what had
happened today. How could it not?

'I've been to see the Douglases,' Dave told Kim. 'It was awful. No other word for it. I think they knew. I really think they knew. But they chose to let their only daughter be abused by their son. What type of despicable parents do that?' Dave's voice rose and he banged the table with his hands, shocked to feel heat in his eyes.

He stood leaning against the bench, his fists clenched. 'Paula couldn't speak. She was frozen,' he told Kim, who reached out to put her hand on his arm for comfort. 'Then she let out this high-pitched wail. I'll never forget it as long as I live. Just full of pain and agony. God!'

He was silent, seeing the scene in his head again.

'Max?' asked Kim quietly.

'Yelled at us to get out. Never once denied it. Not once.'

'They'll leave town, I've got no doubt,' Kim said. 'They can't stay.'

Dave knew that too. Their shame would never let them live under the watchful eyes of the town. The worst sin coming from the minister's house.

'Does Zara know?'

'Jack'll tell her.' Dave reached out and put his arms around Kim and held her to him. 'Sometimes, I've decided, the world is a little dark.'

'It is, my love. It is.'

CHAPTER 33

Emma looked out the window and tried to understand what she'd just seen.

'Are you okay?' Jacqui asked, leaning forwards and putting her hand on her friend's knee.

'Let's just look at this once more,' Emma said. 'I have to be sure.'

Jacqui handed over the phone.

Emma tapped on the Facebook entry and then again on the profile picture. It was a photo of a red Ram ute. There was nothing sinister about that. Kyle drove the ute and she'd seen it quite a few times.

Then she looked at the picture that Gill had used in his online profile on Bumble, which Jacqui had screen shot. She tried to zoom in and check the details. Was the window the same dark shade? Was the bullbar the same? She couldn't see the numberplate—that would have made things too easy.

Betrayal flowed through her. How could this be the same person?

Cash barked and Emma's head came up.

Looking out the window, Jacqui said, 'It's Jack and he's brought Zara.'

Licking her lips, Emma tried to think of something to say, but there weren't words. Kyle was Gill and Gill was Kyle.

Emma was on the brink of starting to see Kyle, while Gill was blackmailing her best friend.

Kyle the kind, hurt man who had laughed with her and spent hours telling her how much he had loved Alice. How much he still, all this time later, missed her. The softly spoken man who enjoyed the same types of books she did and was curious enough to ask and learn about farming because it interested Emma.

Then there were the screen shots of the messages that Jacqui had printed and laid out in front of her: *Front up with the money bitch or that pussy of yours is going on display.*

'This can't be right,' Emma said for the tenth time. 'There must be another ute exactly the same as this. I mean, it's not the only one in Australia, is it?' Her voice rose on the question.

'No,' Jacqui said. 'That's right. And maybe it isn't him, but it's a pretty big coincidence, don't you think?'

Forcing herself to nod, Emma agreed.

'Hello? Anyone home?' Jack's voice filtered down to the office.

'Down here,' Jacqui called back.

Not able to make herself stand, Emma just stared at Jack and Zara as they came into the room.

Jack was wearing a solemn look, while Zara looked upset. Both had blackened hands and clothes.

'Are you okay?' Jacqui asked them both, while Emma caught a whiff of smoke.

Jack nodded. 'Been some trouble in town, but we're working through it.'

At the sound of another vehicle arriving, Jacqui ran to the window, while Emma grabbed a pillow and clutched it to her chest. 'It's not him, is it?' she asked.

Jack followed Jacqui. 'It's not who? What's going on out here?'

'It's Matt,' Jacqui said, relief in her voice. 'It's only Matt.'

Emma gave a small cry and got off the chair.

'Ladies, I need you to tell me what's happening here,' Jack said, looking from one to the other.

Zara had picked up the screen shots from the table. '*You've got one more chance to come good with the money*,' she read.

Matt rushed into the room and went straight across to Emma. He reached out and held her hands. 'I saw Kyle was arrested. I wanted to see if you were okay.'

'Arrested?' Emma's face was white with shock. 'What for?'

Matt shook his head. 'I don't know, but the cop cars were at his cabin in the caravan park. He was being put in the back of a paddy wagon when I drove past.' Looking around, he aimed his next comment at Jack. 'What a bloody awful day.'

Jack nodded. 'You know Kyle?' he asked Emma. Then he closed his eyes. 'Of course you do. He said he was taking you out to dinner when I pulled him up the other day. How do you know him?'

'Here, sit down,' Matt said, leading Emma to a chair. 'I'll get you a glass of water. Anyone else need anything?'

'No, thanks.'

Jack dragged another chair in front of Emma and indicated for Jacqui to come and sit too. 'Let's start at the beginning,' he said.

Emma shakily told her story of the accident and how she'd met Kyle. How they'd stayed in contact to help each other through the trauma of the crash.

'Okay, hold it there. All of you need to let Dave hear this as well.'

~

There was a bang on the door and Dave groaned. 'Who the fuck would that be?'

Kim pulled away and rubbed his shoulder, before going to open the door.

Dave sat at the bench and opened the beer he'd got out ten minutes ago when he'd first walked in after fifteen hours straight on the go.

'Jack,' he heard Kim say. 'Oh Zara, love.' There were muffled words. 'Come in,' she said.

'Beer?' Dave called out.

'Not yet.' Jack walked into the kitchen with Zara. Behind him were three more people. 'You remember Jacqui and Emma? And this is Matt—he works for Emma. Dave, we've got a problem,' he said.

'We're talking about the bloke we cautioned for pulling out too quickly,' Jack reminded Dave, as they all sat around Dave's kitchen table. 'The one with the fat lip.'

'Joel punched him,' Emma said.

'Joel? What? Why? No, don't tell me yet.' Dave shook his head. 'Keep going on this first part you're telling me. But first,' he looked at Matt, 'where do you come into this?'

Matt took his time in answering. 'Nowhere really. But I'll tell you, I never liked this Kyle guy from the start. Thought there was something pretty untrustworthy about him.' Matt crossed his arms.

'Why are you here then?'

'I'm here as support for Emma. To make sure everyone is safe.'

'I trust him implicitly,' Emma broke in. 'I don't trust Kyle now.'

'Right. So you're telling me that Gill and Kyle are the same person?'

'We think so,' Jacqui said. 'I was showing Emma his online profile. I was out at the farm with her and didn't know any of this house fire and stuff had happened. Otherwise, we would've waited until tomorrow to ring Jack.'

Dave could see that Emma couldn't wait for the long-winded story.

'The profile picture is Kyle,' she said simply.

Dave closed his eyes in confusion. 'That's what I thought you said the first time. But how could—' He broke off and looked at Jack.

'Kate told us he was here, remember? That phone call before the blast. I'd forgotten about it. She was sending a team to apprehend him. And they have. They picked him up while we were at the hospital. He was trying to get Jacqui to answer him and—'

Zara waved some of the printed pages. 'There's all this evidence here,' she said. 'It's revolting.'

Dave reached out to take them, all the while talking to Jack. 'Wait on, how come I don't know about this?'

'The other coppers are swarming all over the town trying to help clean things up,' Jack said. 'You know they're here. Computer Crimes thought they'd update you when you got back tomorrow, but Jacqui called me, having already worked it out. I went to Deception Creek to hear what they had to say.'

Jacqui nodded, her face pale. 'He's in jail now, though, isn't he?' she asked. 'He can't hurt anyone?'

Emma spoke, over the top of Jacqui. 'If this is true, I want someone to throw the book at him. Is there anything I can have him charged with?'

Zara held up her hand. 'Actually, I've got something else,' she said.

'Surely not.'

Holding out a small news cutting, she said, 'Kyle is actually Cole Pengilly.'

Jack broke in. 'Joel recognised him when he was talking to Emma in the street. Gave him a real belting, Emma told me.'

Emma nodded, the anger clear in her clipped words. 'Kyle kept saying he didn't recognise Joel, so I just thought he had the wrong guy. Joel was looking really confused, saying, "You don't recognise me?" and that sort of thing.'

It was Zara's turn. 'I found this at the end of the scrapbook Greta gave to Kim. I couldn't understand what it was doing there in the first place because it didn't seem to have anything to do with Joel's case. It's the story of a ute crash.'

Emma snatched the cutting. 'God, that's the crash I was first on the scene for with Kyle. His wife, Alice, she was killed.' She looked from Zara to Dave and back again. 'How can three people be the same person?' She turned to Jacqui and grasped her hand. 'My god, how were we so stupid? Did he know we were friends?'

Raising one shoulder, Jacqui looked at her with tears in her eyes. 'I hope not. I hope it's just some horrible twist of fate.

Matt patted both their shoulders awkwardly. 'You weren't to know,' he said quietly.

'I've spoken to Alice's parents,' Zara said. 'Kyle, or Cole, was stealing from their business. They had the proof, and when that accident happened Kyle and Alice were on the way to the accountant so she could show Alice how he was doing it.' Zara stopped and looked at Emma, who had gone pale. 'They think he drove the car into the tree on purpose.'

EPILOGUE

'I hate funerals,' Dave said. 'And I'm sick of being the one who arranges them.'

Kim leaned over and straightened his tie. 'I think Joel would find it amusing that a copper was giving the eulogy at his funeral.'

She left the room, leaving Dave to stare at himself in the mirror.

He'd been through some hellish times, and funerals always brought back the memory of his mother-in-law's. The shot that killed her was fired by Bulldust, a fugitive who was intent on revenge towards Dave.

Bulldust killed Dave's mother-in-law, but he also destroyed his family. Dave's first marriage ended and he lost his kids with that one shot, and life as he'd known it had changed forever. Which is exactly what Bulldust had wanted, because the same had been done to him.

Dave still felt the guilt of the grief and trauma and pain he'd caused his family.

And now here, the thought of Joel, someone who deserved to live life, finally being free and exonerated only to die hurt beyond belief, more than he would share with anyone. Even Kim.

Because he knew that everyone felt the same way.

'Are you ready, honey?' Kim was back and giving him a sad smile.

'Yeah.' He fiddled with his tie, making sure the back was tucked into the loop, then he followed Kim to the car.

Jack and Zara met them at the front gate, making for a quiet, sombre group.

As they entered the church together, Dave had to hold back his anger at some of the people he could see sitting in the pews. They were there to gawk. To watch. To hear who this man—the man some had wanted to run out of town—had really been.

Does it matter? he wanted to ask them. *You made your judgement long before Joel came back.* Putting his hand in Kim's, Dave walked down to the front of the church, nodding to people he knew, his eyes resting briefly on Jacqui.

As yet, there wasn't enough evidence to charge Kyle Pengilly with the murder of his wife, Alice, but they would work on it no matter how long it took. Kyle, or Cole, or Gill, or whatever he was called, would die in jail, if Dave had anything to do with it.

Dave took his seat next to Greta Kerby, who was staring stonily ahead. He reached out and took her hand. At first she resisted, then she relaxed into his care with a wobbly smile.

⁓

Emma sat in the church with Jacqui and the rest of the girls. She kept thinking of Mrs Hammond, wishing just once she had called in to see Joel and talk to him. Told him how much she'd admired his mother.

She felt movement next to her and looked up. Matt. Her heart gave a little leap. He'd been out to Deception Creek a few times over the past week, helping out. Emma hadn't seen him; she'd been busy giving her statement to the police and answering more questions. But she knew he'd been there.

Cash had been fed and he'd left little messages around the place; a flower on the kitchen table and a smiley face etched into the dust on the dash of her ute.

'Can I sit here?'

She nodded and shuffled over a little.

'I didn't know you were coming.'

He looked at her and touched her leg. 'I thought you might need me.'

A lump formed in her throat as she looked at the steady, reliable man next to her. She nodded and touched his hand while she held his gaze. 'I do.'

'You've got me, Em. You've always had me. We'll work through everything, yeah?'

ACKNOWLEDGEMENTS

Writers are not easy people to live with . . . Or to be friends with! We spend a lot of time inside our heads, talking to our imaginary friends and gazing off into space. Also drinking coffee, leaving the cups of tea on the bench and forgetting they're there. We forget appointments and, sometimes, even where we are supposed to be.

Not to mention having the most warped Google search history! I'm not sure there're many people who could get away with 'How to dispose of a body', or 'How decomposed is a body about three weeks after death?' without the Australian Federal Police taking notice.

In saying that, I've said it before and I'll say it again: I have the best tribe a girl could have.

Love and thanks to Rochelle and Hayden for putting up with me in all states, but mostly the manic one that appears just before a deadline. (I'm sure they'll be glad when they can move out and not have to deal with the irrational mother they have, when I'm in among the last 15,000 words.) I also need to thank them both very much for helping me try to navigate the online world of dating sites in the research for this book—there were many, many strange and funny conversations a mother and her kids probably shouldn't have, but they took it all in good humour, if not with slight embarrassment. But that's what I'm here to do.

Love also to all of this crew: Lachie (see, you can't complain about being on the end of the list this time!), Cal and Aaron, Heather, Kelly, Lee and Paul, Robyn, Jan and Pete, Lauren and Graham, Kay, Donna and Mike, Chrissy, Shelley and David, Bev. The kindness and compassion you all show me on my worst days and the fun we have on my best ones, is above anything I've ever known, and I love you all 'to the moon and back'.

DB, you need your own special acknowledgement. Friend, mentor, listener, ideas bloke. This would be a lot harder without you. Thanks for the idea of burying a raw chop and digging it up three weeks later to answer that last Google search question.

Jack and Rocket—the keepers of secrets, walking buddies and the loudest snorers. And greatest rivals.

Every single one of the Parnell and Heaslip family—love you.

The team at Allen & Unwin—Annette, Tom, Christa, Laura, Sarah, Matt, Andrew, Jenn and anyone else I haven't mentioned but who are part of 'Team Fleur'. There are so many of you who make these books successful and I am indebted to the dedication and care you give. What a wonderful relationship Allen & Unwin and I have had over the past eleven years; thank you to the whole company for the support and belief in me—especially Tom and Annette.

Claire de Medici, who whips these manuscripts into shape and leaves funny little messages, when I least expect them, all through the edits. They make me laugh when I want to cry.

Gaby—we've done sixteen books, ten years, twenty contracts and been through so many things together. You're such a treasure in my world. And, of course, the best agent!

To Bronwen who donated to DVassist to be able to choose a few names in *Deception Creek*, Matt, Jacqui and Cash are here due to your generosity. As with all not-for-profits, we are always in need of help, so if you would like to donate, go to DVassist.org.au. If anyone you know and love is experiencing family and domestic violence and would benefit from the support of DVassist, then please make use of our service.

Anyone who reads or gives these books as presents—I'm so very, very grateful. Our world is busy (and strange) and the fact you chose this book to read in among the other amazing authors who are out there, well, I can't thank you enough. You give me the opportunity to frustrate/annoy my children and friends (LOL) with my vagueness, all the while creating entertainment for all who would like it. What a privilege.

To the booksellers and librarians—none of this would happen without you either.

Wishing you all health, safety and love.

With love,
Fleur x

Broad River Station

FLEUR McDONALD

Mia, a newly graduated constable, on her first post is assigned to Broad River, a small country town. And as certain as she is about her ability to do the job, on day one she's already in conflict with colleagues who believe that women shouldn't be coppers.

It takes the shine off coming home, where her grandmother, Clara, is in the early stages of dementia. Clara is in a nursing home, living between her present and the mist-covered past of her life as dementia slowly steals her memories. Mia is accustomed to their conversations often not quite making sense but when Clara hints of veiled family secrets, Mia isn't sure what she should believe.

In the midst of all this, a local child goes missing and Mia is confined to barracks. When Detective Dave Burrows realises she has skills that could be put to use, Mia's career takes a new turn, and she must decide down which road to walk.

ISBN 978 1 76087 884 9

CHAPTER 1

'Who are you?'

The woman placed her hand on the glass and stared.

There was no answer, just the sound of everyday things. The tick of the clock, the low hum of the TV from the room next door, the muffled conversations of people in the hallway.

'Who are you?' This time she whispered the words, because she knew she was supposed to know the answer.

Her reflection stared back at her. But it wasn't her. Not the way she remembered herself. Who was this elderly lady with hair so white you wouldn't notice snow on her head? Deep lines crisscrossed the image, and the woman's eyes were watery and dull.

The hand touching the mirror seemed to belong to someone else. The skin was paper thin; sun spotted. The gold rings on the left hand were loose.

Confused, the woman shook her head to clear her thoughts.

The door opened silently and a young woman in uniform came in holding a dinner tray.

'Evening, Clara,' she said, placing the tray on the side table. 'How are you tonight?'

She turned at the sound of the voice.

Clara. Yes, that's who she was. Clara, Clara. She silently chanted her name a few times so it would stay in her memory. Clara . . . Worth. Clara Worth.

She smiled gratefully at the woman who'd helped her solve the puzzle. Then she looked at the name badge on the woman's breast. Casey. What a ridiculous name! It made her sound like she was going on holidays.

Another woman entered the room. This one was holding a file.

'Now, Mrs Worth, I've got your medication, which you must take with food.' She put a little white plastic cup on the table next to the food and stood there looking at her.

Clara bristled at her bossiness.

This one's name was Helen. A hard name to go with her hard face.

She regarded both women.

'Come on, Clara,' Casey said gently. 'Come and have your tea. Chef's cooked up one of your favourites: silverside with mashed potatoes, cabbage and white sauce.' The woman smiled in an encouraging way, so Clara moved towards the chair to sit down, ignoring the woman with the file, who had now put her hands on her hips.

The chair was a sandstone-coloured rocking chair with a crocheted rug covering the seat. She couldn't eat there!

What on earth would her mother say if she didn't sit at the kitchen table with her brothers and sisters?

'Where is Brian?' she asked, looking around. 'We can't start dinner without him.'

Brian was her troublesome younger brother, who was probably out in the street playing in the dust or watering the horses that pulled the sulkies for the farmers coming to town to collect their supplies.

Perhaps her mother was serving in the store this evening. That's why she wasn't here.

'Brian?' the one called Helen asked briskly. 'No Brian here. I need to see you take your medication, Clara, and I have many other patients to attend to tonight, so let's get on.' She took a small plastic container of orange juice from the tray and peeled back the alfoil lid, before offering it to Clara. 'Hold out your hand,' she told her.

Obediently, Clara stretched out her hand and watched the white pills tumble into her palm. Helen shook the drink slightly.

'Open wide,' she said.

Clara frowned but did as she was told. *Insolent woman*, she thought. *I'm not a child.*

'Hello, Nana!'

The bright voice came from the door just as Clara swallowed the pills with the orange juice. She coughed then looked around, covering her mouth with her hand. The familiar voice was accompanied by a recognisable face. She reached to the back of her memory.

'Mia. Hello, dear.'

Helen wrote something on her file. 'Your grandmother has just had her medication, Mia, so if you could supervise dinner then we'll leave you to it.'

'Sure thing.' Mia bent down, kissing Clara on the cheek.

Her granddaughter smelled like sunshine and clean air. A breath of fresh air.

Not like this place which stank of disinfectant and pee.

I shouldn't be here, Clara thought. She grabbed Mia's hand, grasping it tightly, while her granddaughter sat opposite her.

Casey took the plastic lid from the plate. 'Enjoy,' she said and closed the door quietly behind her.

Mia leaned towards Clara and whispered, 'They've gone.' She took out a small bottle of whiskey from her shoulder bag and held it out. 'Here you go, Nana. Just what the doctor ordered.'

Clara brightened. 'You're such a good girl, Nicole.' The name jarred her memory. She took a sip and then corrected herself. 'Sorry, Mia. I know you're not your mother.' She put the bottle on the table. 'It's so confusing. One minute I'm here and the next I'm not.' Tears welled in her eyes. 'I'm frightened, Mia. I can't stop it.' Fingers she didn't recognise, but she knew were hers, picked at the hem of her light blue baggy t-shirt. When did she start wearing these types of clothes? Her figure had been beautiful in pants and shirts, Theo Marshall had told her. Now the grey tracksuit pants she was wearing hid her weakening body. She looked at herself in disgust.

'The doctor said this would happen,' Mia said quietly. 'I'm sorry I can't fix it.'

Clara nodded. 'I know you can't, dear.' She took a breath and reminded herself who she was then took another swig of whiskey.

She was Clara Worth, daughter of Gwen Simpson, the woman who had single-handedly saved the family business and raised four children. Gwen had been strong, determined and tenacious and Clara was made of her cloth. There was no place to feel sorry for herself here.

She knew Mia was doing something today. She racked her brains to remember what it was. 'Did you . . .'

Seeing her uncertainty, Mia picked up the conversation. 'I've unpacked and got the new house how I want it, so I'm ready to start work in a couple of days.'

'Do you like your house?' This was a safe subject.

'It's pretty old. The toilet is off the laundry and the bathroom has a cement floor that's been painted green! But I'm happy. There's a bedroom at the front and another small one that I'm going to make into an office.'

Something tapped at Clara's mind. She closed her eyes. Green. There was something green . . .

Her eyes snapped open. Yes! Her mother's outside verandah had been painted green. She remembered the pots that lined the cracked cement, full of camellias that loved the Flinders Ranges heat, and the grapevine that grew over the railings. Those grapes had tasted so sweet, but they had seeds. Brian and she had spitting competitions.

Her mother had pretended to be horrified at her unladylike behaviour, but Clara knew she laughed about it secretly.

Mia was still talking. 'I'm going to the station to introduce myself first thing tomorrow morning.' She paused. 'I'm a bit nervous.'

'Don't be nervous, dear,' Clara said, trying to work out why Mia would be. Which station was she going to?

As if Mia had read her mind, she said, 'There are five other coppers at Broad River Police Station, Nana, and a detective. All blokes. I'm going to be the only female police officer.'

Clara remembered now. That kind lady from the front office had driven her to Adelaide and stayed with her during Mia's graduation service a little while ago. The graduates had reminded her of herself as a youngster. Their wide smiles, enthusiasm and laughter had made her happy. But she'd found it hard. So many words to follow; faces and names that meant nothing to her. She'd been glad to return to the safety of her room afterwards.

'My mother always used to say that, as women, we might be the first one in our family or community to do something and it's our job to make sure we are not the last.' She picked up the whiskey bottle again and took a little sip, enjoying the burn of the alcohol on the back of her throat. 'It's your job to pave the way for other women to become police officers in the bush.' She paused. 'You're a brave girl, Mia. Just like your great-grandmother.'

A flicker of another memory. A key and two thin green doors with glass panelling above the large, tarnished brass handles. Lined, weathered hands putting the key in the large old-fashioned lock and turning it.

Clara could even hear the loud click as the key turned and the doors swung open, almost as silently as the door into her bedroom here in the nursing home.

Mia was talking and indicating the silverside that was on the plate, but Clara couldn't hear her. The memories inside her head were too loud.

She squinted as she heard her mother's voice. 'Now, Clara, here's a rag. You'll need to rub this cedar polish into the dresser to make the wood shine.' She inhaled the smell of bitter almonds as she unscrewed the lid, the amber liquid spilling onto the rag as she upended the glass bottle. Her hands were always oily by the time she'd finished rubbing all the wooden sideboards and furniture.

'Nana?'

Clara blinked, brought back to the present by her granddaughter's voice.

'You need to eat this before it gets cold, otherwise you'll get into trouble with the old dragon.'

Old dragon?

'Helen is so bossy,' Mia continued.

Picking up the cutlery, Clara cut a small bit of silverside. 'She's not very nice. But the other lady—the one who brings the dinner—she's not too bad.'

'Casey. Yeah, she seems very nice.' Mia took a sharp breath. 'I'm sorry, Nan. I'm sorry you have to be in here.'

Clara found the lump in her throat too large to speak around, so she shrugged and cut another piece of meat.

'What did you do today, dear?' she asked. Had Mia already told her? She couldn't remember.

'I finished unpacking the house.'

Ah, that's right, they'd already had this conversation.

'Where is the house?' Clara asked cautiously. She wasn't sure if she should know that answer.

'Two streets back from the river.' Mia gave a quiet laugh. 'Not that Broad River is really a river, is it? Just an expanse of still water that breeds mozzies and ducks and grows reeds.'

'Do the ducks still cross the road at the little dip as you come into town?' Clara asked. 'There was a mother duck who used to herd her ducklings across the road, stopping all the traffic.'

Mia nodded. 'They were there this morning when I walked downtown to get a coffee. Six of them. They're really cute.'

'I guess their mothers taught the ducklings where to cross the road because they've been doing it for years now.' Clara was pleased with that sentence. It was quite long, and she was sure it made sense. She pushed her fork into the mashed potato and tried to shovel it into her mouth. Instead, it fell onto her lap.

Mia leaned forward with a napkin, picked up the splodge and put it in the bin.

Clara tried again. Then she remembered something. 'I've got something for you,' she said.

'Do you?' Mia asked. 'What is it?'

'I've forgotten, but I know it's important.' Pushing her dinner aside, Clara stood and waited until she had her balance.

Pacing the boundary of the room, she tried to think. 'Something,' she muttered, 'something to do with . . .' She stopped at her dressing table and looked at the photos on top. There were three: a black-and-white one—her mother and the four children standing out the front of Simpson's Haberdashery; a faded coloured one of her with her daughter-in-law, Nicole; and a new one, in a shiny silver frame—a bright, glossy photo of her with Mia on her graduation day. Mia stood straight beside the old woman in the photo, her police hat perched on her dark hair, her light blue shirt with the police emblem for South Australia on the arm.

'What was . . . Oh, I remember.' Clara looked at the drawers, bewildered. 'I don't recall where.'

Mia was at her side now. 'What are we looking for, Nan?'

'The key.' She gave Mia a watery smile. 'It's for you, dear.'

Mia started to open a drawer and look through it. 'A house key?' she asked.

'Oh no. No, no, no! *The* key. For the shop.'

Mia stopped. 'For Simpson's Haberdashery? No, Nana, the shop was sold years ago. When we moved to Adelaide. Come and finish your dinner before Casey comes back to get your tray.'

Clara felt Mia take her arm, but she shook her off. 'No,' she said more loudly than she intended. 'No, it's here. I saw it and I need to give it to you.'

She shot Mia a look. Sold? She didn't remember selling the shop. Mia must be mistaken. Clara knew she'd only seen the key a few short days ago, and if it had been sold, she wouldn't still have the key, would she? The new owner would.

There were too many drawers to look in. Her heart kicked up a notch as fear flowed through her. Mia was a clever girl, but she didn't know everything.

Gwen had let her play in the shop out of the hot summer sun often, but Clara hadn't played. She'd *explored*! It was a dark and mysterious place that held so many treasures.

'It's got to be here,' Clara muttered, pulling drawers in and out, quickly. So quickly that she couldn't make out what was inside.

'Nana,' Mia said calmly. 'Nana, stop.' She took hold of Clara's small wrist.

Clara shook her off. 'No! I have to find the . . . the . . . thingy.' She could see what it looked like in her mind, but she couldn't think what the object she was looking for was called again.

The door opened and Casey came in. 'Have you finished . . .'

'Where is it?' Clara rounded on Casey. 'Do you know where I put it?'

'Now, Nan . . .'

'It is here, I know it is.' She grabbed her jewellery box from the top of the dresser and opened it. All the tension left her. Yes, it was here. In this box, somewhere. She thrust the box at Mia. 'In here,' she gasped and sat back down on the chair, picking up her fork.

'Everything okay?' Casey asked.

'We're fine.' Mia nodded.

When the door was closed, Mia handed Clara the bottle of whiskey. 'Another sip might do you a bit of good, Nan.' She turned to the jewellery box.

Clara got the feeling Mia was only humouring her. 'It's in there. You only have to find it.'

'Okay. I'm looking.'

Carefully she took out each piece of jewellery and laid it on the table. There wasn't much—a watch, a brooch and a pin for a pair of glasses.

'Under there.' Clara didn't know where the words had come from.

Mia poked at the floor of the box. It moved. 'Oh, there's a false bottom!'

'See, I knew it was there.' Clara sat back in satisfaction. 'The . . . thingy.'

Mia drew out a large silver key. 'Why have you still got this, Nana?'

Clara heard the reservation in her voice but ignored it. 'You haven't had the shop in decades. We should give it to the people who own the building. How about I take it to them? I thought I'd like to go for a drive to Barker and have a look around. See what's changed.'

Clara relaxed now. The key was where it should be. With the next generation.

'It is with the owner now,' she said.

CHAPTER 2

Mia tapped the key against her hand. Outside, the wind howled around the corners of her house, causing it to creak and moan, as if the ghosts of past tenants were calling to her. A cup of hot chocolate sat at her elbow and her small bar heater was struggling against the night's chill in the large high-ceilinged room.

Taking a sip of the hot chocolate, she wondered why her nan had never spoken of Simpson's Haberdashery since they'd left Barker. Or she'd mentioned it in passing, usually just to share a memory, never in the present tense.

Did she really still own the shop? Mia wasn't sure she could trust what she'd been told. Surely there would have been council rates that needed to be paid and maintenance . . . She knew her grandmother's affairs were taken care of by a solicitor in Port Pirie. George Walker.

Maybe she should make a call to him.

She put the key down carefully and leaned towards the heater, holding out her hands to warm her fingers.

There had been a hard conversation between them years ago in Port Pirie as they parked at the front of George Walker's office.

'There's some things I need to tell you,' Clara had said, her voice wobbly.

Already on high alert—making a trip to Port Pirie had been unusual in itself—Mia had waited.

'I have dementia, my darling girl.' Clara had taken Mia's hands in hers, squeezing for a long moment. The squeeze she'd been giving Mia since she was a little girl, telling her everything was going to be okay.

Mia's tears had come quick and fast, while her nan had sat stoically in the passenger seat, calmly explaining what was going to happen.

'George is going to take over all my affairs. He will have the power of attorney.'

Mia hadn't understood. Surely it should be her?

'You're young, Mia, I don't want you burdened with any of my problems. George can pay the monthly bills, make sure my care is looked after.'

This time Mia had turned in her seat and stared at her grandmother. 'What care?'

Again, the hand squeeze.

'I'm putting myself in the nursing home in Broad River.'

Her words had been matter-of-fact. Clara wouldn't and didn't change her mind. Mia had been there when all the legal documents had been signed with George Walker. Until Clara's death, George was in charge.

There hadn't been any mention of the shop then.

Now, though, the colours from Mia's TV, set on mute, danced over the white walls of the lounge room. Her grandmother's wooden sideboard, made of walnut and dating back to the 1800s, seemed out of place in the room. It was her most valued possession but it looked strange beside the two cheap lounge chairs and unsteady coffee table she'd bought at a garage sale before she'd left Adelaide.

In the kitchen was a dining table her friends had pooled together to buy her, and the fridge was an Engel car fridge that she'd been given for her twenty-first birthday. The police force had covered her moving costs and would pay her rent, but there would be little left over. A constable's wage was pretty small and Mia was still paying off her car, so there wouldn't be much money to spare.

When Mia had found out that her application to Broad River had been accepted, she'd been surprised. She'd wanted to be close to her nan and was over the moon that had happened. But would there be people who remembered her from when she was a little girl in Barker? And if they did, would they take her seriously?

Chris, her friend she'd come through the academy with had reasoned that it was more likely the locals could remember Clara than Mia and so what if they did? She had her uniform.

Mia had still been concerned there might be some tough times ahead.

Still, she wasn't a stranger to be put in hard situations. She got up and turned the TV off just as her mobile rang. The Taylor Swift ringtone echoed through the empty house, causing her to jump. She smiled when she saw Chris's name and the photo of the two of them on graduation day that appeared on the screen with his call.

'Hey,' Mia said, switching off the light and heater in the lounge room and walking towards the bedroom. 'How are you getting on?'

'Holy hell, what a first day,' Chris said with a groan. 'Baptism by fire.'

'Why? What happened?' Mia shook out her hair and sat on the edge of the bed, feeling for the electric blanket switch.

'Car accident out on one of the bush roads. Really untidy. Jaws of life and everything.'

'Ah. Fatalities?'

'Two. Local farmer and his wife. Road was wet, and he lost control going around a corner. Rolled a couple of times.'

She softened her voice. 'You okay?'

'Well, shit, we have to be, don't we?' His low voice ached of pain. Or shock. Probably both.

'Not at your first one.'

There was a silence. 'It was pretty awful, but I don't want to talk about it yet.' He paused. 'How'd you go today?'

'I don't start for a few days. Just finished unpacking this afternoon and I think I'll go to the station tomorrow to introduce myself. Should be an experience.'

'Don't let them get to you before you start.'

'I'm not worried. Hang on a sec.' Mia put the phone down and rummaged around in the chest of drawers, looking for her bedtime t-shirt. 'Sorry, back again.' She got changed and climbed into bed. 'I went and saw Nana today.'

'How was she?'

'All over the place. Sometimes she's with it and other times she can't remember her own name. It's horrible. This freaking disease is a thief.' Mia wriggled against the pillows to get comfortable. 'And it's only going to get worse. There's going to come a time when she doesn't know who I am. Sometimes it's like that now.' Mia knew she was only stating the obvious but it helped somehow to put her thoughts into words.

'Do you know how long . . .'

'No. I haven't seen the doctor yet. And from everything I've read about dementia, I don't know if it's possible to tell how quickly the decline will be.' Mia took a breath, trying to ignore the pain that was squeezing her heart. 'What are the crew like in Burra?'

'Pretty welcoming so far. There are five coppers and one detective here, so it's a reasonably big place. It needs to be though because it's the only decent-sized town between Adelaide and Broken Hill. We've got a fair bit of country to cover. Peterborough is about an hour's drive, but the station there is nearly obsolete—not that far from you really.'

'No, might be thirty minutes.'

There was a silence between them. 'Are you going to go to Barker and have a look around your old stomping ground? See if you can remember any of it?' Chris asked.

The key was now lying on her bedside table. Mia leaned over to pick it up and laid it on the doona. The silver sparkled in the light of her bedside lamp.

'Hmm, I think I will.' Her tone was casual.

'Ah, that sounds like you have something up your sleeve.'

'Nan gave me a key today. To the old store in Barker.'

'And that's significant because . . .'

The question hung between them. Mia wasn't sure how to answer.

'She says she still owns the shop.'

Mia could feel the expectation humming down the line. Chris knew there was more to this.

'I'm guessing Nan's forgotten that she sold the building when we left. She must be mixed up about this like she is with so many other things.'

'You should be able to find out who owns it easy enough. A phone call to the shire or something?' Chris paused and when he spoke again there was humour in his voice. 'Now that you've found out this important piece of information are you telling me you're planning on becoming a shopkeeper?'

Mia laughed. 'Idiot,' she said affectionately. 'Of course not! But it's . . . I don't know. The whole thing has made me curious. I haven't been to Barker since I was a kid.' Her voice trailed off.

'You'll have to go over and see if the key fits into the lock. Bit like Cinderella but a shop not a shoe!'

Mia laughed. 'Of course, and with any luck there's a prince or a pot of gold waiting for me as soon as I open the door.'

'I'll take the gold. Leave the prince for you.'

When Mia spoke next the laughter had been replaced with wistfulness. 'Guess I'll go for a drive when I can and have a look. Nana says there's something she wants me to bring back to her and I'll know it when I see it.'

'Want me to come?'

'Um . . . Not sure. I might be better off going by myself the first time. It'll be strange to go back after so long.'

'If you change your mind, let me know. We'll just have to see if we can co-ordinate our rosters.'

Mia cleared her throat and looked at the silver watch on her wrist. A gift from a boy who was no longer in her life. 'Guess I'd better go to bed.'

'Yeah.'

Mia knew Chris didn't want to hang up. That was how their friendship worked. They'd talked often enough on the phone to know how each other was feeling by the first 'hello'.

'Maybe you should make yourself a hot chocolate.'

Chris snorted. 'That's not very manly!'

Mia laughed. 'You're a Caramello koala, and you know it. Hard on the outside and soft and gooey in the middle.'

'Shh, don't let my secret out.' Chris laughed before giving a big sigh. 'I'll be okay. I keep seeing the ute, that's all.'

'Totalled?'

'Write-off. The SES dealt with the bodies until the funeral directors got there. I didn't see them. Only held the traffic up and then redirected all the vehicles around the accident site slowly after everything was cleared.' He gave a bit of a cough. 'Didn't do much really. Or see anything.'

'There's nothing "only" about what you did, and you know it. Just like you know what happened there. You know that a family is grieving, and someone had to go and tell them. Don't be too hard on yourself. Sounds like the crew at Burra looked after you pretty well.' Mia spoke gently.

'They did.' She could hear Chris shift in his bed. 'In the long run, this is what we're trained to do.'

Mia smiled at his stoic tone. She made her voice gruff and serious, as if she were the Premier about to make an announcement. 'We're here to keep South Australians safe.'

Chuckling, Chris said, 'Exactly.'

'All right, well, I'd better go to bed. Who knows what tomorrow will bring for both of us.'

'True story.'

After they'd said goodnight, Mia let the phone rest on her chest and looked down at the key sitting on the doona cover. She picked it up, thinking about the times she'd spent in the haberdashery shop when she was very young. Before they'd left Barker. She could see Nana behind the counter, a large smile for anyone who walked through the door. Didn't matter if it was Mrs Holder, who was a couple of months late in paying her account, or little Barbara Jones, who had popped in for a five-cent lollipop. Mr Marshall always got a special smile, and Nana would pretend to slap his hand when he slipped it into one of the jars and picked out a couple of liquorice sticks.

She put the key on the bedside table and switched off the light rolling over to get comfortable. A memory nudged her.

There had been something under the counter that she wasn't allowed to touch. A curtain that ran along a piece of wire under the counter and usually hid everything from view, but if you lifted it up you could see Nana's lunch and thermos, next to her cup. There was sticky tape, brown paper and scissors. A gun.

Mia sat up. A gun. She could remember it sitting there. Yes! Right on top of a wooden box.

Why did Nana have a gun within easy reach? she thought uneasily. *And where is it now?*